"MY GOD, JULIE, WE ARE ONE."

With his arms so tight about her, she could not have pulled free if she had wished to. But she pleaded silently with her own body. "Please God, no. Just this once give me strength against my passion for him."

Yet the weakness that came with his touch was already softening her body against his...

She would have resisted his hand at the ribbons of her corselette but she had neither strength nor will. With his lips finding hers, she submitted helplessly to the plunging of his desire...

*Also by Alexis Hill
from Jove*

PASSION'S SLAVE

ALEXIS HILL

THE UNTAMED HEART

A JOVE BOOK

Printed in the United States of America

Requests for permission to make copies of any part of the work should be mailed to: Permissions, Jove Publications, Inc., 200 Madison Avenue, New York, NY 10016

First Jove edition published March 1980

10 9 8 7 6 5 4 3 2 1

Jove books are published by Jove Publications, Inc., 200 Madison Avenue, New York, NY 10016

Rivière

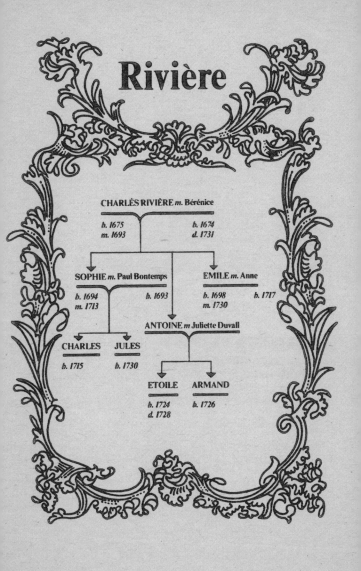

CHARLÈS RIVIÈRE *m.* Bérénice

b. 1675
m. 1693

b. 1674
d. 1731

SOPHIE *m.* Paul Bontemps

b. 1694
m. 1713

b. 1693

EMILE *m.* Anne

b. 1698
m. 1730

b. 1717

ANTOINE *m* Juliette Duvall

CHARLES   JULES

b. 1715   *b. 1730*

ETOILE   ARMAND

b. 1724   *b. 1726*
d. 1728

CONTENTS

THE UNTAMED HEART

Part 1

THE MIRRORED LAND

1726-28

Chapter One

The matched grays that drew the carriage down the Ashley River road toward Charles Town moved along at a dignified pace, maneuvering the sharp curves with an easy, if ponderous, grace. Even if the carriage had not contained three women and a small child on that summer morning of 1726, the pace would still have been well chosen. For although Charles Town had grown apace and many travelers passed along this way, the road remained a rough country lane whose sudden turns could reveal unexpected peril.

Both the man and his mount who followed the carriage gave a startling contrast to its staid progress. For one thing, both man and horse were of astonishing size. The black stallion, his wide nostrils flaring, strained against his reins with the same look of furious impatience that darkened his rider's face.

Antoine Rivière was wigless with his thick hair tied at the nape of his neck and his coat thrown across the pommel of his dancing mount. His shirt was open at the throat against the heat and its fine fabric showed a pattern of sweat on his broad back. As he struggled with his mount, the scowl on his face was as dark as his sun-bleached hair was pale.

"Another damned muggy day," he muttered to his horse. "A man could swim in this cursed air."

Glancing over his shoulder he stared into the west at a bank

1

of gray clouds forming along the horizon. There might be rain. God willing, there would be rain to sweeten the air before nightfall.

Now and then the trees, in full summer leaf, parted to show the broad face of the river glinting with sunlight. Young mockingbirds being forced to flight by their avian parent clung to their branches with desperate claws, screaming in terror.

What a bastard day this was turning out to be, Antoine raged inwardly. It was bad enough to have to spend a day away from his wife Julie when she was so near to giving birth to their child. There was nothing he could do about that. His sister Sophie, along with her maid, needed to ready the town house for the summer move and one day was as good as another for that task. But to leave Julie at the plantation as he had, with tears still fresh on her face and harsh words hanging between them, set him to writhing.

The anguish of their long argument flooded back on him, filling him with despair. It was true enough, as Julie had said, that he and Julie herself owed their very lives to his sister Sophie. It was also true that leaving a beautiful young woman alone to manage a huge plantation made no sense, but God's blood, a man had a right to set forth on his own.

It was Sophie's insane stubborness that was setting all their teeth on edge. How could she believe that her husband Paul, lost since the last Indian war, could possibly still be alive to return to her? Yet she primped for him daily as a bride would do, and refused the sensible offer of a good marriage to wait for a man long gone, if not long dead.

Only because he pressed Sophie to marry did Julie ever raise her voice against him. Only because he loved that willfill wench and their daughter so much did guilt boil in his gut as it did this morning.

At last the walls of Charles Town were in sight. As the carriage slowed for the gate, Antoine kicked the stallion alongside where his sister Sophie raised her face to him at the window.

"After I see you safely inside the gate, I'm going back to the plantation for a quick trip. I'll be back in an hour or two."

"No hurry," Sophie assured him. "We plan to stay in town until late afternoon." A sudden twinkle came into her clear eyes and Antoine knew that some mischievous, probably ribald, thought had come to her. Whatever it was, she

2

banished it, dropping her eyes from his to repeat dully, "No hurry."

The stallion stamped with impatience as Antoine waited to see the city gates close securely behind the carriage.

Pain. A sudden stab of pain came at his sister's stiff way with him. How could he and Sophie have conspired together and laughed together for so many years and still have managed to sour to a formal coldness over this matter on her refusal to forget Paul Bontemps and marry? She was mad on this one point, purely mad.

Paul Bontemps had long ago rotted to mulch in the midden of an Indian camp somewhere in this wilderness. But as long as Sophie fought this hard truth, Antoine himself was honor-bound to be the master of her household even though it meant he could not embark on his own life with his growing family.

With the city gates behind him, Antoine gave the stallion his head. Crouched on his mount's neck with his body low against the lashing of overhanging branches, Antoine pressed the beast with his thighs. Julie. He would at least make peace with Julie before setting out for his day in Charles Town. When that was done, the day would turn fair.

At the plantation, Antoine immediately took the stallion to the stableyard to be sponged of his lather and then crossed the green with eager steps to seek out his wife. As he reached the verandah, he stopped with a quick intake of breath. He had almost passed her in his haste to reach the house. What a fool he was. He should have guessed that the heat of the day would not keep her in. This was never a woman to be trapped within walls as long as there were doors that opened out.

He approached the chaise silently to stare down at her sleeping form.

Would that face ever cease to startle him with its purity of line, its gentle molding? The golden eyes that had ensnared him at his first glimpse of her moved in reverie beneath closed lids. Her perfect ripe mouth stirred in a vagrant smile as some dream image pleased her.

He smiled back at her unconsciously. This child of a woman with the mass of black curls framing her heart-shaped face looked pure and unused, virginal in spite of the great belly on which her fine hands rested lightly.

How could she have come so unstained through the years just past? Their quarrel of the morning had reminded him

3

afresh of the incredible horrors that her short life had held.

She had been a child on her father's estate when he first saw her, the penniless helpless prey of a brutal assailant when he had first lifted her into his arms. She had gone from a falsely accused inmate of Newgate Prison only to be shipwrecked and sheltered by a primitive Indian trader before finally coming into the ruthless hands of her maddened uncle. But still her beauty and humor and—God help him—her spirit, were unscathed.

Her words of the morning echoed in his mind.

"How dare you try to force me to make Sophie abandon her faithfulness to Paul?" she had confronted him, her eyes blazing. "You ask me to do that. I, who happily went through hell waiting for you. What would you have done if I had wed when I was so certainly told that you were dead?"

"I would have widowed you and taken what was rightfully mine," he told her angrily. "But this is different. My God, Julie, this has been going on for years. Look at her son Charles. He was but a child of two when the Yamasee struck the settlement. Now he is grown and off to France for his education and still she waits."

At her stubborn glance, his voice softened.

"What about us?" he asked gently, laying his hand on the great belly that held their second child. "What about you and our daughter Etoile and this one coming? Do we not deserve a life of our own? To be apart from this place to build a home and a life that belongs to us? All my work here, no matter how well I am paid, is labor in another man's vineyard. I need to build an estate of my own, for you and our children."

"I want that too," she replied softly, lifting her face to his. "But I cannot seize our own happiness by forcing Sophie into another man's bed while she still believes that Paul may return."

The scent of her skin close to him stirred in his memory. The helplessness of desire drew him to her irresistibly. His passion for her was a deep, whirling pool that drew him from reason at the touch of her flesh on his. He drew back, gripping his control with clenched teeth. "Jesus," he stormed at her. "How can a man call himself a man when he is so entrapped by women?" He was still struggling to contain his emotions as she pulled herself to her feet and started toward the door.

"Entrapped," she repeated quietly. "Is that how you see yourself?" As she flung open the door he saw the sudden glint of tears on her cheeks. "There. The trap is sprung. Walk out

4

that door. Go and make your fortune in the wide world like a third son in a fairy tale. Your life is your own. Be free of us women."

"Oh yes," he said acidly. "Just walk away, is it? And what of you and Etoile? And that one?" He nodded toward her swelling body.

"An escaped prisoner does not concern himself about the welfare of his jailer," she reminded him quietly.

Fury boiled in him. Why did she not dissolve into helpless tears and start bleating like other women in anger? What a stubbornly independent bitch she could be. He forced his own voice to coldness.

"I realize, madame, that you have managed to enslave half of the men in this miserable colony with your 'innocent' flirtations. I realize that your cousin Jacques DuBois would give his fortune and his life for those same charms that have so thoroughly entrapped me. Is this your plan? To run to your cousin for sanctuary, knowing that his lust glitters for you even while you are great with another man's child?"

Even as he spoke he knew that her anger would rise to match his words, but he could not stem his torrent of insult. He wanted her—God, how he wanted her—and the passion he could not still with her body turned to acid on his tongue. He braced himself for her fury. It did not come.

She stood quietly, her small body balancing the weight of her swollen belly with a curious grace. Her golden eyes were calm and a little quizzical as they met his gaze.

"If you do not choose to walk, then I intend to," she said quietly. Before he could catch his breath and reach out for her, she had passed through the door and closed it against his outstretched hands.

The tears that had shone on her cheeks that morning were gone as she lay sleeping. He watched the faint movement of the child beneath the mound of flowered skirt that concealed her body and smiled with tenderness on that restless unborn child.

Leaning, he lifted a straying curl from her cheek. "Forgive me, Julie," he whispered. Then cursing himself silently for the lust that stirred in him at the caress of that silken strand across his finger, he turned and entered the house.

At his sister's desk he found ink and a quill.

"Julie, my love," he scratched hastily. "I came back to you. As I always do. As I always will. Your own." He did not need to scratch the great flowing initial. She would know.

He slipped the folded note into the open basket of needlework that stood by her lounge chair. She could not fail to see it at once and even if she did, it would fall out when the basket was lifted.

She would be wakened soon enough, he thought, as he called for the horse to be saddled anew. The darkness in the west was clearly rising to a storm that would be at his back as he thundered down the river road to Charles Town.

Chapter Two

The hoofbeats of the stallion were far away before Julie was startled awake, as often happened now, by the strength of the child within her. She did not open her eyes at once, but lay quietly, savoring the scents and the sounds that filled the air about her.

How spoiled she was, pampered both by Antoine and by her sister-in-law Sophie. How could she let herself be driven to such cold fury by Antoine when she loved him with a passion so thorough that her heart caught in her throat at the thought of him? She shook her head. I must not do that, she cautioned herself. I must not think of the angry storms between us; I must not let his thoughtless words upset me. Not in this time of waiting, me needing only joy and strength.

Waiting. Her hand stirred on the roundness of her belly. She opened her eyes and giggled at the flowered mountain that rose before her. The child within was a son. It had to be a son this time, for Antoine. Not that any man could love a child more distractedly than Antoine did their little daughter Etoile. But a man needed a son and Julie was secretely sure that the life that stirred uneasily against her ribs or thumped secret messages during the fretful night was a son who would come from his dark world to become a man of great power and size, as Antoine was.

She was startled to full wakefulness at the sight of a slender Negro girl approaching the verandah steps with a hesitant look on her face.

"Mandy," she cried with delight, struggling upright in the chaise. "Why it is indeed you, child. And whatever brings you

6

here? Nothing is wrong at Monde DuBois, tell me there is nothing wrong."

The girl ducked her head and grinned with delight at the greeting. "All well," she assured Julie. "Your aunt the mistress is still off hobbing and nobbing with her Philadelphy friends. Mistah Jacques say I must bring you a message."

"On such a hot day," Julie said, taking the folded note from the girl's outstretched hand. Whatever could her cousin Jacques want? Surely there was no trouble at the plantation. Since his father's death, Jacques himself had run Monde DuBois and the place had the reputation of being one of the best-managed properties in the area.

"You feeling fine now?" the girl asked gently in her soft, hesitant voice.

Julie smiled at the girl, delighted to realize how the young slave had flowered under Jacques' management of the plantation. Mandy's stick-thin body had filled out and her face had lost the shadow of terror that Julie remembered from the old days when Mandy had been her only friend in her uncle's house. A band of shining sweat stood out on the bridge of the girl's nose and her richly colored cheeks glowed from heat.

"I could not be better, thank you, Mandy," Julie told her. Then, briskly, "While I see what my cousin has to say, you trot in there and tell cook to give you all the cold water you can drink. Then have some of that cherry cider chilling in the well. Tell her I want you to have some nutcakes to go with it."

Mandy hesitated.

"That's really what I want you to tell her," Julie insisted. "Now scat so I can read this."

Her smile faded as she unfolded the crisp sheet of paper. She would know Jacques' handwriting anywhere. Antoine's unremitting jealousy of her cousin made writing their principal means of communication. Antoine had never specifically forbidden her to contact with Jacques DuBois, but it was only because he dared not. Jacques and his mother and her family were her only blood relatives in all the colonies, and he knew she would stubbornly fight any attempt to cut her off from them. But his resentment of Jacques, the way his face darkened at the very mention of his name, kept her contacts with her family at Monde DuBois at an absolute minimum.

She read her cousin's message twice through without stopping. The second time she frowned with disbelief at Jacques' words. Whatever was he thinking of? He was asking her to come to Monde DuBois for some curious unnamed reason. He knew how near she was to giving birth. Surely he knew that bouncing about on rude colonial roads even in the best of carriages was hardly what a woman heavy with child should be doing. Yet there it was in his own hand, the letters joined less flowingly than usual as if they rose from some urgent need. More than anyone, Jacques knew how furious Antoine would be at the very thought of her traveling to Monde DuBois in the best of times and for the best of reasons. She shook her head in disbelief and read the note again, frowning earnestly as if her expression would clarify the meaning of the words.

"*Ma belle cousine*," it began.

Something of possible great urgency has come to my attention. It is not some simple problem that I can send to you by word of mouth. You must come and hear it for yourself. You will only need to be here for an hour. This could be vital to you, my dear Juliette. I have sent my easiest carriage with the steadiest driver. He will take the best of care of you. Only an hour, my dear. Your life could be changed.

An hour that could change her life? How could that be? She seized the bell at her side and rang it vigorously. A maid popped from the kitchen almost instantly.

"Is Mandy having a bite to eat?" Julie asked.

At the girl's nod, Julie lifted her hand. "Would you help me up please? I want to speak to her."

"I can send her right out," the girl protested even as she gave her hand to Julie.

Julie shook her head. "I have to get up anyway," she said, her mind spinning with questions about Jacques' note.

Mandy leaped to her feet, brushing crumbs from her mouth as Julie entered the kitchen house.

"What did my cousin say when he gave you this?" she asked.

"Just that it was for your eyes only and that I should wait." A little tremor of fear stammered her words.

"And the carriage is out there waiting in the road?"

The girl nodded at Julie, her eyes white-rimmed.

"And you have no idea what this is all about?" Julie pressed.

The girl shifted her weight from one foot to the other and her eyes slid away.

"Mandy," Julie coaxed softly. Julie was startled by the sudden moisture in Mandy's eyes. "I really don't know, Miss Julie. If I was to make you my guesses, I be very bad unfair to Mistah Jacques."

Julie measured the girl with her eyes. Mandy's loyalty to Jacques was stiffening her already straight spine. How could she coax Mandy to unfairness to a master who had brought her from a terrified child to this healthy young woman? Julie sighed.

"Finish your cider and we will go."

"Go!" the cook exploded behind Mandy. "You don't real-life say you going to go anyplace out in the heat of this day. You got no lunch in you even. You can't go racketing off all that way for this chile or anybody."

"An hour," Julie told her firmly. "My relative needs to consult with me on a matter which will only take an hour. I will be back and resting in my chair before the others are finished at Tradd Street."

"The sun has touched you," the woman grunted, suddenly turning on Mandy. "What do you mean, chile?" she challenged the girl fiercely. "What you mean coming in here and dragging Miz Julie out in the blaze with no lunch in her and she buried under all that baby?"

Mandy stepped back quickly, as if she feared a blow from the older women.

Julie laid her hand on Mandy's shoulder and shook her head. "Nobody's dragging me," she said softly. "I am going to Monde DuBois for an hour and then returning. But after my rest outside, I need my shawl for the coolness of my aunt's house."

Julie and Mandy grinned wickedly at each other as the cook stamped off grumbling to get the shawl.

Chapter Three

Whatever it was had to be important, she kept reassuring herself. The fact that she was there in the carriage swaying

9

along the road to Monde DuBois represented a dangerous gamble for herself. Only something of critical importance would keep Antoine from wild fury when he discovered that she had left the peace and safety of the plantation. And Jacques knew this, he had to be conscious of the risk she was taking by responding to his summons.

The thought of Jacques melted her heart in a way that Antoine could not understand. How like her own dead father this cousin of hers was. From their first meeting, shortly before her marriage to Antoine, she had found herself drawn irresistibly to this tall slender man whose smoky eyes dwelt on her with the same tenderness that her father's had. At first Jacques had been graceful about ignoring Antoine's furious jealousy, but that passed with time.

"I'm not a man of stone," Jacques had protested to her crossly. "I find your husband's attitude insulting. If that big stud of yours must constantly accuse me of lusting after his wife, of being the viper in his marriage bed, then I will damn well go for the game as well as the name. And he calls the truth fairly, I must admit, except that what he names as lust I know as love."

She had tried to still his tirade, to no avail.

"Love, Julie," he repeated soberly. "Your happiness is the most important thing in this world to me. I am helpless at your every word, your every move. When the day comes that you have had enough of his jealous tirades, come to me. Or better yet, don't bother coming. Call, raise an eyebrow and I will be there for you. Forever."

Knowing Jacques' feeling was a burden whenever they were together. She was always acutely conscious of his eyes dwelling on her. She saw the great effort it took for him to avoid physical contact with her, a quick drawing back of hand after touching, the cousinly kiss that failed to touch her cheek. If their eyes happened to meet she always felt her own heart pounding from the passion in his eyes. Yet she did not love Jacques, not in the way she did her husband. Antoine's brilliant eyes and teasing mouth had been imprinted in her heart at her first glance of him, when she was a child in Middlesex and he was a footman on a gold-and-white coach thundering toward London.

She had barely dropped the curtain again when the swaying of the carriage signaled a turn. Julie knew without looking that the carriage was passing along the tree-tunneled drive that led to the great house at Monde DuBois. Dark

10

memories of her brief life in this place flooded over her, and she shivered as she banished the image of her mad uncle's face from her mind.

An hour, Jacques had said. She need stay no more than an hour in this house in which evil memories hung like eternal shadow.

Jacques was quickly at the carriage to help her alight. The pressure of his hand on her arm was light and his expression cool as she lifted her cheek for his kiss.

"This mysterious business had better be important," she warned him with a smile.

"You mean that you'll catch hell if it isn't, don't you?" he challenged her. "You don't have to put up with that violent temper, Julie, you know that."

She raised her finger to his lips. "Stop that talk or I shall return on the instant. Now, what is this urgent business you wrote of?" Between meetings she forgot how he towered over her, even as her father had. Her heart turned as she looked up at that fine angle of jaw and her father's smoky eyes smiling from his young face.

"I am greatly relieved that you came," he said, his face suddenly sober. "This could mean everything or nothing. . . ." He paused with a perplexed look. "My God, Julie, I just don't know, but I couldn't risk not trying."

"Jacques," she said. "What in the world? You grow more confused and confusing by the moment."

Once inside the hall, with the maid gone off with her shawl, Jacques took both her hands in his and fixed his eyes on hers. "You have a friend here, Julie. I am giving you this notice so that you not be shocked when you enter that room. You have a friend here with whom I thought best that you meet and talk alone."

Her golden eyes studied his face and a tremor of dread stirred along her spine at his words.

"In the parlor, Julie," he said hoarsely. "Go on in. I pray God that this meeting is worth your trip today."

He turned and strode away down the hall, leaving her standing outside the closed parlor door of Monde DuBois.

She stared at the door with apprehension. What mysterious friend was this? She felt her heart racing wildly. What a fool she was to be besieged with terrors when the mystery could be solved by the turn of a brass doorknob.

Julie stared into the half-light, recognizing the shapes of familiar chairs, the delicate desk which no one ever used, the

11

piano gleaming from polish in spite of the absence of its owner. Then a movement against the drape caught her eye and she stepped forward a little, her lips parted in disbelief.

He was standing immobile, in the shadow behind her uncle's chair, his single eye watching her with that thoughtful expression that she had long ago learned to cherish so dearly.

He was so perfectly as she remembered him that for one shattering moment she believed herself to be dreaming. Time and the curtained room slid away from her and she was on a pallet in a rough lean-to in the swampland of Guale. He had come as a solider darkness into a dimly lit room, the mass of dark hair bound at the nape of his neck, the leather clothing and the black patch over his left eye, and the surprising brush of mustache above the unsmiling mouth. Only that time his arm had cradled a gun and a brace of freshly killed fowl had hung at his side.

She felt her legs go weak beneath her and she groped for the support of a chair back. In that swift, silent tread that she remembered so well he was instantly at her side. Her mind was suddenly filled with the bright tune that had always been on his lips. But he wasn't humming, he was speaking to her in that low, calm voice that was dearer than any song to her ears.

"Lady," he said softly. "Easy there, Lady."

How could she be easy? She felt the joy begin like an explosion deep inside her chest. Tears formed in her eyes even as she was overcome by helpless laughter. As he caught her in his arms, the feel of his strong sturdy body against her only made the tears flow freer.

"Josh," she cried. "Oh my God, it is you, Josh. My love, my dear, dear Josh."

The past swept in on her. She remembered the first time he had buried his face in her hair, as he was doing now. She remembered the fine feel of his hard strong legs pressed against her own and the precious scent of his flesh against her face.

What was she doing? Josh had walked in out of her past and swept away all that she had become. Antoine, Etoile, even the child rebelliously kicking under her heart—all dissolved in the shimmering memory of Josh's scent, the rich leather-and-woodsmoke smell that tightened her arms about him.

It was Josh himself who stirred away. He brought a linen from somewhere and wiped her face solemnly, looking at her not at all, only careful at the task like a man mopping up a social error. Then he grinned into her face in his swift bright way.

"Lady," he said softly. "It has been a long sleep between dreams."

A long sleep between dreams. Indeed, she thought, standing there in the loose circle of his arms, their life together had been a dream, a gentle dream in a life more often visited with nightmares.

Josh nursing her to health after the shipwreck, Josh dressing her in Indian leather and bringing her tortuous miles through the wild country to reunite her with her family, Josh honoring her as no other man ever had by letting her make her love a gift rather than forced tribute. Josh leaving her at Maggie MacRae's without even the raised hand of farewell.

"You left me, Josh," she said quietly. "You left me at MacRae's without even telling me good-bye. Oh Jesus." She groped for the chair back again. She must not let the memories flood in on her like that. She must fight back thoughts of the horrors that had followed her arrival at her uncle's house . . . this house which was now Jacques'.

Josh's arms were swift about her again. "Lady, it was what you wanted. It was all you ever wanted, remember? It was your choosing, Lady, not mine."

She nodded. "You are right, of course. And I have lived through it and you have lived through it and—"

"And the man you told me you would always love lived through it too, remember? You were so sure that he was long dead, even then."

"I was sure, Josh," she nodded. "And now we all live."

"Some of us live more fully than others," he reminded her in that calm, soft voice.

She dropped her eyes. "And all of my life is owed to you, Josh. If you had not cared for me after the shipwreck, God only knows . . ."

He caught both her hands in his and his single eye grew sober. "We will have only a moment before your cousin returns, Lady. But I have one thing you must hear. It is I who needs to thank you for my life . . . my real life. It was with you, and it stays with me as long as my mind is alive."

Her lips were parted in protest when Jacques opened the door into the hall. The slave behind him bore a tray covered by white linen.

"I have brought tea for you, Juliette, and something a little stronger for Josh and myself. Remember that you have only

13

an hour. Josh has a story I want you to hear, *ma cousine*. You must decide for yourself if it is a story that might change your life."

Chapter Four

The room was silent except for the clink of silver against china as Jacques, without asking, prepared Julie's tea the way she liked it best. Crisp hot breads and a tray of sliced meat with a pot of Anne-Louise's excellent green pepper sauce lay untouched on the table before them.

Josh sat deep in a chair, staring morosely at the porter in his hand as he swirled the dark liquid in wide arcs almost to the mouth of the glass.

Julie waited, her eyes on his face.

Finally he turned to Jacques with a helpless glance. "Hell," he said crossly. "I don't know where to begin. What do I say?"

"It would be best if you told it just as you did to me. Just to see if Julie gets the same reaction that I did," Jacques suggested quietly.

"I'd like to hear what happened after you left me here in Charles Town," Julie added.

Josh grinned quickly with that flash of white teeth that came like a sudden light in his tanned face. "I had a bad loser of a gambler after me then, if you remember. He was hot after his money and my blood. Since I wasn't interested in making either donation, I lay low for a week or two.

"But I saw you safely into this place first," he said, backtracking. "I watched down there by the drive until I saw your aunt, Jacques' mother, bring you up the drive in the carriage."

His expression turned suddenly pleading. "How was I to know, Lady? When I returned today and Jacques here told me how it went with you, I could have slit my own throat. I had a bad feeling in my gut when I left you, but I put it down to my not wanting to give you up. How was I to know?"

"There was no way that anyone could have known," she whispered. Why did she struggle so hard against her memory of that dread time here at Monde DuBois? Those months were

14

a part of her, of what had made her Julie Rivière, even as her imprisonment at Newgate was a part of her, even as her time with Josh was. Indeed, who could have looked at this grand house and these wide fields and guessed that a madman like Yves DuBois, obsessed by lust and demented by voodoo would turn on his wife's niece and try to offer her as a human sacrifice to a heathen God.

"There was no way," she repeated. "So you hid out here in Charles Town?"

He nodded. "And while I did, I got together a pack train of seven horses loaded with goods for Indian trade. The third week saw me setting out west for Chickasaw country.

"I figured to be gone two years," he went on. "I thought that in two years the wind might blow you out of my head. It has been close to twice that long," he grinned ruefully. "The winds don't work like they used to in the old days."

"But where have you been all this time?" she asked. "Just traveling?"

She leaned forward with her question. She flushed as she saw Josh's eyes move from her face along the line of her throat to dwell on the high roundness of her swollen maternal breasts. Josh stirred restlessly in his chair, pulling his gaze from her with a scowl.

"Not traveling all the time," he admitted. "I traded and traveled some of course, and lived a season with some Chickasaw friends of mine." He grinned wickedly. "I fought a little war with them and could have brought back some scalps if I had had taste for that sort of thing."

He leaned forward, warming to his story. "And I came on a trail I had heard about before but never traveled, Lady. I have known about that path since I first went west into Indian country, but I never went down it before. It ain't a wide road or always a pretty one, but it's a wonder. It's dug deep by foot travelers and horses, and animals too, I guess. Most roads follow the water, but this one is different. It just cuts across the wilderness, winding like a snake past rivers and through forests and marshes until it comes out way west and south on the big river they called the Mississippi."

"There have been feet on that trail forever," he went on. "Some places it is beat down until it looks like a great grave with no end to it. Trees thrust up by its sides, their roots bared but still hanging on while the trail grows deeper. The Indians call it the Trace, the Natchez Trace, after some Indians that live down at the river end of it, in French country."

15

"And did you follow it all the way?" Julie asked.

Josh shook his head. "Not this time," he admitted. "But I followed it down close enough to hear a lot of stories about the Natchez people down there." His glance slid to Jacques. "It was when I was telling some of the tales to your cousin here that he got so excited and sent for you. Damn it all, Jacques," he exploded suddenly. "You got me so tight up about this business that I'm afraid I won't get the story out right."

Jacques nodded. "Let me try." He turned to Julie. "It seems that these Natchez Indians aren't like most of the other savages of this country. They have a king and a noble class, good medical skills, and a civilization of a strange sort. Their king is called the Sun God, even as the King of France is known. The laws of their country forbid the Sun King's family from marrying other royalty. They have to marry the lowest class in the tribe. What did you say those peasants were called, Josh?"

"Stinkards," Josh said quietly. "The members of the Sun God family have to marry stinkards . . . or slaves."

"Indians have slaves?" Julie broke in, astonished.

"It's a big thing with them," Josh told her. "They kidnap from enemy tribes or take people in war and sell them as slaves . . . to other tribes, to the Spanish down in Guale, and even into the islands south."

"There is a particular slave in the head village of the Natchez that Josh heard stories of," Jacques said quietly.

Josh kept his eyes on his hands as he spoke. "Much is made of the fact that the Sun God's sister is married to a tall, fair white man who was sold to the tribe many years ago after being taken in war. He is said to be a man of 'wise head,' with many important skills. He speaks French fluently, and is skilled in the management of animals and crops. He has a child, a girl of about eight years, by his Natchez wife. He is famed all along the Trace, even by those Indians who know him only as legend. The Indians call him PoBotahm."

In the sudden silence that followed Josh's words, Julie realized that both men were waiting for her . . . waiting for her to do what?

"Say the slave's name, Julie," Jacques ordered harshly. "Say the slave's name out loud."

Julie frowned. "Po Bo Tahm," she said tentatively. Her own words echoed suddenly in her mind. It was as if a sudden shower of ice had struck her. She moved her lips helplessly, staring from one man to the other. "PoBotahm," she repeated wildly, "My God in heaven...Paul Bontemps." A shiver moved down her arms and she felt suddenly dizzy. "Paul Bontemps...Sophie's lost husband. My God. My God in Heaven," she sighed, leaning back in her chair.

"There is no proof, Julie. It could be the wildest coincidence in the world. It could be a story made up by Indians to tell around campfires, but there it is. When Josh came looking for you, wanting to know where you were and what had become of you, I told him that you were living at the plantation of Paul Bontemps and he stared at me as if I were wild."

"And he was a slave of war...what war?" Julie asked.

"The Yamasee War," Josh said quietly.

"But he has stayed there," she protested. "Surely in all this time he could have gotten away." She thought of Sophie rising each day in hope and lying down alone each night to tears of loneliness. "Surely he could have gotten away to come back home."

"The Indians are still savages," Josh reminded her. "There is a custom they have to prevent runaway slaves. They cut the tendons on the ankles of strong men. They can hobble to work but they haven't a hare's chance of fleeing."

"What can we do?" Julie asked quietly.

"If he were an ordinary slave, we could buy his freedom," Josh explained. "A slave is a piece of merchandise to be bought and sold. The fact that he has fathered a child in the royal line makes it a little harder."

"Kidnap?" Julie asked.

Josh grinned at Jacques' look of surprise. "That is possible, as are many things. My friends the Chickasaws are old allies of the Natchez people. Who knows what deal could be made? If it is the right man."

"What are the odds, Josh?" Julie asked. "Tell me the odds."

His grin brought a nostalgic skip to her heart. "That's my Lady," he said proudly. "A real gambler's woman." Then he sobered. "There's always a chance in anything, Lady. This one I would put about one in five thousand, of getting there, getting him loose, and getting him home. If he is the right PoBotahm."

"My God," Julie shook her head. "I am in a kind of shock. Sophie...what about Sophie?"

Jacques frowned. "Josh and I talked about that. It is no secret that there is bad blood between your husband and his sister over her refusal to marry Henri Beauchamps. Perhaps it

17

is not Sophie who needs to hear this story but her brother, your husband Antoine. It seems that it is Antoine who has much to gain from the return of his brother-in-law from the dead. Her hopes seem high enough already."

Julie breathed out slowly, nodding. "Any further raising of Sophie's hopes with no better odds than these would be cruel. But oh, you are right about Antoine. What joy it would be to hand the responsibility of his sister into her own husband's hands. What can we do now, Josh? What can we do today?"

Both men laughed, but Josh sobered quickly. "You have to remember that this was only one of many tales I have heard until I heard this man's name from your cousin. I have promises to keep with the Chicasaws and am soon to go back to Indian country for that. Now I will go farther down the Trace. Now I will follow the details of the story to confirm what Jacques and you suggest. Once we know it is the same man, then we will explore our options."

"One in five thousand," Jacques reminded them quietly. Then he rose and approached Julie's chair. "I will not ask you how you will approach your husband with what you have heard here today. But I will remind you that I asked only for an hour and the time is already a little past."

Chapter Five

The storm that had crouched above the wooded hills to the west moved in closer. From the doorway Jacques eyed the heavy-bottomed clouds that had pushed all the sky's lightness to the sea. Wind rattled in the vines against the porch and whipped the branches of the giant trees lining the drive.

"Rain," Jacques decided aloud in a disgusted tone. "It will come in fast too. Is it possible for you to stay?"

"You know better than to ask that, Jacques," she reproached him. "I am glad I came, though, and my heart has new hope." She rose on tiptoe to press her lips to his cheek.

The wind loosened tendrils from her ribbons and sent them curling about her face as she turned to Josh. Whatever words she could have found for him stilled in her throat as she took both his hands in her own. "Josh," she murmured, her heart in the name.

His own soft voice was suddenly hoarse. "Lady, my Lady. Your cousin here will know when I get back. Godspeed, Lady."

Blinded by sudden tears, Julie let herself be lifted into the carriage by Jacques and Mandy. Josh would not say good-bye. He could no more stand to hear a farewell than he could stand to have anyone tell him they were sorry. He was Josh and her tenderness for him had not lessened with time or her marriage or her new and glorious role as mother.

"Perhaps you could tell the driver to hurry as much as possible," Julie told Mandy. Once in the carriage a whole range of frightening possibilities had occurred to her. What if Antoine and Sophie and the others had seen the storm coming and rushed home to the plantation? What if they were already there and the maid had told them that she had gone to Monde DuBois without explanation?

"As fast as possible," she repeated to Mandy.

"I tole him already," Mandy said, her eyes solemn on Julie's face. "He say that no horse alive is gonna beat this rain to your place, but he aims to try with what he got."

As if in agreement with the driver's prediction a slow rumble of thunder sounded above the hoofbeats of the horses and the rattling of the carriage wheels. Within minutes, drumming rain began on the roof of the carriage. It settled into a steady, even rhythm, like an accompaniment to the beat of the hooves.

"You might as well sit back," Mandy said quietly. "It don't shorten miles to brace up stiff like that."

Julie grinned at her. "My mind is already home," she admitted, leaning against the cushions. She could not really relax.

The speed of the carriage seemed to multiply the ruts in the road so that she was pitching about in spite of a firm grip on the handles.

"Want me to tell him slow down?" Mandy asked. "The rain is already coming anyway."

Julie shook her head stubbornly. "I am late already. It is not all that bad."

"I can't even tell where we are," Julie confessed, trying to peer through the sheets of rain coursing down the carriage windows.

"Not far enough, I can tell you," Mandy replied quietly.

Julie schooled herself to self-control. It was hot in the carriage. The rain striking the sunbaked earth turned to steam that brought a fine line of sweat to her upper lip. It was hard to breathe. Every yard that the carriage traveled seemed like a mile to her. Why couldn't she breathe? The dull low ache that had begun to press in her lower belly had to be from the jolting of the carriage as the storm went on unabated.

Sharp rolls of thunder seemed to speak and answer from all about them. The explosions of sound were accompanied by staggered shafts of brilliant light that glowed eerily through the curtains.

"The worst of the storm is still behind us," Julie kept telling herself. "We are outrunning it with every mile."

She heard the driver's shout of alarm as the bolt of lightning struck the road just ahead of them. Even as her eyes clamped shut with terror and her head seemed to burst from the crashing sound, she felt Mandy's imperative hands on her shoulders. Together they were thrown back hard against the cushions and the horses screamed in terror and panicked in their shafts. She heard the shouted curses of the driver as the rampant horses hurled the carriage from side to side.

As the carriage was thrown over, she lost her grip on the door altogether. She could find no breath to scream as she was thrown back and forth with Mandy's hands still clinging to her.

But she stayed conscious . . . conscious of Mandy's slow desperate sobbing and the scream of an injured horse. It was while she struggled for words to comfort Mandy that the pain came. It was strange that she could clearly see the pain in her mind, a thin and flexible steel stiletto held by a ruthless hand. The pain struck at her waist and tore through her body toward her legs.

"No," she screamed as she shivered from the passing of the pain. "No. No. No."

She tried to face the enormity of what had happened. Tears blazed behind her eyes. She knew that if she for one moment released her grip on herself she would dissolve into hysterical weeping. The memory of the pain lay like a scar across her mind. Her baby. Her baby was coming and where in hell were they in the mud and the storm with no help for miles?

"Mandy," she said fiercely. "Stop that noise this minute."

She heard the girl's sharp intake of breath and a strangled gasp.

She heard a scratching above her. She tried to look but the

awkward angle in which she had been thrown hid that part of the door from her view. She heard the click of the latch and saw the broad dark face of the driver appear above her. A draft of cold air swept about her and rain dampened her face. "My God, mistress," the man groaned prayerfully. "My God. My God."

"Pull the girl out," Julie ordered firmly. "Reach in and pull the girl up."

Julie herself could not move. A great indolence held her in place as she saw the driver's strong brown arms reach down for Mandy, watched the swirl of petticoats against Mandy's slender brown legs as the girl was lifted away from her.

The driver stared down at her doubtfully. "I don't know if I can lift you, ma'am," he confessed.

If only there were a moment of quiet. But the growling and the terrifying crashes of the storm continued unabated and always, from beyond the shell of the carriage, came the cries of the injured horse, a wordless screaming that tore through Julie's head.

"You must lift me out," she told him sternly. "NOW."

His arms moved down toward her, his face greened by fear in the strange light of the storm. She worked her arms up until she could lock them firmly behind his neck. The strength in the hands that gripped her about the waist was reassuring.

Just as she felt his hands tightening about her waist, the pain began again. She moaned and froze as the agony tore down her body.

"God," he cried, his eyes white-rimmed above her. "God."

She moistened her lips and raised her face to him.

"You can do it," she told him firmly. "I know you can do it."

She felt the child as a great swaying weight as he lifted her through the door. A flood of moisture coursed hotly down her legs, as if her own blood were afire.

Mandy, her eyes wide with terror, crouched by the carriage wheel, her lips pressed tightly as if to still an outcry.

One horse had struggled to its feet but the other, still screaming with pain, lay on the ground with is back leg at an off angle.

"You have to kill it," she told the driver. "Are you armed?" He shook his head.

"A stone," he muttered with his face twisted. "I could use a stone."

"Is there a house near?" Julie asked. "Anything to keep off the rain?"

"Once a house was here," the driver said. "And buildings.

The Indians burnt them and the people was run off."

"There must be some shelter left," Julie insisted.

"A shed maybe," the man agreed.

"You'll help us there," she told him. "Then take the horse and go for help quickly."

Only after the driver had helped them across the sodden field and into the rude open shack and then gone with the horse did Julie realize what she had done. She had given the man no directions. Antoine. She needed Antoine and Sophie and the great cross slave Susan who had been so much help to the midwife when Etoile was born. But the man was gone and rain drummed steadily on the tired roof of the open shed.

Chapter Six

A strangely heightened consciousness pressed in on Julie as she entered the shelter. It was a lean-to, nothing more. Once it had boasted a door, but now there were only the twisted leather remnants of crude hinges and a single rotten board falling awry.

The roof leaked. Having removed her undergarments and folded the petticoats against a later need, Julie lay on the uneven floor and stared at the darkened circle of stain where the rain was coming in. It was only a small hole, so the drops of rain came in singly, like musical tones set to measure a few seconds between drops. Each drop chimed as it fell into the shallow pool that testified to other days, other storms, since the building had fallen into disuse.

There had been life here before. The driver had told of a plantation being set here and a family started, only to have all lost and destroyed during the Indian war. They had passed a chimney set in the rubble of the field outside. Vines clasped the chimney's bricks, as if the forest itself were trying to hold up whatever was left of this place where humans had labored and lived and borne children.

In pain. Julie clenched her hands fiercely, feeling her nails break into the flesh. What had first come as a stiletto was now a broadsword cutting its searing path down her body. Mandy, kneeling at her side, watched helplessly, her dark eyes awash with tears.

"What can I do?" the girl pleaded softly. "What can I do?"

"Wait with me," Julie tried to force her voice to a calmness that would reassure the girl. "Just wait with me and help will come."

"What if it don't come?" Mandy whispered.

"We don't think about that," Julie told her. Then in an effort to distract her companion, she asked. "Listen, Mandy, what bird is that?"

"That's just an old mockbird," she said with disdain in her voice. "He don't know anything but singing. He don't even have his own songs, he's so dumb. He just grabs onto other fellows' songs and sings away like he was somebody. He's so dumb that he's like to drown out there with his face up and the rain falling in."

Julie laughed softly as Mandy's frustration at their predicament spilled out in her attack on the high sweet song that was rising and falling through the rhythm of the unremitting rain.

"I like you, Mandy," she said softly.

The girl's troubled eyes slid away from Julie's gaze. "I like you too, missy," she said softly. "But I don't much like myself this day. If I was to know what would happen I would never have given that letter to you from Mistah Jacques. I would have just tore it up even if it meant I got whipped bad."

"Mister Jacques would never whip you," Julie rebuked her.

"He's got a right," Mandy reminded her. "Just like his daddy before him, he's got a right."

The pains were coming closer together. Julie counted the drips of the leaking roof between them. At first there were twenty chimes in the pool between pains, then fifteen, and finally every tenth drop of water into the pool was the signal for the pain to start again. She could feel her body squeezing the child toward birth like a great independent fist.

"Wait," she whispered silently to her own body, panting between the waves of agony. "For the love of God, wait."

Either the rain-drops were falling farther apart or the pain had quickened until there was no spell of peace at all, but only pain tripping over pain. She had to struggle for each breath, keeping her eyes tightly closed and fighting back the screams that lay behind her lips.

The baby would not wait. She imagined that she could feel the very bones of her body widening like a great anguished flower to release the child into the world. Other births flashed

23

through her mind in scarlet waves . . . the coming of the child in a fancy London townhouse when she had been a helper to her dear friend Margaret. That mother had been given certain opiates and her lids had been half closed in sleep and still she had rent the house with screaming. She reminded herself that she had borne Etoile safely. She clung to the thought of her daughter . . . her own little star. She forced herself to see the child's face, that heart-shaped face whose great sapphire eyes were so exactly like Antoine's. But Etoile had been born in the great bedchamber of Sophie's plantation house, where she had been conceived. Julie herself had been given something bitter to drink and there were nurses there and a midwife with great strong arms like a man. And Susan had been there, sage and crossly tender.

Mandy, seeing Julie's tongue pass uselessly along her lips, rose in her silent graceful way and disappeared. She returned with water cupped in her hand. Julie drank from the curve of the girl's palm, the coolness flowing like balm down her burning throat.

"What can I do?" Mandy whispered again. "That baby coming, ain't he?"

Julie nodded, stuggling for breath between the onslaughts of pain.

"Have you ever seen a baby come?" Julie asked.

Mandy shook her head sadly.

"He will come," she told the girl between gasps. "You will see his head first and then the shoulders curved like a man carring a great burden. Then you must slip your hands about his shoulders and pull, helping him to come. In blood," Julie added firmly, holding the girl's eyes with her own.

As if the child itself had heard her words, the pain of its coming grew suddenly fierce and tearing. The sword sliced and a fire blazed in Julie's belly as the muscles tightened and loosened, forcing against the child. Julie ached to grip Mandy's hands, as she had the hands of the nurses by her side when Etoile was born, but she could not. She must leave Mandy's hands free to help with the child. She straightened her arms stiffly and gripped her own legs, digging her nails into the tender flesh.

"Oh Jesus," Mandy moaned. "Oh Jesus."

"The child," Julie gasped. "Help the child."

Like a great torrent breaking past barriers, Julie felt the child plunge from her body. She felt her own muscles continue to grip and loosen and then grip again. Her eyes were

24

working strangely. She saw Mandy rise as if she were suddenly a long distance away. She saw the girl hold the birth-stained child before her with a stunned expression, it's cord trailing to her own body.

"Upside down," Julie gasped. "Hold it by the feet and slap it on the back. Quickly."

She tried to rise to her elbows but the strength was not there.

"Hit him?" Mandy asked, as if from some great distance.

"Hit him," Julie hissed desperately. A drum began in her head, a slow steady cadence of death. He must cry. He must not lie in the girl's arms like that, a curled silent bloodstained doll in the dim light of the shed.

"HIT HIM!" she screamed.

Mandy gasped. Then with her mouth still agape, she seized the baby by its feet and turned it over. Julie saw him sway from the grip on his ankles. She saw a twitch of movement in his arms. In the silence the sound of flesh hitting flesh was an astonishment to her ears. Then the other sound, the sudden mewling of complaint, and the baby coughed and gagged and began to scream.

"He lives," she whispered in disbelief. "He lives. Antoine has his son."

With her dress all the way unfastened, Julie laid the baby against her own warm flesh. He was curled as if to sleep, his face scarlet from his screaming. His hands clutched themselves into fists, as if he were gripping treasure. She pulled the fullness of the dress over the two of them like a coverlet. They were still joined and yet he lived apart from her, a small sleek head, dark and smooth as the body of a mole, resting between her breasts.

She felt her lashes drop with exhaustion. She would sleep. She would sleep with her new child on her breast until Antoine came.

The mockingbird sang and the child stirred against her flesh. Her eyes flew wide at the sound of horse's hooves outside the shed. Her heart thundered with excitement and relief. Anoine. Antoine had come and all would be fine now.

Then the figure came in the door. Her cousin Jacques, his face pale with horror, stood in the opening.

She stared at him dumbly. Shock came over her in dark waves and she began to wail. "Antoine," she wailed. "Where is Antoine?" And the darkness closed over her.

25

Chapter Seven

The warehouse of the merchant Ethan Weston was on the first floor of his double house on the Battery. The back rooms were piled to the ceiling with barrels and crates, but the front room, which served as his office, was barely less cluttered. A coil of ship's rope had been set against the door to the office to hold it open in the hope that some vagrant sea breeze would stir the heavy air of the room. Ethan himself toiled over a desk that was buried under piles of accounts, some held down by empty and crusted ink pots. At his right hand stood an open decanter of rum, but no sign of a cup or glass.

Antoine Rivière, having settled his sister and her maid into the house on Tradd Street for a day of cleaning and dropped his child Etoile and her nurse at the Scotswoman's house, made his way to the Battery with a lighter heart.

Julie would waken, read his note, and, as always, the gentleness of her spirit would overcome her petulance. She would be eager to come to his arms by day's end. The clouds that had been at his back had gained speed until the last tinges of blue had been pressed from the sky. What sounded like the faint rumbling of thunder came from the west. Indeed there would be rain, and both man and earth would be more comfortable for it.

Antoine stood watching the merchant a long minute before Ethan was aware of his presence. God only knew where Weston had taken that name from. He certainly looked more gypsy than Englishman, scowling darkly at the work under his hand. There was a mystery about the man and his sister, a darkly voluptuous young woman with smoldering eyes who came and went with the whimsy of a seafaring man. The townspeople whispered dark things of the girl, but Antoine had noted that when she swung along the street, her slender neck held high, there were none who dared to accost her.

For his part, he liked Ethan, having grown to know him well while marketing the produce of his sister's plantation. Antoine smiled at the small wiry man fiercely scowling at the desk before him. Although a shadow fell as Antoine's bulk filled the door, Ethan did not even glance up.

He only muttered, "Hold. Hold," crossly, working down a line of figures before him. Then totting, he pushed the paper aside, grinned up at Antoine, and rose.

"They match. Those bastard columns of figures match." Only then did he squint into Antoine's face with delight. "Good God, Tony, what brings you here between harvests?"

He seemed to be all about Antoine at once, seizing a stack of papers that had flown to the floor at his rising, jerking a chair from between two barrels to offer to Antoine, and handing him the rum decanter after a quick wipe of its mouth.

"For God's sake, sit down. Drink, man!" he ordered. Then remembering, he peered about fiercely. "There ought to be a glass or cup somewhere about for a snob too good to tilt a bottle."

Antoine shook his head and sat in the chair. "Never mind that, Ethan. That rotgut of yours won't go down my throat unless it's stiff with lemons."

Weston, back in his own chair, spread his knees wide and planted his heels on the floor with a sigh of satisfaction. "Damned if it isn't good to see you. How are things, anyway?" Then he pitched forward in his chair. "The babe. Has your wife had the babe you were waiting for? And if so, what did it come?"

"Not yet," Antoine grinned, "but it could happen at any minute now. She swears it is a boy, but I don't really give a damn myself. Another charmer like Etoile would suit me fine . . . for now, anyway."

Weston reached for his pipe. "With such a beauty as you have with that one, who could complain? But in the end a man needs sons."

"And a somewhat for them to inherit," Antoine added soberly.

Weston prodded the rough tobacco into his pipe bowl, thoughtful at Antoine's tone. This was a new line to hear from Antoine Rivière. The man had seemed content enough to run that great rice plantation for his sister these past years, far more content than an ordinary man would be to manage the fortune of a man as apt to return as a sow is to fly. Weston was convinced that Antoine must draw a steady percentage from his work, but that would be a pittance to what a man of his strength and wit could do on his own. But now it seemed that Tony was bending his mind to his own purse. Interesting.

"Are you thinking of seating a river for yourself and your

growing family?" Weston asked.

Antoine hesitated. "I need a place, of course, but I had more thought of something inside the walls—just a house, really. I'm not as eager to get into growing as I am to try the shipping end of this business."

"A bastard gypsy from God knows where," the townspeople said of Ethan Weston. But as Antoine laid his thoughts before the man, he was impressed as ever with the earthy, animal swiftness with which Ethan's tongue cut through words to the bare white bones of logic that lay beneath.

The sky darkened beyond the open door and the first spattering of raindrops bounced along the walkway while they talked. A clap of near-thunder starlted Antoine and he leaped to his feet.

"Good God, that storm has sneaked in on me. Now I'll have to get those women out to the plantation in a downpour."

"Not your wife, surely?" Ethan asked with dismay.

Antoine shook his head. "She's safe at home at least," Antoine assured him. "She had no mind to come and it's just as well. She's too near term to risk being bounced about on roads like ours."

"So it is to be shipbuilding," Ethan said thoughtfully as he took Antoine's hand. "As I said, it's only the new capital that will hold you back."

"I would appreciate your asking around a little . . . naming no names of course," Antoine told him. "There must be someone about with idle pounds to invest."

Weston shook his head. "Those are gambler's pounds you are asking for, Tony," he reminded him. "Between the storms and the Spanish and the pirates, a man can lose money on ships like dice tumbling on a table."

"Or win fortunes," Antoine reminded him. "There's more rice and stores stacking up in this port than there are ships to carry them. That's a need you can't gainsay."

By the time Sophie and her maid were loaded into the carriage and Mrs. MacRae had clucked little Etoile in on the seat beside them, the rain was sweeping along the streets in sheets.

"Tony, please ride inside," Sophie pleaded. "Your horse can be led behind. There is no haste for a carriage on such roads, anyway."

"I'll not melt," he promised her genially. "I haven't a dry thread on me now and you would all be the same if I got in there with you."

Sophie had been right about the rain-drenched road.

Antoine felt that hours had passed by the time they arrived at the plantation. Leaving the carriage to be unloaded by Ben, Antoine took the stairs two at a time to seek his wife. He paused at the door of their room, then turned the knob carefully, lest she should be sleeping. The windows had been closed against the storm and the curtains drawn shut. The air was sweet with Julie's scent, but the bed was empty. He left a wet trail on the floor as he strode across the room to look for her in Etoile's small adjoining nursery.

Shrugging, he peeled off his wet clothes and dressed hastily before going to seek her downstairs.

"How can Julie sleep through this storm?" Sophie laughed as he ran down the stairs.

"She's not up there," Antoine replied. "Haven't you seen her either?"

A small line of concern came between Sophie's brows. "Nowhere down here," she admitted. "Is her shawl up there? She might have gone over to visit the Beauchamps rather than spend the long day alone."

Antoine turned to the stairs again, only to return after a moment. "I'll send Ben over for her in a carriage. But good God, she surely wouldn't have walked that far today, not the way she was."

The look of concern on Sophie's face deepened. "Let me check with Meg in the kitchen. She must know where Julie is off to."

As Antoine turned to follow his sister, his eyes fell on Julie's sewing basket, which had been set on the floor just inside the hall door. At once he saw the pointed edge of the note he had slipped into it for her. Of course it was possible that she had found it and read it and replaced it in exactly the same fold of the embroidered dress, but it was unlikely. His heart plunged. Damn it all. If she hadn't seen his note she would have gone this long day with no reassurance from him.

The rain pelted on his shoulders as he ran from the rear door to the kitchen house, where Sophie had gone to seek Meg.

Sophie's face was expressionless as she turned to him.

"Where is she?" he asked roughly. "What's wrong?"

"She left early," Sophie said quietly. "A little before noon."

"But where?" Antoine asked crossly, irritated at the careful way his sister's words came out.

"In a carriage," Sophie almost whispered. "For Monde DuBois."

"Monde DuBois," he repeated the word fiercely. "God in

Heaven, what have I done?"

"Come into the house, Meg," Sophie ordered quietly, with a warning glance at Antoine. "Come and tell us exactly what happened."

Antoine, scowling fiercely, listened with impatience to Meg's careful retelling of Mandy's arrival and her own cautionary words.

"'Only an hour,' she told us," Meg said slowly, avoiding Antoine's eyes. "She say she gonna stay only an hour."

"Then what in the name of God has happened to her?" Antoine lurched toward the door, then turned. "Tell Ben to bring my horse around here fast. And I'll need a cape."

"Horse," Sophie said with astonishment. "What good can you do hauling yourself up to Monde DuBois on a horse dripping wet? Do you have it in your mind to bring Julie home like that, in her condition? We'll take the carriage and I will go too, and so will Susan." She barely paused for breath as she rang for Ben. "And pillows and a little brandy. Even if it is only the storm that has delayed her, she will be weak from exhaustion."

"I will kill him, Sophie," he said softly, as Meg scurried from the room to get Susan. "If that Jacques DuBois has laid a hand on my wife, or if she is hurt in any way from this foolish adventure, I shall kill Jacques DuBois with my own bare hands."

Sophie tried to soothe him. "Julie knows full well how you feel about her cousin. She would not have made this trip up there if it had not been a matter of some real import."

Antoine stared at her thoughtfully, then nodded. "Her aunt," he decided aloud. "If something had gone wrong with Anne-Louise's health, for instance, and she needed Julie's healing skills."

"But Anne-Louise isn't—" Sophie began to speak and failed to stop her words in time. Her hand flew to her mouth as she stared back at her brother.

"Out with it, Sister," Antoine almost shouted. "What were you about to say? Anne-Louise is not what?"

"She is not in residence at Monde DuBois," Sophie said lamely. "She is in Philadelphia, visiting with friends."

Sophie felt herself blanch at the look of black fury in her brother's face. Hearing the call from the door, she scurried toward the carriage, careful not to meet Antoine's eyes again.

Chapter Eight

The wheels of the carriage sucked and slid through the mired ruts of the road that led to Monde DuBois. The storm-blackened sky that pelted the carriage with wave after wave of chill dark rain was at least occasionally brightened by streaks of lightning.

Ben fought the terrified horses valiantly, but the carriage rocked and jolted from his battle to keep the beasts in their traces and the wheels on the road. Sophie, who had made this trip to Monde DuBois several times in the years since Julie and Antoine were wed, marveled that miles could be so magically lengthened by the presence of the storm and her brother's glowing fury at her side.

She had quite given up hope of anything ever happening when she heard Ben's frantic shout and felt the tossing of the carriage as the horses reared against the tug of his reins. The carriage shuddered violently. Before it settled back onto its wheels, Antoine was wresting the door open to look out.

"Where are we? What the devil is wrong?" he shouted.

"There's a carriage blocking the road," Ben shouted back. "There's no way to get by."

Antoine was at once out of the carriage and into the rain. A dull weight of despair settled on Sophie. "Susan," she said softly, "I simply can't stand any more...." Susan sobbed bleakly in reply, a sound that only added to Sophie's distress. Sighing, Sophie pulled her mantle up over her carefully curled white wig and leaned out from the door to discover what Antoine and Ben were shouting about.

The carriage was indeed blocking the road and in the tangle of broken wood and leather Sophie saw the eyes of a great bloated horse whose mangled head lay in a puddle of water stained by its blood.

"How do you know this carriage is from Monde DuBois?" she heard Antoine shout furiously. Ben's dark hand pointed to the small crest blazoned on the door that was cocked open so that the pouring rain was filling the coach like a bucket.

"And empty," Ben said. "There's nobody in there."

"Where?" Antoine shouted. "Where could they have gone in this wilderness?"

The carriage was deeply mired. With the traces all the way free, they finally shifted the carriage aside to give room for passage.

"The other horse," Antoine explained, calling back to Sophie. "She had to get away on the other horse."

After Herculean effort, the road was finally cleared. Antoine, thick with mud from head to toe, mounted the box beside Ben. It seemed to Sophie that the carriage had barely started again when it heaved to a sudden stop.

"What is it?" Sophie called from the open window, heedless of the rain. "What is wrong now?"

"Another carriage," Antoine called back. Then she saw it herself, a light chaise whose horse had been so hastily secured to a roadside tree that he could not even reach down to crop the wet wild grass that grew alongside.

Then she heard Ben's cry. "Look. There are people over there...out by that shed."

Even from that distance Antoine recognized the tall spare form of Jacques DuBois. He felt his hands tighten into fists at his sides and the fury of murder coursed crazily across his mind. "Bastard," he groaned to himself without slackening his pace. "Rotten son of a madman."

But Jacques was moving toward him, his hand raised like a cleric pleading for peace.

"Easy," he called out to Antoine. Easy."

"Easy," Antoine gasped, lunging for the approaching man. "You dare to caution me 'easy.' Where is my wife? Speak up, you son-of-a-bitch, where is my wife?"

Jacques stepped lightly away from Antoine's grasp. "Your wife is all right," he assured her, motioning to the shack a few yards away.

Antoine, really looking at the shanty for the first time, stopped dead in his tracks.

He was barely a step from the open door when he heard the faint, unmistakable mewling of an infant. He froze where he stood. Etoile. This was how Etoile had sounded when she had burst forth stained and flailing from Julie's body.

Then he stood silent at the door. Although twilight was yet an hour away, the interior of the shanty was so dark that he had to squint to see what lay within. At first he saw only the broad square back of a woman bending toward the floor. Some soft murmuring exchange was passing between the woman and her patient, who was totally hidden from him.

He stared about the room desperately and caught the eyes of a slender Negro girl clutching a bundle to her breast as she stared back defensively into his face.

"My child," Antoine said dumbly to the girl.

Mandy's lips tightened and her eyes brimmed with tears.

"Your son, sir," she stammered in a low voice. As the girl's gaze left his face he followed her eyes to see Julie, her black hair in a tumbling frame about her face. Her golden eyes were warm on his face and he barely caught her whispered words.

"I knew you would come," and she smiled.

The large Negro woman grunted as she hefted herself erect. Antoine's stomach lurched to see her hands and arms scarlet with Julie's blood, but the woman was smiling. "Mistah Jack knows I do all the babies around there so he brought me fast. Nice clean birthing," she reassured Antoine, nodding. "Mandy and your lady done a nice clean birthing. Cord's tied now and everything fine."

Antoine's murderous rage seemed to withdraw into the darker shadows of his consciousness. There was room only for relief. He knelt by Julie, careful to keep the mire of his mantel away from her.

What could he say? Behind him the infant had set up a rhythmic howling. He could hear the midwife's shushing sounds and Mandy's stuttered pleading. Then Sophie was there and he heard her cry of astonishment and a spate of chatter among the women. Yet he could not take his eyes from Julie's face. She lived. There was a son. But God in his Heaven, Julie lived.

He saw her try to raise her arms to him and fail in strength. He saw her draw a deep breath to rally some power to speak. "You," she finally said softly in that same tone of delighted discovery with which she had turned to him when they first joined in the passion of lovemaking. "You," she repeated. "You."

"Always, Julie," he groaned with relief. "Always." The desire to fold her in his arms was a physical pain but he dared not touch her in his muddy state.

He called to Ben to come to bear her to the carriage. Jacques DuBois broke in. "I can carry her," he insisted.

"We will do it my way," Antoine said coldly through clenched teeth.

Once Julie was inside the carriage braced against Sophie's protective arms and the child was clasped in Susan's arms beside them, Ben mounted to the seat. Antoine had a leg up to join him, then thought better of it. He left the carriage to approach the chaise where Jacques was readying to return to Monde DuBois.

"Great gifts make men generous," he said coldly. "Whatever caused you to lure my wife from her home in this desperate case is between you and her. But you have my word on this, Jacques DuBois, that if you ever contact my wife again, or enter our home, or send the smallest message whatever to her for any reason, I shall demand the satisfaction of your life. This is a challenge, Jacques DuBois, suspended only in time."

Chapter Nine

When it was over, and she and the child were safely settled in the airy bright rooms of Sophie's plantation house, Julie found herself unable to seize on any coherent memory of the events of that afternoon or the days following.

The storm she remembered vividly enough because it rose again and again in her dreams. Always it began with the faint spattering of furtive drops, only to grow steadily more furious until she would waken moaning, her hands tight against her ears to block out the crash of thunder that rolled about her in that place lit only by eerie greenish light.

Wakening from such a dream, she sat up in the bed she shared with Antoine. She caught her milk-laden breasts in her hands, barely suppressing a moan of pain. She sighed, glancing toward Antoine's side of the bed, wondering that the storm in her head had not been loud enough to startle him awake also.

Awake he was, although he gave no appearance of having been startled. Instead, he lay with his arms behind his head, watching her. She smiled at him. Even the weak moonlight that lit their room was enough to throw the lines of his face into sharp relief. His hair, bleached even fairer by the hot sun of the Carolinas, seemed to contain its own light in contrast to the bronzed darkness of his flesh.

Bracing herself, she freed a hand to raise it to his face. He flinched at her touch and stirred restlessly away.

"My God, Julie. Don't do that," he ordered. Then he left the bed hastily, pulling his shirt from the chair and ramming his arms into its sleeves. His movements were not swift enough to keep her from seeing that he was swollen with desire for her.

"I am sorry, love. You looked so—"

"Don't tell me how I looked," he cautioned her. "Try to imagine how you have looked to me these past days with your breasts rosy with life and your body turned slender again. A man does not turn eunuch when he sires a child, you know."

She ignored the crossness in his tone. "It was the same after Etoile," she reminded him. "After all, it will be soon."

"One man's soon is another man's forever," he grumbled. "But tell me why it is that you start from sleep like that? That dreadful day comes back to terrify you, doesn't it?" His voice was rough and accusatory.

"The storm," she corrected him. "It is only the storm that haunts me in my dreams." She hoped that he would not sense the concern in her voice. When the dream came back again and again, it had begun to worry her. Could it be an omen? Could it be some sign that their child, born in such tumult, would be cursed with a troubled life?

"Only the storm," he repeated acidly. "You never dream of the events of the day, of the overturning of your carriage ... of your son's birth with only a half-grown girl sniveling in a filthy hut with you?"

"There is something I should tell you about the birth of our son, Antoine," she said softly. "No sane woman would have chosen such a way or such a place for childbearing. I would have been too great a coward to choose it myself. But I feel that I am richer for it happening the way it did."

She raised her eyes to his, pleading for understanding. "You must remember how long I worked with my friend Margaret in London learning to be a healer. Since I have been so protected and supported by your love, there have been times when I feared that I might have lost all my carefully won skills. When the signs showed me that the baby was coming I was afraid. But it turned out all right. I was able to talk to an untrained girl and help her bring the baby forth. When I heard his first cry during the lashing of the storm I felt a great surge of pride!

"Don't you see, Antoine? Our Armand was born, not like the pampered son of a French nobleman but like a

35

colonial . . . roughly, independently, in a crude setting in a savage land. It was a strong beginning, Antoine, for a strong man."

"Oh my God. If my father could hear you talk this way," Antoine laughed bitterly. "My father who reveres his title and his lands and his privileges above his honor or his life. You are a strange fey woman, Julie Duvall Rivière, and I waver like the wind itself between warring urges of love and fury with you."

"But since our son has come, you have borne a greater weight of fury than love," she told him quietly, hoping he would not realize how painful it was for her to speak those words.

"For God's sake, woman, can I be blamed?" He strode to the window, staring out at the path of moonlight across the lawn.

"Don't you think that we should talk about that day, Antoine? Do you have questions that are keeping you sleepless on your own pillow?"

"I have no questions," he said flatly. "I know all that I need to know. I know that your cousin sent you some message . . . probably something of spurious importance. But the very fact that he called to you made you forget your obligation to me and to our unborn child to go racketing off about the country in the teeth of a rising storm. That you risked yourself and our child for that beast DuBois."

"You know only what you wish to think," she corrected him. "What if I were to tell you that the message that Jacques sent was about us . . . you and me? Let me tell you why I went. Let the truth be out and you will understand."

"Not on your life," he said furiously. "Once I let you force your unwelcome truths on me after we had been apart for the long years. I still have enough trouble living with your infidelity of that time to hear more of that from you. I never want to know, Julie. I never intend to hear why you flew to that cousin of yours. I only know that I will not have his name said in my presence ever again. I have told him to contact you or enter my house or have anything to do with you again only if he is ready to be dead at my hand."

"Hush, Antoine. You'll waken the baby!"

Her warning came too late. The indignant howl from the next room stilled their voices. Julie tightened her shoulders at her husband and grinned wickedly at him.

"Listen to that," she whispered. "He is a little terror."

36

He nodded, anger slowly leaving his face.

Together they listened to the creak of boards as Susan struggled awake, then the patient slap of her feet on the floor as she crossed and recrossed the room, carrying the child and crooning softly to him even as his screams grew more murderous with each moment.

"What if you should feed him?" Antoine whispered.

"How could it hurt?" she giggled.

Sliding into his trousers, Antoine rapped on the door of the adjoining nursery. Julie heard Susan's apologetic voice turn to register protest. Then Antoine returned victorious, carrying the child who was livid with rage, his fists pummeling wildly.

Dropping the ruffled neck of her gown, Julie pressed her nipple against the baby's scarlet cheek. Armand's mouth turned to it unerringly. His cry ended in a strangled gulp as he seized her and began to nurse vigorously.

"He's like a damned alligator," Antoine said, eying the boy proudly. "I don't remember that Etoile ever behaved like that."

"Ouch," Julie replied, easing the baby's grip on her flesh. "Etoile was never like this." She shook her head. "But look at him, Antoine. Look at those great hands, his barrel of a chest. He is a monstrous child, and so fierce."

The infant's belly swelled as he drank. Then, as suddenly as he had begun, he ceased. The tension disappeared from between his lips. He stirred and grunted and began snoring softly, his cheek still pressed against Julie's breast.

"Come here, you little tyrant," Antoine whispered. "You sleep on your plate like a drunken bandit."

Julie slid the limp child from her own arms into those of his father, who returned him to the nursery.

As he fell asleep, Armand had bathed the front of Julie's gown with warm milk. While Antoine was returning Armand to Susan, Julie slipped out of the soiled garment and pulled a fresh one from the chest. She had it lifted above her body when Antoine returned to the room. Seeing him there, his eyes intent on her naked body, she grew suddenly clumsy, unable to find the sleeves with her upraised arms.

He chuckled softly at her predicament and crossed the room to her. "How can such a body have been the vessel for that wild young man in there?" he asked softly. Then, with his hand on her waist, he turned her body to the light. "Where are the bulges that new mothers are noted for, good wife?" he asked. "Where are the deforming stripes that mark a mother?"

He slid his hands down from her waist, stroking the smooth unblemished skin of her hips. His voice was husky with passion.

"Tell me, wife, you who are skilled in the arts of medicine and healing, how long must a man be swollen with lust without great damage coming to him?"

Julie trembled at his touch. She felt the nipples so recently soft from nursing, grow tense with passion. That familiar sense of melting moved along her loins and she felt her breath quicken with desire.

Julie lifted the gown from about her shoulders and tossed it away. She slid within the panels of Antoine's loose shirt and pressed herself against the hard rod of his desire. The wildness of her passion seized her. Unable to reach his lips, even on tiptoe, she pressed her open mouth against the hard line of his throat just below the ear. She slid one leg in between his thighs, curling the other tightly about his own.

"Witch," he cried, pulling her up into his arms. "Witch and temptress."

On their bed, with her arms tight about him, he struggled against his own passion.

"God in Heaven, Julie. I would not hurt you for the world."

"Only a touch then," she said, arching her body against him.

"A touch," he agreed, guiding himself into that warm nest.

Theirs was a new lovemaking. Julie knew pain when he entered the bruised places of her body, but once within her, he stayed very still. Her need of him, her desire for closeness after having been so long denied moved in waves about him. Her very belly clasped and loosed on him with a strength she had not known she could summon. From his stifled cries she knew that his rapture was equal to her own.

"My love, my love," he moaned against her hair.

Laughing softly, she caught his head between her hands and touseled his fair hair. "What joy, what joy, my love."

"Hush, you wanton," he grinned down at her, writhing against her bare flesh. "Susan will think us mad."

"But will she know the half of it?" Julie teased. She buried her head against him and nuzzled his neck. "It is over, Antoine. It is all over and in that room beyond sleeps that boisterous son of ours."

"And Etoile," he reminded her gently. He pulled away and turned her body so that the moonlight played on the star-shaped scar just above her waist. He laid a finger on that star that was his eternal reminder of how nearly he had lost this woman whom he was convinced had been destined to be his. It was for that star that he had named their first child.

She giggled. "Sometimes I think you cherish that tiny girl of ours more than you do me."

"If such were possible," Antoine laughed. "But it is not. And I must say that this brute Armand has a job to do to win me the way his sister has. Even to think of her, that miniature coquette seems a doll quick with life. It is magic that a child could be so flawlessly beautiful."

"You would certainly not wish a son like that," she reminded him.

"Good God, no," he snorted. "It is enough to have a brother that simpers like a girl and grows coquettish at the sight of a handsome new male. I'll take that rowdy little hellion in there and fight him to my last breath rather than be disgraced like my father has been humiliated by Emile."

"And the last thing you needed right now is another woman in your life," she reminded him. She slid her hand along the line of his flat belly and into the warmth between his thighs.

"Woman," he warned her. "Best you know what you are doing, lest you waken a serpent you do not wish to conjure with."

She only pressed tighter against him, her swollen breasts blazing against his nakedness.

"You are serious," he whispered with astonishment.

She closed his mouth with her own as he turned to her with a chuckle.

"You are incorrigible," he whispered down to her.

"I had a masterful teacher," she reminded him.

Chapter Ten

In spite of every effort to rid her mind of the obsession, Julie's thoughts kept turning to the storm that had raged the night of Armand's birth. Her fear that it had been an omen of disaster haunted her days and brought sudden tears to her eyes on waking.

Armand was little more than a month old when the first of a

series of events occurred to deepen her sense of foreboding.

Unlike her daughter Etoile who had quickly fallen into a pattern of meals and sleep and gurgling play, Armand was a demanding infant from the first. His prodigious appetite so drained Julie of strength that she had little for anything but feeding him. He grew apace, his long limbs filling out with fat. The thoughtful bright eyes in his fine, square-jawed face studied his mother carefully. Susan, into whose care he was given during his hours of wakefulness, chuckled with pride.

"A giant," she told Julie with satisfaction. "You watch that boy, he'll make a giant. And with that fired-up head of hair he got."

And indeed, the dark fine hair of his birth was replaced by rich red curls that matted on his moist scalp while he labored at nursing.

"My sister's mark," Antoine commented, lifting a red curl to watch it snap back into place on his son's head. "But he will make two of her long before he is grown."

Julie marveled at the difference in Antoine's attitude toward his two children. One could only say that he openly adored the girl Etoile. No conversation was so absorbing that Antoine's voice would not trail into silence to watch the child enter the room. His face softened with tenderness as he reached out to catch that elf of a girl into his arms. When his eyes met Julie's over Etoile's riot of soft pale curls, his expression was that of a totally seduced male.

Toward Armand, however Antoine assumed a different stance. He stood above the cradle studying the child, as if he thought to trace a man's future in the lines of an infant face. Pride and speculation seemed equally balanced in his measuring glance.

But those were lonely times for Julie. It was a rare morning that Julie did not waken to find an empty pillow by her side and know that Antoine had risen before dawn to gallop his stallion to Sophie's plantation to oversee his sister's rice crop. Within only a few hours Sophie herself would follow to spend her days at her desk in the almost deserted plantation house. Sophie would return at twilight to bathe and rest a little before dressing for their late dinner they all took together. Sophie and Julie were often already at the table when Antoine slid into his chair with a mumbled apology for his tardiness.

Julie, thrown back on her children for companionship and entertainment, seemed to exist in some special soft place of clinging arms and soft voices.

40

This unreal bubble was burst with startling suddenness.

Julie had been enjoying the last hour of sunset with her children on the piazza when Sophie came to join them. The sea breeze carried the scent of summer flowers onto the open porch and Julie's heart hummed with contentment.

As Sophie entered, Etoile was poised on tiptoe, staring into the crib at her sleeping brother.

"What do you think of your small brother?" Julie asked her daughter as the child's blue eyes stared soberly into the crib.

"He's strong," Etoile said, turning an apprehensive face toward her mother.

Julie laughed. "That is very true, love," she agreed. Then she raised a thoughtful glance to Sophie. "Was your son Charles like this, Sophie? Did he show great will and stubbornness even before he was weaned?"

Sophie stopped and stared thoughtfully into the trees beyond the piazza ledge, then shook her head. "He was more like Etoile, more eager to please, much less anxious to have his own way. Paul used to worry about him, saying that Charles was too gentle to be a man of this rough country. I think that must have still been on my mind when I made the decision to send him to France to be taught. That way, at least he has his choice of the two worlds."

Though she turned her head quickly to hide them, Julie saw the quick glint of tears come to her sister-in-law's eyes.

"I miss him," Sophie confessed softly. "I miss my fine son. The reports from his tutors, from my own mother and father, are all so grand. They say he excels at fencing and horsemanship and shows great aptitude for the management of money affairs. I know I should celebrate his successes, but instead I only miss his face and voice and grieve that Paul's son, who was but an infant when his father left, is growing to manhood without his father and me."

Julie's heart ached for the pain in Sophie's face. How much she longed to reach out and comfort her about her husband, but what could she say? The secret hope that Paul Bontemps still lived, even as a slave of a distant Indian tribe, burned in her mind.

What had Josh said . . . one chance in five thousand? The enormity of the odds of ever finding the man, of his being the right white man, and of freeing him were overwhelming.

She could see her sister-in-law still struggling to keep from weeping at the thought of Charles. Her hands grasped the back of the chair so tightly that her knuckles gleamed white above the emerald ring she always wore.

"Come, my pet," Julie said to Etoile. "Go and find your Maggie. Tell her that Mother and Tante Sophie would have a quiet time here together."

"What about your making a trip to France to see Charles?" Julie suggested soberly. "You could get there to be with him easier than he could leave his studies to come here."

Sophie's eyes widened with astonishment. "But Julie. That is impossible. What if Paul should return while I was away?"

"You went away from here to England to buy Antoine's release from Newgate Prison," Julie reminded her.

"That was different," Sophie protested. "That was a matter of life or death for my brother. This is only . . ." When her voice trailed off, Julie looked up at her. She was startled to see that a strangeness was on her sister-in-law's face.

Julie rose swiftly and went to Sophie's side. Sophie did not even see her move, but continued to stare into space with a strange absorbed expression on her face. Her great fine eyes stood out like dark smudges. Even as Julie leaped to her side, she found her own mind racing.

My God, how thin she is. How long has it been since I really looked at her? The dark shadows beneath her eyes suggested many nights without sleep. The careful spots of makeup that Sophie always wore stood out starkly against the pallor of her skin.

"Julie," Sophie said in a sudden hushed tone. Then her voice rose and she repeated the word: "JULIE!"

Her eyes widened and she turned to stare at Julie as if to steady herself with their exchanged glance. Then she reached out for Julie with one hand. But before they touched, she gave a small moan and with her head drooping like a tired flower, she slumped to the floor of the piazza.

"Susan! Maggie! Betty!" Julie called with desperate urgency, naming everyone she could think of to help her. Even as she heard fast steps approaching, she knelt over her sister-in-law who lay limp and white on the floor.

Sophie was not in a simple faint, she was really ill. Sudden panic filled Julie's breast. A bird called wistfully from the darkening garden beyond the piazza. Antoine. My God, it was night and Sophie was terribly sick. And where was Antoine?

Chapter Eleven

With the help of Susan and Maggie MacRae, Julie was able to get Sophie into her own bedroom. She hastily removed the ornate white wig that Sophie always wore, releasing the rich masses of auburn hair hidden beneath it.

"There must be a physician near here," Julie said desperately when the harsh odor of salts held under Sophie's nose elicited no response.

"There's a Jonathan Marlowe person," Maggie MacRae said in her rich, burring voice. "He's young and new to Charles Town and not much known as yet. The ladies told me . . ."

Julie should have known. Maggie, with her circle of gossiping woman friends, knew every dot of business that was done in Charles Town before the ink was dry on the line.

"Tell Susan where he lives," Julie ordered. "Have her send along a messenger on the run. Tell the slave to say that this is urgent and we beg his attention at once."

Once the room emptied, Julie loosened Sophie's tightly bound bodice and turned back her own ruffled sleeves all in a bunch. Moistening a cloth, she cooled Sophie's head with it while she knelt by the bed, rubbing her sister-in-law's wrists furiously. To Julie's instant hope, Sophie moved her head distractedly on the pillow before lapsing again into unconsciousness.

Shutting Etoile's cries from her mind, Julie grew oblivious to the sounds of the house about her. She was suddenly startled by a man's deep voice close behind her.

"Move aside, mistress," she heard. She scrambled to her feet and backed away.

The man who took her place at Sophie's side did not waste a glance about the room. Instead, he pressed the prostrate woman's wrist and listened, frowning, to her pulse. After opening her eyelids one at a time with deft hands, he laid his head carefully against Sophie's chest to listen intently.

"Brandy," he ordered tersely without glancing about. "And have hot coffee brewed at once."

When Julie had overseen the delivery of the brandy and

43

sent someone scurrying to the kitchen, she seized a moment with Etoile, who was still crouched in the hall sobbing quietly with her eyes glued to her aunt's closed door.

Etoile had allowed herself to be tugged to her feet as the door opened again. Terrified by the strange man filling the door to her aunt's room, she raced away to seek her nurse.

Julie went swiftly to the physician, her eyes wide with concern. "How is she?" she asked breathlessly. "What is wrong?"

Whatever words had been on Jonathan Marlowe's lips were swept away with alarming suddenness. Instead, he stared at Julie incredulously, his large dark eyes moving from her hair to her eyes and then to her lips, finally to pause at the curve of her breasts whose roundness rose from the low throat of her gown.

Julie felt the color rise to her cheeks at his open admiration.

"Now that you have examined both of us, Doctor, what is your diagnosis?" she asked.

"Forgive me, mistress," he said quietly. "I have not been long in these colonies and I must confess that I was startled by as all men who see you must be. Surely this is not an unusual reaction to a person of your attributes."

"I thank you for your compliments," Julie said, furious at herself for being flustered by his candor. "But the subject of Mistress Bontemps' health is what interests me most."

He frowned soberly and stood aside for Julie to enter the room. Sophie's head lay back on the pillow in a much more relaxed attitude. Even from the door Julie could see that her breathing was deeper and more regular. Although the startling pallor remained, Sophie seemed otherwise in a deep and natural sleep.

"There are some things I need to know," Dr. Marlowe said quite professionally, as if their exchange in the hall had never happened. "Is your friend with child?"

Julie's eyes flew open in astonishment. "Oh no, sir, that is not possible."

"Then she is not married?" he asked quietly.

"Oh, indeed," Julie began. Then with a glance at Sophie's sleeping face, she paused. "Perhaps it would be better if we were to speak somewhere else," she suggested. "Lest we disturb her rest."

Although the sun had set since she had taken Sophie from the piazza, the last of the light lingered in a heavily perfumed dimness. Sophie thought passingly of sending for a lantern,

44

but was too distracted by her concern for Sophie.

"I feared she might not be totally asleep," Julie explained. "My sister's husband was lost in the Indian wars many years ago."

"Then she is widowed?" he pressed.

Julie shook her head. "She still hopes for his return. And waits." She tried to explain, but her words sounded somehow lame even as she spoke them.

"And how long has this been?" he pressed.

The intentness of his scrutiny made Julie edgy. "I fail to see how all this affects your opinion of her illness," she said almost crossly.

"It is quite pertinent," he assured her. "I would say that your friend—that your sister," he corrected himself, "is suffering from great grief or stress. She is obviously exhausted and of such painful thinness as to suggest," he looked back at the room he had left, "that in this house at least she lacks appetite or interest in food rather than suffering from a forced hunger."

Julie frowned, considering his words. "She does not sleep well," she confessed. She raised her eyes to him. "Often in the night I hear her stirring when all others are asleep."

"Then you yourself do not sleep well," he suggested.

She grinned at his words, her mind turning to that lusty Armand whose hunger knew no clock. A deep dimple flashed in her left cheek as she replied, "I assure you that I have reason to be abroad at night. And as for eating," she paused with a frown, "I fear I have not noticed. She breakfasts alone and we dine quite late with much conversation that distracts me from such attention."

Julie could see him trying to absorb the details of the household. "She works very hard," Julie added, attempting to be more helpful. "Each weekday she goes to her plantation early and works over her accounts until late in the evening."

"Although this does not sound like an average woman's life, desk work alone does not usually produce the kind of exhaustion that I see in Madame Bontemps," he said quietly, watching Julie's face with an expression that bordered on doubt.

Jonathan Marlowe stared at her thoughtfully. "It is not a physician's business to pry, mistress," he said quietly. "But the condition of your sister concerns me a great deal. It is almost as if she finds life insupportable. When I was able to rouse her to consciousness, her eyes clung to my face for a moment and

45

then she turned away in protest. She acted as if the return to life was something she did not desire. She must rest. She must be coaxed to eat nourishing food. But most of all, whatever is plaguing her spirit so grievously must be removed if she is to be restored to health and strength."

The suddenness of Antoine's appearance at the door startled Julie. His face was dark with annoyance and his tone acid.

"Am I interrupting something?" he asked.

Julie fled to his side, slipping her arm inside his own. "Oh my dear," she said. "I am so glad you have come. My husband, Antoine Rivière, Dr. Jonathan Marlowe. Dr. Marlowe came instantly to our call for a physician for Sophie."

Julie hoped that Dr. Marlowe would think it was the darkness of the piazza that prevented Antoine from seeing the physician's outstretched hand.

"Sophie ill?" Antoine said with disbelief. "Impossible."

"Oh, quite the contrary, sir," Dr. Marlowe said in a tone that suggested that he was not unconscious of Antoine's rudeness. "Your sister is suffering from exhaustion to a most critical degree."

"Vapors," scoffed Antoine, then he turned to Julie. "This is only some new aspect of her madness." He nodded curtly to the doctor. "If you will excuse me, I shall dress for dinner."

"Your husband refers to a madness." He inflected the words like an unspoken question.

Julie caught her lip between her teeth. "They do not get along too well these past few years," she said lamely, trying at the same time to be honest with the doctor and loyal to Antoine. "He considers her clinging to the hope of her husband's return a sort of madness."

The thoughtful way the doctor's eyes dwelt on her face gave her the curious feeling that he understood, without her telling him, the stress that Antoine brought to bear on Sophie.

Then he shrugged. "This must make it very difficult for the patient," he commented. Then, as if rousing himself, "I repeat, she must eat good nourishing food and stay in bed for at least a week. Anything that can be said or done to raise her spirits would be the best of all medicine." He grinned, his face suddenly boyish. "Even laughter, if such can be had."

When he was gone, Julie ran swiftly up the stairs to Sophie's room.

As Julie tiptoed to her bedside, Sophie's head turned toward her.

46

"He called me, Julie," Sophie whispered softly. "One minute I was there on the piazza with you and the children, and the next moment I heard Paul calling my name. His voice was the same, Julie, the same as it ever was."

Julie could not reply. She only held the frail body close to her own until Sophie relaxed. When she was laid back on the pillow, Sophie fell into instant sleep. But her words kept echoing and re-echoing in Julie's head. "What does it mean?" Sophie had implored her. "What does it mean?"

As Julie closed the door to Sophie's room behind her, she realized that Antoine was waiting for her in the hall. She didn't want to see him. She didn't want to fight anymore. She was too drained by her concern for Sophie.

But he did not come to argue. Instead he reached for her there in the darkness and buried his face in her hair. "Forgive me, Julie, please forgive me," he pleaded. "I am genuinely sorry for the way I behaved. Maggie MacRae and Susan have told me what happened and how capably you cared for my sister."

"It was just that coming on the two of you . . . that strange young man and you, there in the dark, upset me. I am sorry, my love, I am truly sorry."

For the first time in all their love her mind went to another man as Antoine held her. Josh's small tune came humming into her ears unbidden. His words came back through all the time and his voice was even the same, cross but without anger, as he spoke.

"I have to tell you, Lady, that sorry is not my favorite word. Sorry is mighty easy to say if it is just that surface kind. Inside sorry has to be acted out."

Chapter Twelve

Sophie's return to strength was not a matter of days or even weeks. The sweet indolent days grew shorter and autumn blossoms replaced the summer flowers in the garden beneath the piazza. Time came for the return of the family to the plantation house for winter and still the insidious weakness kept Sophie dreamily prone on a chaise, a complete contrast to the vibrant energetic woman that Jule had always known.

Dr. Marlowe, while becoming a familiar figure at the house on Tradd Street, was clever enough to schedule his calls only at those hours when Antoine was not to be found at home. Although Jonathan Marlowe was equally gallant to both women, Julie was uncomfortably conscious of his glance lingering on her face and the way he followed her every movement when they were in a room together. His attitude toward Sophie was teasing and prideful as he watched her slow return to health.

"You are grown radiant," he told her, lingering over her hand. "I shall lose my most favored patient if you continue to do so well."

Sophie laughed merrily, her rich, low voice filling the room. "I hope you do not delude yourself that you have affected my cure, Doctor. It is my little court here who have brought sunshine back into my life." She waved at Armand, who was flailing like a turtle on his belly in his efforts to crawl. The ethereal Etoile, her memories of her first meeting with the doctor still alive in her mind, was always struck dumb in his presence.

"They are beautiful children," Dr. Marlowe agreed. Then with an appreciative glance at Julie, "But how could it be otherwise?"

Julie flushed and fabricated an excuse to leave the room. To her annoyance, the doctor rose to follow her. Thinking he might have some word about Sophie's care, she paused in the hall to let him catch up with her.

"Do I imagine that you are avoiding me?" he asked softly when they were abreast at the top of the stairs.

"Do I imagine that you only come here to stand about ogling me when my husband is absent from the house?" she countered.

His smile dropped momentarily before he burst into laughter. "I could point out that few men are at home less than your husband, madame," he said quickly. "But since that would be quite rude, I will only commend you on being such a forthright woman. You cannot imagine how startling your words can be from such an angelic face." Then he grew serious. "I sincerely wish that you could realize how earnestly I try to conceal my feelings. It is grievous to realize that my ardor for you is so transparent when I make such great attempts to keep it privy to myself."

Julie, still smarting from his off-hand remark about

Antoine's many absences from home, came back sharply. "And let me then say that I hope that my lack of interest in your attentions is even plainer than your feelings are for me. Did you wish to speak to me about my sister?"

Recoiling from her stern rebuff, his tone turned suddenly solemn. "Indeed I do. As I told her just now, I feel that she is gaining strength rapidly now. And as much as I shall miss having you both here so close to town, I realize her desire to return to her home up the river."

Forgetting her self-consciousness at this hint of good news, Julie dimpled with pleasure. "Oh, Dr. Marlowe, are you saying that she is ready to return to the plantation?"

His eyes lingered wistfully on her a moment, then he shook his head. "Not quite," he cautioned. "But I do have a prescription for her that can only hasten that happy day. And you will have a great part in it."

"She needs more open air and an opportunity to make herself strong by moving about," he explained. "I would prescribe that she take a small promenade daily, or perhaps every other day at first, and then increase the distance by easy steps."

Something unspoken seemed to lurk behind his words. She studied him quietly. "That is good news because both my sister and I enjoy walking. Do I understand that she can begin this program at once?"

"The sooner the better," he nodded. "With careful attention against overfatigue, of course."

Standing there beside Jonathan Marlowe, Julie could clearly see why Antoine, with his hateful jealousy, was so inflamed by this man's constant presence in his house. Dr. Marlowe was undeniably a fine figure of a man. She could not stand in conversation with him without being conscious that not only was he impressively handsome but his carriage was magnificent. The combination of his almost military bearing with his finely shaped body gave him an air of impressive power.

"I would suggest late afternoons," he said with a strange closed expression on his face. "That way, there will be no danger of the sun sapping her limited strength."

Why did his words seem so carefully chosen and why did she imagine that his eyes were mocking as he bent over her hand in farewell?

Sophie fairly bounced with the news. "We won't even tell Antoine," she decided firmly. "Since he's always out at the plantation anyway, he will not have an idea what we are doing. We shall go out and march about and I shall get very strong. Then one day, as a great surprise, I shall just get into the carriage and go back home again." Her face grew suddenly serious. "Oh Julie, you must know that I realize how lonely you are for Antoine when he is gone early and late on my business. I cannot say it to him, but it grieves me for you and the children."

"He is happy to do it," Julie said numbly. She had hoped that Sophie had not realized her own growing sense of separation from Antoine. With the onset of Sophie's illness he seemed to have given up on his campaign to marry her off to her neighbor Beauchamps and resigned himself to be manager of Sophie's property to the exclusion of all else.

And strangely, in spite of his long hours of work, he had returned to a level of passion that she could not recall since their earliest time together. Nights when she had drifted to sleep after lovemaking he would caress her awake and press against her once more.

"What a stud you have become," she teased him nestling into his embrace, winding him about with her legs so that he had to struggle to have his way with her. His low chuckle vibrated against her flesh.

"I cannot sleep for the richness of life," he told her, pressing his lips against the star above her waist and moving downward with his warm mouth against her flesh.

"The richness of life," she pondered, when he finally slid away from her into sleep. Was this the same man who only months earlier had railed at his life as entrapment? Just having a son could not have made the difference, for Armand had only made his restlessness to make his own fortune more acute. She longed to talk to him about these things, but there was never time.

The gentle conspiracy to keep Sophie's growing strength a secret from Antoine worked like a minor miracle. First they walked a block together with Sophie giggling all the way at how her feet prickled after these long months on a chaise or the rugs of the house. In order that Antoine not rebuke their bravery when he came to learn of their adventures, Sophie had Betty and Eban the stable boy accompany them on their walks.

When the brief trip did not even shorten Sophie's breath they ventured farther afield until their excursions carried them to St. Phillips, which had been rebuilt into a handsome new church by the town wall north of Sophie's house.

"It is strange to me that you should choose to walk in that direction," Dr. Marlowe commented when Sophie reported to him on her progress. "There is much more to see if you walk the other way along Bay Street. There the ships are coming and going, people pursuing their business . . . it is interesting and educational."

"And the roustabouts from the ships reeling drunkenly along the streets and the pirates hawking their silks and what else you couldn't guess," Julie scoffed, piqued as always by the vague sense that Jonathan Marlowe spoke only half of what he was thinking when he talked with her.

"For heaven's sakes, you already go escorted," he reminded her with a lift of the eyebrow. "And with two such compelling beauties abroad as the two of you, you could be sure that there would be five gentlemen to defend you from any ruffian who dared to accost you."

Spurred on by Dr. Marlowe's suggestion, they followed Bay Street along the Cooper River toward the Battery. Julie heard Betty and Eban grumbling behind them as the wind caught at their clothes, and smiled at their sighs of impatience as Sophie stopped here and again to chat with a friend or stare at some merchandise shown by a street peddler.

The little party was nearing the Battery when a sudden commotion along the street caused them to draw back against the shelter of a house. A horseman was approaching, whipping his mount into a lather and going at an insane pace for a street busy with pedestrians. The people who dived for safety shouted at the man angrily as he passed, but he paid them no heed. He only bent closer to his mount's neck as he raced along the thoroughfare, the mare's hooves striking fire from the cobblestones.

Julie heard Eban's astonished cry, but did not understand it until Sophie herself cried out. "Ben," she said with astonishment. "What in the name of God is Ben doing here?"

By the time Julie had her wits about her enough to focus on Ben, he had reared the horse to a stop about a block away. Sophie seized Julie's arm as they watched the overseer from the plantation spring from the horse and disappear into the first floor of a warehouse.

"Something is wrong," Sophie said flatly. She started off after Ben in a brisk walk. Julie laid a restraining hand on her arm but Sophie only shrugged it away. "Something dreadful has to be wrong at the plantation for Ben to ride into town at

51

this hour, and at such a speed."

"You cannot rush in there after him," Julie told her. "Wait until he comes out and you can ask him what is happening."

Her thought had only been to restrain Sophie from an exhausting run after the mounted slave. But her own mind was spinning too. Antoine was at the plantation as he always was. It must have been Antoine himself who sent Ben on this errand. And Antoine would dispatch Ben only on an errand of great import.

As they watched, a young Negro boy ran out from the door of the warehouse. Within seconds he returned, leading a stallion. Julie caught her breath with shock. That could not be. The beast the lad was leading was like a carbon copy of Antoine's own horse. But at that same moment, Ben emerged from the door to mount the foaming mare he had ridden so perilously down the street.

Then she saw him. He was wigless and apparently had been taking his leisure, for he drew his jacket over his half-buttoned shirt even as she watched. His fine pale hair was touseled and his face flushed, as if with drinking. He moved unsteadily, as if someone were clinging to him, trying to hold him back.

As he was full clear of the doorway, she saw him turn and speak to someone following, and the two of them burst forth from the door into the clear light.

The woman was clinging fiercely and possessively to Antoine with her face raised very close to his own. She was gripping him with all her might, as if to hold him back as she pleaded with him passionately in words Julie could not hear.

But the girl herself was enough. It was her face that Julie saw first, a fine long face with high dominant cheekbones sheltering deep-set dark eyes that glittered as she spoke. Her rich bright mouth, open in unheard protest, revealed perfect white teeth that glistened in the light. She was dark, not dark as a Negro would be but that richly bronzed gold of a gypsy's skin.

As she clung fiercely to Antoine, his sleeve caught against her, tugging her low blouse aside to reveal the unbound opulence of a fine full breast. The scarf that bound her head and trailed down her loose long hair was the same bright Moorish pattern of the skirt that swirled about her bare ankles.

She was shouting and pleading with Antoine, pressing her full figure against him frantically. But Antoine would be free of her. Julie watched as his hands clasped the girl by her bare arms and pushed her from him. He held her thus for a moment, then, as if relenting, he caught her in a full hug and pressed his lips against her face before setting her aside almost roughly.

Once on his horse, Antoine wheeled and shouted something back at her. Then he grinned that blinding smile that had so many times turned her own heart to jelly in her breast. Then the stallion reared and whinnied as Ben mounted his mare.

It was Sophie who caught Ben's attention. Her clear sultry voice was unmistakable above the chatter of the crowd. Julie saw both men glance about with puzzled frowns. She saw Antoine's jaw go slack as he stared at his sister. It was Ben, struggling with the reins of the mare, who shouted the explanation.

"Fire," he called. "Fire at the plantation house."

In that one split second before the horses got their heads Antoine's eyes found Julie's face. Knowing that he would read the hurt and the fury in her face even from that distance, she turned away, avoiding the gaze of those clear blue eyes. It was only as she whirled blindly that she realized that a man was standing very close behind her. Her quick movement threw her against his chest and he caught her gently by the arms to steady her.

"Easy there," he said, his lips close to her hair.

She gasped and pulled herself free with a wrench. But it was too late. Antoine's quick eyes could not have missed that quick protective embrace as she turned toward Jonathan Marlowe.

"Beast," Julie hissed at him. "You dirty rotten beast. You planned this. You planned this from the very start."

He was laughing, his handsome face very near her own in the crush of the crowd. "Of course I planned it, my dear." His tone was acid with sarcasm. "I set your sister's plantation house on fire. I sent her Negro here to raise an alarm. I even deliberately pressed your husband into the arms of the gypsy whore Marta. You do think I am pretty clever, don't you?"

"I only told you that a walk this way would be more interesting," he reminded her with a grin. "Or did I say educational?"

Part 2

THE STORM

1728

Chapter Thirteen

The sound of the horses' hooves receding seemed to act upon Sophie like the whip Ben was applying to his mare. Seizing Julie by the arm, Sophie quickened her steps to walk swiftly, almost at a run, along Bay Street toward the house on Tradd Street.

"Come," she said curtly. "There is no time."

With Betty and Eban panting as they trotted along behind, Sophie swept Julie into the house. Moving as if she had never had a sick day in her life, Sophie swept up the stairs shouting out a stream of orders in her deep rich voice.

"The carriage, Eban," she ordered. "Hitch it and have it ready at once. Betty, bring the medicine bag from my room along with all the old linens you can find and some barrels of salt. Tell Ned he will drive and we must leave for the house on the river within minutes."

"But what are you going to do?" Julie finally asked, trailing helplessly as Sophie flew into her room and began changing from her walking suit to a sturdy cotton dress.

"Go fight fire," she said angrily. "I should have known better than to leave only slaves in charge of my home."

"But we both thought that Antoine was there too," Julie protested, forcing herself to put the truth into candid words.

The import of those words hit Sophie hard. She turned to Julie, her arms caught in the dress and her eyes suddenly

55

brimming with tears. "Oh Julie, my love, what hell this must be for you." Then with lightning swiftness, her mood shifted and veered. "That bastard brother of mine. Who would have thought he would leave the plantation to carouse away his afternoons with a waterfront gypsy whore?"

"It could have only been this day," Julie remonstrated, trying sickly to justify Antoine.

"Today, hell," Sophie snorted. "This has been going on for months, almost since Armand was born...most certainly since I fell ill. Oh Julie, these slaves are more given to gossip than the wind is to singing in trees. I knew he was leaving the plantation every day a little after noon, letting us think he spent the whole day working with Ben."

Her look was beseeching. "I simply didn't have the guts to challenge him when he has labored so hard for my interests for so long. I...well, I made up things to tell myself, I guess. As God is my witness, I never thought it was anything like this...that slut!" she finished explosively.

"What did you think he was doing?" Julie asked. "Where did you think he was?"

"Well, I think I listened to him too closely," Sophie admitted. "I heard his great restlessness to begin establishing an estate for you and the children. I decided he was making plans for that aim, perhaps seating a river place to make a fortune in rice or establishing himself with merchants to equip an Indian trading venture...I really didn't know. But I certainly figured it was money he was after, not flesh."

After Sophie, still shouting, careened away in the carriage, Julie sat down quietly in the room she shared with Antoine. She heard the clatter of the carriage fade. She heard the fluting tones of Etoile's voice in conversation with Maggie MacRae. And she was cold.

She looked about the room with a shiver. She could not stay in this room where Antoine had filled her nights with joyful lovemaking. Had he come straight from the gypsy wench to her? Was this why he had said that life was so rich? She shuddered, feeling, as she had a few minutes earlier on Bay Street, a desperate need to run, to escape.

But where could she go? What was she to do?

She was still sunk in thought when Maggie MacRae rapped at the door and asked entry.

"Hot tea," the Scotswoman said softly, her native burr deepened by the emotion in her voice. "Just a spot to warm the chill from you."

She raised her eyes to Maggie, who sat solemnly staring at her own feet as if to read a message there. The Scotswoman's face had a strangely downy look, as if all of her flesh, even her highly colored cheeks, might feel like velvet to the touch. Although time had left creases at the corner of her mouth and across the high round forehead, Maggie MacRae was still a warmly attractive woman. Her eyes, hazel with glints of reddish auburn, met Julie's thoughtfully.

"What can I do?" she asked Maggie simply. There was no reason to tell Maggie what had happened. Maggie, bless her, could be called a gossip and a tittle-tattle and any number of ugly things, for, like Julie's old friend Ellie in Newgate, Maggie was a person who always knew what was going on. Right now, this was very convenient for Julie.

"The better thing is to ask what you want to do," Maggie countered.

Julie grinned wryly. "That is simple enough. To lie down on the floor and kick and scream and wail at Fate and maybe spit at the wall."

Maggie leaned forward with a chuckle. "That has helped many a woman in this world, I'll be bound. But after that, what would you want to do?"

Julie swirled the leaves in the bottom of her cup. "I wish that I could read these fragments like gypsies do. I cannot even seem to think clearly. What do you think?"

Maggie pursed her lips and rolled her eyes to the ceiling.

"What do you see?" Julie challenged her, handing her the cup.

Maggie hooked her thumb in the cup, but her glance did not go to the tea leaves. Instead she stared across the room to where the window stared bleakly back at her. "I see very muddied water," Maggie said quietly. "I see a fine figure of a man who wants to do what man has been trained to do since Bible days...make a shelter for those he loves and cosset them with the fruit of his labors."

Julie stared at her in astonishment. "You are talking about Antoine. What about me?"

"I'll get to that," Maggie said a little impatiently. "You asked what I saw, do you really want to hear now?"

Julie nodded meekly, wondering as she did so if she was really ready to face the brunt of this shrewd woman's vision.

"This man," Maggie warmed to her subject, "is fierce in love with the girl he moved Heaven and Earth to find when he thought she was lost to him." She stared at Julie piercingly for

57

a moment, then, satisfied with Julie's expression, went on. "Having found her, and having a man's natural ambition to cosset her, he is beset by dead ends on every side ... by loyalty to his sister, by the great amount of gold it takes to start a venture in these times, and by a great and furious terror that someone or something might take his world from him before he gets it tight enough in his hands."

"So he canters down to the waterfront and fools around with a gypsy wench," Julie put in acidly.

"Love," Maggie said thoughtfully, "did you ever watch a kettle with the pot tight on and the wood blazing higher by the minute? There comes a time when that lid is going to tilt and the steam and the hot water go flying all about. God knows where it will run or who will be burned by it."

Then Maggie began to speak again and Julie wondered if the woman's mind were wandering.

"If he had not been killed so young by the Indians like he was, my man and me would have had a babe or more just like you," she said quietly. "The babes a woman bears grow in her mind first. When no real babe comes, that child you dream about is still there." Her eyes were full on Julie now. "The girl child I would have borne, the one I dream of in my head still, is the spit of you, lovey. Now she would be no wise as lovely to look on as you are," she added quickly, "for himself had a noticeable weakness about the chin and a neck a little longer than a body would choose, and I myself have never fired a bridge with beauty, but inside that girl would be the spit of you. She'd be gentle and given to testing and always have an ember of fire ready to fan into spirit. Like a true Scot. And if the truth be known, I'd be surprised if you yourself didn't have a wee spot of Scot running in you somewhere, for you're much a Scot in your hidden heart."

"That's the nicest thing to say to me," Julie told her softly, touched by Maggie's words.

"You came to me dressed like a simple farm girl, remember? But hovering over you with his great love was that fine Josh Simmons. I seen him yearning to shelter and protect you and all the time he didn't even know you had a strength the same size as his own. That same strength kept you alive through those terrible times with that mad uncle of yours, until you was back with your man and married."

When Maggie paused, Julie felt her eyes on her, waiting.

"What are you saying to me, Maggie?" she asked.

"I'm saying that you may think that Josh Simmons and that

58

cousin Jacques of yours and your own husband love you for that pretty face or because you have that body men hunger for. They think they do and you are both wrong. What they love has nothing to do with a face or good tits or yellow eyes. It's your strength and purpose as a whole person that they yearn after. That you can't be put down, can't be beaten, can't be owned like chattel. A man never quits chasing what he can't quite get ahold of."

Julie stared at her. "You are telling me to fight. Me, with a suckling babe at breast and a baby of two to worry over, that I should fight against a strong-willed man and his wily gypsy wench?"

Maggie nodded fiercely. "Hard. Tooth and nail. Stand up to the fact of it and give them the what-for. It's your way, lovey, and if you lie down now you're a soaked biscuit for the rest of your days."

"All I really want to do is run away," Julie admitted bleakly.

"You could make worse choices as a fighter."

Julie stared at her, astonished.

Maggie shrugged. "He's probably out there right now fighting that fire with his left hand and his right while he gets his words ready to coax you down. He knows you are here and as long as you are here, in his sister's house, right alongside his bed, he's winning."

"I'm not the easiest in the world to coax," Julie reminded her.

"That's true enough, but you must surely know by now that words are like the bite of a sick dog: they fester and leave bad scars that never heal over."

"But my God, Maggie. I have no place to go. If I were to go to Monde DuBois, after the threats that Antoine made when Armand was born, he would kill Jacques or be killed. I have no other family and no friends."

"So what's wrong with that little place of mine?" Maggie challenged fiercely. "Sure it's not so grand as the plantation and the sheets on the beds are the same that I had from my own mother's dower and as white as ever except for some sea stain when the water got into the hold on the trip over and there's never been enough sun to bleach it out yet."

A sudden rush of tears caught Julie off guard. She jumped from the chair and seized Maggie with a boisterous hug. "Oh Maggie, Maggie," she cried. "What have I ever done to deserve such a friend?"

59

Maggie was sniffling too. "Land, lovey. If we women got what we deserved, we'd all be in chains from about the age of six on up."

As the carriage turned the corner onto Maggie's street, Julie remembered seeing the house the first time . . . with Josh. The tune came into her head and echoed its rhythm in the rumbling of the wheels.

Josh. Now what odds would Josh give her on the success of the risk she was taking this night?

Chapter Fourteen

Once outside the city gate, Antoine spurred his mount and left Ben on his winded mare to follow as he could. But even as Antoine goaded his horse mercilessly toward his sister's plantation, his mind clung to the confusion of the scene he had just left.

What were they doing there? How had they come? And why in the name of God did that cursed Marta have to pick that public moment to exhibit her wildcat possessiveness? It had been plain enough from the start, from the very first day that Ethan Weston had drawn his sister into the discussion of capital for his venture, that the woman was possessed of a restless animal appetite. Everything about her proclaimed her for what she was, the swing of her hips in walking, the teasing moistness of those full lips. Jesus. The memory of her warm flesh under his hand as he turned to reassure her burned in his mind as he knew it burned in Julie's.

But it was Julie's own fault. It was Julie alone who had driven him to coax and cajole a gypsy whore for capital for his shipbuilding enterprise. If Julie had played the part of a decent, loving wife, she would have thrown her influence with his against Sophie. By now Sophie would be disabused of her mad hopes, safely married to her dull planter Beauchamps, and he would be free to take the capital he needed as a loan from the pair of them with no risk of stripping Sophie into penury if the market should break or the rice crops fail for a season or two.

He saw the billowing smoke first. It rose in a massive

cloud, dispersing itself in the brisk wind. Tatters of smoke trailed the path of the river and the smarting fragrance of it dipped here and there along the road he traveled. When he saw the first tongue of scarlet flame lick above the trees, he kicked his stallion to renewed speed.

Wheeling about, Antoine studied the situation. The cooperage had been charred, but the damage was so far small. No flames rose from the structure, only dense smoke that showed where a late fire had been drowned. He heard the wail of women from the dependency house.

"Hildy's gone," one of the slaves called to him. "Got blown up in there."

"Blown up?" Antoine asked. "What in hell was there to blow up in a cookhouse?"

The man shook his head without breaking the rhythm of the buckets passing through his hands. "Don't know. Wax maybe."

Even as he watched, blazing cinders broke from the cookhouse to rise in the smoke and dive into new patches of fire in the dried brush along the roadway.

His voice was raw from shouting and the choking heat of the fire by the time Sophie's carriage rattled up the drive. By that time he had wagons brought to the house, filled with the largest barrels he could find. By carting that greater quantity of water steadily from the river, the slaves were finally making inroads on the flaming pyre of the cookhouse. The air was filled with the ominous hissing of scalding steam as barrel after barrel of water was fed into the flame-spouting windows.

With scarcely a glance passing between them, Sophie threw herself into the thick of the fray. With grudging admiration he watched his sister direct the hurling of the salt onto the flames.

"Sand!" she shouted. "When the salt is spent, refill those barrels with sand from the river."

She was right of course. The cookhouse, with its storage barrels of oil, would produce a blaze that water would only tease. Salt or sand would damp the fire that a river of water would not kill.

The last he saw of Sophie, her trim figure was walking swiftly, with a scampering young slave at her side, toward the row of houses where the injured slaves had been carried.

A tentative moon peered through the smoky sky by the time the last glint of red flame was damped in the ruins of the cookhouse. One wall of the four was left standing and the cooking hearth yawned blackly from the mess of twisted metal, broken pots, and charred wood half-buried under the steaming sand.

He was turning to seek Sophie even as she approached him across the littered lawn. The quickness was gone from her step and as she approached, he caught the sharp scent of that raw medicine she used to heal wounds. Her face was ashen in the light of the lantern Ben had brought him.

"Quite a party," he said without smiling. "Many injuries?"

"Only two that are really severe," she replied tiredly. "And another two slaves with bad smoke in the lungs. Some painful burns and, of course, Hildy."

"Figure out what happened?"

"Candles," Sophie said. "Putting wax on too hot a fire to heat and then turning away. A common enough story."

"For an invalid you moved with some celerity," he commented mildly.

She looked up at him. Her lips formed a rueful smile that did not extend to her eyes. "It was a surprise for you," she said quietly. "Every day I have been walking a little farther, gaining strength. We meant to surprise you."

They stared steadily at each other for a moment. It was Sophie who dropped her eyes. She reached out and laid her hand on his arm. The suddenness of her gesture revealed that she was swaying with fatigue. He caught her in his arms and pulled her close for a long moment.

Sophie. Jesus. How much they had been through together as brother and sister, as conspirators against their father in their youth, as friends in their young adulthood and as open enemies for the past year or so.

"Come, sister mine," he said, forcing his voice to lightness. "You must be tucked into a carriage and hied off to your home."

She stared at him soberly. "And you?"

"I will be along within the hour unless something wholly unforeseen happens. Things look well under control. Does this mean you must remain the rest of the winter in the town house?"

She smiled wanly. "I have decided not to think about anything until tomorrow. Fortunately we built the cookhouse and the laundry house separately. The meals can be cooked on the laundry fires, for a time at least."

"Tomorrow is plenty of time."

Antoine was conscious, as he had been so many times in their lives, that their minds had turned to the same place at an identical moment. He tightened his arm about his sister's slender back and turned to propel her toward the carriage.

"I love her, Sophie," he said quietly. "I love her even more than life."

"I know," she sighed. She clung to him a little overlong as he lifted her into the carriage.

He watched the carriage lights wink along the river road until they disappeared altogether. He tried to whip himself back into the anger that he had felt when he saw Julie turn away from him and into the arms of Jonathan Marlowe, but it did not work. Instead he saw only the shock and pain in her eyes clinging for that one startled moment to his face.

He cursed and turned and shouted for Ben.

Chapter Fifteen

The moon was half hidden behind a distant hill before Antoine felt safe with his arrangements at the plantation house. Every bone in his body ached as his mount cantered along the river road toward town. He had become a man of ash. His smoke-blackened clothes scraped at his flesh, as if they had been dipped in lye. Each breath reminded him that his lungs were the same hue as his blackened hands. To swallow was to feel a sword plunged toward his belly, which ached with a dull heaviness that was half hunger, half raw anguish.

But at last it was Tradd Street. He let himself in as quietly as possible. A single taper shone from the sitting room upstairs. He grinned wryly. A candle for the wanderer's return, he told himself silently. That would be Sophie's trick. His steps echoed hollowly through the downstairs rooms that were so seldom used because Sophie, like the other people of Charles Town, believed that malaria was unable to climb stairs.

He grinned as he stood in the door. He had been right, all

the way right. The little vixen had put the candle on the table by the decanter whose color suggested the finest brandy that Sophie's wine cellar boasted. The flame of the taper wavered as he entered, sending sparks of light from the glass she had set out for him.

He poured the glass half full and drank it down in a single scalding gulp. Then he refilled it, sighed, and held it close to his face to savor the headiness of its perfume after the acrid smoke of the past hours.

It was then that she spoke. Her voice sounded very small and young, like the girl she had been at sixteen when he had first conspired with her that she could elope with Paul Bontemps. The same timorous fear moved that he remembered from that time in her voice, and something froze in him at the memory. He turned slowly to look at her.

The white wig was gone. Her auburn hair tumbled about her shoulders like a young girl's. She was tucked up in a chair with her feet drawn up under her from the chill of the floor.

He willed himself to walk toward her, but thought better of it and went back for the candle. He set it on the table by the massive chair in which she was crouched. Her eyes, in that clear light, shone with terror and grief.

Her hoarse voice answered his unspoken question.

"She's gone." Then she shook her head distractedly, as if at her own stupidity. "They are all gone," she said heavily.

"Gone!" he shouted. "What do you mean 'gone'? Where have they gone to?"

She did not caution him to silence. Who was there to be wakened? She only shook her head.

He wanted to seize her, to force from her some more satisfactory reply, but the look of anguish in her eyes stayed his hands.

"But the slaves," he said. "The slaves must know where she took off to. What about that Scotswoman, Maggie?"

"She's gone too."

"That is impossible," he shouted. "A woman and two children and a nurse cannot disappear into thin air like that." Then he paused.

Twice before he had left Julie and come back to find her gone. Once in Epping Woods, when he had been fleeing the King's men, he had left Julie with Titus, his man. Later the innkeeper told tales of a maid and a dwarf who had disappeared into the thin air. Once in the year just past he had returned to find her gone, and she had been at Monde DuBois and was lying in her blood with the newborn Armand in a filthy shack. The thought brought him to his feet, flaming with fury.

"Monde DuBois," he shouted. "She has fled to that lascivious cousin of hers in a fit of pique. If she has gone from me to that man's house, so help me God, Sophie, I shall beat that woman like a runaway slave."

Sophie stared at him with astonishment. As she rose, she seemed to be uncoiling herself from her peignoir like an oleander spreading its petals to bloom. When she stood before him she was barefooted and ridiculously small for the imperious dignity in her voice. The blaze in her eyes was unmistakable.

For the first time in his life he saw his father in his sister's face, the stern resolve, the brutal fury that he thought had missed them both, coming to rest only in the foppish man-hungry Emile whose temper was that of a madman. The fury in Sophie's eyes smelt of madness, too.

"Your brandy speaks," she said coldly, her low throaty voice making the words sound even more scathing. "But mark my words, Antoine Rivière, if you ever, for any reason, lay your hands in violence on Julie, I shall personally horsewhip you to within a breath of your life."

Cursing, he took the brandy decanter by its neck and raised it to his lips. It dripped as freely along the flesh of his own neck as it flowed down his throat but he didn't give a damn. When it was empty, he threw the decanter across the room.

He would get out of these filthy rags and into something that did not claw at him like a chorus of devils. He would saddle that stallion and go to Monde DuBois and take back what was his own. Sophie would see who would raise the horsewhip in this family. He reached the door of the sitting room on the second try. The hall was a simple obstacle, lacking only something to support him across its wide open center. Then he reached the stairs.

At first he didn't try to stand. He crawled from step to step like an animal, heaving his heavy body behind him. Then at the landing he drew himself erect. "I'm a man, not a goddam eel," he told himself furiously.

The first step was his mistake. He brought his foot down heavily on the edge of the riser, only to have it slide away from his touch. He spun to reach for the bannister and failed to find it. He fell heavily down half the flight, landing finally with his leg twisted painfully beneath his body. After a painful effort to jostle the leg free, he felt a swinging giddiness join the sharp pain of the leg and he fell into darkness.

Chapter Sixteen

The baby's whimpering wakened Julie into the half-dark room. She was conscious that Armand's slowly rising complaint had stirred her from dreaming. Pulling her robe about her, she groped her way across the unfamiliar room in Maggie MacRae's house. The curtains had been left tightly closed, for Maggie's good reason.

"There is no call to make our presence here common talk any sooner than it need be," she explained.

Not until she lifted the heavy child onto her shoulder and settled back with him against her pillow did she realize that a heavy hard pain was pressing inside her own chest. She breathed deeply and pressed her hand against the knot of pain before loosening her gown to release her nipple for the baby's searching lips.

After a grunt of satisfaction, Armand's eyelids fluttered shut.

The pain was a coincidence, Julie told herself. It had simply come because of the hurt and shock of the previous day. She did not want to remember the other time in her life when such a pain had come and stayed until it was so much a part of her that she thought she would never be without it.

She had been in London then with her friend Margaret. The pain had come without reason on a certain day. It was only by chance gossip that she later learned that at the same time Antoine had been captured by thief-takers and prisoned in Newgate to stand trial for highway robbery.

It seemed only minutes before her son grew restive at her breast. Troubled. Julie lifted him to her shoulder. He protested in such great shrieks that she feared both Maggie and Etoile would waken in alarm. "Hush, hush," she coaxed, and lured him to quiet with the other breast.

When his eagerness was again quickly exhausted, Julie glanced up to see Maggie, ghostly in a long gown, watching at the door.

"I don't understand it," Julie told her. He nurses only a few minutes and then grows furious with me. He screams and acts as if he were hungry but will not nurse again."

Maggie stood above her, looking at Armand, now scarlet with rage. Then she laid a gentle hand on Julie's breast, which was still moist from the baby's mouth.

"Your milk," Maggie said thoughtfully. "It seems to have gone away."

"Oh, but it can't be, Maggie," Julie protested, her eyes widening in panic. "Maybe it is just that I did not eat anything last evening. Perhaps when I have had a little tea and bread." Her tone was hopeful.

Maggie shook her head. "Now you know better than that, lovey," she chided her. "You must have heard how a mother who has a great shock will find the milk gone all at once from her!"

The pain in Julie's chest seemed suddenly more intense. The wails of the child stabbed at her heart. "But what can we do, Maggie. What can we do?"

"There is not a fresh cow in all of Charles Town that I know of," Maggie mused aloud. "And if there was one, its owner would be more apt to sell the cream for butter, dear as it is, than provide milk for a stranger." Then she halted suddenly, her eyes narrowed in thought. "But my good friend Matilda has a maid named Sally with a fine new boy. Perhaps she would sell her services to us until your milk returns. It would not be costly," she added hastily. "Matilda is beholden to me for many things and the girl is only a cook's helper anyway."

"Another woman nurse my child?" Julie shrieked.

Ignoring her, Maggie went on: "We need only keep this young man from howling until the day is full and I will go over and talk to Matilda myself." She laid the sleeping baby back into his bed. "In the meantime you might be getting yourself dressed in case someone should come by. I have a feeling it has been a long night over there on Tradd Street." She left the room with a note of triumph still hanging in the air.

As hasty as her packing had been, Julie found all that she needed to array herself for a chance caller. Since the yellow flower-patterned was a favorite of Antoine's, she put it on even though it was a bit summery for the season. She was finally able to get her long rebellious hair under control so that only a few springy curls strayed about her face. She stared into the mirror and then slapped her cheeks softly. The pain had given her flesh an unbecoming pallor.

With the shawl about her shoulders, she slipped out to Maggie's cookhouse. During the summer Maggie rented her house to people who feared to spend the season on the river. Now that they had returned to the country the kitchen looked bare and unused and no hint of fire glinted on the hearth. Julie frowned about her, seeking for something to feed Etoile when she stirred awake. She knew Maggie kept some stores in the place for those days when she would slip off with Etoile for a quiet day in her own home.

By the time Maggie brought Etoile out for breakfast, Julie had set out a fine repast of crisp biscuits with honey in an earthenware pot and a plate of dried fruit preserves whose cherries glittered like jewels in the sweet liquor.

Maggie grinned broadly at her.

"A fine little housewife was lost when you married that proud Frenchman," she said. "All that is wanting is a spot of tea and we'll have that when my near neighbor is astir to borrow fire from."

By noon the house was in full operation. A pot of stew fragrant with barley simmered on the hob and in the corner, her dark eyes apprehensive, Matilda's girl Sally held the greedy Armand to her full dark breast.

When the girl had returned to her house, "only a skip away," as Maggie said, Armand settled in for his long afternoon nap. Maggie, with Etoile in tow, set off to replace her stores for their evening meal.

They had been gone from the house less than an hour when Julie heard a clatter of horses' hooves on the quiet street. Her heart began to pound unaccountably. She stood very still to listen, struggling for breath.

But when the fine strong pull rang on the bell, her heart failed her. She froze to the spot, unable to move. What could she say to Antoine? Even if he had come to seek her, that did not mean that he could explain the strangeness of his acts, his deceit. She must remind herself that she had not observed a one-time chance meeting with Marta but that he had deceived her for months, letting her think he was laboring at the plantation while he was whiling away his hours only a few blocks away in Charles Town.

The second peal of the bell sent her flying to the door. She knew it would be Antoine. She had already braced herself for the flood of emotion she always felt when she faced him even after a day's absence. She was ready for the fine bulk of his body towering over her, the brilliance of his eyes. But even as she swung the door wide, she felt her own face change.

Equally astonished, her aunt, Anne-Louise DuBois stared back from the threshold. The older woman frowned at Julie a moment before she cried out in relief.

"Oh my dear, how delighted I am to see you," her words tumbled out quickly. "I was mad with concern for you and came to see if perhaps my friend Maggie MacRae knew aught of you."

Then stepping inside swiftly, her aunt caught Julie in a tender embrace.

"It was barely light when the man Eban came to Monde DuBois searching for you and the children. We have been so concerned. Jacques has done nothing this daylong but pace the floor and curse with concern for you. What has happened, why are you here?"

"Was it the fire?" her aunt pressed. "Are the dear children all right? When we passed the plantation and saw the signs of the fire from the road, my heart was ready to burst. And is dear Sophie all right?"

"We are all fine," Julie finally managed to say. "Armand is asleep in the next room and Maggie and Etoile are out for some stores." She paused. "Antoine deceived me and I ran away."

Her aunt had her bonnet half off at Julie's words and she stared at her in amazement. She eased into a chair without taking her eyes from her niece's face.

"Ran away?" she asked quietly.

Julie nodded, ashamed to realize that her eyes were flooded with tears.

"Oh Tante Anne-Louise, I am so miserable." Julie fell to the floor by her aunt's chair and laid her head on the older woman's lap. "I am so miserable without him."

"Deceived you," the woman said thoughtfully. "Julie could you possibly be wrong?"

Julie shook her head. "For months he has been letting me think he was working at the plantation when he has been down on the waterfront... somewhere else."

"A woman," Anne-Louise guessed softly, aloud. "Why must men be such pawns, so stupid?"

"Stupid?" Julie challenged her. "He was smart enough to

fool me all that time, to come from her to me claiming he had the richest of lives."

"No," her aunt shook her head. "They are stupid. Let something tilt their world only a little awry and they feel that their manhood is threatened. They can think of no way of proving themselves except by leaping into bed with the nearest female."

"But his world was not awry," Julie began to protest.

Even as she spoke, she saw the reproach in her aunt's eye. "His world will be awry, Julie, until he has the four of you together with your future all in his own hands alone."

Julie slumped against her knee. "But how can that be? Poor Sophie." Her aunt's caressing hand on her head stopped suddenly. "But my dear," she said gently, "have you forgotten about your friend Josh Simmons?"

Julie raised thoughtful eyes to her aunt. "That is such a long chance, Tante," she reminded her.

Her aunt nodded. "But I have hope too. When I first returned from Philadelphia and Jacques related that story to me, I had grave doubts. Since then Jacques himself has convinced me that through Josh your sister and her husband will be reunited."

"I don't understand why Jacques believes so much."

"Because he wants to believe," her aunt said softly.

Julie sighed. "And I don't understand that either."

"Don't grieve, child," her aunt said. "He cannot help himself more than you can prevent his devotion. But your unhappiness is his unhappiness, Julie. He would do anything in his power to see you happy . . . even if he is forbidden the sight of your face. To know you are happy is his great dream, even if you find that state with another man."

Chapter Seventeen

Antoine was jarred to consciousness by hands lifting him, by a flood of pain so universal that he could not at once figure out its source. For one thing his head throbbed miserably and his throat felt swollen shut from the inside. The linings of his

70

eyelids felt scalded and even the slightest attempt to open his eyes resulted in a blurred scratching sensation that made darkness preferable.

But the worst was his leg. A sharp stabbing of pain plagued his right leg a little below the knee. He groaned and tried to reach for it, only to hear Sophie's throaty voice cautioning, "Don't move, Tony. Don't try to move at all."

With great difficulty he forced his eyes open to focus on her. She was almost eye level with him, which was startling enough. Also, she was crisply attired for morning with her white wig in place as if she had been abroad for hours. He frowned at her.

"Jesus, Sophie. Where am I? What in hell is wrong?"

"You're either halfway up the stairs or halfway down," she replied, her tart words belied by the look of concern on her face. "I would guess that you tried to make the trip with at least a pint of brandy more than a tired man with an empty stomach could handle."

In spite of her warning, he tried to curl his body to see his leg. "Good God," he cried, falling back in a sweat.

His mind began to work laboriously. "Julie," he said with sudden urgency. "Where is Julie?"

"I know no more than I knew a few hours ago," she told him. "I was just coming down to start...well, to start something. In the meantime you have to have help. The doctor should be here soon."

He felt his aching muscles tighten. "Not that son-of-a-bitch Marlowe," he menaced.

She shrugged.

Antoine groaned. "Then you have sent for him."

She nodded, still frowning. "I do wish you were in a better place."

"I can damn well move it," Antoine boasted. "Just give me a minute."

Bracing himself against her, he slowly straightened the injured leg. Then slowly, supported on each side by a stout slave, he managed to hobble down the half flight of stairs to collapse, drenched with sweat, on a chaise in the lower room that Sophie had covered with white linen to protect it from the soot and filth of his clothes.

"Monde DuBois," he said fiercely, when he was able to catch his breath again. "Send a message to Monde DuBois and ask for Julie."

She nodded. "I have already done so. Eban should be back

71

within the hour with whatever he has learned. I also sent a messenger to Maggie MacRae's home," she added. "I could think of nowhere else to inquire."

"MacRae's," he repeated, nodding. "That's very clever, I might not have thought of that."

"Not so clever, as it turns out," his sister replied. "Susan was there and back already today. The curtains are shut tight, as Maggie leaves them when she is gone. There is no sign of life at all, no smoke from the house or the cookhouse and no one astir."

"Jesus, Sophie," he moaned. "What a hellish mess I have made of things."

The sound of the bell and voices in the hall relieved her of the necessity to answer.

"That will be Dr. Marlowe," she warned.

Why did the man have to look so damnably shaven and immaculate standing there in the door? He wasn't smiling, but Antoine sensed a smile tugging behind the suntanned creases of the man's carefully sober face. The doctor bowed to Sophie, then turned to Antoine with an uplifted eyebrow.

"Good day, Rivière," he said. "The leg, I presume. Do you really want me to attend him in here?" He glanced about incredulously at the elegantly appointed room.

"It is the best for now," Sophie assured him. "What are your needs? Hot water, linen, scissors?"

"All of those to begin with," he nodded. "And possibly two flat wooden boards the length of your brother's lower limb."

With his clothes cut away, Antoine watched the doctor move his finger carefully along his leg. Antoine kept his eyes determinedly on the doctor's face, willing his body not to flinch or betray the pain of the examination by any sign. But he could not repress a sigh of relief when Dr. Marlowe rose to stare down at him.

"It appears that you have been more than a little lucky," he said in an unhurried way. "While one bone of the leg is clearly broken, the other holds firm. This will promote a much speedier recovery."

"How long?" Antoine asked.

"Oh, no more than a month or two," the doctor replied blithely.

"Two months, Jesus Christ," Antoine groaned. "My God, that is a lifetime right now."

By the time the injured leg was bathed and treated with a chill ointment that bit into his flesh, then bound immobile in fabric-wrapped slabs of wood, there were small rivers of sweat streaming down Antoine's back and chest.

His instructions for Antoine's care were terse and reasonable enough. He did advise brandy for the pain, "in reasonable amounts." He said this with his eye on the decanter still lying empty against the wall of the room. The damned meddling bastard had had to stand there and gossip like an old crone. Even as the doctor stood in the doorway with the full morning sunlight flowing past him across the sill, Eban slid into the room and caught Sophie's eye. The Negro's flesh shone from the speed of his travel and he bowed at Sophie, avoiding Antoine's eye.

"No words of the mistress at Monde DuBois," he said quietly. "No word at all."

Antoine refused to look up again when the doctor bowed himself out. But he knew he could feel the man's eyes on him, aloof and amused and a little triumphant.

Chapter Eighteen

It was Susan who found them. Distraught for Armand's safety, certain that even if they had found a safe place to stay no one could care for the great lusty boy as well as she, the nurse had set out to find Julie and Maggie and the children herself. It had been bad enough when the child Etoile had been taken from her care and given to Maggie MacRae to raise, but no one was going to separate her from the baby Armand by just walking away with him. She simply stole away from the house on Tradd Street and prowled the back doors of Charles Town probing for gossip.

"Don't know anything about a lady and two children," a cook told her, "but our girl Sally was put out to nurse a little white boy today. Fine big baby, she said, built like a plow horse with the bluest ever eyes."

"He's mine," Susan had howled and run straightaway home, barely restraining herself from shouting the news to strangers along the way.

But with Susan's return home, all pretense of peace disappeared. Susan rapped, or rather hammered, on the door of the sitting room and then entered without being summoned.

"They all right," she howled, still breathless from running all the way home. "They over at Miz MacRae's, all right, and the lady's milk has gone away. I know it for sure. Can we go get my baby even if it means that we got to take that other girl too?"

"What other girl? Who? At Maggie's?" Sophie was on her feet in a minute, trying to make sense of Susan's garbled report.

Antoine rattled his chairs and roared. "Come around here where I can see you, goddammit," he shouted. "Now start again, where is my wife? But wait. Tell Eban to saddle my horse..."

"Stop that noise and let's get Susan's story straight," Sophie told him tartly. "Tell us all about it, Susan."

Including every detail of the search she had made, even reporting on a runaway pig which had almost upset her over on Montague Street, Susan finally finished her recital.

"And so Julie's milk has stopped," Sophie said thoughtfully. "That's really not too surprising. But are you sure it is them? Did you see them yourself?"

Susan paused. "Not with my eyes, I didn't," she admitted. "But this cook over there, she say their girl Sally nursed a big white baby as pale as the sun in his hair color with those blue eyes."

"You go down and settle yourself a few minutes, Susan," Sophie told her quietly. "We'll get back to you in just a few minutes. And Susan," she added softly, "we thank you very much for what you have done. My brother thanks you too in his own gracious way," she added with a sly grin at Antoine, who was swelling as if about to burst.

"Now what in the name of God did you do that for?" Antoine challenged her the minute the girl was gone. "There is no 'few minutes' about it. So we use the carriage because of this damned leg, but we go this minute and bring back Julie and my children."

"They are her children too," Sophie reminded him mildly. "And as for the carriage, you are no more able to get that leg into a carriage than onto a horse. For a while you are stuck right here. That is what we need to talk about."

"No talking," he shook his head firmly. "Just send the carriage over and bring Julie back here. Tell her I want to see her."

74

"The question, dear brother, is whether she wants to see you or not. She is the one who left, if you remember."

He stared at her, flushed, and fell into a sulky silence.

"What can I do, Sophie? Tell me what I can do to get this straightened out."

"I don't know, Tony," she told him frankly. "But unless you can get Julie to understand, as you have me, why you have deceived her all these months, what your involvement really is with Ethan and his sister Marta, I don't think you'll make much headway in healing the scars you made last night."

"What about my wounds?" he flared at her. "What about my looking around on a public street and seeing my own wife being escorted by that lecherous doctor of yours. My God, she turned into his arms like she knew the route by heart."

"Oh, escorting, hell," Sophie snorted. "He was just there, even as half of Charles Town was to see what the action was. And as for her turning into his arms, she was probably blinded by tears. Would you think better of him if he had let her stumble on the cobbles and fall on her face?"

He wasn't listening. She could almost see his mind working at double pace. He lifted the empty wineglass to his lips, then thumped it down with disgust. Then she saw a glimmer of brightness in his expression.

"All right," he said quietly, out loud to himself. "All right, that is what we'll do. Sophie, would your cook be able to handle a couple of extra guests for dinner?"

"Tonight?" Sophie asked, surprised.

"Tonight," he said firmly.

Sophie thought a moment and then nodded yes. "What are you going to do?"

"Gamble," he replied tersely.

"If you are talking about gambling with Julie, you are playing with what I call dangerous stakes," Sophie warned.

He seemed not to have heard her. "Look, Sis, would you get me quill and ink and something to write on and send Eban up here in just a few minutes?"

"Of course," Sophie said, rising with a puzzled expression. "What are you going to do?"

"I'm going to get the principals together and lay all the cards on the table at once," he said quietly. "That way, Julie will get a chance to make up her own mind about what kind of deception has been going on behind her back."

"But Antoine," Sophie protested, "does this really seem right to you? When there is such a rift in a marriage, do you

75

really think that airing it before strangers makes any sense? Wouldn't it be better just for you and Julie to talk it over together? It is such an emotional thing."

"I intend to take full advantage of my wife's gentle upbringing. We'll thrash this thing out before strangers. Her unfailing good manners and that unbelievable self-control of hers will give me the chance to show her how things really are with both of us," he paused and flushed, "being betrayed by our emotions."

Sophie only shrugged, but Antoine could not miss the look of skepticism in her eyes. "How do you propose to get her over here for the show?" Sophie asked.

His eyes pleaded with her. "I am going to have to depend on you for that, sister Sophie. And since you know how much it means to me, I have no doubt at all of your success."

She groaned as she let herself out to get all his wishes dispatched at once. She stopped at the door and returned to retrieve the wine bottle. She smiled at him prettily as she carried it out with her. "I have no intention of handling this evening with you half-crocked like you were last night."

She was comforted by the sound of his chuckle as she shut the door behind her.

Chapter Nineteen

Sophie was astonished to realize that her palms were damp with nervousness as she and Susan approached Maggie MacRae's house. How silly to be afraid to face Julie. After all, her sister-in-law had been her closest female friend and a member of her household for nearly four years! Yet Sophie was the first to concede that Julie Rivière was too deep a pool for her to fathom.

But now it was she herself who must pit herself against that will and try to get Julie, who had deliberately left in anger, to return meekly to see her husband.

Thank God for his broken leg, she thought ruefully as Susan stepped forward to pull Maggie's bell cord. She might be saved by Julie's compassion when all the wheedling in the world would flow past her like warm honey.

When Julie opened the door Sophie saw at once her quick flash of disappointment that it was not Antoine who faced her across the ledge.

"How are you, my dear?" Sophie asked, not presuming entry until she was invited.

Instant contrition crumpled Julie's set expression.

"Oh Sophie, Sophie," Julie cried. "Do come in, you and Susan both. I am fine ... it is you I am concerned about. The fire. Do tell me that you did not lose your beautiful house."

At Susan's expression of mute appeal, Sophie laughed. "Is it all right if Susan goes straight back to Armand?" she asked.

"All right!" Julie laughed. "It is wonderful. He has been just impossible these last hours. He is warm and dry and full and still he screams. It can only be you that he needs, Susan."

"And I really am fine, Julie," Sophie assured her as Susan disappeared down the hall. "There is nothing like a fire to remind one to be thankful for what has been saved. As it was, the blaze was contained in the cookhouse and few people were even badly hurt."

"How fortunate," Julie agreed.

"But I did not come here to talk about the fire," Sophie began bravely. "I came to invite you to join my brother and me for dinner this evening."

"We especially wanted you to come," Sophie said quietly. "There will be other guests, some business friends of Antoine's."

Julie's chin tilted a little at the mention of her husband's name, but she could not seem to pronounce it herself. "I am sure that your brother will be able to entertain his business friends without any assistance from me."

Sophie was suddenly reminded of her youth in France, when she had stood at gaming tables and played her cards this same way. She could almost feel the fact of Antoine's broken leg flat beneath her thumb, like the missing king in a royal flush.

She smiled as brightly as she could. "It isn't that he needs you there, my dear. It is more that he wants you there."

Vague suspicion warred with irritation in Julie's face. "It seems strange that a grown man should send his sister to entreat for something he sincerely wishes," she said pointedly.

"Under other circumstances it would never occur to him," Sophie agreed quietly.

"Other circumstances." Julie's mind worked quickly. The fire. He had been on his way to the fire when she saw him last.

Sophie had mentioned injuries in the fire. Without even being conscious of it, her fist tightened against that pain that had hung in her chest since she first woke. She fought the panic she felt at the veiled suggestion behind Sophie's words.

"Something must be wrong, then. He has been hurt. Tell me how he is, Sophie," Julie's words spilled out breathlessly, all pretense of disinterest gone.

While the softness was still there in Julie's face Sophie spoke quickly. "You see, that is why Antoine sent me to extend his invitation. It is only because he was unable to rush to you himself, or come in any way until the braces are off his leg."

"I must speak to Maggie," Julie said, backing away with a strange, distracted look on her face. "Please excuse me for a moment."

Maggie was holding Etoile when Julie entered. A book lay closed between her fingers as the child's head lolled against her breast in sleep.

"You heard?" Julie asked.

Maggie nodded. "I'm sorry about his pain."

"There will be other people there," Maggie reminded her. "He would have rushed here for you, you heard her."

"You can always insist on being brought back here if you decide not to spend the night there," Maggie added softly.

Startled by the suggestion implicit in Maggie's words, Julie tossed her head smartly. "Of course I shall return."

"Either way, I think it would be well to go," Maggie advised, tugging Etoile into a position so that she could rise.

Julie nodded, her mind obviously on other things.

Julie was still struggling with the wild beating of her heart as the carriage neared Tradd Street. A hundred questions battered at her mind. How had Antoine been hurt? Was it by falling lumber? Too well she remembered the terrifying fires of London and the screams of the men pinned under the falling buildings. Julie didn't understand why her sister-in-law urged the carriage driver with such haste until they were inside the house. Julie was startled to hear a strange male voice from the sitting room beyond.

"They are already here," Julie cried in dismay, her hands quick to her hair. She glanced down at the yellow sprigged dress which was wholly suitable for an evening at home alone but not what one would wear to receive dinner guests.

"Don't give it a thought," Sophie whispered. "Believe me, you will be the best-dressed woman here."

"But my hair," Julie whispered.

78

Given no time to protest and with Sophie's hand firm against her back, Julie found herself being propelled into the room.

She knew that other people were there, but she had eyes for no one but Antoine. She watched him brace his weight on his arms to rise and then fall back with a wince. His eyes were hollowed from fatigue and his long, bandaged leg stuck out awkwardly on the extra chair before him. His voice was careful as he called out to her.

"Come in, my dear. We have waited eagerly for you to join us."

Julie flushed. It was as if she had never made her bold move at all. He made it sound for all the world as if she had been upstairs all the time simply dawdling over her grooming. She crossed the room and coolly offered her cheek for his kiss. His grip as he caught her hand made her wince. She did not meet his eye as she tried to pull away.

"You cannot imagine how I curse this impediment," he said, still clinging to her hand. "Julie, may I present Marta Weston and her brother Ethan?"

Marta, her mind repeated with a dull shock. Marta had been the name of the woman at the pier. The woman was deep in her chair, as relaxed as a great sleepy cat. She raised her jewel-heavy hand to Julie, and her head cocked a little as she returned Julie's astonished stare.

She was dressed in a deep green silk whose color changed to a peacock blue when the light struck its folds. The fichu of lace at the low bodice of her dress was the finest French handiwork. Cuffs of the same fine lace fell in ruffled folds over her long slender fingers. The great mass of richly colored hair that had hung loose under her scarf the previous day was elaborately coiffed in great gleaming mounds held just high enough to display the glinting jeweled earbobs that swayed against her graceful bare neck.

"Mademoiselle," Julie murmured politely, feeling as if a wintry river had been injected in her veins. And Sophie had said she would not be underdressed. She felt like a simple milkmaid in her gown with its profusion of ribbons lacing the yellow corselette.

"I hope that your children are all well," the girl said civilly enough, with her amused eyes on Julie's face. Her voice was as deep as Sophie's, but with a different, almost musical accent that fell strangely on Julie's ear.

"In the most excellent health, thank you," Julie replied. She

79

had been trapped into the room with this bawdy. Antoine and Sophie together had trapped her. This capacity for duplicity in the two people closest to her heart startled her into cold fury. With Antoine's hand still gripping her own she could not even move free of contact with him.

"Please make yourself comfortable, Mr. Weston," she said with as sincere a smile as she could muster. "I will myself sit down when my husband remembers that my hand will not fall loose to grow anew like a lizard's tail."

Ethan Weston bent forward with a roar of laughter. "By God, Tony, she is as bright as she is beautiful. Let her go, you selfish bounder." Weston leaped to Julie's side and took her by the arm. "Come and sit by me where you will be out of reach of that scoundrel."

"Have you been long in Charles Town, Miss Weston?" she asked quietly.

The woman sighed as if she found the inquiry tedious. "I come and go," she said tiredly.

Her brother laughed. "What my sister means is that she is a true traveler, restless of spirit. The Barbados, London, Lisbon...you name it and Marta comes and goes there."

This peculiar conversation was mercifully interrupted by Sophie's arrival to announce that dinner was served. Julie turned to Antoine with a catch of concern, only to see a stout slave helping him to his feet.

"Do go ahead and be seated," Antoine urged. "I am still too new at this form of locomotion. Julie. Would you give me a hand, my dear?"

Startled, she moved to his side, instantly conscious of the warmth of his arm pressing her close to his body.

"Oh, come now, Tony," Ethan Weston said, starting forward. "Let me help you." Antoine's soft laugh rumbled against Julie's arm. "Do not make the mistake of judging this woman's power by her size, Weston. Julie and I will do fine."

"I cannot tell you how much I appreciate your coming on such late notice," Antoine told his guests as the soup was being served. "Especially since, with this new handicap of mine, I felt that it was time for all of us to discuss our new venture together."

The air was festive. As the wine was being poured and Antoine lifted his glass for a toast, Julie felt a rising sense of expectancy in the room. Ethan Weston and his sister exchanged glances so joyful and conspiratorial that Julie felt as if a cold wall had closed between her and the others. But she smiled purposefully and raised her glass with the others as Antoine announced a toast.

"May all winds blow fair," he said solemnly, "for the *Sojourner*." He touched his glass first against her own, but even as he did his eyes exchanged a smile with Marta across the table. Julie set her wine down untasted.

Chapter Twenty

Julie's fingers froze on the stem of the goblet.

Sojourner ... traveler. Her mind slid back to Ethan Weston's description of his sister Marta, "A traveler, restless of spirit. ... You name it and Marta goes there." She stared at Antoine, unable to accept the conclusion that struck her mind.

Antoine laughed merrily at her expression, mistaking her dismay for simple astonishment. He reminded her suddenly of Sophie's son Charles when she first met him, eyes alight and glittering with excitement, flesh glowing and a tremor of exaltation behind his words. Antoine was no child, but a man. His excitement, instead of infecting her with the same joy as Charles' had done, chilled her to withdrawal.

"She is a ship, Julie," he explained. "The *Sojourner* is to be our ship, ours and others'. She will be the first of many ships which will build an empire for our son Armand and for ourselves."

It was Sophie who found her voice first. "A ship!" she cried with astonishment. "One of many? What kind of ship?"

Antoine's merry glance moved to his sister. "I might tell you at once, Sophie, that the *Sojourner* will not be a delight to the eye. She is designed more like the Dutch flute than any other craft, with a broad beam and a wide, flat bottom. But such ships are cheaper to build and need only a crew of a dozen men to handle them ... perhaps a few more if we need to add firepower against pirates.

"But the big thing is that this ship will have the advantage of a crew that will fight for her to the last man if it comes to that," Antoine concluded.

"How can you be so sure of these things, Tony?" Sophie asked. "It is common enough knowledge that almost any able seaman can be easily recruited by those pirates. I have heard that the pirates are even willing to supply these men with certificates of impressment in the event that the sailor later falls into the hands of the authorities."

"That is true enough, Sophie," Antoine replied. "But therein lies the difference between the *Sojourner* and the other merchant ships that ply these waters. These men will have their own fortunes tied to the craft even as mine are. They will fight for her as if she were their own because she will be."

"Now I *really* don't understand," Sophie admitted.

"We spoke of pirates," Antoine reminded her. "I actually pirated the idea from the buccaneers themselves. On pirate ships there stands the rule that every man shares in the prize. That is the very reason that it is so easy for a pirate to recruit.

"An ordinary seaman, however able, gets little more than a pound a month, and that for all his life. His life is one of steady hardship, enduring the discomforts of evil weather, the uncontrolled brutality of bad officers, diseases, starvation, and fevers. Does he earn five hundred pounds in his whole life for this?

"But, ah, the pirates. When booty comes the way of a ship, the captain and quartermaster get a share and a half, each man an equal share of the rest. Why, it is their custom to sign a man on with the pledge that he be free to leave when he has accumulated a thousand pounds. That represents twice what he would expect to draw between his first day on board a merchant ship and his grave.

"With our men it will be the same. The first share will go to repairs and to repay capital. After that, all men (and our capital source as well) will share equally. There will be no quick fortunes made at first, but steady earning for as long as a man has a stomach for the seafaring life."

"Time is with us over here in the colonies, Sister," he told her. "As long as that wide sea stretches between us and the rest of the civilized world, we have the winning hand. This endless land can produce lumber and tar and pitch and tobacco for the world, if need be. Do you know how many barrels of rice left this small port here in these past years?"

"Ah," she raised a hand to caution him. "But the navigation laws limit where you can sell things, remember."

Antoine shook his head. "Those laws will have to be repealed. They will be. We will bury that small island of the King's with rice if they are not. And when the laws are changed so that Carolina rice can be sold outside of England, the *Sojourner* and her sisters will be ready." He glanced at Julie. "I am even willing to wager that new capital will be clamoring to be in on our business before three years are out."

"But the beginning," Sophie asked. "Where does the money come from in the beginning?"

Julie saw Antoine pause, refill his glass and lift it to Marta, who smiled lazily into his eyes before she drained her own glass.

The conversation swirled about the table. Sophie, her good business head engaged by the enterprise, plied the three partners with a stream of questions about the ship and their method for recruiting this novel group of men. The answers came haphazardly, with Ethan and Antoine and Marta interrupting each other in mid-sentence. They shared the intimate glances and smiles and nods of agreement that are characteristic of those welded in an adventure from which all others are excluded.

The meal which had been so hastily enriched with special dainties from Sophie's larder was eaten as heedlessly as if it were the humblest of repasts. The wine bottles were replaced again and again and the tapers burned low.

"I only hope that you have not underestimated the danger of pirates," Sophie said mildly during a break in the flow of talk.

"The great golden days of the pirates are past, Mrs. Bontemps," Ethan assured her. "When Black Bart's fleet was run down by that fleet of pirate chasers, the end was already in sight. And once Blackbeard's head went north on the prow of Maynard's sloop with his great headless body still swimming in circles in Ocracoke, it was the same as all through."

"After them have been only bunglers," Marta said acidly. "Amateurs setting out in rusty tubs with less skill than a cabin boy. They turn tail at the sight of a cannon or the threat of a decent fight."

"Who then is this Battery John?" Sophie asked. "That's the name I hear all the time since Bonnet was hung. Does he not have a fleet of his own even as Blackbeard had in his prime?"

Ethan nodded. "Battery John is indeed a different sort of pirate, ma'am. He's not a wild-eyed beginner, that one. But it is said of him that there's a mentor that rules him . . . some wise head that controls him and his fleet with an iron hand. And he's got this curious rule that keeps me from worrying about him. He and his fleet prey only on other nations, the Spanish in particular. He will not have his flag run up against an English ship no matter how rich the prize."

"But what of our men of Charles Town who have run afoul of him?" Sophie challenged.

"They played a fool's trick," Marta said quietly. "They ran up a strange banner, thinking to conceal their cargo. Once aboard, no captain would have kept the men from plundering. It is the flag of Spain that he will go out of his way to bring down."

Julie, watching and listening, pondered on the girl across from her. Marta was beautiful, there was no gainsaying that. She had a wild animal beauty that seemed to burst through the proper richness of her attire. Lisbon, London, Paris, her brother had said. Yet this woman who wore the finest silks and jewels seemed even richer in pirate lore than her brother, whose life was lived there among the gossip of seafaring men.

A sense of stifling helplessness overwhelmed Julie. This creature, all woman and yet half-man in her bold glance and seafaring knowledge, was suddenly too many things to Antoine. He had taken money from her and Julie well knew what a man of honor Antoine was when it came to debt. It was even possible that Antoine's fortune was tied to a ship which was named in a private joke for her wandering ways. Julie felt a complete, unneeded outsider. Yet, even as she struggled to conceal her dismay, she felt terrible guilt that she was unable to be happy for Antoine's sake. How long had it been since she had seen such fire of joy light his face?

When the men, flushed with food and wine, adjourned to the sitting room with the help of a sturdy slave to get an unsteady Antoine resettled, Sophie turned to Marta.

"Please join us upstairs while the gentlemen have their port."

Marta, her fine body stiff, looked about at the men with a thoughtful stare, then smiled. "No, thank you. Since I am very fond of both men and port, I shall remain with them."

"If it were not so impossible it would be funny," Sophie suggested, removing her wig upstairs to brush an errant curl into place.

"I am not terribly amused," Julie admitted. "Sophie, where in the world would such a young woman get so much money to lend to Antoine? Obviously not from her family, if Ethan is a sample."

"Probably by marrying and burying old men," Sophie

suggested. "She has the equipment for that."

"But why should she risk her capital on a man with no property to put as security against it?"

"A native gambler," Sophie suggested. "Clearly she stands to make or lose much in the turn of the same wind."

Julie sat down limply on the side of the bed. "Do you think it is possible for me to be seized by a sudden attack of vapors and not go back down for coffee?"

Sophie turned her eyes to her sister-in-law. "Possible but not characteristic," Sophie said. "Antoine tried, Julie. He got this party together to show you how hard he is trying to do what he thinks is best for you all . . . to explain that his contact with Marta is based on business alone."

"Then he cannot see the challenge she throws me with her eyes? With her familiar gestures toward him? Is he blind?"

Sophie shook her head slowly. "Not blind, Julie, not in the normal way. He is only blind to all but his own wants, as all people are. Everyone wants to win, Julie. Antoine wants his enterprise, Ethan wants a profit, and Marta wants a profit and Antoine. It is simply up to you to decide what it is that you want."

Julie stared at Sophie a long moment. A strange light moved in her clear yellow eyes, a hard implacable light that did not match the sudden dimpled smile that came to her face.

"Actually," she said lightly, "I want to go down and have coffee with the gentlemen. With brandy too, of course."

Chapter Twenty-One

"This," Sophie said quietly as the door was shut behind their departing guests, "has been one of the longest days of my entire life."

"And mine," Antoine echoed from his chair.

Sophie rose with a sigh. "I am going to celebrate it by going the way of all exhausted ladies, straight into bed. If you want anything, Julie, just ring the bell. Eban is up. The same is true for you, Tony."

"But where shall I sleep?" he asked, as if he had just that

85

moment realized the insuperable obstacle that the stairs presented. Sophie giggled.

"I had a bed made up in the music room. That can be your private quarters until you escape from that box. I do hope that you are able to rest without pain."

"Ah, good girl," he said. "And good dreams."

Just before his departure Ethan Weston had produced a large, carefully painted picture of the projected ship the *Sojourner*. Propped as the painting was upon a low table with a taper set near, the picture dominated the room. The least waver of the candle flame seemed to fill the sails with life and stir carefully limned ocean with new turns of color.

Julie turned from the picture to see Antoine's eyes on her from across the room. "The worst pain I feel at this moment is the absence of you from my arms."

She had to ignore him. She had to seize this moment while it was here to let him know where she stood with him, with this yet unrealized ship and with Marta whose animal vitality had lingered in the room like an alien scent after she had left.

"This whole evening represents the fulfillment of a dream to you, doesn't it, Antoine?"

He nodded. "Even as you were during all that time that we were apart."

She turned her eyes to him. "Dreams have a way of fading with the day," she reminded him.

"You never have faded for me," he said quietly.

Why must she remember his voice raised in anger at her? Why did the black fury of his attacks on her have to come so swiftly to her mind? She took the lie from him with steady eyes until he dropped his lids, his voice growing plaintive. "Come and sit by me, Julie. I cannot talk with you clear across the room like that."

"You know the girl Marta is in love with you."

"You talk like a jealous wife."

"A jealous husband deserves a jealous wife," she goaded. "You do know that she is in love with you."

He stirred in his chair. "She is not in love with me, she only wants me. Like she wants to be in Portugal for a certain festival, like she wants a gown of red velvet with pearls sewn along the hem."

"And so you used her weakness to borrow money to build this ship?"

"She is no child, Julie, believe me. She went into this arrangement with her eyes wide open. She is gambling too. In fact she is the greatest gambler of us all. I can lose time and credit. Ethan can lose time and his patience, probably. She can lose a cool fortune in English pounds."

"English pounds," Julie repeated incredulously.

"She made some sort of a killing in Bristol," he explained.

Slave trading, Julie decided to herself. Then she sighed and rose from her chair. The light illumined only one side of her face, casting the rest into darkness so that her expression was hidden and mysterious.

"I have not had it in my heart to help force your will on Sophie all these years, to coerce her into marrying a man she does not love." Julie's voice was heavy with fatigue. "I have not had it in my heart to try to persuade you to accept the ample capital resources that my aunt has offered again and again because I knew that you would not consider being in debt to . . ." Her voice wavered and she finished lamely, "my family. By these means I have lost all right to protest what you are doing now.

"But Antoine, Marta knows and I know that the battle for your allegiance has only begun between us. I will fight for you against her wiles and against the power she has over you by your taking her money. But I will fight only as long as I think you want me to be victorious and not a moment longer. I am tired of fighting, Antoine."

"Jesus Christ, Julie," he shouted at her. "You are grown as mad as Sophie. If I have ever looked with lust on another woman since we met, my God strike me dead."

"Yesterday is dead, Antoine. Tomorrow is the problem."

"Is yesterday dead, Julie?" he asked quietly.

"Just by being yesterday, it is gone forever," she reminded him.

He fell silent, watching her in the wavering light of the taper.

"Would you please hand me the bell, Julie? I wish to summon Eban."

She wasn't thinking clearly. She crossed the room with the silver bell in her hand and held it out to him. As quick as a cat he grasped her by the arm and dragged her body across his. His voice was almost frightening in its intenseness. "You are mine, Julie. Do not stand across a room from me and make pronouncements about war and embattlement. My God, Julie, we are one."

With his arms so tight about her she could not have pulled free if she had wished to. But she pleaded silently with her

87

own body: *Please God, no. Just this once give me strength against my passion for him. Just this once.* But the weakness that came with his touch was already softening her body against his. His voice stirred the loose curls about her face. "We are one, Julie," he repeated fiercely. "We are one in the magic of our Etoile and in the rough strength of that terrifying child Armand, but most of all, Julie, we are one together."

She would have resisted his hand at the ribbons of her corselette but she had neither strength nor will. With his lips finding hers, she submitted helplessly to the plunging of his desire deep in her throat. She barely stifled the moan of pleasure that rose to her lips as he slid his hands in eagerness around the smoothness of her hip and in between her thighs.

Then, to her horror, he rang the bell.

She leaped to her feet with a cry of outrage.

He grinned wickedly as she fought to cover the breasts that he had released to glow in the candlelight. "It is for this, my dearest," he told her quietly. "That God invented shawls."

Nervously, with the white lace shawl careful about her shoulders, she assisted Eban as he supported Antoine into the music room where the bed was laid back with fresh linen.

All her inhibitions left with Eban. She was conscious of a heady power over Antoine that only fed her passion for him.

As he lay helpless on the bed she undressed slowly, standing a long time to fold each garment carefully as she removed it.

"Jesus Christ, Julie," he stormed, "would you drive me to madness?"

She smiled at him. "I am only trying to figure out the mechanics," she explained, grinning over her shoulder at him.

"Mechanics, hell," he said. "When I first made love to you, you were as sick as a dog."

"Ah, but I was in fever," she reminded him. "One writhes a lot with fever."

"I like writhing," he confessed, grinning.

"But that," she stared at his wood-encased splint. "Whatever are we going to do with that?" When he reached for her, she jumped nimbly away.

"You are no lady to tease like this," he told her with mock displeasure.

"And you are certainly no gentleman to stand up so straight in such a particular place when a lady is present."

Without warning she moved swiftly to the bed and slid in

upon him, her mouth open against his throat and her hands tight upon him.

"God, Julie," he moaned.

"It's nice on top," she purred when the flood of his passion filled her and she felt his body grow limp beneath hers.

"I could have told you," he murmured, pressing her close to him, marveling that flesh so satiny and frail could contain such passionate energy.

"You did indeed," she agreed softly, "but I have never tired of the tale."

He softly slapped her behind. "And neither do I."

Sophie, stirred from sleep by the laughter from the room below, moved against her pillow. Her loneliness for Paul returned swiftly like a windswept cloud, engulfing her with grief. She wept bitterly into her pillow for the man she had waited for all those interminable years.

Antoine was half asleep when Julie's drowsy voice stirred him.

"I am afraid I have to know what Marta was shouting at you as you ran off to the fire yesterday."

"Do you really want to know?" he asked mildly.

"Really," she murmured.

"She was screaming for me not to be a fucking fool and if I went out there and got my ass burned off she would have my head on a stake."

"Shades of my old friend Ellie," Julie giggled against his chest.

Chapter Twenty-Two

As passionately as Julie loved her husband, she was far too honest to herself to endow him in her mind with qualities that he did not possess. Nothing that she knew of Antoine Rivière suggested that he would be capable of patience. Even as he was an impetuous and demanding lover, so had he attacked all life by hurling his mind and body at problems as if the force of his siege itself would save the day.

How astonishing it was for her to see him quietly accept the long weeks of inactivity that it took to mend his broken leg.

When Ethan Weston came to work with Antoine at the house on Tradd Street, wreathing the rooms with clouds of acrid tobacco smoke, Antoine became all shipbuilder. Their voices echoed along the hallway in laughter and excited planning. Ethan's friend, the shipwright from Dorset, had agreed to join the team. There was word of a sailmaker in Albemarle whose sails were stouter than those of the King's navy.

When he was able to walk, slowly, with a cane in his hand, he led Julie along the Battery to dream about the day when that sea would carry his own ship. They watched the smoke signals from Sullivan's Island, and studied what craft nudged at anchor in the harbor. He was touchingly pleased when Julie grew able to distinguish a sloop from a schooner and at last to know a three-masted square rigger from an East Indiaman.

Julie had had less of a problem with Ethan's sister Marta than she would have dreamed possible. Shortly after their first meeting Marta disappeared as she had come. Since neither of the men mentioned her going, Julie had to swallow her pride and inquire of her from her brother.

His response was a hearty laugh. "Excusing the expression, Mistress Rivière, but God only knows. She comes and goes like the wind, that woman. I am just glad I am not elected to try to keep an anchor on her." He frowned. "She did mention Martinique. I know she has firm friends there. And Paris. She does seem to take to the French with some degree of spirit."

But not only the sea absorbed Antoine's healing weeks. He managed to stay as involved with Sophie's plantation as he was with his ship.

"Look here, Sophie," he called her. "I have drawn this plan."

"Why, it's a new cookhouse," she realized, studying the picture. "But it is brick and tile."

"I have strong feelings about that," he admitted. "I think you should build only for the long time. If brick is too dear, then we can train our own slaves to make it." He handed her a second sheet with another sketch and a small map. "See, this would be the colliery and here is where it could fit comfortably. Much of the same equipment could be used for the making of tile. That way, a fire would never torch your buildings."

By Armand's first birthday, the boy had reared himself onto his feet to lurch about with an amiable grin, terrifying the

90

barn fowl and keeping his sister Etoile dancing about like a wind-blown seed with concern for his safety.

But as the toasts were poured on that festive day, Julie grew pensive, remembering the day of his birth.

Antoine, always quick to her mood, slid his arm about her waist. "Where is your mind, love?" he asked. "With such a fine strong son to your credit, why are you so quiet?"

She smiled up at him, her hand straying unconsciously to his throat, tanned by the summer sun. How could she tell him that she had been thinking of Josh? For it had been a year to the day since Josh had told her the story of the white slave of the Natchez who might possibly be Sophie's husband, Paul.

"Such a good life," Antoine sighed. There was a choke in his voice as he caught Etoile and swung her against the blue of the summer sky. "And within a year . . . maybe a little more, the ship will be on her first voyage."

By the time Armand's birthday came again, more changes than any of them could have guessed had come about. A new king was on the throne of England, to Antoine's great jubilation. "Only wait," he said happily. "Only wait and you will see that those outmoded navigation laws will be repealed, for the good of us all." Armand had lost much of his look of babyhood and become a great amiable boy who was as playful as he was strong. The *Sojourner* had grown under the tools of the workmen in the heat of a summer unusual not only for its blazing sky but also for the severe rains which threatened all the crops that could not grow as rice did, knee deep in mirrored water.

Admiring the work on the boat with her arm wound through Antoine's, Julie marveled that the skeleton of wood had been clothed into such a vast seaworthy craft by the hands of simple men.

They were turning to start away when Julie felt Antoine's hand tighten on her arm.

She stood watching them from the dock. The wind caught her full, patterned skirt and whipped it about her slender ankles and bare feet. Her hair was loose as it had been that first day Julie saw her, pulled back carelessly under a bright scarf. The thin fine cotton of her low blouse was shadowed by the faint pale brown of her nipples pressing against the cloth. Julie felt a flush rise to her cheeks at the careless bold way Marta's eyes swept Antoine.

"The little family out for a stroll?" she said. "I must say that it is good to see you upright on the stems again, Tony."

91

She approached them in a loose, swinging walk that was more like the gait of a sailor than a lady. When she turned to Julie, she feigned astonishment. "What, are you still in trim? Where are those fine sons you boast would man our ships?"

Julie flushed at the suggestion, but Antoine laughed easily. "All in good time, Marta, all in good time. Have you enjoyed your traveling about?"

'Yes," Julie put in. "How did you find Paris?"

It was such an innocent question to evoke the strange response that came. Marta's look of astonishment was followed by an expression of dark fury. "My goodness," she said in an icy tone. "My private business does seem to be noised about just anywhere, doesn't it?" Then she looked steadily at Julie. "Paris was enchanting, as you must surely know yourself. You have traveled in France, haven't you?"

The girl had such a knack for putting her tongue on Julie's sore spots. But before Julie could stammer her admission of having never been there, Antoine spoke up, turning toward the boat. "How do you approve the progress during your absence? It has been a slow but satisfying time."

"She looks magnificent," Marta admitted. "And I am all the more impressed that you started from an invalid's chair." Her smile was sly as she caught Antoine's free arm in her own. "Haven't got drunk enough to fall down any more stairs lately? What a dull life."

Julie felt Antoine stiffen at Marta's words, even though the woman's tone was jesting. "Come off that, Marta," he snapped. The tightening of his arm against her own caused Julie to stumble a little on the rough stones of the street.

Marta shrugged. "Lost your sense of humor along with your splint?" Then without pausing, she tugged at the loose neck of her shirt with her free hand. "Jesus, what a sultry day you have here. The air lies heavy on my skin. If I had known what weather you were having, I would have stayed on those shaded avenues until time for the launching."

"The hottest weather in anyone's memory," Antoine said, obviously eager to change the subject from his broken leg. "One old wharf rat keeps telling Ethan and me that it is hurricane weather. He has become so hysterical about it that it is a local joke."

"It's probably those rice fields steaming up the air," Marta shrugged. "Come along and have a drink with Ethan and me."

"Thank you," Julie said quickly. "We are expected at home."

Marta gave her a long straight look, then shrugged. "Of course, I forget you are bound by those domestic rules." Something in her tone started that vague anger in Julie again, the same irritation she had felt at Marta's strange remark about Antoine's drunkenness.

"Antoine is certainly not bound," Julie said quickly. "He could come back as soon as he drops me at home."

But Marta shrugged. "Oh, never mind. We'll have nothing but each other's company in the weeks to come." She smiled wisely at Julie as she tightened her arm on Antoine's.

Julie would have asked Antoine that moment about Marta's remark, but he hastened her home so quickly that she was almost breathless.

"I have promised Etoile a tale," he grinned down at Julie. "That little sprite cannot know that I look forward to those story times as much as she does."

The entire house was too warm to be comfortable and the heat in the dining room when the warm food was served was oppressive. The three of them toyed with their food. Sophie, worn from the heat, ate only a few bites and sat solemn and unsmiling. Unable to erase Marta's remark from her mind, Julie finally put anxiety into words.

"Tell me what Marta meant about your falling downstairs from drunkenness," she said. She saw the quick exchange of glances between Antoine and his sister, and heard Antoine's muffled expletive.

"That girl has a big mouth," Sophie said wearily. "Among other things."

Julie looked from one of them to the other. "Whatever she refers to obviously has not been kept privy to the family," she pointed out. "How did your leg get broken, Antoine?"

"After the fire," he replied slowly. "It was after the fire."

"That is *when*," Julie prompted him. "Now I guess I would like to know *how*."

"It's all over and past, Julie," Sophie said tiredly. "Why do you want to drag it out again?"

"Because I didn't 'drag it out' the first time," Julie said, a little annoyed at the way they seemed to have joined forces against her on such a simple case.

"It was after the fire," Antoine said quietly. "The night was well spent and I was exhausted. Sophie and I talked . . ." His voice faltered. What had they talked of, Julie wondered, that made him unable to meet her eyes a year and a half later?

"So I was sore and filthy and angry and I drank too much."

She stared at him, remembering Sophie at Maggie MacRae's door, hearing her invitation . . . so carefully stated. How could she be so incensed by something from so long ago? Only much later did Julie realize that it was not so much what happened but that she had learned it from Marta's intimate jest. It was starting again. The girl was barely there and already she had driven this wedge into their intimacy.

"I am astonished that you would do that to me, Sophie. That you could come to Maggie MacRae's and lie to me about Antoine and the fire."

"I didn't lie," Sophie protested, unable to meet her eyes. "I was careful as I spoke and your concern for Tony filled in the blanks." Her tone was pleading.

"Would you have done it differently, Julie? Would you have come to Antoine if you had known the truth."

Julie stared at her thoughtfully. "Probably not," she admitted. Then, with Sophie's gaze still speculative on her face, Julie felt the slow flush of shame rise on her cheeks.

And oh God, how she had come back. She remembered that night of lovemaking in the music room and felt suddenly cold. Suddenly it seemed as if she were dining with strangers. She saw them waiting, both of them, Antoine with words poised behind his lips and Sophie with wary eyes.

Julie slid from her chair and rose. The words of her careful upbringing came softly from her lips. "If you will excuse me now, I think I shall retire."

Antoine was on his feet instantly, his hand on her arm. "Julie, darling," he began.

She did not flinch or move away. She knew what fury rose in him whenever she moved away from his touch.

"You might enjoy the piazza," Sophie said in a quiet, half-scared voice. "It is the only place where there is a breath of air these nights."

Sophie did not follow. Just outside the door, in the dark of the piazza, Antoine turned her roughly, seizing her with such urgent force that she felt the breath jarred from her body. His hands moved along her back and his lips were on her throat and her quickly bared breasts. Noting the stars through the leaves that shaded the area, she was conscious of the exposed place where they were, and she struggled against his hands loosing her dress. The urgency of his passion was thrusting against her belly as he lifted her skirts aside.

"Antoine," she begged in a fierce whisper, hoping to bring him to his senses.

Ignoring her plea, he lifted her against the wall that separated the porch from the room within. The force of his passion came like waves, crushing her against the hard surface of the wall. Nothing. No part of her stirred to his frantic lovemaking. Instead, she felt strangely above and apart from his frantic rutting.

But he did not know. When she felt the groan of his satisfaction and felt the warm flood of his seed down her bruised legs, he sighed with that same satisfaction that had so many times signaled their mutual ecstasy. He did not know that he had brought no response from her.

But she was limp against him, held by his great strength against the wall. Did she imagine a note of triumph in his voice when he whispered against her neck.

"I cannot bear it when you turn from me, even for a moment as you did back there. I am sorry, Julie, sorry that I had to deceive you like that, but I cannot live without you. You are mine, Julie, don't you see that? Mine."

"I am yours," she echoed faintly. But it was a joyless truth. The disillusion was there, still a hard painful place between her breasts, far more hurtful than the bruises he had made by pressing his passion against her in that strangely public place.

And the song was there. What had started it in her mind? A chance series of notes from an experimental mockingbird in the vines beyond the lattice? Or the word, again, the word that was only a word and therefore could be spent on the air like false coin.

Sorry. Sorry. Sorry.

Chapter Twenty-Three

Marriage, Julie decided wistfully, is like a long slow journey through an uncharted land. You simply keep walking at the same unchanging pace while the very earth beneath your feet changes invisibly. Since the trees and sky hold their color, you do not notice that the rhythm of the bird song is changed until you look to see a hill as familiar as your hand and find that you have passed it beyond recall.

As little as she wished to, she did not easily heal from the hurt of Antoine's having tricked her back into his arms. She could not completely trust his great ardor after she realized how consciously he had exploited her passion for him to make peace with her.

But on the surface all remained the same, the summer an endless procession of sultry days with scarcely enough breeze to flutter the flowers that hung in the vines. What rains came were sudden heavy downpours that somehow failed to cleanse the air as summer showers were supposed to do.

Only Antoine, drunk with excitement over the completion of the *Sojourner*, seemed impervious to the weather. He bounded forth in the morning in high spirits, returning at evening with his vast energy seemingly undiminished.

Sophie chuckled. "I have to say I do prefer this particular madness to his former foul moods." Then, with her eyes on her sister-in-law's face, she spoke softly.

"Julie, I do hope that you realize how difficult it is for me to say tender things, no matter how true they are. I have always had a voice to which curses came easier than compliments, which is an unbecoming thing for a woman. But, my dear, there is so much that I want to thank you for."

Julie's golden eyes flew wide before she burst into laughter. "Oh indeed, Sophie, you are greatly in debt to me," she mocked. "You rescue me from certain death at my uncle's hand and shelter me in your own home. You wed me to your favored brother when I had come without a pin of dowery. And as if that were not enough, I have bred two children who also live on your bounty as carelessly as birds in trees. Yet you say you are in debt to me. I certainly would not have such an accountant as you to tot my books."

Sophie chuckled. "How you can twist things about, you minx. You know very well what I mean. Without Antoine to manage the plantation as he has these past years, I would still be deeply dependent on my neighbor Beauchamps. That poor man's patience is strained beyond comfort and I do not blame him. It is enough for a man to court a woman for so many years without having to assume the burden of the management of her affairs at the same time. Antoine has released me from this debt to him. And as for you, my dear, I am not deceived by your serene demeanor. I know what hell Tony has put you through trying to get you to throw your influence into making me marry again."

Julie's eyes were sober. "Having waited so long for Antoine, I can certainly not fault your constancy to Paul."

"He will come, Julie," Sophie whispered, suddenly leaning toward her friend. "That dream comes again and again, but it is more than that. It comes with my eyes open and wakeful. A heaviness forms in the air like mist and I can feel him there beyond my seeing. I hear his voice calling my name. He will come, Julie. I know he lives and will come again."

A faint shiver moved over Julie's flesh in spite of the day's heat. It was time. It was time for Josh to have returned with his report of the man they thought might be Paul Bontemps.

"You are strangely silent," Sophie observed, her eyes curious.

Julie looked up with a start. "You must remember that I have never met Paul," she said hastily, searching for a subject to distract Sophie's mind.

"To have seen our son Charles is to have seen Paul," Sophie told her quietly. Then, in her maternal way, the talk drifted to her son in France, to his successful studies and the astonishing fact that he had made peace with his grandparents.

"When we ran away like we did, Antoine and Paul and I, all those years ago under such clouds, I never thought our father would cast a friendly eye on us or our children again."

"He is grown old," Julie reminded her.

"And sick," Sophie added quietly. "Charles describes his grandfather as an old sick man given to strange humors."

"Does he say what kind of humors?" Julie asked.

"Charles does not say right out," Sophie confessed. "But from what I read between his lines I would say it is some sort of scheming. He has always loathed Emile as a son as much as Tony and I have despised him as a brother." She shivered. "I was terrified of him as a child and still am, all these miles away. But the name of Rivière and the title and land that have been claimed in that name all these generations are more important to Father than the blood of any outsider. So now he is pitiful, having only that sniveling Emile to claim as heir. It would not be strange that he battles against his fate with wiles and ruses as well as his notable rages."

"But you tell me that he has received Charles cordially," Julie said. "Isn't it possible that he might be able to name your son as heir?"

Sophie shook her head vehemently. "Not in a million years. Paul would never permit it. Even thought he was disinherited by his own family, he is still as vain of his name and lineage as my own father is. But there is Armand."

Julie's eyes flew wide in astonishment. "Armand!" she

laughed. "That is a truly ridiculous idea, Sophie. Antoine would never entertain such a thought. His father has been the same as dead to him since he repaid the debt he owed. 'Buying myself free,' he called it. Consider his passion for building an estate for Armand. Is that the work of a man who would meekly send his son into a yoke of which he tore himself free?"

Sophie shrugged. "With each year a man lives, his ears become more sensitive to the siren song of gold."

"But it is his own gold that Antoine is eager for," Julie said. "Not his father's bounty."

Sophie shrugged and rose, fanning her skirts irritably. "Their eyes fail a little too, as they age," she said mildly. "They do not search as carefully where the gold is coming from."

Julie eyed her husband's sister thoughtfully. Was Sophie thinking of Marta? It was true enough that Antoine had stiffly refused loans from his own sister and any possible help from her aunt. Yet he had put himself thousands of pounds into debt with that gypsy woman, like a blind man not seeing what hand filled his cup.

She shrugged. The hostile truce that lay between herself and Marta had somehow managed to hold. The *Sojourner* lay at anchor beyond the bar. The crew who would man her were even now aboard. How painfully Antoine had chosen these men and enlisted them in his enterprise. And what a good crew it was: Captain O'Reefe whom Maggie MacRae said was as solid as the hill he sprang from, with his son Timothy as lieutenant; the quartermaster John Snell was a sober man whom Julie herself had instinctively liked and trusted because he reminded her so much of her father's banker, Henry Furlong in London. Down to the lowest seaman they were fine, solid men, each one of them as excited as Antoine about this great adventure.

So as little as she liked Antoine's debt to Marta, what could happen now with the longboats already loading the ship for its first passage.

"If it were not for that damned cloud of mosquitoes that hovers over the river like a miasma, I would pick up and move us all back to the plantation this minute to escape this heat," Sophie said crossly. "This city brags on its sea breeze and I'll be bloody hanged if I can feel anything but steam waves. Look at that sky, that hideous overcast. The air is an oven and it is only noon."

The overcast grew denser by the hour. By the time the

children were laid to their naps, fretful from the heat, Julie realized that the sky had grown dark beyond the curtains.

It was ridiculous. How could twilight come at midafternoon on the fourteenth of September? Yet she could hear in the distance the far rumblings that presaged storm. Hearing Sophie and Eban in spirited conversation in the hall below, she stopped to listen.

"That would all be fool's work, Eban, and in this miserable heat. We cannot disturb an entire household because of the doomscrying of every old madman in Charles Town."

"He say the hurricane is coming," Eban repeated stubbornly. "If he be right we need to carry the food and fresh water up above where the water going to come rolling. He say that God is taking the water out of the sea to wash the sin from this wicked city and the fornicators and the lawyers will all die."

"Eban, for God's sake," Sophie almost laughed. "Fornicators and lawyers indeed. I would be interested in knowing how he made that particular order for sinners."

The stark terror in Eban's face and the tremors of his voice caught at Julie's heart. And even as he spoke she could see black clouds slowly swinging in from the southeast, moving like a shroud toward the cluster of mast in the harbor. Antoine was out there on the *Sojourner*. But surely they had seen the storm coming. They would all be safely ashore by now, with everything battened down on the ship.

"What is it that he really wants to do?" Julie asked curiously.

Sophie shrugged with annoyance. "He wants permission to fill the entire upstairs with food stores and casks of water. He says that when the hurricane hits there will be hunger and death in the wells." At Julie's solemn expression, she shrugged. "He is right of course, if a hurricane really comes."

"Is this the old man down by the wharf who is saying all this?" Julie asked. "Surely you know he has been saying the same thing all summer long."

Eban nodded. "I know. I know. Only now he is sitting down there in a boat with biscuits and dry meat and a basin of water waiting to be washed away. And praying," Eban added. "You have never seen such praying in your born days."

Sophie herself was now staring at the darkness that was folding itself over and over as it moved in toward the town.

"Very well, Eban," she decided in a brisk voice. "Tell all the slaves to come above and bring with them all the food they can carry. And all the casks they can find are to be filled with water. But you also tell them that this is your idea and I am only humoring you. When that storm passes over, the lot of you get to carry all that stuff right back down and put it away without a whimper."

"Yes, ma'am," he nodded vigorously as he started down the stairs. "They already got stuff out ready to carry. They got seven casks filled and still drawing. Such praying," he added as he disappeared down the hall. "You have never heard such calling on the name and the horses coming in all colors."

"It can do no harm," Sophie said, almost shamefaced. "It will at least keep them from getting hysterical when this storm actually hits.

Still. Not a whisper of wind stirred as the darkness spread over the harbor and into the city. The bird song, so much a part of Charles Town that one ceased to hear it, had disappeared. There was not the screech of an insect to be heard in that stillness. There was only the far thunder and a stillness like a scream crouched in a madman's throat waiting for release.

When it came it was like the cry of a giant beast whose lungs had the air of the world for its breath.

"Sophie," Julie cried. "Sophie, come and see." Her own mind went all places at once, to the *Sojourner* swaying at anchor out there beyond the bar, to her children twisting in their beds.

Once, long ago, when she and Josh were till together, she had tried to put it into words for him, telling him that fear lived in the center of love. That cold center of her many loves was spreading, making a icy panic that flowed splintery through her veins. Desperate tears flooded her face. "Sophie!" she screamed.

At her side Sophie stared at the sable cloud with horror. "Oh God," she said softly. "Dear God, no."

The roar filled the air, almost drowning her voice. The black cloud seemed driven by some irresistible force that swirled and tumbled it. The thunder, once so distant, was now close and imperative. Shafts of lightning pierced the darkness of the cloud and even as Sophie dragged her from the window Julie heard the rain begin. The branches of great trees flailed at the air like whips, snapping and moaning from the force of the wind-driven rain.

Sophie was everywhere at once as shutters were nailed shut and the doors braced with wooden bars against the wind.

The slaves wept or wailed as they worked and a voice Julie did not recognize began a low sibilant incantation, part prayer, part appeal and part terrified gibberish.

Julie, frozen at the window, peered between the cracks of the shutters watching the rain that swept about the besieged house. The world seemed at once half fire and half flood as lightning illumined a street already deep with swirling water. A runaway horse galloped down the deserted roadway, skidded and lost his footing to be thrown against the corner of a building by the force of the water. He was unable to rise again and Julie saw the water cover his head, as his great jaws opened and shut in screaming appeal that could not be heard for the clamor of the storm.

"Antoine," Julie moaned. "Antoine."

Etoile was screaming in terror. All attempts by Maggie and Susan to calm her were useless while the slaves in the room beyond vented their own fear in bloodcurdling screams.

"Sing," Sophie shouted to Eban. "For God's sake get them to sing."

Eban's voice was drowned by their din as they ignored his pleas. Then Maggie MacRae set Etoile down firmly and went to the door of the room where the slaves were huddled. Seizing a glass bottle, she crashed it against the lintel of the door. A room full of startled eyes stared at her.

"You shut up that savage caterwauling this minute," she said fiercely. "You start over there, Eban, and the rest of you better join in. I want singing. I want praising to God that He can hear over this bloody storm of His. You sing heathen or you sing proper, but the first one that stops singing is getting his heart cut straight out by this bottle here."

Eban's voice rose quivering, but singing. Then another voice joined, and another. Gasping and sobbing and clinging, they sang while the wind crashed against the house and the water rose in the streets outside.

Sophie, like Julie, stared at the blackness beyond the shuttered windows. Then she turned away and groped her way to a chair where she sat limply.

"It is the Gulf Stream," she said quietly. "I keep remembering stories of the storm of 'ninety-nine. The water is already halfway to the floor of this story."

"What in God was that?" Sophie whispered tensely.

Julie's voice was calm. It was too incredible to be important anymore. "It was a ship, Sophie," she reported quietly. "It was a ship coming up Tradd Street. It only brushed us but it went all the way into the house next door."

"A boat," Sophie corrected her sanely.

Why was it so important to be accurate? "Actually it was a ship, Sophie. It was a schooner."

"What can we do?" Julie asked.

"Wait," Sophie said quietly. "We simply wait."

"How long?" Julie pressed.

Sophie shrugged. "Until it is over."

"But Antoine," Julie began, that spiral of terror starting to rise again in her chest.

Sophie's voice turned stern. "We wait," she insisted, as the wind howled and the trees hammered at the house as if their limbs had been endowed with life and were clamoring for entry.

There was neither night or day as the storm battered the city walls. Beyond Julie's cramped view the wind whipped the waves of the sea to incredible heights, forcing the water into the bay and along the rivers that bounded the city. Wharves broke and houses tumbled like blocks in the path of the current. The sea, rushing along the streets, swept everything in its wake, rising until the second-story windows seeped water into rooms of terrified citizens.

Men who had lived with this sea all their days were agape with horror. There was no ebb. There was only the ceaseless relentless driving of the water drowning the city in its path. Palmetto trees that had towered over grown men appeared on the crest of the water like low-growing bushes.

Then, as suddenly as the wind had come, it turned about. The same violence that had blown west turned to the east. A ringing started in Julie's ears that almost brought a scream to her lips. Over the sound of the wind came the sucking rushing sweep of the water in the town being drawn back into the sea.

There was no hope. No hope at all. All was lost. It could not be otherwise.

Chapter Twenty-Four

It was night as the water receded from the city. It was night and there was nothing to be done.

"I cannot stay here," Julie said flatly. If no one will go with me, I will go alone."

"I cannot stay here," Julie repeated dully.

With Eban at her side she picked her way down the stairs, past the stairs, past the drenched furniture of the lower rooms and into the streets of Charles Town.

Eban's was only one among many lanterns moving among the smashed boats and coops and clutter that had been left on the streets by the receding water. Death was everywhere, both man and animal.

Julie looked but did not see as she walked toward the wharf. Or where the wharf had been. Every vessel that had stood within the harbor was cast ashore, some broken and some whole, but set at heedless angles in among the ruins of the wharves. But the face of the sea was calm, dark and leathery under the light of a hesitant moon.

Even as she walked the streets of Charles Town without actually seeing the particulars of the ravages about her, she heard the voices of the townspeople without absorbing the sense of their words.

To walk through Charles Town was to abandon hope that one frail ordinary life could have been saved from among so many. She saw Antoine pressed inside the lids of her staring eyes, Antoine as a footman blazing with fairness and color, passing on a white coach when she was a child in Middlesex...Antoine as lover in the haunting woods of Epping...Antoine, Antoine, Antoine.

"It does no good to walk," Eban reproached from her side. "Your children wait for you."

Her children, Antoine's children. Etoile, that elf of a girl who had wound her father's heart about her smile until he was a great soft plaything in her grasp. That sturdy Armand for whom Antoine desired empires that his son might leap into manhood with the same lusty strength that he had leaped from her body.

And always the voices of strangers wailing loss. She envied them the strength of their grief. Her own mourning was a voiceless weight that stumbled her feet along the cobblestones.

Dead Dead. Dead.

Then among the voices was one calling her name. "Rivière," she heard, "Madame Rivière."

She did not at once recognize the surgeon that Antoine had enlisted to serve on the *Sojourner*. This man with his shirt awry and his face haggard with strain bore little resemblance to the crisp Francis Arlington who had bent so gallantly over her hand at their first meeting.

"Arlington," he said quickly. "Francis Arlington from the *Sojourner*."

A limpness overwhelmed her. She clutched at his hands helplessly. "From the ship," she cried. "Oh God, tell me."

Compassion filled his face as he caught her arms to support her. "Some of us had come ashore," he told her. "A little before noon, your husband and Timothy O'Reefe and I." She struggled with the name and then remembered: Timothy . . . the fresh-faced son of the captain.

"Even as we left I heard the captain say that if the wind yielded what it promised, he would cut the mast."

What did it matter? What did any of it matter now?

"And my husband?" she asked.

"We left him at the warehouse with Mr. Weston and his sister."

"The warehouse." She gripped his arm. "Then he was already on shore when the storm hit?"

"Oh yes," he nodded. "As I said, we came early. There was something about the rigging and young O'Reefe came along and a man who was called Venner."

The spiral of hope flamed hotly. "And my husband, where is he now?"

His glance slid toward the rubble that remained of the double house containing the warehouse. "I do not know, madam," he admitted dully. "I do not know."

The leathery face of the sea seemed to crease in small sly undulating smiles.

Sophie, her eyes ringed with shadows, handled Julie as if she were a wounded child. When the food she offered would not pass Julie's throat, she enticed her with a glass of strong wine with a few drops from her special vial in it. Within minutes she watched Julie sink into a dark, drugged sleep.

Titus was there. She watched in the haze as the dwarf who had been her great good friend hobbled across the clearing on his bandy legs, his face hidden by the angle of his humped back. She called out to him but when he turned, his face had become that of her crazed uncle raving with madness. Flames rose from the tunic he wore and she began to scream.

When the arms closed about her, she fought furiously against them only to have them tighten like a rope about her. She screamed at the strength that held her. "I will not," she screamed. "I will not live without Antoine." Then the mouth of her captor closed on her own and the lips were Antoine's.

She clung to him, feeling her mind grow crafty. Antoine was dead. This time he was most truly dead. If she could only manage to cling to him, she could stay with him. Who would notice one living creature among so many dead?

The spectre that was Antoine spoke into her dream in protest. "You are choking me, love." The voice was gentle. "Hold off a little so that I can breathe."

She obeyed him lest he should take his arms away. The dream faded in the warmth of his arms and she rocked gently in a careful sleep, fearful that she might waken and startle away both Antoine and the dream of his closeness.

She wakened to sunlight and Antoine's sober face staring into her own.

She seized him frantically. "Dream," she gasped.

"It was no dream," he comforted her.

He bent and nuzzled her across the cheek with the roughness of his beard. "No dream, my love, no dream."

She struggled herself upright. "But how? I saw the warehouse."

"I live because of Marta," he admitted humbly. "We had come ashore from the ship, Arlington, young O'Reefe, Venner, and I..." he shrugged. "They left me off at the warehouse to go about their business. God knows how the rest of them fared."

"But you, what is this about Marta?"

Antoine shook his head. "That woman is a hellcat but not without wit. She was raving when I got there, cursing like a drunken pirate and slamming books and records together while she screamed at her poor brother. There was no gainsaying her. Before the first rain struck we were on horse hauling the records and the gold upriver for safety. Once there I could not return until the ebb came. When I got here, you had already been sent into the demon sleep that my sister prepared for you."

Julie smiled at the picture he presented and he held her close.

"We live, Julie. How can we be so blessed? It is that star we met under, I swear it is. That bright particular star that brought us together from the first. As long as we have that star, we will win."

She nodded and curled into the warmth of his body, wanting him all about her like a glove. Then the sadness caught at her throat. "What of the others? The crew?"

His face darkened under her gaze. "Only time will tell."

Chapter Twenty-Five

When Julie was newly come to the Carolinas, her aunt Anne-Louise DuBois had described the Charles Town settlement to her.

"We are small pockets of humanity pinned to the endless cloth of a savage country," she had said with a note of warning in her voice.

Anne-Louise's words came back again and again in the weeks following the hurricane. Living on the bounty of her sister-in-law, sleeping in fresh graceful rooms and dining from a well-stocked larder had dulled Julie's senses to how frail and helpless this colony and its people were against powers larger than themselves.

But in the weeks following the storm she saw the truculent courage of these people in stubborn action. Great need seemed to lend superhuman strength to their hands.

And nowhere did she see a bolder expression of this strength and persistence than in Antoine.

The morning after the storm revealed a single craft bobbing at anchor in the harbor beyond the bar. Spyglass in hand, Julie watched as the battered longboat, lifted from the side of a house in King Street, rowed out bearing Antoine and his companions to the *Sojourner*.

Of the nine men who had been left aboard the ship only four were ever found. She stood beside Antoine at the burials in the churchyard, the first ill-fated crew of the *Sojourner*. Captain O'Reefe's son Timothy wept unashamed as his father's casket was committed to the sodden earth along with the others. Julie knew that the names of these men would be imprinted in her mind forever. For those whose bodies had not been found they set only stones with the earth undisturbed.

Then Antoine turned, like the other people of Charles Town, to restoring the drenched and foul city clinging to that bar of land between its two rivers. Their faces twisted with loss, the survivors set to work on the new wharves and fortifications.

"Sharks and Spaniards never sleep," they commented as the cannons were dried and hauled back into position on the Battery.

Many who had been dragged from the swirling water failed to survive their injuries. Many who had been wounded, perished. But even as the turning of fresh earth for graves never seem to stop, neither did the drumming of anvil and hammer for the rebuilding.

There was little food and less water within the city walls. The cypress dugouts that in normal time carried the rice and produce to the city for sale came down the rivers now with food and water from the plantations, those outlying pockets of life that undertook to supply the beleaguered town.

Young Timothy O'Reefe was named the new captain of the *Sojourner*. Only his father's wisdom in sacrificing the mast before the storm struck had saved the shell of the ship. With the new mast being fitted, Timothy and Antoine set out to assemble a new crew and replace the cargo that had been almost completely destroyed during the storm.

But even as the city dragged itself erect after the pummeling of the storm, a new and more insidious enemy began to take its toll behind closed doors.

The sailing men who had traveled with this spectre to every port in the world called it yellow jack. The doctors, Jonathan Marlowe and the ship's surgeon Francis Arlington, called it yellow fever.

Sophie was already organizing her household for the retreat to the plantation when Armand fell ill.

Julie, startled from sleep by Armand's anguished cries, joined Susan at his beside. The child shivered with cold even as he screamed in pain.

"Perhaps he have very bad dream," Susan said hopefully.

"Maybe we make him very warm and cozy he shut right up."

But the morning brought fever and vomiting that racked the boy's small sturdy body. There seemed no end to his agony. Just when Julie, distraught and exhausted, was certain that the child's small frame could survive not another hour of this punishment, the fever abated. He slept, his round cheeks still stained with the screams of rebellion he had made against his anguish.

Antoine, leaning over the crib, smiled up at Julie in relief. "My God, he had me scared. But he will be fine. See how sweetly he sleeps. Nothing can happen to us now, Julie, nothing can happen."

Julie could not respond to Antoine's optimism. She could not give him the reassurance that he sought.

"Remission is common with this fever," she told him. Then to encourage herself, she added, "But he is a great strong child, a sturdy strong child."

And the fever did return, darkening Armand's fair face with the bilious yellow for which the fever was named. A long day and night passed before Francis Arlington rose stiffly from the child's side.

"You have won," he said quietly. "He is weak and must be carefully tended, but now you have won."

That night as Julie leaned aginst Antoine's chest, watching from the piazza as the first star of evening came into view, she made a secret wish that their trials were at last over. Antoine was wholly confident. "You see that star, Julie?" he said brightly. "It still shines, our star still shines."

As if invigorated by his misfortune, Antoine proceeded with the work of preparing his ship for passage. The cargo which was to fill the ship the second time was harder to come by in a city stripped of its resources. New sails had to be stitched and every laborer's hour cost more than the same man's time would have cost when there were fewer jobs about the wharf.

"Is there to be no end to this expense?" Marta railed as Antoine coaxed more and more money from her to repair and equip the ship. "I laid out what I wished to invest in the first loading. I damned well do not intend to be made penniless by this enterprise."

Antoine's assurance soothed her only a little. "What kind of a gambler are you to throw one bet on the table and walk away grumbling?" he asked.

"I did not look on this as a gamble," she said crossly. But she brought up the extra capital, her bold eyes suddenly secret against his glance.

And then Etoile wakened screaming, her face flushed and her skin painful to the touch.

This time it was Antoine who pushed the nurse aside to hover at the bedside. He lifted the fevered child into his arms with fury on his face. "She will not be sick," he insisted. "By God, nothing will touch this child with pain. Get Francis Arlington over here this instant. And that damned bastard Marlowe, just in case."

He was a madman while her fever raged, refusing to leave her side to eat or drink. During that brief respite when her disease seemed to have passed, he sat day and night, nestling her in his arms, smiling into her eyes.

"Tell me a tale, Papa," she pleaded in her weakened voice that was suddenly like a baby's voice again. "Tell me the one about the fox and the rabbit."

Even as his voice droned into harshness with one tale after another, his eyes sought Julie's for reassurance.

"Armand lived. See how he thrives. It will be the same again."

Because he did not leave Etoile's side through all those days, Antoine was haggard from exhaustion when the frail respite ended. She was in his arms when the fever stirred her to complaint. He watched the yellow ugliness supplant the fairness of her skin. When she began to retch and the black vomit was torn from her throat, he grew ashen. It was as if all his strength and will faded with Etoile's strength. Blindly he wavered between pleading and fury.

"Are there no doctors?" he screamed. "Where are your proud healing arts, Julie, while your babe lies dying?"

Julie, herself exhausted by grief and nursing, waited stolidly while he raged.

She felt her heart turn with agony in her breast when she saw Etoile's small head roll back against her father's arm and heard the hollow rattle in her throat. His look of horror as he raised his eyes to her brought tears to Julie's eyes and she reached out to him. He brushed her hands aside and rose like a blind man, groping his way to the door.

He neither ate nor slept until the child's burial. But he drank steadily. When he was not restlessly astir, his shoulders hunched against his grief, he sat vigil by the small casket staring at the small golden doll of a child who had so lately been fair and laughingly responsive.

"I cannot bear it," Julie whispered to herself as she fell exhausted into the bed he had so long been away from. "I cannot live with his pain or the loss of my child."

"It is the shock of grief," Sophie assured her. "When the burial is past he will come slowly back to where he was. Still lonely," she added quietly, "but back."

Her aunt Anne-Louise who had buried so many of her own children stood by Julie as Etoile's grave was being heaped with flowers. Antoine stood apart, his great face cadaverous with loss of flesh, his eyes dull and unseeing.

Anne-Louise brought comforts for Armand, who was soberly puzzled by the absence of his beloved sister. She brought fresh white flowers woven into the shape of a star for Etoile's grave. For Julie she brought the whispered news that Josh Simmons had returned from his long trek to the towns of his Indian friends.

"He is sure of this information?" Julie asked.

Anne-Louise nodded. "Can you imagine Josh sending the word to you if he were not sure? He is even now equipping a train to attempt the journey to the village where the white man lives with his wife the Sun Queen."

'His Indian friends have encouraged him to think that the white slave with the name of PoBotahm can be brought back."

"But how?" Julie asked.

"They have word that the Natchez are having great problems with the French who encroach on them ever more steadily in spite of every Natchez effort to be fair and friendly with these invaders. They fear the need for a great war and will be easy to trade with if arms and guns are offered."

Julie sighed. "What a hard choice to make between the Indians and the people of one's own blood."

"It is easy to choose the life of one you love over the death of a multitude of strangers," Anne-Louise said quietly.

She raised her eyes to her aunt's face and shuddered. "How long has Josh been back?" she asked.

"Nearly a month now," her aunt replied, dropping her eyes. "There never seemed to be the right time to talk with you. But now I thought this small thread of hope might be helpful."

Julie laid her hand on her aunt's and pressed it softly. "The smallest thread brightens this dark fabric. When does Josh intend to make the journey? Where will the money come for the arms and goods?"

"You are not to worry about the money," her aunt said firmly. "It is Jacques' great honor, and mine. The delay is due to the shortage of goods since the storm."

"God go with him," Julie said softly.

"Your blessing is all he requires," her aunt replied.

A semblance of normalcy was restored to the house on Tradd Street. Life resumed its quiet rhythm and Sophie, deprived of Antoine's help, began to depart at dawn to the plantation desk even as she had in the years before Antoine's coming to the Carolinas.

And the days turned to weeks and the friends and neighbors' calls of condolence gradually ceased. But Antoine still did not stir from the house by day. Only at night did he stagger drunkenly down the stairs and lurch out into the empty streets of Charles Town.

And all the while the *Sojourner* lay at anchor, waiting.

Chapter Twenty-Six

The bell rang into the silence of the house on Tradd Street. Dinner had been cleared away, a solemn meal served to Sophie and Julie alone at the long table that had seen so many evenings with Antoine filling his armed chair at the end. Sophie, pleading fatigue from her long day at the plantation, had gone to her room. Thus it was Julie who watched from the stairway above as the slave opened the door to Marta Weston.

Marta stood in the doorway, her ripe body twitching with irritation as she glared up at Julie.

"I have just this evening returned," she said bluntly. "What in hell is going on here? I must see that stupid lout of yours and at once."

Julie started down the stairs quickly, hoping to quiet the woman's tirade. She would not be stilled. She stood squarely in the doorway where her husky voice tunneled through the hall and into the upper-story rooms. "What is going on?" she repeated, her eyes flashing with rage. "Nothing is happening on that ship. It hangs there in the harbor for the worms to

111

gnaw at her hull. Not one of those dumb bastards will make a move without him."

Julie tried to shame her to silence with her eyes.

"A little time," she pleaded quietly. "He is in great grief."

"You call this a little time?" the girl raged. "My God, that kid was planted before Christmas and the year is now well turned."

With a cold stab of panic in her breast, Julie was conscious of Antoine's silent emaciated figure by the child's bed in the room above. He must not hear. He must not hear.

"Don't try to shush me, you yellow-eyed witch," Marta sneered. "What kind of man do you have anyway, to desert his work and snivel in a corner because a child is dead? A child!" The girl's rage seemed to be fed by the sound of her own voice as it rose into a high pitch, filling the rooms.

"It is you," she spat suddenly. "It is you who have cut the cock from that great stud with your lily-livered goodness. Jesus in Heaven. It was only a babe. Babies are to be had for the twist in the sheets, but a fortune swings in that harbor."

Her words, screamed in fury, were a mistake.

Both women glanced up at the sound of the door being slammed in the upper hall. Antoine, unshaven and disheveled, swayed unsteadily at the top of the stairs. He made his way down the steps slowly, gripping the railing firmly for support. He moved carefully, his eyes never leaving Marta's face.

Julie tried to bar his way, but he thrust her aside with a rough arm, throwing her half across the hall.

"Only a babe," he said softly, close to Marta's face. His voice was low and slurred from drink. "Only a babe . . ."

Even Marta seemed a little in awe of the fury in his face and would have stepped back if he had not caught her by the arm. "Slut," he said viciously. "You vicious, raddled slut. How dare you put your rotten mouth to speak of anything as pure as that child?" Either a cough or a sob broke his voice and Marta, straining to be free of his hold, spat at him.

"It might have been your seed, you thankless bastard," she said. "But it is my gold."

"Shit on your gold," he said fiercely. "There is not gold in all these colonies, not in all the world, worth the breath of that child. I would see you in Hell to have her breathe again."

Marta, with a swift movement, pulled free of him, leaping from his grasp and rubbing her arm where he had bruised it.

"You will be in a hell all your own, Antoine Rivière," she

112

sneered. "Unless you get your manhood together and go about your work."

She smiled, tossing her head, a reckless look of triumph on her face. "Are you fool enough to think that you charmed money from me with your handsome face and your great lusty body? Fie on your man's conceit, Tony. I knew where there was money to make good that bond before I ever slid a pound into your greedy fist. Hell, you vain bastard, the world is full of great studs to be had for the flick of a hip. It takes more than a fine high cock to loosen my pursestrings.

"Didn't you wonder what I was doing in Paris, Tony? Didn't you think I could find your old man, coughing and spitting his lungs out? And didn't you think that perfumed pervert brother of yours would pay handsomely to buy my note? Wouldn't he, though? With you in a debtor's prison and your son in Emile's hands, he would have nothing between him and the estate. Lucky for me it was the girl who croaked instead of the lad, that would have weakened my position a good bit."

Antoine reeled at her words. For one horrified moment Julie feared he would lose his balance. But his rage seemed to stiffen his spine. He lunged for the girl just as she slammed the door of the house flat against his face.

He was struggling with the knob when Julie intervened. "Please, Antoine," she begged, catching his arm. "Don't go after her, please."

She had never seen him this drunk. When he seized her she realized that he could not actually see her. His eyes stared flatly back at her. She felt that shiver that presaged death move along her spine as she struggled to disengage herself from his grasp.

He struck her a stinging blow across the head with the back of his hand and as she fell he seized her, throwing her back on her feet to be struck again. It was as if in his drunken rage she had become Marta to him.

"Only a babe," he screamed as he belabored her shoulders and breasts with the massive strength of his balled fist. There was no escaping his blows. She heard Maggie's astonished cries and then her footsteps on the stairs. She could not rise to her feet and this time he did not pull her up. Instead he kicked her fiercely with his heavy boots, again and again as he panted like a wounded animal with each blow.

Then came a low whine. Julie did not see the whip until it

113

curled about his face, leaving a quick spurt of blood from the line it made. Dragging herself away from his boots, she heaved against the door and clutched for the knob. She heard Sophie hailing her slaves as she slid through the open door into the cool night air.

The pain of her beating made her too giddy to stand. Instead she clung to the wall and worked her way along the house to the alley beyond.

She could hear cries from the house and the glint of a lantern showed at the door.

She must not be taken back. She would not be taken back.

She curled in the darkness, stifling the tears of hysteria until she heard the street grow silent as the searchers went farther afield.

Hearing the path they took, she resumed her flight in the opposite direction, toward the waterfront. Thank God for the cover of dark. She had to place one foot carefully before the other to stay erect and still she panicked each time she took a step. Her head throbbed unmercifully. At the sound of approaching footsteps she flattened herself against a wall.

As the footsteps passed and then stopped, she held her breath. There came no other sound and after a long time, she loosed her hand from the wall and began to walk again.

He had been waiting. When she came abreast of a tree he stepped forth suddenly. She stifled a scream as he seized her arm.

"Mistress Rivière? Julie?" It was a question.

With her eyes swollen from blows, her vision functioned strangely. But she recognized the voice.

"Jonathan," she breathed with relief, "Jonathan Marlowe."

It was refuge she wanted, refuge from pain.

She drew a painful breath to say what she must say. "My aunt," she breathed. "My aunt at the plantation Monde DuBois."

Even as she heard some murmured response, the spinning in her head overcame her senses. She felt his arms tighten solidly about her as her legs gave way.

Chapter Twenty-Seven

When Jonathan Marlowe's trap drew up before the gates of Monde DuBois, the great house lay peaceful in its shadows. A single upstairs window gleamed with light where Mandy, not certain that her mistress would not need her services again, yawned over handiwork in her own room. Anne-Louise herself sat at her piano in the sitting room, playing with a single finger, over and over, the small catchy tune that rose to Josh Simmons' lips so unconsciously.

Into the peace of that house came the urgent clamor of the front doorbell.

Startled by the thought of a caller at such an unseemly hour, Anne-Louise called up the stairs for Mandy before going to the door herself since all the slaves but Mandy had been sent to their quarters for the night.

The man in the doorway held Julie like a child, her dark head half buried against his lapel and one graceful hand swaying limply.

"Dr. Marlowe," Anne-Louise managed to say, stepping back quickly to admit him.

"She has been hurt," the doctor said tersely. "I shall need a bed, and hot water and linen of some kind."

"My bedroom," Anne-Louise called to Mandy, who stood wide-eyed halfway down the stairs.

When she had done all that she could to supply the doctor's needs, Anne-Louise stood in the shadows by the bed, her heart torn by the condition of Julie's young body. As gentle as Dr. Marlowe's hands were in his ministrations, Julie, poised on the edge of consciousness, moaned and writhed as the linen cleaned her wounds.

When she cried in pain, Dr. Marlowe motioned for brandy. Julie, temporarily roused by the bite of the liquor at her lips, opened her eyes briefly. She stared dully at Anne-Louise, her words coming in quick gasps.

"Tante," she cried. "He must not find me. He must not."

Anne-Louise nodded as the girl's eyes fluttered shut. Then, hearing the door bang in the hall below, she went hastily downstairs.

"Whose trap is that in the drive?" Jacques asked tersely.

"Dr. Marlowe from Charles Town," Anne-Louise replied, wishing she had taken only a moment to compose herself before coming downstairs.

"And why is he here?" Jacques pressed with a tinge of annoyance in his voice.

"He brought Juliette," she said as levelly as possible. "She has been hurt."

"Hurt?" Josh challenged. "How hurt?"

"That goddamned Rivière," Jacques exploded.

"You don't know that," his mother challenged.

"Of course I do. If it were anything but that bastard husband of hers she would never have come here."

Josh, his face sober, looked from one to the other of them. "How badly is she hurt?" he asked.

Anne-Louise swallowed before answering, "He suggested that maybe a week or two..."

"A week or two," Josh exploded. "Good God, what happened?"

"Listen, you two," Anne-Louise said tiredly. "That is all I know. But I did have a thought as I came downstairs. "She looked at her son appealingly. "Since the children are all off at school, and since only Mandy will know that Juliette is here..."

The men exchanged a knowing glance. "Then it was Rivière," Jacques said bitterly.

"I don't honestly know," Anne-Louise admitted. "But if you remember, the time she was missing from the house at Tradd Street, a slave was sent here to inquire."

"You could caution them not to talk about it," Josh suggested.

Jacques' laugh was short. "You could tell the wind not to blow, too. Mother is right. If we mean to keep her presence here a secret, and we surely should until we find out what is going on, then we must keep it from the other slaves."

"But what of Mandy?" Josh asked.

Jacques laughed. "Mandy would never betray Juliette."

"It is easy enough to arrange," Anne-Louise plotted aloud. "I shall simply be struck with a fever during the night. That will explain the doctor's coming here if anyone happened to see that. I will be fast in my room with only Mandy to tend me. The others will be eager enough to avoid the extra work of that part of the house as well as the risk of fever."

Jacques nodded approval, then glanced again at the stairs.

"God in Heaven, he is taking forever. Are you sure that everything is all right?"

"I can go and see," Anne-Louise offered. "In the meantime enjoy the wine there. I'll be back when I can."

It was Dr. Marlowe, rising at last from the side of Julie's bed, who suggested that he be let out privately. "Surely you have a convenient back exit?" he asked.

"Yes, of course," Anne-Louise replied, confused by his request.

He did not meet her eyes. "There is common talk of bad blood between your son and your niece's husband," he said blandly. "I hardly think that any honest exchange between the two of us tonight would help that situation."

"Then it was not an accident?" Anne-Louise asked, a little sick at his implication.

"It was not an accident," he said firmly. "You will be taking care of her, I presume. I think you will agree when you realize the extent of the... brutality... she has been subjected to."

"Will she need further medical attention?" Anne-Louise asked as she stood by the young doctor's carriage in the clear starless night.

"Not unless some of her abrasions become infected," he replied. "Oh, and Mistress DuBois, when she regains consciousness again, which should be within the hour—it was a light potion that I gave her so that I would not pain her during the treatment—I would appreciate your giving her a message for me."

"I would be happy to."

"Just tell her that it was my honor to serve her and that I remain her humble servant."

Anne-Louise watched the trap as it disappeared behind the trees of the drive and shook her head. "Well, that admirer was one she needed," she said wryly, returning to Julie's room the way she had left it, by the back stairs to the servants' quarters.

To her astonishment, Julie was awake and smiled wanly at her when she entered the room.

"I came to see Josh," Julie said after a while.

"He is here. He and Jacques are much concerned about you, my dear."

"Tell him that I will grow strong again very quickly. Then we will go together to seek Paul Bontemps."

"Julie!" her aunt cried. "That is madness. He won't let you go."

"I am not going to ask him, *Tante*," the girl said soberly, her

117

eyes implacable. "I am going to tell him."

Both men were instantly on their feet as they saw her enter. She answered their mutual unspoken question quickly.

"She is going to be fine. The young doctor knows his business. She is strong and eager to heal."

"And you still don't know what happened?" Jacques asked.

She turned away to fill her own wineglass. "Not really."

"Then I will get it out of the doctor myself," Jacques said, starting toward the hall.

"It is no use," his mother said calmly. "He is gone. I let him out myself."

His eyes narrowed at her. "That seems peculiar for you to have done that." His tone was challenging.

"Peculiar only if you are set on revenge or retribution," she said quietly. "Personally I am more interested in Julie and what she needs and wants than in anything that is past."

"You must know why she came here," Jacques said, only a little mollified by the rebuke in her voice.

"She came to see Josh."

The Indian trader watched her warily.

"She knows my plans to make the expedition, doesn't she?" he asked, his voice thoughtful.

Her dark eyes watchful, Anne-Louise nodded. "I told her of it at the burial of her child Etoile."

"So why has she come to see Josh?" Jacques pressed with a note of irritation in his voice.

Anne-Louise swallowed. Why should her throat be dry? Why was she doing this so badly? There must be some easy way to persuade them that Julie was serious, that Julie was not to be deterred from what she had decided. I understand what she is doing, Anne-Louise told herself. I cannot explain it to these two men but I understand it.

"All right, Mother," Jacques said tiredly. "Out with it."

Her eyes fell. "She says she is going with you."

After a stunned moment, Josh exploded into an expletive. "God in Heaven, has my Lady lost her mind? Does she know how many hundreds of miles that trail runs? Does she know of warring Indians and wild beasts and vipers? Her with her lace petticoats and her fine soft flesh . . . follow the Natchez Trace to the village of the Great Sun? Impossible. No woman, anyway no white woman, has ever tackled that trail. You tell her *No*."

118

"Her head is clear as a bell," Anne-Louise said.

"Do I understand that you agree with what she wants to do?" Jacques asked, incredulity in his voice.

"I understand that Juliette has earned the right to do with her life what she damned pleases, that's what I understand," she said, feeling the rush of anger rise in her cheeks.

"Jesus," Jacques snorted. "I would like one day to know where women's heads are."

Anne-Louise stared at him coldly. "Right behind their eyes, which is more than I can say for blind young men like you."

"But her safety," Josh protested softly.

Eyes. Safety. The two words seemed to fuse in Anne-Louise's mind, and she grew crafty. Her voice was suddenly softer, indicating that she would make peace with them.

"Would you like to see her?" she asked. "The doctor gave her a draught for sleeping. It would do no harm for you to look in on her before you both retire. Just to assure yourselves," she added.

The two men exchanged a startled glance. "Are you sure that would be proper?" Josh asked.

"I see no reason why not," she said lightly, starting for the stairs.

From the doorway she didn't even appear real. Her dark hair was fanned out on the pillow with her face turned a little away. The candle's shadow across her throat left half the graceful curve of her breast in darkness.

"You can go nearer," Anne-Louise urged. "But quietly."

"I shall kill him," Jacques said levelly. "I shall kill Antoine Rivière."

Josh could not speak. Julie's graceful body was draped with such a pale fine fabric that none of the discoloration of her skin was secret from them. He let his eyes travel down the fine round arms which were blackening from beating. He saw the swelling along her temple and the raw abrasions where the boots had torn the flesh on her legs and thighs. A giddiness spun his head.

"You would send her back?" Anne-Louise asked.

While Jacques splashed whisky into glasses for himself and Josh and poured a fresh glass of wine for his mother, Josh left the room in that silent animal way that never failed to astonish Anne. When he returned, he handed a folded stack of what appeared to be leather to his hostess.

After glancing up at him, she examined what he had

119

handed her. It was leather, but the softest finest leather that she had ever touched. The pale shirt was trimmed with quills in an intricate design of gold and brown. The skirt was of a darker leather with a silken fringe of finely cut leather. The shoes were trimmed with the same pattern of quills along with tiny beads.

"If you just leave them out where she can find them," Josh said quietly, "my Lady will know what my answer is."

Part 3

CHILD OF THE SUN

1728-29

Chapter Twenty-Eight

The pack train had left at dawn. Josh, on his own mount, with six sturdy horses loaded with double packs, had already made a half-day journey along the hill road before Jonathan Marlowe's trap stopped at the porch of Monde DuBois. The vines of the porch lattices which had rattled death all winter were knobbing with new growth and the green scent of spring herbs wafted from the woods beyond.

Jacques, having left the window above his desk open to admit the gentle air, was in the hallway by the time the manservant answered the peal of the bell.

"I am Dr. Marlowe," the visitor explained, handing his hat and coat to the servant. "I have come to check on my patient." His eyebrow rose quizzically at his own careful words.

Jacques nodded cordially, taking the man's hand.

"I will take the doctor up myself, Ned," he told the slave. Then, on the stairs, he spoke to Jonathan Marlowe.

"My mother is still confined to her room and I am certain she will be delighted to see you."

Anne-Louise, answering Jacques' rap on the door and seeing who accompanied him, stepped back quickly.

"Dr. Marlowe," she said with genuine delight. "Do come in. We have a visitor, Juliette," she called softly.

Julie turned from the window where her slender figure was silhouetted against the light. "Jacques and Jonathan

Marlowe," she cried, crossing the room in swift steps. "How good to see you both."

The welcome in her voice stabbed Jacques painfully. Damn it all, why must he be so possessive of his cousin? He certainly had no exclusive right to that dimpled smile, that bright-eyed delight at the sight of them in the doorway. He was a fool but at least he was conscious of his own foolishness. The past weeks, with Julie hidden away upstairs in his own home planning to take the long trek west with Josh, had been a steady torment to him. Only when they reluctantly conceded that another man might be helpful in their plan to rescue Paul Bontemps had his anguish lessened. But only a little. There was always Antoine in his mind and then Josh and now Jonathan Marlowe . . . was there no end to this army of men she had enslaved, not even counting himself?

After dispatching Mandy for coffee and cakes and the ordinary civilities had been exchanged, an awkward silence fell over the room.

"I have restrained myself as well as I was able," Dr. Marlowe confessed to Julie with a smile. "I could only presume that you were healing satisfactorily or I surely would have been summoned."

Julie smiled warmly at him. "I am fully healed," she admitted. "In fact, I am grown strong and fat in this safe place."

"It is indeed a safe place," the doctor nodded, exchanging a glance with Anne-Louise "It is no secret in Charles Town that a great and diligent search has been made for your whereabouts with no success."

"The man from the Bontemps plantation has come here steadily making inquiries of the slaves," Jacques told him.

"And your slaves have been waylaid in town and quizzed and a watch been kept on your woods from the road beyond," the doctor added wryly. "Your sister-in-law seems convinced that you are here in spite of all evidence to the contrary."

"Evidence to the contrary?" Julie asked curiously.

"I can't really say how this got around town," the doctor said mildly, carefully examining the ring he wore on his right forefinger. "But I do remember mentioning to a merchant along the street on Bay that it would be simple for any woman to escape Charles Town unnoticed. As much traffic as this port enjoys, she would only need to drape her head in weeds and board any ship with a damp handkerchief before her face

122

and she would be gone for good with none the wiser."

Jacques' great frame vibrated with laughter. "Our great healer is also a sly fox," he observed with approval. "Let me congratulate you on both those skills."

"I do bring reports that are based on more truth than that one, madame," he told Julie, his face turning suddenly serious. "Your son Armand is growing apace under the care of that worthy Mrs. MacRae. He is happy and adjusted in spite of your absence. I do not bring this report to distress you, but rather to assure you that the child is well and not grieving."

"I appreciate that very much," Julie said quietly. "And the others?"

Jacques felt his body stiffen involuntarily at this veiled reference to Antoine.

"Madame Sophie is well, greatly concerned over your disappearance but working again at the old pace she used to before her recent illness."

"And her brother," Julie asked with only the faintest tremor in her voice.

"I have to admit that I have not seen Rivière," the doctor replied levelly. "He has not been at the home when I have been there to call on Madame Sophie, but I understand he is recovering nicely from his incapacitation."

Jacques' sympathy for the shock in Julie's face brought him to the question that he feared she could not ask.

"Incapacitation?" he asked.

"He was injured the same night that I brought Madame Julie here," he said calmly. "Severely injured, I am told. He was removed from his sister's house to the quarters of Francis Arlington, the ship's surgeon for the *Sojourner*. He is only now able to rise and walk about with some celerity. More than once Madame Sophie has mentioned to me that the search for her lost sister-in-law would have been considerably more intense if her brother had not been unable to move from his cot. Her phrase has been that he would have torn up the world looking for his wife if he had not been injured."

"Injured," Jacques repeated thoughtfully. "How injured?"

Jonathan Marlowe lifted his coffee cup, studying its painted rim with the same attention he had earlier bestowed on his ring. "It seems that he was horsewhipped," he said levelly. "I believe the common expression for his condition is that he was horsewhipped within an inch of his life."

Astonishingly, it was Anne-Louise who gasped softly.

123

Julie's golden eyes widened almost perceptibly but she only nodded as if his words had brought her some sudden understanding.

"But apparently he is healing nicely under Dr. Arlington's care," the doctor finished almost brightly. "When he is in the fullness of his strength, I expect his search for Madame Julie here will become his concern. I understand from my friend Dr. Arlington that his patient is deeply smitten with guilt, even to the point that his recovery has been delayed by his restless impatience to find his wife and make amends for his lamentable treatment of her while maddened by grief and drink.

"That is a noble effort, Dr. Marlowe," Julie said quietly. "I am able to hear my dear Sophie's phrasing behind your words. You have performed this act of friendship for her with concise gallantry."

Julie rose suddenly. As always, Jacques was amazed that a figure so dainty and womanly could achieve such great dignity in motion. She passed to the window where she stared out into the woods as if she were seeing another time, another place. When she finally spoke, her gentle voice was weighted with such pain that Jacques felt deep compassion for her.

"However, this particular ruse has been used before to get their way with me. Sophie cannot possibly expect that I would be twice hurt and twice drawn back in sympathy by such a strategy. But I confess I am curious as to how she got this careful message to you."

Dr. Marlowe nodded. "She mentioned that you had few friends in this country and since I was numbered among them, she wanted to tell me how things stood . . . just in case."

"But not with any particularity?" Jacques asked.

"Possibly at first there was particularity," Dr. Marlowe conceded. "But when the word came back through the slaves at the plantation that Mistress DuBois had been taken with fever and was mending but slowly, she became dissuaded from her suspicion. When she also was informed that you, Jacques, had postponed a planned trip to the North pending your mother's recovery, she was even more fully convinced that her suspicions had been false."

"They do chatter on . . . these slaves," Anne-Louise commented wryly.

"At least that," the doctor agreed, smiling. "She also told me that she had been informed that you, Jacques, had made an investment in a pack train leaving for Chickasaw country."

Jacques laughed merrily. "I suppose it is a poor knife that cannot cut two ways."

He saw the doctor's eyes flick over the packs that were strapped and piled in the corner of the otherwise immaculate room. "Then you do intend a journey?" he asked.

"I do indeed," Jacques replied. "The slaves were even right about the pack train. It left Monde DuBois only this morning."

"Good fortune to your endeavor," the doctor said, rising. "I must not overstay my leave." After bowing over Anne-Louise's hand, he took Julie's into his own.

"I cannot tell you how delighted I am to see you in this more comfortable condition. Whatever course you choose, please remember that you have a friend with me. And a co-conspirator, if that be your specific need."

After touching his lips to her hand, the doctor followed Jacques from the room.

"Now she will weep," Jacques told himself as he watched the trap disappear behind the trees of the tunneled drive. "Now she will break down and weep for what is lost to her...for that fine son and that great madman of hers."

Upstairs, Julie calmly refilled her cup from the last of the coffee cooling in the silver urn.

"You were magnificent," her aunt said quietly.

"I was grateful for his coming," Julie confessed. "And I might have dissolved into a torrent of tears except for the way he so carefully quoted Sophie's words. They were her words, Tante, and thinking of her saying them reminded me of that night again. It had all been very hazy in my mind. There was the terrible pain of his beating and suddenly the whine of a whip in the air and Antoine's scream. It was Sophie...Sophie herself stood at the top of the stairs with the whip in her hand."

"She is your friend," Anne-Louise reminded her.

"But she is also his sister," Julie replied. "In the fever of rage she is all my friend, but in the cooling of that fever, faced with his misery, she is not only his sister, but a repentant one, aching to make amends."

"Why are you going?" Anne-Louise asked suddenly. "I have not asked you before because it has not mattered to me other than that you have earned the right to your own life. But why are you making this dangerous and taxing journey? Can you think that even if you succeed in bringing back Paul Bontemps that Antoine will ever forgive your traveling like this with another man, or men?"

Julie set the cup down and stared at her aunt thoughtfully.

125

"You did not hear the words that Marta shouted at him, the threats. She warned that if he did not make good on the voyage of the *Sojourner*, she would sell his debts to his father or his brother who is a scheming perverted creature. If the brother, Emile, gained control of the notes, Antoine would certainly languish in prison while Emile took charge of his affairs and his son. This man will stop at nothing to inherit the estate that his father is trying to keep from him."

"That is all very terrifying, Julie," her aunt admitted. "But I do not see how this trip can stop what course events will take."

"Only with Paul Bontemps back at the head of his family, standing behind Sophie against Emile and the others, could Armand be saved. Paul's connections in France are equal at least to the power of the Rivières. Emile might take Armand from Sophie but never from the two of them."

"Then you are doing this for the child, not for Antoine at all," Anne-Louise said quietly.

"I said there was more than one strand to this line, Tante," Julie told her quietly. "All that I am as a woman belongs to Antoine Rivière, always has and always will. But there is more than being a woman to being a person, Tante. I will lose Antoine, I will lose even my own life before I will submit to a life in which I am a pawn to be used as a player chooses." She paused and laughed softly. "How dreadful this sounds, Tante, but I may never have this chance to be honest with you again. I have learned the skills of docility. I would make a fine falcon until the rope was loosed because I can pretend, even as a falcon on the wrist can pretend, to be tamed. But I am my own person, Tante, I am not only untamed but I fear I may be untamable. So I will take the wild way, throwing all I have on the table in the desperate chance of winning all. I may lose, but the bitterest loss of all would be to return to Antoine's wrist now. If I save Armand, I have won enough. If I live to return and Antoine takes me back, it can only be as a person, for the woman he married died that night in Jonathan Marlowe's arms."

The last light had been extinguished in the slave quarters behind the great house at Monde DuBois. Smoke from banked fires brushed their paleness against the star-spattered sky. As the two mounts threaded their way along the logging trail that led west through the forest, owls warned their kind in the trees ahead, setting up a soft chain of cries sounding before them into the wilderness.

They had gone a half-hour's ride past the last of the logging trails when Jacques reined in his horse.

"See that clump of birches?" he asked. "That is the last edge of the DuBois property. From here we venture into strangeness."

Julie stared at the cluster of white trees, then smiled at her cousin.

"You can still go back," she told him. "Josh and I will understand if you wish to go back."

He shook his head. "I want to be a part of this."

"But how about Tante Anne-Louise?"

"My mother is fully in the saddle of that plantation. She even has those miserable kids brought around at last. I have had papers drawn that leave her as fully in control of that property as King Edward left Philippa on the throne of England when he was off warring with the French."

"But why, Jacques?" she pressed softly. "There is so much danger ahead, and so little for you to gain."

"I would rather share danger with my Juliette than comfort with any other soul," he said quietly.

Chapter Twenty-Nine

They saw the smoke first, a thin pencil of smoke drawing a pale wavering line in the dark sky. When they drew their horses to a stop a little short of the clearing, Julie heard the soft hum of Josh's song broken only by the stamping of the pack animals and the faraway cries of night birds.

He smiled into her face. "You look to be bearing up all right, Lady," he said as he set her lightly on her feet.

"One night's ride," she scoffed, restraining her inclination to rub her backside which was numb from the saddle's pressure.

"We'll take it easy," he promised. "Was it a clean getaway?" he asked Jacques, who was tethering the horses at the edge of the clearing.

Julie lay flat on the cool earth, listening as the men discussed the news brought by Jonathan Marlowe.

127

"So now for all the world to know you are off to the North on business," Josh nodded approval. "The pack train is gone and I guess your mother will begin to make herself public right away."

"She plans a trip to Charles Town tomorrow," Jacques replied. "Seeking news about her missing niece."

Josh laughed softly. "What a great web of intrigue you wove to let this bird escape."

Julie chuckled. "And having begun so well, how can we fail?"

"Only by carelessness," Josh said quietly. "Out here failure is only another word for carelessness. You always know what you are going to do before the need comes to do it."

"What do you mean by that?" Julie asked, rolling over to stare at him.

He shrugged. "Some simple things like never being alone. At least away from the camp. In your case, we won't leave you alone." He paused. "Things like never firing your gun unless you got a second one loaded at your side."

This time it was Jacques who looked at him in surprise.

Josh shrugged. "Never undersell the brains of a native. When you hear a gun being shot that usually means the man holding it is unarmed until he gets it loaded again. They know that too."

"Then you do expect Indian trouble?" Julie asked, conscious of a vague prickling of fear joining her other discomforts.

Josh grinned at her. "Lady, I expect what comes. Traveling like this with a pack train is always the safest way. Natives all trade with such as I and they like having the goods come in. The problem with the three of us is what a mixed bag we are. There's been time enough now that the natives have mostly chosen up sides. The Creeks and the Choctaws trade with the Spanish and the French and consider an English scalp a fair prize. The Cherokees and the Chickasaws tend to line up with the English and wear a French or Spanish scalp at their waists."

"And the Natchez?" Julie asked.

He shook his head. "Natchez break all the rules. They even look different. They're taller and fairer and more finely built. They live different and worship different." He shook his head as if distracted.

"Take this uneasy peace they have had with the French all these years. They have helped the French build forts and fed them in bad harvest times. They have taken punishment from that French colony that a saint wouldn't stand still for, but they stay downright amiable. But don't conclude that they are not a savage people. They guard an eternal fire and kill great numbers of their own tribe as sacrifices when a ruler dies. They cripple their slaves and torture their captives and turn around and act like Christian gentlemen the next half-hour. Who knows what is in a Natchez head? But they are proud like the Creeks and keep their own counsel."

He grinned over at Julie. "Because I am the only one of us fluent in the native languages, we'll stay in Cherokee and Chickasaw country. We're safest there."

It was strange to lie on her blanket between the two men, strange to lie in this wild place with the sounds of the beasts in the woods around them and the pale stars, beyond counting, glowing in the sky above her.

From their breathing she could tell that both men were as wakeful as she. A long time had passed when she heard a rustling from Josh's side and a whisper, almost as soft as the sweep of the wings of the night birds.

"Lady," he called softly.

"Yes, Josh," she whispered back.

"I'll be damned if I can go to sleep until I get this thing off my mind." He rose on one elbow and stared down at her. "Just having you lying there reminded me. Remember how you used to scream at night when we were together before. There was a name you always called out when you were just getting well from the shipwreck."

"Ellie," Julie told him. "It was the name of my friend who was separated from me when the ship began to go down."

"Jacques' mother told me it was that girl who had something to do with you and your man getting together again. So she must have lived through that shipwreck in spite of what you thought."

"She did indeed," Julie replied. "I've never found out how and I've never been able to locate her, even though I am sure that she is somewhere in the colonies. Sophie and Antoine ran into her along the seaboard when he first came over, but we have tried without any luck to find her ever since. She seemed to have vanished like he appeared. Her name means nothing to anyone."

"Ellie you called her," Josh mused. "Was she alone?"

Julie chuckled softly. "They said she had a great lout of a sailor in tow, a tall man who was built like a bear but with the face of a bearded good-natured schoolboy."

Julie giggled and turned away.

From his breathing she knew that Jacques was still awake and couldn't help having heard their conversation. Did she imagine that the open friendship, the easy camaraderie between the two men had grown steadily more tense as the day of their departure drew nearer? She had dreamed that, she decided stubbornly. The two men were simply tense, even as she was, at the coming of the long trek ahead. She heard Jacques sigh and then, finally, the slow even breathing of sleep.

The land changed with the days. When Julie became accustomed to the rolling hills of the Piedmont, the trail became suddenly steeper. Their pace slowed so dramatically that Julie felt that she could stop at the end of the day and still look back at where they had begun at morning.

"If we could only travel without the pack train," Julie told Josh wistfully.

"Natives are like other men," he said drily. "You don't get nothing for nothing from them."

She noticed that he had never used the word "Indian" since they had left Charles Town. He always referred to these peoples as "natives" or by their tribal names. When they chanced to meet them on the trail, he always acknowledged the hunter or group by clan, speaking in a strange musical tongue that sounded more like the passing of water over smooth stones than human speech.

Natives were like other men. Josh said this often and she grew to agree with him wholly. They were comely men with rich coppery skins that glinted in the sun. While their features were strong for her taste, they were singularly unlined of face except in great age and their expressive dark eyes shone with curiosity and amusement. In the chill of the high land, their bodies were draped with fine skins and although they traveled many miles bearing onerous burdens of weapons or provisions, their hands always seemed free.

And neither were they more shy with her than other men. Often when she glanced at a young brave she found him staring steadily back at her. No matter how swiftly she averted her eyes, she was never fast enough to miss the slow smile of approval with which he returned her gaze.

When they encountered the same band of Cherokee men for the second time, Julie was careful to keep her eyes from the bold young man who had smiled at her. After Josh smoked with them and they had passed on, she turned to him with excitement.

"Does this mean that we are nearing the town?"

He shook his head. "They have been back to the town and reported our passage. A friend of mine in the town sent them to invite us to a great ball game. There will also be dancing," he added. "Would you like me to teach you the steps?"

Julie, tired from her saddle, guessed she would settle for being their most delighted spectator.

"Is this friend of yours Cherokee too?" Jacques asked.

"A squaw man," Josh replied.

"And what is your friend's name?" Julie asked.

"Taylor," Josh replied. "He must have had a Christian name once but it has been long forgotten. He is called Horse Taylor by the Cherokee, for his great skill at breaking the wild horses." He grinned at Julie. "His wife's name is Little Spring, for the way she babbles on and on without ever giving offense or threat to anyone."

Traveling as they were, with six pack animals, the choice of each night's camp was a serious decision. There must be water for both themselves and the beasts and grazing for the weary horses. Even though both men rode with loaded guns across their saddles, only rarely did a wild thing cross their path to provide fresh game for their evening meal. What game might have strayed in the path of a single rider or two was early alerted by the laboring passage of the pack train. Except on those rare nights when they chanced on an abandoned Indian hunter's hut, they made camp in the open in late afternoon. While Julie nursed a budding fire to flame, Josh set forth into the woods to augment their provisions with fresh fish or game.

It was on such an evening, as she knelt feeding small twigs into a struggling campfire flame that Jacques confronted her. She had been conscious that he had been watching her. She had even felt some tremor of a strange emotional state but she was not prepared for the harshness of his attack.

"Juliette," he said suddenly from the side of the fire. "I have to speak to you about your behavior with Josh."

"Behavior?" she repeated with astonishment. "What are you talking about, Jacques?"

"Intimacy," he said furiously. "I am talking about your intimacy with that man. It is clear to me now that I intruded by asking myself along to accompany you. I have even begun to wonder if this whole trip is not just an elaborate ruse for the two of you to travel together, as you did before, as husband and wife."

Julie leaped to her feet, suddenly ablaze with anger. "Jacques DuBois, what a rotten filthy thing to say. Good God, if I had the need to bed a man other than my husband, would I be fool enough to launch myself into the wilderness to achieve it? Oh, think not so. I am no less clever than any other adulterous wife. I would simply hie myself off with a maid and a buggy for an afternoon abroad and set up my dalliance like the proper wives of Charles Town do."

"You see, it is on your mind. You have made yourself a student of such affairs."

"I am a student of people," she told him crossly, kneeling again to her task as she saw her weak fire struggling against the damp wood. "And *I* would say that you are behaving less gently than I would expect of a man like you. Name one impropriety with Josh. One. I challenge you."

"One," he scoffed. "Am I deaf that I do not hear your giggling whispered confidences at night? Am I blind that I cannot see his hands cling to your waist as he draws you from your horse, how he shelters your arm when you take two steps together."

"And is it not the same with you?" she asked fiercely. "I have not noticed your dropping me from the saddle like a potato burning your hand. Your hand is as quick on mine in gentleness as his. But wouldn't you protest if Josh rebuked me for this?"

"There is a difference," he protested in a surly tone. "As unsuitable as it may be, the man is obviously in love with you. God knows what lay between you before . . . in that time that you both refer to with such obvious pleasure. Look at this adventure. Who but a madman would undertake such a trip as this unless he thought to capture the woman he desired by the act?"

Julie stared at him thoughtfully before laying her hands on his arms. "And you, Jacques? What madness lured you into this undertaking? Did you think that by generously equipping this train and making this arduous journey that you might capture the woman you desire?"

With her face close to his, Jacques' spirit broke. He slid his arms around her and pulled her tightly against him. "Good God, Julie, do not taunt me with my own words when I am

132

ablaze with passion and envy. I have never denied my love for you nor my lust. But this trip . . . this whole endeavor is solely for your happiness. But to ride by you and sleep by you . . . it has grown too much for me to endure."

When he released her suddenly to stride away to fill his pipe and lean to light it by the fire, she stared at him in confusion. Then she saw Josh emerging from the wood, coming as he always did, swift and silent on his Indian shoes, carrying a pair of freshly killed game birds in his free hand. Josh was curiously silent as Julie took the fowl from him and cleaned them as he readied the spit above the fire.

Only when the meal was finished and the three of them were sitting silent and stiff by the fire, did Josh speak more than a perfunctory word.

"While we are in Cherokee country, before we take the more dangerous path through the country of the Creeks, I think we might break out a bottle of our wine and share it together."

Jacques glanced at him in surprise.

Josh shrugged. "Perhaps we should even get out cards and play a little by the fire. After all, why should we do nothing but labor and sleep this long spring away. You would not happen to have a set of cards in your pack, would you, Jacques?" he asked guilelessly.

Before Jacques could protest, Josh slapped his fist in his hand and laughed. "Where is my head? I do think I might even have one myself, tucked in here or there." When he returned from his pack he was humming his small song and carrying a bottle of red wine in one hand and his cards in the other.

"There," he sighed as he dropped down beside the fire. "All the ingredients for a real party. A little booze, a little game, and a beautiful wench."

"Well, I like that," Julie laughed.

"So do I," Josh said softly. "So do I."

It was a strange game that Julie watched from her post against the mossy tree. Jacques won and then he lost and then he won again. Then with a streak of remarkable luck he won steadily until the small pile of stones that had been designated as silver florins was all by his side except for a single stone by Josh's knee.

"Are you tiring, Lady?" he asked quietly. "Would you like us to shut up this tavern for the night?"

Julie, half dozing from the fire's warmth, laughed softly.

133

"The scent of wood smoke and the warmth of wine turns me to a pudding," she confessed. "But I am still game for what games you two can play."

"We will finish this up," Josh said briskly. "Then we will close off with a tale by the fire."

Within moments Julie's drowsiness had fled. As the hands were dealt Josh began to win. Knowing his skill as a card dealer and knowing what enemies he had made with such winning streaks, she watched like a hunting bird for the slightest sign that he was dealing wrongly or cheating. But she saw nothing even though only minutes passed before Jacques, with a white line of fury about his jaws, handed the last smooth stone to Josh and threw up his hands.

"I don't know how in hell you did that, but I am out for good," he admitted.

Josh laughed softly as he stowed his cards and poured the last of the wine into their cups. "Now for the story I wanted to tell," he said indulgently, leaning forward to stare into the fire.

"He was a friend I had in another life. He was a black, a runaway slave. He lived in the swamps below the Carolinas that the Spaniards call Guale. He ate off the land and bartered for his other needs with the natives of that country and with me. Much of what he bartered with came in on the tide from the sea. One of the treasures he dragged from the waves was our friend here."

Jacques sat up stiffly, staring at Julie in astonishment.

"She was near enough dead that I was able to buy her for a few paltry skins," Josh grinned at Julie. "Later he might have rued the bargain but he was a man of honor."

When he began again it was as if Julie were no longer between them. His words were wholly for Jacques and Julie recognized the import of what he had to say by a subtle change in his tone.

"One thing he said of this particular piece of flotsam was that she was cursed by something he called Batakatsi."

Jacques frowned at the word in that moment of silence.

"This word from his language meant evil . . . anything that was evil or caused evil to flower in other people. He told me this word about my Lady was a warning.

"He was right, Jacques. We have both seen evil visited on this girl from no fault of her own. We understand that the evil that hangs about her is not of her own doing. But by bringing out the evil in men she becomes the victim of it."

Jacques would have protested but Josh held his hand up in

134

warning. "We who love her, Jacques," he went on soberly, "must constantly war against the evil in ourselves that rises from that very love. We are poor gamblers who have taken on this enterprise together. If we war among ourselves, we are already lost."

Jacques sat in silence a long time. When he rose, his shadow fell across the coals and blended into the darkness beyond. As he leaned to offer his hand to Josh, the trader leaped to his feet and shook the proffered hand solemnly. Then Jacques leaned to the fire and relit his pipe with a smoldering coal. He handed the pipe, stem first, across the fire to Josh.

"Calumet," he said quietly. "Isn't that what your friends call their bowl of peace?"

"Calumet," Josh nodded. As he drew on the pipe a thick cloud of smoke billowed in the air. Julie hugged her own shoulders in an ecstasy of satisfaction.

Chapter Thirty

To Julie, limp in her saddle from exhaustion, it seemed that the day would never end. Josh had passed any number of sites which offered everything needed for a comfortable camp and still the pack train moved on, up, always up wooded slopes whose crests seemed to recede as they approached. When she had quite abandoned hope, and indeed ceased to pay much attention to what was about her, her mount, in a burst of renewed speed, crested the hill they had been climbing daylong.

She stared at the Cherokee town that lay in the valley below, scarcely able to credit her eyes, Having seen nothing more elaborate than the rude shacks of the hunters hidden in the folds of the hills, she was not prepared for the size of the settlement.

The town, probably a hundred buildings, lay on both sides of a swift mountain river. These were not simple shacks but long wooden buildings carefully constructed of trunks of trees shorn of their bark and sealed by some mortise the color of the soil. The only edifice that varied greatly from this design was a large rotunda on the other side of the river. This impressive cone-shaped building was set on a high mound of earth so that it towered over the single-storied buildings around it like the church spires of an English village dominate the surrounding cottages.

Around the settlement on either side of the river stretched level fields, some green with the pale growth of early crops, some freshly tilled and readied for planting. It was an orderly peaceful scene that seemed singularly unthreatening in the late-afternoon light.

But Josh, with a look of sober concern on his face, drew up his mount to stare solemnly at the village below. Julie and Jacques followed his gaze curiously.

"Why so sober?" Jacques asked. "That seems a decent enough place."

Josh shook his head. "Something is amiss," he said in a thoughtful voice. "It is too serene. Where are the children, the barking dogs? There are not even any squaws going about their tasks."

"War?" Jacques asked.

Josh shook his head. "Village life goes on even when the braves have left on the warpath. This is something else."

"If you and Julie can get the train down this slope without help, I will ride ahead and see what is going on there."

By the time they had completed the tortuous descent and were wending their way closer to the village, Julie saw Josh emerge from one of the houses, mount, and start toward them at a rapid canter.

"A pestilence is on the village," he said tersely. "We must make camp outside of town, out of the wind lest it be borne that way."

"What kind of pestilence?" Julie asked, dismayed to realize that Josh had already exposed himself to whatever disease had stilled the life of the tribe.

"It is a flux," Josh said tersely, "where a man's own body drains the life from him through his bowels."

"But have they no medicine for this?" Julie asked, her mind turning quickly to what herbs and drafts her friend Margaret had used when her London patients were afflicted with this wasting through the bowels.

Josh grimaced. "Their medicine man is an old priest who is jealous of his craft. He has performed his rites and administered what powders he knows of and still even the chief himself is near the point of death. My friend Horse no

136

more glimpsed my face than he asked desperately what medicines we carry."

"Only a little quinine," Julie said thoughtfully. "And those herbs I always have." She shook her head. "I have no red oak bark; that makes the best tea for flux."

Josh slumped on a pack and stared at the ground. "God, what a scene that is back there." A look of great distaste crossed his face. "There in that hogan, Horse's wife Spring lies like dried leaf, her eyes hollow in her face. All about her are old crones wailing and howling death while the poor girl helplessly clings to life."

Jacques shook his head. "Your friend Horse must be out of his mind with helplessness."

Josh nodded. "They have children, you know. The son is four and the little girl barely weaned."

A stab of anguish struck Julie as she remembered her own children stricken with the fever in the season just past. She turned away with tears stinging behind her eyelashes. Almost without thinking, she went about the business of making camp, performing the familiar tasks absently while her mind groped for a memory that continued to elude her. There was some remedy . . . not an herb, not a chemical, but some simple household remedy that Margaret had turned to when all else failed. But what was it? And even if it should come to her, what chance was there that the required foodstuff would be among the limited stores that they carried in their packs?

The fire was lit and Josh drawing near with a fresh armload of wood when the thought hit her. With a cry she seized the pack and began to search through it desperately. For a moment she was terrified that Josh had talked Anne-Louise out of packing it. "It takes too long to cook rice," Josh had insisted. "Such a grain is useless on a trek like ours."

Josh watched her curiously. "What's up, Lady?" he asked. "What have you lost that puts such a high color in your cheeks?"

"Rice," she cried. "Oh Josh, please tell me that you didn't leave that sack of rice behind."

He grinned at her as he turned away. "I brought it, all right," he told her. "But since I figured it to be no good on the trail, it is in the other pack. But why is it so urgent?"

"The flux," she babbled. "Oh hurry, Josh. Build the fire higher. We can use the water we have started. Bring the rice quickly."

137

Josh nodded and turned away to do as she asked. "More water, Jacques," he called. "And larger staves for the fire."

Jacques grinned at him. "God, what a hold my cousin has on you, friend. Have you this much blind faith in a simple girl's home remedies?"

The moon had passed over the valley by the time the rice had boiled to a soft pulp. Josh watched curiously as she pressed the milky fluid from the sodden grain with the back of a flat spoon.

"It seems strange that there might be healing magic in such a common pap," he said. "But I would be the last to deny the magic of simple things, Lady."

Looking up at him, Julie felt a warm flush arise to her cheeks, which were already flamed by her nearness to the fire. From the restless movement of Jacques beyond the flame, she knew that her cousin had not missed the yearning tenderness in Josh's tone.

"Let me take it to her myself," Julie pleaded. "I am not afraid."

"Not on your life, Lady," Josh said firmly. "If the pest is in the air then I alone have been exposed to it. We'll keep it that way. But don't wait for me. It has been a long day and night to follow."

When an hour had passed and then another, Jacques brought fresh wood for the fire. "If you insist on waiting for him like a nervous mother with a virgin abroad, you might as well be comfortable."

"I haven't seen you yawn," she jested with him, leaning back against a rolled pack and making herself comfortable.

She was wakened by Josh's gentle touch on her hand. Dawn was just beginning. The faintest streaks of color had begun in the sky that framed his head. The song of a lark sounded very near, its song like a celebration.

Smiling sleepily at Josh, she whispered, "How is Spring? Is the broth working?"

He nodded. "She is even sleeping now," he assured her. Only then did she realize he was not alone. She struggled into a more formal position as she met the eyes of the young Cherokee brave whose glance had been so bold at their first meeting.

"This is Moon Gift, Julie," Josh said quietly. "He wants you to make some more of the broth, this time for his father, who is at the point of death."

Julie threw her robe aside and caught Josh's hand to rise.

"The coals are still hot," she said. "Quickly, bring wood."

The pillar of flame brought Jacques from sleep with a grunt of alarm. Then, taking in the scene with narrowed eyes, he rose to help Josh with the feeding of the giant fire. Moon Gift sat motionless as Julie stirred the bowl of cooking grain. When the heat of the fire licked against her wooden spoon, he rose and left only to return with a polished arrow shaft to which he had bound a wooden spoon with leather thongs.

"The chief has lost many sons in war," Josh explained while the young brave was gone. "Only this one brave, who was born late in the chief's life, is left. Those are two close men, Moon Gift and the old chief."

Julie's face felt parched from the blaze of the fire and by the time the grain was cooked, her whole body ached from leaning over the boiling pot. As she pressed the fluid from the grain Josh watched her, musing. "You might put a few magic words in there with that pummeling, Lady."

She glanced up at him. "I wonder if you know how much I wish I could."

"We all join you in that wish," Josh grinned crookedly. "Moon Gift is here in defiance of the medicine man and his priests. The old man, embarrassed by the improvement of Horse's wife, has tottered about warning the villagers of the bad magic of a yellow-eyed witch."

"How can they do that? They haven't even seen me," Julie said in amazement.

"That's something more you can learn of these natives," he laughed. "They may look taciturn but they are hopeless gossips. Let a deer be shot fifty miles away and someone will describe its antlers for you."

Moon Gift, frowning a little at his exclusion from the talk, spoke quickly to Josh. As Josh explained their conversation the young man's face became disfigured in a scowl and he spat in derision, his spittle singing suddenly in the hot coals.

"I gather he is no friend to the priest," Jacques laughed softly.

"He called him a fool and a man who loved his own gut and several other colorful things that I am sure my Lady would prefer not to have translated."

When Julie rose with the half-filled bowl of thick broth, Moon Gift nodded soberly and took it from her hands. Watching him leave the campfire with the bowl carefully between his hands, Josh laid his arm across Julie's shoulder.

"Want to give me the odds, Lady? If he lives, we will all be basking in honor. If he dies, you will learn why these people are called savages even by their firmest friends."

Chapter Thirty-One

Having defied the counsel of his medicine man and drunk the broth prepared by the yellow-eyed white woman, White Eagle, the great chief of the Cherokees, rallied from the flux and turned his face toward life. Within a few days he was able to rise from his pallet and stir about his rooms. Within a week he was able to walk about on the arm of his son Moon Gift and see his fields of corn rising green by the bank of the river.

The same thrust of life that turned the Cherokee fields green stirred the land of the Natchez that lay on the bluffs above the Mississippi River. The gently rolling fields of the Natchez sprouted green with Indian corn that grew well, safe even from the natural peril of spring flood by its position two hundred feet above the bed of the swift wide river.

On those same bluffs, near the river, stood the French fort named Rosalie. The newly appointed commandant of the fort, Captain D'Etcheparre, mounted his horse and rode out through the palisades of the fort to study the Natchez land.

He knew himself fortunate to have obtained this appointment after being removed from other posts on charges of arrogance and injustice both to his men and the natives. He also knew that he owed this position to the covetousness of Commissioner General Perier, with whom he had made secret agreements to use his power as commander to obtain rich settlement lands for both Perier and himself in this territory.

All of the land along the bluff was level and fertile but much of it had already been claimed. As he passed the plantation of M. DuPratz he looked with envy on the productive tobacco fields and the nearly fifty acres of hickory trees that stood knee deep in verdant grass. But the DuPratz land had been first cleared by the Indians.

But the land around the Indian villages, long cleared of trees and the high thick cane of the region, were fine open fields that yielded rich crops. He passed the village that lay on the banks of St. Catherine's Creek. This settlement was called the Grand Village and the Sun King who ruled it was a young man whose father had been a French soldier from the fort. D'Etcheparre, known to all the colonists and Indians as Chopart, sat on his mount and stared at the village, at the great house from which the Great Sun came each morning at dawn to make his obeisance to his brother in the sky.

He rode back to the fort sunk in thought. It was important not to provoke new trouble with the Natchez, but rather to manage them by degrees. In the past there had been blood spilled between the French and the Natchez, and he must not let such trouble disturb his plans. They were a proud strange people for all that they were heathens, a nation of tall strong warriors and delicious women of easy virtue. But still heathens. Did they not strangle their own families and servants at funerals? Did they not eat the flesh of dogs?

He would first demand of them, not the Grand Village but a village a few miles away called White Apple. The Sun King of White Apple was an old man who might be easier to handle than the young buck at Grand Village. Once he had obtained White Apple for Perier, he could start working towards getting control of the Grand Village land for himself.

Delighted with his plan, he refreshed himself with a bottle of good French wine while he sent a messenger to summon the Sun King of White Apple village to come before him.

Since the Sun Kings of Natchez did not touch their feet to the ground but were borne on litters by strong warriors, some hours passed before the old man reached the fort. By the time the Sun King arrived, Chopart was deep into his second bottle of wine. Flushed with alcohol and his own cleverness, he watched the old man, clad in a loose garment of Limbourg cloth and wearing the feather crown of his caste, stand inside his door, waiting for Chopart to invite him to be seated.

The Suns, being governors themselves, were skilled at diplomacy. They were sensitive to tone and manner. It was trying to the old Sun to hear this arrogant young captain address him in a tone that the Sun himself would scarcely employ with a slave.

"The ships are even now leaving France with new settlers," Chopart told the old man. "These people will need more land that is convenient to the fort. The village of White Apple must be moved."

"But the village cannot be moved," the old man protested. "The bones of the generations are there. It is a sacred spot."

Chopart looked slyly at the old man. "Then we leave the

141

village of White Apple and will take the land along St. Catherine's Creek. Those huts must be cleared away and moved elsewhere."

Concealing his astonishment at the interpreter's words, the old Sun phrased his reasonable answer carefully. "Surely you are speaking in jest, to test the response of my people. The Natchez have lived in that village for more years than there are hairs in the twisted queue that hangs from the top of my head to my waist. This second request is more astonishing than the first. We have lived with the French in peace and friendship. We have given freely of our stores and sold fairly in commerce.

"There are other lands to spare. Take them with our blessing. But the Grand Village of the Natchez must be left untouched. Our temple stands there, the bones of our fathers have slept there since our people first came to dwell in this place."

Chopart, flushed with drink and irritated by the steady eyes of the dignified old man, turned away and spat on the floor. Who was this scrawny old savage to tell him that a village "must be left untouched." By God, he would have the Grand Village and he would have it immediately.

"Don't give me this prattle of temples and bones," he said angrily. "We want the village and we will have it. If the huts are not cleared from the land in a matter of days, you and your people will repent of it."

As he finished, Chopart lurched to his feet, turning his back on the old man as he left the room in a gesture of disrespect.

The old Sun, dropping his eyes so that the interpreter could not see the fury and loathing he felt, left a calm message for Chopart. "Tell your commander that I shall assemble the old men of the village to counsel on this affair."

When the old men gathered in sober counsel to discuss the demands of the Frenchman, the old Sun King defined the problem as he saw it.

"Although Chopart was drunk when he spoke, I believe he will speak the same when his head is cleared. We need to buy time from him. We cannot yield the Grand Village but we need time to plan how we will handle this demand."

This was the first of many counsels which were held in the week to follow. Patiently the old men made decisions. Patiently the Sun carried their words to Chopart, only to return again for the counsel and rebuff.

"The corn is only a little out of the ground," they told him the first time. "And even now the hens are laying in their nests. If the village is moved now, there will be no fowl to cook or corn to grind when winter comes."

Chopart responded with a curse. "If those damned huts are not off the land within a matter of days, you shall indeed reap a harvest of French violence."

After that meeting, the old men and the Sun spoke together well into the night.

"We must find a way to appeal to the man himself," he suggested. "The lowliest slave knows that Chopart is a greedy and lustful man. We will appeal to his greed."

When the Sun again spoke to Chopart, he brought a handsome offer from his council.

"Winter is the time of hunger for the French as well as the Natchez," he reminded the commander. "If you will leave the village and its fields alone until the harvest is in and the corn dried, there will be plenty for all. Each hut in the village will bring a tribute to you...a fowl and a basket of corn from every household will be yours alone. Even if your settlers are on the sea now, they cannot arrive until the Month of the Bison which the French call November. Give us until the Month of Bison."

Chopart, remembering the close rations of winters past, tried to conceal his delight at this offer. What a bounty this would be! He would have grain and poultry to sell and still have the village lands in exchange for only a few months of patience. In his greed he did not question why the old men had suddenly grown so generous. Instead, he accepted the offer, even adding a great discourse of flattery. He spoke of the long friendship between the French and the Natchez and pretended that he hoped this alliance would extend to their sons and their son's sons.

The old Sun nodded his thanks for the flowery words, but his eyes were unreadable on the young captain's face. When he was taken back to the village by his swift-running litter bearers, he called the old men together for one more meeting.

"We now have time," he told them. "And I have thought of a plan."

143

Chapter Thirty-Two

After the healing of the Cherokee chief White Eagle, a great ceremony of thanksgiving was held in honor of the yellow-eyed woman. When the ceremonial fires were all ashes, Josh loaded the packs on the fresh horses supplied by the grateful chief and the pack train started west and south toward the Natchez Trail.

The vague fears that she had felt during the early part of their trek were gone. Julie knew that beyond their fire stood silent watchers guarding over them, emissaries sent by White Eagle to insure their safe arrival at the Chickasaw dominion.

Curled in the elaborate fur robe that Moon Gift had presented her upon their parting, she battled against the memories that seemed to form into living scenes in the smoldering fires.

Strangely, she never saw Antoine as he had been when she left, gaunt with anguish and raging in violence. It was the old Antoine who returned to her, his eyes defying the brightest blue skies of noon, the pattern of his laughter, and the urgency of passion he roused in her with his touch. Sometimes she was startled by the smooth vibrancy of his flesh against her only to realize that her longing for him was so strong that the smooth lining of her robe became his flesh against her own.

But there was no turning back. There were only endless campfires and shadowy groves with Jacques and Josh stirring in sleep beside her.

Safe in Chickasaw country, having bade farewell to the last of White Eagle's warriors, Julie was astonished to find they were treated with great honor and ceremony.

A great fire was lit for a festival of welcome. There was feasting and long speeches were made in the strange tongue that was like the Cherokee only a little lower in tone and more pleasing to the ear.

The girl who sang could not have been more than sixteen or seventeen years old. She was smaller in stature than the other squaws in the group and her clothing was meaner.

"She is a slave," Josh explained in a whisper. "She is a

daughter of the Choctaw who has been taken in battle. Choctaws are widely famed for their songs."

Jacques and Julie, sensitive to their roles as honored guests only listened attentively to the girl's strange unintelligible lyrics, but Josh, after the first few lines, leaned forward in undisguised excitement. Julie was startled to feel his hand grope for her own and clasp it tightly as if in fear.

"What's up?" Jacques whispered, his tone mildly resentful as it always was at Josh's slightest overture toward Julie.

"Hush," Josh whispered urgently, listening intently to the song.

The last note had barely died when Josh was on his feet, moving in that swift silent tread toward the side of the chief. Julie watched him make careful obeisance and saw the chief nod approval as Josh spoke to him. Then Josh returned with the Choctaw slave girl walking behind him, her face impassive but her eyes wide with fear.

When he had persuaded her to sit and passed the bowl to her, he began to question her in the fluting dialect that seemed second nature to him.

After they had spoken for what seemed a long time to Julie, Josh rose and took a trinket from his pocket and presented it to the girl.

"What in the name of God was all that?" Jacques asked, having grown impatient with curiosity through the long exchange.

"It was her song," Josh said quietly. "I was asking her about the song she had sung for the company. She says it is a new song that was brought to her village only days before she was captured and brought to this place. It is a song of a spirit." He glanced at Jacques and then Julie. "Did either of you catch any of the words?"

Julie shook her head. "Not a word."

"Nor I," Jacques agreed.

"The song she sang was very different. Most Indian songs about squaws are stories of great courage or love songs with unhappy endings. This is the song of a spirit. It tells of a great noblewoman, a daughter of the chief Sun King of the Natchez. This woman was fair of face and graceful as grass stirred by wind and had great gifts." He glanced at Julie with a shy grin. "She was said to give the love of her body as freely as the river gives water, both to the men of her own nation and to the white men who had power."

Jacques whistled softly. "That is indeed a different story. I

145

thought a hard fate was set for a squaw who was careless with her marriage vows."

"Not so with the Natchez," Josh told him. "But in any case, because she was blessed with great gifts and because she was a daughter of the Sun, she was free to lead a life of her own."

"What were these great gifts?" Jacques asked.

"Healing," Josh said shortly, with a shy glance at Julie. "She was a great healer who could stop death with the flat of her hand to save those people she cared for."

"It is a spirit song," Josh said again. "The song says that La Glorieuse, having died and her bones dried in the sun, has come to life again to walk on noble feet even as she did before. It is sung that she sleeps with two men at the same time and has held death back with the flat of her hand from White Eagle, the great chief of the Cherokees."

Julie almost choked at his words and Jacques laughed merrily.

Josh nodded. "There is no laughter in the song. It is a spirit song and in the song they refer to Julie with the same name that the French gave the woman who lived before...La Glorieuse. They say that La Glorieuse has returned to life in the yellow-eyed white woman at your side."

Josh sighed. "If they accept my Lady here as the spirit of this Natchez healer returned in another form, they will expect an ungodly amount of skill from her. She will be obliged to heal, and if she does not heal she will be accused of killing."

"But tell them," Julie insisted. "Tell them this is all a wild idea someone had. Tell them I am a simple woman with a few lucky skills."

Josh smiled wryly. "I asked the Choctaw slave where the song had come from. She said it had risen like the wind of late afternoon, blowing at once to all the nations. The Creeks sing of it as well as the Choctaws. The song is the same everywhere, she says." He paused and then went on. "The only difference between these songs, Lady, is that among the Natchez you are called 'La Nouvelle Glorieuse'...the new Glorieuse."

146

Chapter Thirty-Three

And indeed the song and the story of the woman called La Glorieuse had been carried even to the Grand Village of the Natchez on the banks of St Catherine's Creek.

Since the women of the stinkard class had little leisure, they chattered ceaselessly to each other as they went about their labors. They whispered the stories to each other as they prepared the evening meal.

"Yellow eyes," one young girl repeated wonderingly. "But La Glorieuse in life had eyes of the glossiest, most beautiful black."

Her companion glanced around before replying, "But in other ways she is said to be the same. They say she has a small, beautifully formed body designed to draw men's eyes and that she sleeps with two men at a time."

A nervous chorus of giggles stirred among them.

The tongues of the noblewomen were no less busy than those of their servants. The Sun Queen of the Grand Village, a ripe lithe girl of eighteen, stood admiring herself in a glass while her slave combed her waist-length hair before binding it with ornaments of beads and feathers. Her dark eyes danced as she listened to her noble friends repeating, for what must have been the twentieth time, all the stories that had been heard of the yellow-eyed white woman known as La Nouvelle Glorieuse.

"There have been cold beds among the officers at the fort since La Glorieuse was strangled at the funeral of the Great Sun," one of the women said thoughtfully. "Do you suppose that this woman would lie down with such men as they are?"

"There can be no Glorieuse," an old woman spoke up roughly. "I myself saw the tobacco put into her mouth and watched the blood run from her severed neck at the funeral of my brother the Great Sun King."

The young queen looked at the old woman with respect. Seldom did a woman of the Natchez live to such great age as the Tattooed Arm had. It was said of her that she had been a great beauty in her youth and scarcely less winning in her prime. If she had wed among the Natchez she would long ago have been a sacrifice on the death of that husband, but by mating with a Frenchman she had survived. The cheeks that had once glowed with vibrant color were seamed with wrinkles and her eyes, while quick enough to sense the faintest change in a person's smile, were rheumy, with limp flesh beneath them that sagged on the folds of her cheeks.

"No one really claims that this woman is the same," the young Sun Queen told her mother-in-law gently. "They only say that her spirit walks in this woman. That she can heal a great chief when the shadow of death is already on him, even as La Glorieuse could do."

"La Glorieuse is with her master," Tattooed Arm repeated crossly. "And if any such woman came here, she would be severely chastised for claiming the name of the worthy dead."

Tattooed Arm braced her sinewy arms on the earth and pulled herself to her feet with a rude grunt. "The wind is in your skulls, you giddy creatures," she rebuked them. "Here you sit and babble of spirit women and lovemaking while some great mystery takes place as the men sit in council daylong."

The young Sun Queen drew her mouth into a rebellious pout. "And nightlong too, it seems to me. My own husband is become a stranger to me because of councils...always councils."

Tattooed Arm studied her daughter-in-law's face with narrowed eyes. "And who knows what they are speaking of? Does your husband ever reveal what the nature of these councils is?"

The girl shook her head with a pleased smile. "Believe me, great Princess, your son is not yet of an age when he comes to our bed with affairs of state on his mind."

Drawing apart from the chatter of the other women, Tattooed Arm pondered the events of the weeks just past. The men, even as the young queen had complained, had been daylong and nightlong at council for many weeks, yet nothing of their talk had been reported to the people.

Having been sister to the Grand Sun and even now the mother to his successor even though the boy had been begot by a Frenchman from the fort, she had always been party to the inner secrets of the tribe. Always in her life she had managed to know even the smallest gossip of the village before any other ears. She smiled wickedly to herself. How simple the young Sun Queen was. Ah, when she herself had

148

been eighteen as this girl was with her ripe breasts high and her skin like the feathers of a dove, no man could have kept a secret from her even if the telling would have cost him his life.

Why could she not be left in peace? All she wanted was to know what was afoot. Was that too much to demand in her great age? Her son was thoughtless. He knew she had other concerns on her heart. He knew that she was greatly worried about the health of the young Sun Princess Techou, who lived in White Apple Village. This was a young woman whom she loved dearly for her gentleness of spirit and easy grace. But now Techou was great with child and the carrying was not going well. Perhaps it was her concern for the princess Techou that made the talk of La Glorieuse so maddening to her. How many times had she thought that if La Glorieuse still lived something could be done for her dear Techou. She would have known what herbs and potions could keep the flesh from swelling about the girl's ankles and stop the aching in the head that plagued her.

But no, she was worried and pained and resentful and still her son sat in his councils and came forth with a secret face. She was able to learn only what could be seen with careful watching. She had known when that brute Chopart had sent for the old Sun of White Apple Village. She had not thought much of the council that was called after that meeting, for all the tribe knew of the stupidity of the French commander.

But always her own son was in these councils. He was a stubborn headstrong young man, but she would get it from him in the end.

She rose painfully and went to seek an old nobleman friend who might have heard something she had missed. To her astonishment, her friend's wife explained that he was absent from the village.

"Absent," Tattooed Arm cried. "Why would he be absent from the village at this season?"

"He was sent away," the wife explained. "I do not know where he went or why. I only know that he and many other nobles left in the first light of dawn to be embassies somewhere."

It was then that Tattooed Arm hobbled furiously across the compound and demanded an audience with her son.

"The embassies I sent forth?" he asked with that winning smile that for a brief moment brought the memory of his father to her mind. "Indeed I did send embassies. I am not your son for nothing, my wise one. It has occurred to me that

149

we have no regular intelligence of the affairs of neighboring nations. Your brother the Great Sun was careful to keep such contacts alive and I must do the same. I have sent noble embassies to strengthen the bonds of old friendships."

"And that is all?" she pressed. "There is nothing else afoot?"

"Afoot," the young Sun laughed, hugging her thin shoulders. "What is there to be afoot? What is more important than keeping our nation's friendships in good repair?"

Having no answer, she took her leave, determined to learn more when the embassies returned to the village. But in the meantime there was much to occupy her. The princess Techou had rallied from her illness and the child still moved in her belly. Tattooed Arm, fearful that the girl's slaves might neglect her, traveled almost daily to visit Techou and carry extra fine foods to build her strength.

And so it was that the Festival of the Peaches came and passed. The last of the embassies returned by the time the Festival of the Great Corn took place. She waited for her son to announce an open council that the village might hear the news from abroad, but no council came.

This time she accosted her son in anger, only to have his words slide away from her like eels in water. She turned her eyes away so that he would not read her fury.

"One does not save the honey by striking the hive with a stick," she reminded herself, accepting his explanations silently.

Chapter Thirty-Four

The fullness of summer lay on the land. Not even the dense woods through which the Indian trail wound could provide respite from the oppressive heat that glued Julie's leather clothes to her damp body. To uncover even an inch of flesh was to invite the swarms of mosquitoes that hung in the darkness of the trees humming with warning.

"Not much longer," Josh assured them nightly, watering the horses in brackish pools and measuring their own water carefully for their daily use. "This section really is the worst part," he added hastily at Jacques' wry look.

Finally, in desperation, Julie began wearing a soft cloth over her head. It fell about her shoulders like a widow's veil and turned the path ahead into a vague fused lightness of blurred shapes. But at least she was not constantly slapping and fanning at the pillared clouds of insects that raged for their blood as they passed the shadowy places.

"Aha," he cried. "Good Lord, what have we here?"

Throwing back her veil, she looked ahead curiously.

The forest was suddenly gone. Before her stretched a wide field of freshly cut corn stubble. Jacques, kicking his mare, was already halfway across the field, riding toward a grove of trees and high gleaming cane. She turned to see Josh watching her with a smile.

"Fresh water," he told her. "That grove hides a fresh creek." With sudden seriousness, he drew his horse alongside hers. "This has been a long journey, Lady," he said softly. "But now it is through."

"Then we are there?" she asked in disbelief.

"As close as we can be," he nodded.

"What will happen now?" She asked quietly, a sudden chill coming along her spine. Once she would have answered that question for herself. But that was when she had known so little as to propose this journey boldly. Looking back at the months that she could barely contain in her mind, she wondered at her own innocence. If she had been this unconscious of the vast land that lay between Charles Town and this place, how wrong had she also been about their chances to free the white slave named PoBotahm?

"If I have followed the map truly, the village beyond that grove is called White Apple," Josh said quietly. "My friends among the Chickasaw say that the Sun of this village is the oldest and wisest of his people. They say he is as kind as he is wise and will deal with us fairly."

Julie pondered his words. Over and over during the long trek, she and Jacques had questioned Josh about the strange nation they were seeking. Having stayed so long with the Cherokee and been the guest of many Chickasaw villages, Julie had lost her old primitive fear of what Josh called the "natives." But everything she had heard about the Natchez filled her with wonder.

"Not chiefs, but Suns," Josh always corrected her. "They consider themselves the family of the sun itself and the Sun of each village speaks daily to his brother in the sky."

151

"The village of the White Apple," Julie mused, her golden eyes thoughtful as she stared across the open field.

"The white slave is reported to be dwelling here with his family," Josh told her. "Why don't you ride ahead after Jacques and have some fresh water. I will free the pack horses for drinking and be along after you."

The trees stopped as she drew nearer the river. Leading her horse, she followed the trail of bent and broken cane that Jacques had left in his wake. She gasped with delight when she reached the smooth bank of the stream.

Jacques turned to her, his hand still on the bridle of his drinking horse. "I have even located a place for bathing," he told her. "A little farther downstream is a deep place just designed for that long-desired pleasure. When the horses have been tended we must take turns. Ah, to be clean again." He knelt and filled his flask with water from the stream.

"This will be your toast to journey's end," he said as the water gurgled into the neck of the flask.

"Then you knew where we were," Julie said.

"I have been studying the map Josh got from the Chickasaw," he replied. "I realized we had to be getting very close." He dropped the reins of his mount to bring the flask to her. The old passion that she thought time and close association had dampened blazed suddenly in his face as he looked down at her.

"A toast to the goal we seek," she said, taking the flask and drinking without meeting his eyes. The cold sweet water was as heady as wine after the brackish portions of the past days.

"Now you will toast me, *ma cousine*," Jacques said quietly. "You may phrase it as you will, but I have earned a flattering commendation for the way I have controlled myself these past months."

She looked up to see a fine line of sweat along his jaw. "I have walked by you and ridden by you and slept under the stars with you, Juliette. I have ached for you like a man in Hell through all these things." He sighed. "And now that the end of this part of the journey is near, I am fool enough to grieve its passing."

She was relieved to hear Josh approaching through the canes with the pack horses.

The pool that Jacques had decided was a bathing tub was indeed a sight to behold. Shielded by overhanging branches, Julie let herself all the way down into the chill sweet water, giggling at the curious pressure of the mouths of small fish

152

against her naked limbs. With her hair piled high, she lazed in the water, guiltily conscious that the others waited beyond the screen of the cane, Josh on guard with his gun across his knees.

It seemed barely moments before Josh summoned her softly.

"Are you through, Lady?" he asked.

"If I need to be," she replied in a whisper.

"You need to be," he replied with unmistakable urgency.

Rising from the water, she hastily wrapped herself in the length of cloth she had brought for a towel. She had only slid her wet feet into her moccasins to shield her feet from the knife edges of the broken cane when he called out again. "Here, lady," he urged. "Come here quickly."

He had no eyes for her. Instead, he stared intently into the darkness gathering in the canes on the other side of the creek. "Take this," he said, thrusting the gun into her hands. "And keep it trained on me."

With no further explanation, he plunged into the stream and crossed it in swift strides, keeping his eyes trained on the same spot on the opposite shore.

Then as suddenly as he had left, he disappeared into the high stand of cane on the other side.

Julie was surprised with the speed that the curse rose to her lips. "Dammit," she whispered. "How can I keep a gun on you if you fly off into the brush?" She jerked the linen up about her knees and waded over the creek after him. Her sodden moccasins sloshed as she followed his trail through the cane. He heard her coming and raised his hand to warn her to silence without even looking back.

Then he called something in the native dialect, clearly a command of some firmness. Instinctively, Julie swung the gun around to train it on the section of cane he was staring at.

When he spoke again, curtly, a frantic rustling began in the brush before a figure stepped forth.

It was a girl, very young and dainty, clutching a water jar to her chest as she stared at Josh in terror.

She was gracefully formed with fine rounded arms and the barest beginnings of breasts showing beneath the loops of shells and feathers that ornamented her bare chest. Clad only in an apron of Limbourg cloth, she would have been any lovely ten-year-old except for the deep black scar cut across her nose. Her hair defied description, hanging to her waist in a silken gleaming black bounty.

Her first sound was a hollow cry. Then she wailed,

153

"Glorieuse," in a terrified tone. At her cry, she dropped the jar, breaking it into a multitude of brightly colored shards. Then she turned. With the black hair streaming behind her like a banner, she fled unheeding through the giant cane.

The cane around them seemed suddenly astir as if by a local tumult of wind. They broke forth all at once, not wind, but a circle of warriors. The tall golden-skinned men whose bodies were decorated in intricate colored designs stared impassively at Julie and Josh. With a swift movement Josh knocked the gun from Julie's hand to lie on the broken cane. This was not a circle of unarmed savages that surrounded them. With guns leveled at their prisoners, the men closed in around them.

Chapter Thirty-Five

The sun rose in a shimmer of blazing heat. The old Sun Princess Tattooed Arm stared crossly into the clearing beyond her door. She had observed that the fullness of sunlight seemed to bring on fresh attacks of Techou's sickness. She wished she were free this day to journey to White Apple Village and warn her beloved niece to remain inside, away from the rays of the sun. But she had other plans, plans she had been carefully making since the last of the embassies returned from the other tribes.

She knew there was conspiracy afoot. It hung in her nose like an evil smell. She could sense it in the faces of the old men as their eyes slid away from her own when they passed in the village. She would not even be surprised if her son's soft-bodied wife knew what was going on. The girl had grown very silent with her lately, almost to the point of avoiding her company.

It was her son's stubbornness which had forced her to make the plan that she would put into effect this day with the sun so hot that their heads might be addled by its rays. She needed only to get the young man apart from any other company to wrest the secret from him. And didn't she have a right to know, a blooded princess of her great age and wisdom?

"My relative the Sun Princess in the Meal Village lies ailing," she had told her son, arranging her face carefully to show great concern. She did not mention to him that this same relative had been ailing for almost as long as she herself could remember, being one of those women who preferred illness to health for the attention it yielded.

Her son the Grand Sun was quick to sympathy. "This saddens me," he told her. "I certainly hope that she will soon be rid of whatever plagues her."

"I can find no peace in myself until I know that she is being well cared for," she told him.

"I mean to go and see her," she said quietly.

He frowned. "But is that wise? It is a long journey for such a hot season."

"I had hoped that you might accompany me," she confessed. "With you as my companion the journey would be swift and pleasant in spite of any turn of the weather."

He would have explained why he could not make the trip with her, but she was too crafty for him. "Of course, if you feel that your duties are more important than your mother's happiness . . ." she began. "Or that the concerns of your family should be shrunk to smallness since you have the responsibility of governing this village."

He flushed with embarrassment and protested quickly. "No duty is more important to me than your happiness. My family has lost no stature since I have been made Sun King. My love and esteem for you remains unchanged."

She had wreathed her face with delighted smiles. "How could I think that such a fine son would disappoint me?" she asked aloud. "We will leave early in the morning, after your brother the Sun has received our obeisance. This way we will be back at our own fires long before the twilight."

She did not speak of what was on her mind during their trip to the Meal Village. Instead she told stories of his youth, weaving him even closer to her with the web of loving memory.

But when they had spent their time at Meal Village and left her ailing relative promising that health would surely follow the visit of such illustrious kinsmen, she fell into silence.

The young Sun, accustomed to his mother's constant prattle, eyed her with concern. "I fear that the heat has been too much for you, Mother. You have grown overtired. Aren't you at all comforted by this visit to your relative?"

She shook her head. "I was comforted, but now that the

concern for her welfare has been lifted from my heart I find an old sadness returning to fill its place. I find myself thinking again of how you and the other Suns no longer trust me."

When he started to protest, she shook her head. "I know that I have become a person of no account in your eyes, like a stinkard of no class. The honor of being the mother of a Great Sun like yourself and all my privileges as a princess seem as nothing when my own people treat me thus. You treat me as if I were French. And while it is true that I lay with a French lover to conceive you, the blood of the Natchez is my true blood. Thus it wounds me that you and the others are plotting against the French and trying to keep the truth from me."

He stared at his mother in astonishment. "Come, Mother," he pleaded. "It is not common for even a Great Sun to reveal to his mother what is done in the men's councils. I must be careful to give a good example of secret-keeping for the others. And as for my own French blood, it is as nothing to me, now that I am Sun King. But since you have already discovered our affair, I must caution you to hold your tongue at every cost."

"Are you saying that I am a babbler?" she challenged him. "I am only greatly concerned for you in this matter. We both know that the commander Chopart is a man of small wit and less grace, but I wonder if you and your men realize how great and powerful the French nation is. They have more warriors and resources than all our villages could summon together."

"Cease your fears," her son told her earnestly. "Let me assure you that other tribes know of our plans and approve them. Those among the Choctaw who have been mistreated by the French have pledged to join with us and act on the same day that we do. The Chickasaws to the north are equipped with the selfsame bundle of sticks to set their joining in this attack against the common enemy."

She kept her eyes on the path, horrified that her guess had been correct and even more appalled at her son's calm words. He was a fool. Her own son was a fool who had been lured into this insane scheme by bad counsellors. She was certain that any design to destroy the French could only fail and bring misery and death to the Natchez. She must take steps. She must move with great care, but the French must be warned that the nations were planning to rise against them.

After taking leave of her son with flowery words of gratitude for the pleasure of his company, Tattooed Arm hastened to White Apple Village even though the sun was already low in the sky.

She was not a Sun Princess for nothing, she told herself proudly. The bevy of young girls, setting out together for the night at Fort Rosalie, were flattered when she stopped them on the roadway. When she had praised their glossy hair and the beauty of their ornaments, she added a laughing note. "Such fine Frenchmen we women have to bed with. Remember that the Great Sun, my own child, was born of such a moist sweet night in the arms of my gallant. Only be sure that your French lovers keep alert against enemies, remembering that even long times of peace do not last forever."

One maiden, cleverer than the rest, studied her face with concern. "What are you saying, Princess? Is there a warning in your words for the French?"

The old woman laughed. "Old heads have long memories," she told them. "There have been wars before between the Natchez and the French. I simply would not have you lose your fine young studs because of their careless soldiering."

Tattooed Arm was well satisfied with her evening's work by the time she made her way to the house of her niece Techou. She saw at once that the girl looked somewhat improved. There was less swelling in her kinswoman's face and Techou's voice was strong and more vibrant. But the child who usually played happily outside the door was nestled against her mother in an attitude of fear.

Tattooed Arm nodded at the child's father and went to the girl. "What is wrong with my little plum?" she asked gently.

Techou's hand strayed lovingly across her daughter's forehead. "She had a great fright this afternoon and her heart still beats repidly from that."

"Was there an alligator in the creek?" the old woman asked. "Did some brave dare to make advances to you?"

The old woman saw Techou's eyes stray to her husband's face. When she spoke, her words were hesitant. "This is supposed to be a great secret," she confessed, "but I see no reason why it should be kept from one of your station. There are strangers in this village...a woman and two men with pack horses that came from the east. Our Great Sun has hidden them away and wants no word of their presence known to anyone. Even as the Sun's warriors moved in for

157

their capture, our child stumbled upon them on the bank of the creek and was startled."

"Strangers hidden? Captured?" The old woman could not believe her ears. She turned to Techou's husband. "What is this silly business? What is this silly business? Why should strangers be seized and hidden? What do you know of this, PoBotahm?"

The tall man shook his head and smiled at the old woman.

"It makes no more sense to me than to you, great Princess," he admitted. "Perhaps the Great Sun has taken this unusual step because the woman with the pack train is a strange white woman with yellow eyes. From what our child has told us, she is the one who has been spoken of. La Nouvelle Glorieuse."

The Great Sun whose acts had struck the old Princess as such "silly business" lay silent on the bed in his house. Because he was a man who enjoyed good company around him, he was irked by the emptiness of his rooms. But he had made pledges to the Great Sun God in the sky, promises of fasting and self-denial to insure that the coming campaign to destroy the French might be visited with success.

He had fasted painfully to gain his God's approval. Even with the goose-down mattress beneath him he could feel the hard wooden supports of the bed pressing on his bony form. He was a man with a great appetite for fine food. When the cook fires grew hot in the village and the rich scents of spiced meat wafted past the terminals of his door, he found his mouth filled with the spittle of furious hunger. Yet he had fasted for seven nights and days without a single bite of warm food passing his lips.

He had sent his wives from his bed. As weak as his body was, lewd dreams still haunted him. He thought of the sleek rounded limbs of his latest wife and how her quick tongue moved against his flesh, rousing him to fulfillment. Yet he had not seen a woman nor lain his hand along the curved line of a shapely limb for seven days and seven nights.

There was nothing he would not suffer to insure the success of the plan he had made against the French.

But he stirred on his bed and groaned, pained by this problem that had come to him this day past. His scouts had alerted him days before that the pack train was moving along the old trail. They brought word that the woman known as La Nouvelle Glorieuse was one of the three and that they came in search of a slave.

Even though the Chickasaws who had reported this news were men of good repute, he questioned this story. Slaves were known to be plentiful in the east, why should these strangers come to seek a slave in a land where even the French grumbled that there were not enough hands to turn to the tasks of building and cultivating food?

His great hope was that the pack train would turn aside and visit some other tribe. Instead they had headed for his own village of the White Apple, as if they had been led. They had come to the bend of the White Apple Creek to be surprised there by a child going for water.

Never in his long reign had he imprisoned a stranger without cause. Never had he tried to conceal so great an event as the arrival of a pack train from the people of his village. But even now in a sealed hut behind the chinaberry tree he had the three strangers hidden in darkness.

He had no choice. What if the French of Fort Rosalie learned that traders had entered the village carrying pack loads of arms and ammunition? What if they learned that people from the English colonies in the Carolinas were sheltered in his village? He had sent a messenger to the Great Sun of the Grand Village to help him with counsel. Until the messenger returned, the strangers must lie hidden in darkness.

The Sun Princess Techou was wise and kindly and her white husband not a man to babble about the village. As for the child, they had promised to keep her within doors until some decision was made.

If he could only sleep.

He knew well enough what could bring sleep to his pillow. If he had the dripping joint of a roasted fowl to eat or a bowl of rich stew; if he could ease the pressure in his groin into the moist cave of a woman's body, he could sleep.

He cursed and turned again on the bed which had become damp with his own sweat.

Chapter Thirty-Six

Julie was stirred awake when Josh lifted her head from his lap. Tugging at the loose cloth that was still all the clothing she

159

wore, she sat up quickly. But already Josh was only one among the shadows that stirred against the dim light at the door.

"Hold fast," he called back at her softly. "Hold fast, Lady."

When she saw the boards set once more against the rude opening, she peered about the darkness but could discern nothing.

There were no windows in the hut. By standing on tiptoe with her face almost pressed against the uneven boards, she got a narrow-slitted view of the village. There were many huts along the palisades in the distance. In the center of the area was a large green space rather like a park. At the end of this space was a large mound, taller than a man in height. There was a door set into the side of this mound and at the other end of the clearing, facing the mound, stood a huge hut whose roof boasted carved statues of eagles.

Even as she watched, an old man emerged from the large conical house and stood immobile facing the rising sun. He was painfully thin and walked as if weakened by hunger or disease. After making three loud cries like a strange greeting, she saw him raise his pipe, draw deeply, and then blow out the smoke, first toward the rising run, and then toward the other corners of the world.

As if this ceremony were a signal for the day to begin, people began coming out of the huts, young women with babies and half-grown boys and girls clad carelessly if at all.

But there was no sign of Josh or Jacques, who had been thrown into the same dark hut with her after their capture at the edge of the creek. Food and water were brought and the jars and basins carried away. She spoke to the guard in French, but his only acknowledgment of her words was a slight elevation of his eyebrows.

She marked the days on the floor of the room with a sharp dark splinter she had tugged loose from the wall. Seven mornings she watched the old man make his solemn obeisance to the sun and seven times she marked the floor while there was still light enough for her to count her own markings. When darkness had fallen on the seventh day she heard the door open suddenly. After being pulled from the floor by rough hands, a covering was thrown over her head and a hand clamped roughly over her mouth. As she was carried through the darkness she heard horses stamping quietly and the distant baying of wolves. Then, as suddenly as she had been seized, she was thrown to the ground, free of any restraint.

She tugged the covering from her head and stared around her. A single rude torch lit the room. A few yards away stood a tall thin white man, clad only in a brief fabric apron. His hair, dressed in a native queue, was snow white and hung nearly to his waist, and his eyes, studying her face, were a clear cold blue. In spite of his thinness, his face was ruggedly handsome. He watched her dispassionately as she struggled with the cloth which had been tugged away from her body when she was thrown on the ground. At last, seeming to have reached a difficult decision, he came toward her in curiously awkward steps and held out his hand to help her up.

"I am Paul Bontemps," he said quietly. "What do you want of me?"

"I came," she said quietly, "to try to obtain your freedom from this place."

He frowned. "On whose authority?" he asked. "You are a child in size and a woman of lewd reputation. You have come suspiciously far to seek a man who is unknown to you."

"Oh, but . . ." she began. Then, at his stern glance, her tone grew sober. "You are well known to me through your wife Sophie, your son Charles, and your brother-in-law, Antoine Rivière."

At each name she spoke his face underwent a change until, by the time she was through, he was staring at her with pained disbelief. Then he turned away. She heard him whisper her words, repeating them as if they formed a strange new incantation. "Sophie . . . Charles . . . Antoine."

"I am Antoine's wife."

A slow smile tugged at his mouth. "Antoine married? Oh, come now."

"With a child," she added resentfully. "A son who is a great boy by now." She thought of Etoile but remained silent of her.

"Sophie," he repeated softly. Turning away, he sank to a low stool where he sat silently for a long time, his eyes off into the darkness. "Tell me then of Sophie. Has she not wed? And the baby Charles."

Careful of her words at first but growing more free with each minute, Julie told him of Sophie's long faith, of the prosperity that had come to his plantation, of Charles being sent to France for his education.

"And Antoine?" he asked, still amused at the thought. "Tell

161

me about your husband Antoine. He was in England having all sorts of misadventures when I last heard of him. One of the men with you is surely Antoine."

"No," she admitted. "He was in Charles Town when I left. We had differences."

For the first time he chuckled softly and a brief amused light softened his blue eyes. "I would propose that it would take some hellish sort of a difference for a wife to plummet off into the wilderness with two other men."

"It was a hellish difference," Julie conceded. At his questioning glance she tried to put it into concise words. "He foolishly got himself deeply in debt to a woman who threatens to destroy both him and our son."

"There has to be more to it than that," he said. "Why would Antoine go into debt with a stranger if Sophie is doing so well with the plantation as you say? Debts can be paid," he added ruefully. "I should certainly know, having had my own freedom bought by Antoine himself."

"Sophie and Antoine do not agree on all things," Julie said carefully. "This was a private debt which its holder threatens to sell in France."

He eyed her thoughtfully. "And who in France wishes ill to Antoine? His father? His brother?"

"One or both," Julie replied. "But if Antoine were thrown into prison, our son and I would fall under the control of Emile in time, because Antoine's father is old and in failing health."

"And Emile? Has he grown to be the disgusting monster that his childhood promised?"

"I gather that he has," Julie replied quietly.

"You have seen me walk."

Julie nodded.

"Do you know that I am married?"

She nodded again.

"Her name is Techou," he said softly. "She is not only a woman of great grace but also of tender and wise spirit. When I came here as a slave from the Yamasee, she pleaded with her father that I be given to serve her. When we grew to know each other she begged his permission for us to be wed. Do you know what it means to be the mate of the daughter of the Sun?"

Julie shook her head.

"Among other things it means that at a word my wife Techou could have me murdered. Or at another and different

162

word she could divorce me with a simple expression of farewell."

"That is not all," he cautioned her. "She is also great with our second child. I know little of these things except that she has been very ill and the old ones who do know of such things are sure that both she and the child will die. When she dies, I go with her," he went on matter-of-factly. "I and her servants and her near friends and our child."

"No," Julie breathed softly. "That must not be."

He went on as if she had not spoken. "Techou has always been thoughtful about my capture and mutilation. She remembers the early days when I raged against my fate and suffered for my separation from Sophie and the boy. If she lives, Techou will most freely send me back to Sophie. She is that kind of a woman."

"She need not die," Julie said softly. "She must not die."

Paul stirred restlessly. "This brings the conversation back to you. Aside from myself and our daughter, there is one other living soul who loves Techou devotedly. She is an old woman, a meddler with an evil temper and a devious heart, but great power. She was a near relation—a sister, I think—of the woman called La Glorieuse. She is consumed with rage that another woman should be called by that honored name. She is blazing with fury that the simple people of her tribe repeat the stories of your healing and name you as the returned spirit of her dead relative. That old princess, whose name is Tattooed Arm, had you brought here tonight."

Julie stared at him in confusion. "But why? Why did she do that?"

"If it had not been that Techou is so terribly ill, Tattooed Arm would have had you killed by now. But she stands in mortal terror that Techou will die. She brought us together for me to give you a message."

"And the message?" Julie asked, trying without success to keep her voice level.

"She told me to remind you that if indeed you are the returned spirit of La Glorieuse, you will have it in your power to heal Techou and bring her safely to term. If you are not what you claim to be and Techou dies, you will be strangled by Tattooed Arm herself at the funeral service for Techou."

Julie sat quietly, weaving her fingers in her lap. She felt his glance on her, waiting. She was too tired. She was too exhausted by the long road behind her and the long journey ahead to be weighted with this unfair burden. Finally she raised her eyes to him with a sigh. "I have made no claims for myself," she told him dully. "I am no spirit but a simple woman trained in a few healing arts. Without her threats I would use all the skill I know to heal this woman you so obviously love. What else can I say?"

To her astonishment, his eyes were gentle on her and he was smiling, suddenly looking, in spite of his age and gauntness and the strangeness of his dress, a little like an older Charles.

"You need say no more, wife of Antoine. But you are more than you claim to be. You are a graceful beautiful young girl of unusual daring who has been caught in the deadly web of a strange and marvelous culture. Tell me, my dear, aside from La Nouvelle Glorieuse, what are you called?"

"Juliette," she said quietly.

"When I rise and tap at that door, two guards will come. Not even the Great Sun himself, who is the son of the Tattooed Arm, will know where you are from this moment on. You will be taken to the house I share with Techou and my child to care for my wife. You will be prisoner and healer, Juliette. And you will walk out of that house as free souls or as sacrifice to the dead."

Julie studied him thoughtfully, then nodded. "And what of my friends, my traveling companions?"

He looked at her strangely. "Ah yes, your friends. What was their motive in coming, Juliette?"

"Only that they are my friends," she told him. The Indian trader, Josh Simmons, first heard the Indian name for you—the PoBotahm—and guessed that it might be you. The other is my cousin Jacques DuBois."

He leaned forward. "DuBois?" he asked in a puzzled tone. "Is that the son of Yves DuBois of Charles Town?"

"In blood and name but not in spirit," she replied.

"I will try to get word to them of your safety and your whereabouts, along with a warning. Tattooed Arm is not a woman to try to deceive."

Chapter Thirty-Seven

The old princess known as Tatooed Arm walked along the wooded path, her bare feet gripping the earth she had walked for all these years.

"Is this then what it is to grow great with age?" she asked herself bitterly. She had not blamed her son the Great Sun for not heeding her warning. It was natural that a young man would prefer the counsel of other men over that of a woman. She had not been too surprised when the soldiers who slept with the girls from the White Apple Village had tossed away the girls' words of warning like they did their own trousers at the coming of the young Indian belles.

But she had also made harder and more dangerous efforts. It had been weeks since she had encountered a particular soldier on the open road.

"I have a message for your commandant," she told him in careful French. "Tell him that the Natchez have lost their minds and he must be on his guard. Tell him that the smallest repairs on the broken fences about the fort or the smallest show of strength would be enough to frighten the Natchez into abandoning their wild and bloody schemes."

It had been only a few days later that she learned through the gossip of the young women that the Commander Chopart had been thrown into a rage by the soldier's warning.

"You are a coward who sees an enemy in every bush," he railed at the young man.

She had even sent an unsigned message to the Lieutenant Commandant in hopes that he would have wit enough to hear her warning.

To no avail. To no avail.

And now the Month of the Bison was at hand. It was common talk that the French expected new settlers to arrive by ship in the Month of the Bison which they called November. She had seen the bundle of sticks grow smaller and smaller on the temple table and knew that with the loss of each stick the day of the attack grew nearer by one day. Her son had said that the other nations were rallying to attack the French posts on that same day.

There had been no course open to her but to steal a stave or two from the bundle in the temple while there were still enough that their number would not be missed. This way the Natchez would go into battle alone. There would be a chance for some of the French to escape and warn their fellows.

Why had this burden fallen on her who already had more concerns than her mind could hold? Her relative the White Apple Sun had launched a great search for the yellow-eyed woman who had been secreted from his own hut in the dead of night. It was of necessity a secret search, but his threats against the person who had interfered with his governing were terrible to hear.

It was for Techou that she had done this dangerous thing. Never mind that the woman's companions had grown frantic with concern for her. Never mind that the Sun himself groveled with embarrassment at his inability to manage his own village. The yellow-eyed woman tended Techou well and Techou had thrived from her nursing. Whether she was La Glorieuse returned in spirit or not mattered no longer. Techou's child was due in the Month of the Bear and each day that she survived increased her chances to live through the delivery.

Tattooed Arm only wished that in her haste to pull the staves secretly from the bundle in the temple she had taken time to count how many remained. It was soon. She walked with dread into every twilight wondering if the attack against the French would take place this day or the one following.

Chapter Thirty-Eight

Julie, wearing a costume of Limbourg cloth that Techou had provided from her own wardrobe, sat quietly watching Paul Bontemps in conversation with his Indian wife.

What a great love lay between the two of them. When her illness racked her with headaches that thundered like drums behind her eyes, Paul hobbled back and forth in a helpless rage against her anguish.

Paul interrupted Julie's reverie. "Techou has asked me to tell you that she grieves for your absence from your friends. She weeps that all our attempts to locate them have failed. She has decided that the Sun himself has them imprisoned in his quarters where only his most trusted warriors are admitted."

Julie nodded and smiled at Techou. "Please tell her that I understand, Paul. Tell her that I appreciate all the efforts she has made even though they have come to nothing."

"There is more," Paul went on quietly. "It is a belief of my wife that to use love is to damage it, but in this case she is finally driven to that course. She has asked me to send for her younger brother whose love she trusts. She says that even if they are being held in the quarters of the Sun, he can take a message to them and tell them that you are safe."

The long days had stretched into weeks. It was as if Josh and Jacques had disappeared from the earth that night they were withdrawn from the hut. Paul, who moved about the village freely, had seen or heard nothing. He had heard hints of a frantic secret search for the yellow-eyed woman which no one understood because no one in the village had ever seen her.

The brother came at twilight bearing gifts of food for his sister. He was a tall handsome youth of some twenty years. The scars on his cheeks and the tattoos on his arms showed that he had already gained much distinction in battle.

"He will tell your friends that you are well and where you are being hidden," Paul translated for her. "For now that will have to be enough. He knows the men well, having been charged with guarding them.

"I just don't understand it," Julie said with sudden frustration. "Why has the chief held them secretly? What have we done to have been made prisoners?

Paul shook his head. "There is some great mystery here, sister," he admitted at once. "I have watched the traders come and go all the years I have been here. *Les couriers du bois*, the natives call them. They welcome them as friends, heal their wounds, and flatter them with feast-giving. Techou says the same. She names it as a great mystery that the Sun has treated you and your friends so strangely.

"Paul Bontemps," Julie said quietly. "You are a man blessed by the love of fine women."

Paul grinned a little ruefully. "An embarrassment of fine women, I might say. But to Techou this brings no pain. Her own father had many wives and loved each in her own way."

167

Julie's mind went to Sophie, Sophie of the rich copper hair and flashing eyes, Sophie in laughter, Sophie at the head of the wide stairway with a bullwhip in her hand.

Paul watched her face and smiled a little. "Yes, Juliette," he said quietly. "I know. I know."

The tapping began very late, long after midnight but still before dawn. It was a slow careful drumming, like the feeding of a crested bird on tree bark. Listening from her pallet, Julie sat upright, troubled that the sound came and went as if whatever made it stopped to listen between beats.

When the tapping was replaced by a tune, a softly whistled melody, Julie gasped and flung the robe from her bed.

Paul's urgent whisper came from across the room. "What is it, Juliette?"

Her voice faltered as she struggled with a garment to cover herself. "Josh," she whispered. "It has to be Josh."

Pressing herself against the panel, she started to call out and then thought better of it. Catching her breath, she tried to whistle the same tune in reply, only to have her breath fail after a few tentative notes.

But it was enough. Instantly Josh was in the room, with Jacques close on his heels. Forgetting his companion and unheedful of who might be watching in the dark room, Josh took Julie into his arms, folding her close against his hard body, his face buried in her neck as he called softly. "Lady, Lady. My God, Lady."

When she was released, Jacques' embrace was no less fervent. Throughout this, Techou and her child watched with wide eyes from the darkness. Paul Bontemps, leaning against the post of the door, searched the two men with his eyes, waiting.

"Josh Simmons," Julie finally gasped, "Jacques Du-Bois...this is Paul Bontemps."

"But how is it that you are here?" Paul asked after taking the hand of each man in turn. "Did you elude your guards?"

Josh pulled his gaze from Julie's face to frown at Paul in a puzzled way. "They left. It made no sense to us either.

"And the old man," Jacques began, then stopped and corrected himself. "The Sun was gone from his room that adjoined our own. The place is empty, not a soul remains there."

Paul turned to his wife, speaking swiftly in their soft, fluid tongue. She smiled as if satisfied at his words. "The brave who brought word to you is my wife's brother." he explained. "She was happy that he was able to serve you."

"My wife suggests that we lay out robes to hide you in case a search is launched," Paul explained. "She herself will stand by the door to prevent anyone trying to enter."

"There is no one there," Jacques repeated quietly. "They have all gone."

Julie stood with one arm about Techou's waist as they stared into the silent darkness. Finally the veriest strand of color stirred the darkness in the east. Then another came and another until a vast skein of brightness wove across the sky. The cock crowed and his fellows answered, even as they had on her first dawn in the village. The light angled in at the door, brightening Techou's face with glowing color. Julie saw Paul's arm tighten about Techou as he looked down at her. Then, like an old man painfully mounting a difficult crest, the scarlet sun climbed over the trees that flanked the outskirts of White Apple Village and Techou's face paled with disbelief.

Without knowing her words, Julie understood her message to Paul.

He was not there. For the first morning in all the dawns of his life the White Apple Sun was not there to greet his brother sun at his rising.

Though they stood a long time waiting, no one came forth from the Sun's house or the temple. The cocks continued to cry morning and a yellow dog wandered across the plaza. Finally Paul, restless and confused, ventured forth to accost an old woman who had walked from her hut to settle herself in the sun.

"War," she cackled at him, her hand pointing to the west where St. Catherine's Creek curled about the Grand Village of the Natchez on the bluffs. Toward the Mississippi River where Fort Rosalie poised behind its ruined palisades.

"War against the French and Chopart," she cackled at him.

Chapter Thirty-Nine

The twenty-ninth day of November in the year 1729 dawned late as early-winter days were wont to do along the Mississippi. The sun rose leisurely through a sky streaked with bands of brilliant color.

Having slept in an unfamiliar bed and having imbibed perhaps a touch more wine than his head could take, Father Du Poisson wakened early. Stepping from his quarters at Fort Rosalie, he paused to contemplate the morning. Although his real work was as missionary to the Arkansas Indians, he had spent the night at Fort Rosalie and agreed to perform some parochial services there before resuming his journey south to New Orleans.

From the face of the Mississippi River a fine wavering steam rose, curling into the hollows below the bluff, swirling into spidery nests of trapped light. The strange birds of this country rattled among the rushes at the river's edge and a fish leaped, shone, and flopped again into the water. Father Du Poisson smiled. What better place to waken on the eve of the feast of a saint who had himself been a fisherman, a brother to St. Peter?

Later it was said that M. D'Etcheparre, commandant of Fort Rosalie, more commonly known as Chopart, was drunk even at this unseemly hour. This was a defamation. True, his head was swollen and painful from the drink and revelry of the night before and a certain uneasiness stirred in his belly from having eaten richer food than it had required. But there had been guests at the fort, the banker M. Kolly from Paris and his son, and the priest, Father Du Poisson from the Arkansas.

As a matter of fact, Chopart was feeling rather well in spite of his dissipation. He had handled the matter of the Natchez land with consummate skill. With the Month of the Bison drawing to a close, the corn should be dried and would soon be brought to the fort along with the promised fowls. Once he

170

was in possession of this tribute that the White Apple Village Sun had so foolishly offered, he would seize the villages according to plan.

When he glanced out his window, he did not at once notice that there were more Indians around the fort than usual. After all, they had been free to come and go as they pleased since the early days of the fort under M. De Bienville. And it was not as if they were all in a group. Some stopped at one house and others along the way.

When, within a few minutes, it did dawn on him that there were a great many Indians about, he realized the cause for this with some satisfaction. They were bearing corn. It was time for the tribute to be paid. In his pleasure at this thought he did not pause to ask himself why this debt was being paid so freely, without even the inconvenience of his own men being sent to collect.

Even as he preened himself on his cleverness in dealing with these worthless heathen people, he realized that the young man at his door, clad in the full regalia of his office, was that half-breed upstart that they called the Grand Sun.

It was tedious the way these people barged in and out as if they owned his own quarters. He had set down his coffee and risen to protest when he realized the Sun was not alone. Among those with him was a man bearing a handful of live fowl.

The man with the fowl was dressed in the manner of the stinkards, the lowest caste of these people. The fool extended the cackling birds toward Chopart with a wide smile on his face, that ingratiating grin that always set Chopart's teeth on edge.

"Get those goddamned chickens out of here," he shouted. "What in hell are you doing, carting your livestock into my quarters?"

"Tribute," the man replied quietly in French as he laid the thrashing chickens on the floor at his feet.

Chopart thought of the stench of the chicken shit lingering in his room. The carpet that covered the rough floor would be hopelessly stained.

"Jesus Christ," he shouted in a fury as he leaned over to seize the clattering chickens and throw them from the room.

It was at that moment that the stinkard reached inside his loose garment and withdrew a club. He struck the commandant across the head, killing him so quickly that, as Chopart

171

fell, his bleeding head was pillowed on the startled poultry who cackled with protest.

It was eight o'clock in the morning on the eve of St. Andrew.

There was no way for the French at Fort Rosalie to defend themselves. Even as the Grand Sun gave the signal the inhabitants of the settlement looked up to find tomahawks raised above their heads or heard the whistle of spears aimed at their heads.

The order from the Suns and their councils had been to destroy all the French who would not serve well as slaves or concubines. The orders were methodically fulfilled. The coopers at their staves and the clerks at their books were felled in like manner. Men and women were caught in flight. Women heavy with child were thrown to the earth. When the unborn babes had been torn from their mother's wombs, their heads were smashed and thrown to mix with the gore of their mothers.

M. la Loire de Surins, a former counsellor, was abroad from his home when the attack was begun. He spurred his horse into the fray and managed to kill four Indians before he himself was cut down.

The war cries and the shrieks of the dying created a din of horrifying confusion as three hundred lives were destroyed in the space of an hour or two. Only a few terrified young women and children were spared, to be herded into stockades to be dealt with later.

By the time the heavenly sun was high in the sky the stench of blood and death rose along the length of the bluffs. Plantation doors had been burst open and tillers in their fields watered their crops with their own blood.

Tattooed Arm had seen the warriors begin to pass toward the fort a little before dawn. Driven by her curiosity, she had followed to see the full horror of the attack.

She saw her son's handsome young face twisted in bloodlust as he moved among his warriors. She heard the sickening sound of human flesh being rented as the French soldiers were beheaded and their dripping heads arranged in a great ceremonial circle. The center of that circle had been reserved for Chopart. With his skull smashed, a black stain where the blood had leaked from his open mouth, his eyes bulged wide to stare at the proud triumph he had gained over the Natchez.

172

Tattooed Arm gripped her own elbows and moaned. Lost, all was lost. There would be warnings sent to the French downriver, she herself had seen to that by making certain that not all the tribes struck at once. But the village and the tribe of her childhood and youth were gone forever. Her son, who even now was leading his triumphant warriors to break into the stores of the fort and loot at will, would be harried from this day to his grave. She saw doom like a cloud moving across the sky of her people's future.

Among the French stores was brandy. Alone among the Indian nations, the Natchez were not drawn to drinking. They despised the wines that the French swilled like hogs at a creek bed. But the flavor of brandy was something they took to easily. With the stores of French brandy open to their taking, they passed the bottles among themselves gleefully, staggering until at last they slid on the slippery gore that filled the compound, falling to grovel in the thickening blood of their enemy.

Tattooed Arm turned away and plodded back to the deserted Grand Village. Kneeling on the floor of the temple whose shelves held the sacred bones of her ancestors, the great war chief Tattooed Serpent, the last Great Sun, and the Princess called La Glorieuse, a great pain came in her belly. She clutched herself and cried out, her breath fluttering the sacred flame which must never be allowed to die.

The dancing would begin and the revelry continue at the fort. The Frenchwomen would be raped and despoiled while the fort itself would be torched to flame, dropping the charred wood cinders into the face of the river below like a beacon.

She understood the pain in her belly. It was her own womb rebelling against her child. For it was sunset for the great Suns of the Natchez and the blame for this day must lie on the child she had borne from the seed of a Frenchman.

Chapter Forty

"This war at least explains our imprisonment," Josh pointed out. "If the French had discovered a six-horse pack train of fresh guns and ammunition coming into a Natchez village, all hopes of a surprise attack would be over."

"And surprise is the primary Natchez war weapon," Paul agreed.

Julie listened silently to their talk, her mind trying to reach from this talk of war to its consequence. She fed Techou and the child and dressed Techou's long, glowing hair. As Techou smiled gratefully at Julie, Julie leaned over and touched the Indian woman's cheek with a gentle hand. To Julie's surprise, Techou caught at her hand and pressed it to her lips. Julie felt a rush of hot tears across her wrist.

"Are you in pain?" she asked Techou with quick concern, kneeling at her side.

Paul, her ears always attuned to his wife, turned in time to see her nod, biting her lips to hold back her cries.

"She says that her heart is running away from her," Paul told Julie.

Frowning, Julie laid her head against Techou's breast. To be sure the girl's heart was hammering at an alarming rate. It seemed to Julie that Techou's body, usually so lithe and pliant, had stiffened.

"Come and comfort her," Julie told Paul. "I must brew a tea that will stay that racing of her heart."

Before the tea was even steeped, Techou seized Paul's hands in a painful grip. She cried out as she began to twist on the pallet. Her face twitched and her dark eyes rolled wildly from side to side. Josh was quick to join Paul in trying to hold the writhing girl on her sheets. The flesh of her face turned a strange blue and she gasped helplessly to control her tongue before the spasms began to subside. Once eased, Techou wilted under their hands to lie gasping, her eyes closed.

Paul raised stricken eyes to Julie's face, but she dared not meet his gaze. This was the convulsion she had fought all these weeks to prevent. Unless some miracle occurred, this would

174

be only one of a number of such attacks that would take her to death. The look on Julie's face brought Josh to her side. She smiled at him when what she earnestly desired was to turn to him, to lean against his leathery warmth and give in to her grief.

Techou still lay resting with her eyes closed when the scrape of a foot was heard at the door. Before Paul could cross the room, Techou's young brother appeared in the doorway, his chest heaving and his hair awry. His body was stained with blood and his eyes were white-rimmed with horror.

He was a man suddenly aged, Julie realized. His young eyes sought out his sister's face with an expression of glazed nausea. With a cry he knelt by her side and buried his head on her chest. Techou, roused from her lethargy, stroked his head and spoke to him gently in their own tongue.

Once his words began, they flowed in a torrent. Paul, his face stiff with disbelief, gaped as the recital continued.

"Good God, man," Josh finally pleaded. "Tell us what has happened."

Having no time to organize his shocked thoughts, the words fell from Paul's lips in the same hysterical way that he heard them from the young warrior. Julie felt her stomach heave as she groped for support. Jacques caught her, bracing her against his encircling arm.

It was Techou's voice that stilled them. Weakened as she was by the convulsion just past, her voice came even gentler than before. But the tone was one of absolute authority. For all the time that Julie had stayed with her as nurse and friend, Techou had spoken only in her native tongue. Now she suddenly spoke in a halting and accented French which Julie realized she must have learned from her childhood among these people.

"My brother knows where your horses are hidden," she said calmly. "My brother knows where there are food stores for your journey. My brother will lead you past the final village of our people toward the country of the Chickasaw— but it must be tonight."

Paul spring forward. "But my love, can you travel?"

Julie watched Techou's eyes go in tenderness from his eyes to his lips and back, like a caress.

"I will travel, PoBotahm," she said gently. "But only from here to the temple, to remain there. Your Glorieuse knows that I am dying. There must be an extra horse for PoBotahm," she said to her brother.

"My brother protests that you must stay and die with me since you are my husband." she smiled at Paul as she struggled upright and reached for her brother's hand. "*Attendez*," she told him fiercely. Then with her eyes only on Paul, she spoke a single Natchez word, loudly and firmly. Both men started at the word and Paul cried out in distress.

"No, Techou," he pleaded. "No."

She shook her head and turned to Julie. "I have divorced your brother PoBotahm," she said quietly. "In the sight of my brother and these witnesses, I have cut your brother off from our marriage and our bed. It is Natchez law. Now you must take him across the miles to his other wife."

But Paul was on his knees beside her pallet, clasping her to him, murmuring endearments in both her own tongue and in heartbroken French. Even as she clung to him, she denied him.

"You have heard me speak. I am no longer wife to you. Take your companions and your horses and be gone from my house."

The young brother hesitated, his eyes going to Techou and then to Paul in confusion. Then, jarred from his apathy by his sister's firm command, he left the room.

It was a long vigil waiting for the night. Techou, exhausted from her rally, slept with her hand in Paul's. The taper had been lit against the falling light when the cry was once again wrenched from Techou's throat.

This time the convulsion was mercifully swift. Her body writhed in anguish for only a moment or two before she lapsed into a sudden coma. Then, almost immediately, Julie felt the pulse stop in the girl's limp wrist.

Paul Bontemps did not really mean to go with them. He did not even realize what was happening as he was led from the house and helped onto his mount. He stared vaguely ahead like a man in a painful trance.

It was only when Techou's brother led Paul's horse from the clearing toward the place where the pack horses were loaded and waiting that Paul roused from his reverie.

"My child," he cried. "She must come too."

The young warrior laid his arm across the shoulder of the sober little girl and shook his head.

"She is no longer your child, PoBotahm. She is a princess of the Sun and will stay with her people."

*   *   *

As they rode out north from White Apple Village the flat bluff gave way to rolling hills. It was on a promontory of one such hill that the riders paused to look back at the red glow dominating the sky behind them.

Fort Rosalie was a giant torch, staining the night sky the color of blood.

As long as the soil gods smile on him and to Villico the god
that represented the thing. It was on a mountain, and it was
on a hill that the gods were—and my finally it did fall over
the mountains . . . I think I'm right.

For Willico was a giant tomb, standing the relief of the
robe of Ishtar.

Part 4

THE TRACE
1730

Chapter Forty-One

The crude map Josh drew showed a tangle of serpentine rivers. With his fire-reddened knife tip he drew the lines carefully on the small square of tanned leather.

"There's no way I can write the names out for you," he told them, "so you must remember the rivers' names from their shape. The long snake to the left is the Mississippi. That cross there at the top is north. The big winding river east of it only a few leagues away is called the Pearl."

He paused to stab a number of dark points beside the river called Pearl and drew a line to show where the Noxubee drained into it.

Jacques frowned intently at the sketch. "Then we are traveling in an expanse of land between those two rivers."

Josh nodded. "Those spots I made are the sites of Choctaw villages." As he spoke their names the Choctaw words sounded strangely the same to Julie's ears as the words of the Cherokees and the Natchez.

"Nanih Waiya," he intoned quietly, still marking the map. "Caffeetalaya, Scanapi, Loucfeata, Yanabi."

When he had finished the first map, he set it aside and laid his knife into the fire to heat it again.

"But if the Chickasaws are north of us, why can't we go directly there instead of winding through this enemy

Choctaw country?" Jacques argued, still studying the crude map.

"You got to have a trail to follow," Josh said quietly, touching the hot knife to the second square of leather. "Once you light off into this wilderness and leave the trails, you are the same as done for. These traces are not here by accident but for good reasons. They have to run high enough that you won't get drowned when the rains come like they do here in a great rushing river that would seem to wash away the world. They have to go over the safe cushions of the marshes where a misstep will plunge a man into a quagmire that will pull him to his grave. They have to cross creeks and rivers where they can be safely forded. A trace like this may look like a poor thing when you're traveling it, but what lies beside it is a helluva lot worse. And a week or two ought to get us past the worst of it."

"A week or two," Jacques laughed. "My God, that's no time at all. I don't see why you are going to the trouble to make all four of us maps."

Josh continued to pierce the leather with his knife. "For the selfsame reason that the stores will be divided up tonight into four packs . . . one for each horse. There's got to be food and water and ammunition on every pack horse equally."

"But my God," Jacques exploded. "There's no way we can split up and still travel, not with Julie." He would have added Paul but caught himself in time.

Josh sighed. "We don't aim to split up, Jacques. I am just saying that if we do get split up, we need to have a chance. And while we're at it, there's another thing to remember. If we get split into two pairs we got to agree what to do. The rule is that if you hear two guns fired, you don't look back. You just keep on traveling, fast and careful."

"We can't do that," Jacques protested. "Who is to know what two gunshots mean? It could mean nothing."

Josh nodded. "And if it means nothing then that pair will catch up in time and all's well. But if there has been trouble and both guns are emptied why should the other pair walk into a trap and lose all?"

Paul, who seldom emerged from his grieving silence, looked curiously at Josh. "Even when we arrive in Chickasaw country, how can we know we are safe?"

Josh grinned at Julie. "We travel on Lady's pass here. As friends of La Glorieuse, we will be under the protection of all the friends of White Eagle of the Cherokee . . . all the way home to the Carolinas."

180

"We weren't this careful on the way down," Jacques pointed out, rising to dampen the fire for the night.

"The Choctaws weren't on the warpath then," Josh reminded him mildly. "They are friends of the French at Fort Rosalie. My guess is that they won't take that scene at the fort without spilling a little blood on their own. If they aren't at war with the Chickasaw by now they will be soon."

As Julie rose, Josh looked at her thoughtfully. "I wish to God we had been able to find your other clothes, Lady. Not only is that cloth gown pretty weak garb for what we are going into, but it looks Natchez, not a healthy way to look for a good hundred and fifty miles."

"It will be a long time before we can hope for fresh horses from the Chickasaw," she told him reasonably. "Since Paul must ride and the passage goes slowly anyway, why not let me walk? That way we can rest one horse every day."

The great rain that thundered through the forest in the night soaked through even their leather covers. By the time the sun finally appeared in late afternoon the earth was a sponge under their feet and the creek that followed the trace was a roaring river.

They always moved in pairs, as Josh had insisted. When Jacques and Josh went out for game, Paul and Julie, with guns loaded at their sides, made camp.

Julie yearned to talk with Paul of the old times, of Sophie and Charles and Antoine. But the open, friendly man who had watched her tend his Natchez wife had retreated behind a face closed by grief.

They were long on the trail before Paul himself finally broached the subject to her. She was bending over the fire turning squabs on a spit. The rich scent of the broiling fowl filled the air and smoke billowed about her face, turned rosy from the heat.

Paul spoke suddenly from his post by the tree. "You are a remarkably beautiful woman, Juliette Rivière. Antoine might have chosen you for that alone."

Julie looked at him in surprise, then smiled, the dimple coming in her cheek. "That was very prettily said," she told him. "And since I came without dower, he must have chosen me for that reason alone. Is there another way?"

Paul nodded. "There are other reasons. If I were to choose you I think your beauty would be among the least of my reasons. But then I am older than Antoine. Older than anyone in the world I sometimes think."

181

"Surely Sophie's beauty was not among the least of your reasons for falling in love with her," Julie rebuked him. "Have you forgotten the magnificence of her hair, the way her eyes light up with mischief, and the quick fire of her wit?"

Paul rose and approached the fire in that careful hobbling gait. "I have not forgotten," he admitted soberly, bending to stare at the fire beside her. "I find myself more in fear that I have forgotten the Paul Bontemps who was captured all those years ago by the Yamasee. I am not the same man." A sudden anguish came into his voice. "I am a different man altogether, and it is not only Techou that I think of. My values are changed, all of them. What if this great adventure of yours shall have been in vain, Julie? What if the Sophie who has fathered my child and become the manager of a successful plantation and waited so patiently for my return does not love the man who comes back to her?"

"Impossible," Julie said hotly. "Love doesn't come and go like a summer storm."

"You say that because you have the same fears inside yourself," he told her. "You loved Antoine."

She turned on him. "I *love* Antoine," she contradicted him, mindful of the sudden flush that was added to the color that the fire had brought to her cheeks.

"But you left him," he reminded her. Then he leaned back. "This has been a strange journey, Sister. Both of your companions have talked to me of Antoine because I asked them to. The man they describe to me is a different man than I remember. To Josh, Antoine is some kind of a magician who has worked a spell on you in spite of his brutal mistreatment. To Jacques, he is a great selfish baby given to drunken rages and jealousy."

Paul smiled almost indulgently. "To me, Antoine has always been a little larger than life. Raging at injustice, frantically loyal to those he loves, given to wild dreams and schemes to fulfill his ends. You must know that when your father-in-law broke my betrothal vows to Sophie, when my own family let me be thrown into prison for gambling debts, it was Antoine, still practically a boy, who calmly stole money from his father to pay my release from prison and then helped smuggle Sophie and me out of the country." He nodded, smiling. "I see Antoine as all a man should be and a little more, larger than life."

His words evoked Antoine so vividly that Julie could not reply for a long moment. When she did, her voice was thick with emotion. "So he has seemed to me," she admitted, "so he has always seemed to me."

"Yet you left him," Paul reminded her quietly. "You left him to plunge into the wilderness with two men whom Antoine must surely loathe for the love they both bear you."

Julie nodded, smiling ruefully at the way he placed his case. Paul seldom touched her. She had sometimes thought that he made a conscious effort to avoid physical contact with her. Now, for no reason, he leaned close and laid his hand gently on her arm.

"Does it strike you, Sister, that you and your husband are cut in different patterns from the same piece of cloth? And until you find a way to join together, really join, not in name alone, you will both be hopeless tatters?"

She raised thoughtful eyes to him. It had not occurred to her that this adventure of hers was in any way like Antoine's acts to get Sophie and Paul together.

"May it be soon," she whispered with a crooked smile. "Please, God, may it be soon."

Chapter Forty-Two

Rain. Julie, sliding along the wet trail, her pony balking at puddles, his hooves sucking and sliding on the earth, felt as if the very sky was conspiring against their passage. With their leather cloaks pulled over their heads and tied with thongs at the neck, she and Josh and Jacques appeared like strange Oriental drawings of old men slogging through rice paddies.

Then Josh announced that they could light no fires.

"Good God, man," Jacques protested. "How can we rise to walk with every stitch wet and not even a warm cup in the belly."

"Look at your map," Josh explained. "We are too near the Choctaw villages now. Nanih Waiya is only a few miles from this place. We risk enough by staying on the path without sending a smoke signal to tell them of our passing."

On the third evening without a campfire, Josh, laying his hard biscuit and smoked meat aside, held up a cautioning hand.

The other men, tensed with listening, watched Josh's face. When the call came again, from a little to the left, Josh rose silently to his feet.

"Quick," he whispered. "While it could be nothing, we can't take chances. You, Jacques and Paul, mount and take your horses along the trail a ways. Withdraw into the trees and wait until we join you or you hear a signal from us."

The fresh horse dung breathed steam into the chill air as Julie covered it with wet leaves and debris. Then, her heart pounding, she followed Josh off into the near impenetrable woods. After tethering the horses a little way from the trail, he led her along the stream bank to where a cave, carved from the earth by violent waters, had formed in the overhang.

The space below the overhang was barely large enough for the two of them. Only by curling inside the circle of Josh's arms could they fit into that concealing darkness. A steady drip of rain fell in a sheet from the grasses that crowned the embankment, shutting off the outside world with a flowing curtain.

"The accommodations aren't first rate," Josh whispered against her hair, "but I sure do appreciate the company."

"I'm not complaining either," Julie whispered, grateful for the warmth of his body close to her own.

The owl cry came again, only to be echoed as before. When it sounded the third time it was farther away, along the path that Jacques and Paul had taken.

"I hope to God they had wit enough to hide," Josh breathed. "Jacques should know enough by now."

"It could be only birds," Julie reminded him.

"That was a Choctaw scout," he said.

She heard the approach from many yards away. Julie cringed in Josh's arms as the sound grew nearer, heavy ponderous steps as if the walker were crashing through the woods unheedful of overhanging branches and tangled underbrush. Josh moved free of her to bring his gun into firing position, pressing her abruptly against the hard wet earth behind her.

When the massive dark shape emerged from the wood to approach the stream, Julie felt Josh's muscles relax. "Bear," he whispered. "Stay very still."

The beast rolled towards the stream on all four feet, paused at the water's edge, and stared upstream, pensive. When he had drunk, he sat back and clasped himself with his huge hairy arms to scratch. The scrape of the long yellow claws on his flesh grated on Julie's ears. With his vermin thoroughly attacked, the bear drank again, sloshing great quantities of water about on his tongue. Then he turned the swaying mound of his round back toward them and the whinny of the pony sounded from the woods beyond.

"Jesus," Josh whispered softly.

The bear turned and stared at the woods where the horses were tethered. Cocking his head as if in sober thought, he wheeled about and changed his course to cross the stream less than five feet from where they lay hidden. His weight, passing through the stream, sent small waves lapping up into their caves to puddle about their legs. Then he was gone into the brush.

Josh stirred swiftly from her side. "Wait here, Lady," he whispered urgently. "Don't move out of here for nothing. I'll be back, you just wait." He started to leave with his gun on his arm and his knife at his waist.

"No," she whispered urgently. "We stay together. You said so."

"Not this time," he shook his head. "Don't you move from this place no matter what. I'll be back." His tone turned coaxing. "Come on, Lady, do as I say. I always come back, you know that."

He stepped off into the woods in the direction that the bear had taken. Within moments she understood his haste. The scream of the horse rent the quiet night as his companion neighed and whinnied in distress. Julie realized that any scout within ten miles would hear that din which grew steadily louder from the rough bellowing of the bear.

The sound of Josh's gunfire swept her into action. A man alone against a bear would have no time to reload. She knew the slender knife at his waist was no match for the raking claws of that giant. With her own gun loaded at her hip, she followed the sounds into the forest.

She was trembling so wildly that when she sank to her knees she had to brace the gun against the trunk of a tree to hold it steady. There, against the wet bark, she raised the gun into firing position and tried to train it on the weaving animal.

Even as she moved the barrel of the gun back and forth trying to keep the skull of the animal in her sights, she saw the other man. He was crouched as she was at the other side of the clearing, watching the mortal combat. In the dim light she

185

could not make out the features of his face, only that a pair of feathers rose from the crown of his head and that his own gun was trained on the clearing.

The screams of the injured horse tore through her as she watched the scene before her. The bear, blinded by pain and still gushing blood, was beginning to weave unsteadily. Even as she watched, it reeled toward Josh, forcing him to step back toward the spot where the Indian was waiting.

She barely stifled a scream as Josh danced aside to avoid the falling beast. But even as the animal fell, she saw the Indian lay his gun aside and leap on Josh's back.

There was no time or way to warn him. Josh's knife flashed as they grappled in combat. The Choctaw was a taller man than Josh and heavier of build. She saw the knife drop as the Indian twisted it free of Josh's grasp. Then she saw the man stoop a little, catch Josh in his arms and throw him across the clearing to land, crumpled and unconscious, against a tree.

The Indian, after staring at Josh a moment, picked up Josh's knife and raised it above his head as he approached Josh's body.

Julie, sighting carefully along the barrel of the gun, fired.

The blast, so near her head, deafened her and momentarily distorted time. She saw the Indian's arms rise as if in a mute skyward appeal. She saw the knife describe a graceful arc as it flew from his hand. She saw him crumple and go down gracefully like a woman kneeling into her skirts.

She waited a long time, until the blast of the gun ceased to echo and re-echo through the trees. Until the horse, bled white by its wounds, finally twitched into silence. She listened for the cry of the owl lest another warrior be close.

When no one came she began to slip carefully from tree to tree, circling the area where the Indian and the animals lay in their blood.

Loosening Josh's jacket, she slid her hand in to rest on his chest. Warm, and his heart was beating. She could not lift him but she could drag him, a few feet at a time, from the clearing into the woods beyond. His eyes were closed and he did not move but he was still alive. After what seemed a very long time she managed to drag him over the branches and stones and dirt to the cave by the stream's edge.

The hardest part of all was going back to the clearing. Once there, she loosed the packs from the dead pony and found Josh's knife in the leaves where it had fallen from the Choctaw's hand. With the pack safely stowed in the cave, she

186

retraced her steps for the last time, ruefully conscious of how much she had learned from Josh. Moving carefully backward from the clearing, she removed all sign of her passing, throwing mud and dirt on the torn places in the earth where she had dragged Josh's body.

Only when she had done all that she could to conceal her passage did she crawl exhausted back into the cave with Josh. She found him as she had left him, his head back against the wet earthen wall, his hands limp in his lap.

In that dim light she could hardly make out his features, yet her love for him overpowered her. Bracing herself so that she did not press her weight against him, she laid her lips on his in a gentle caress. He did not move but she imagined that his lips stirred under hers.

She had barely pulled her lips away when she heard his sigh. His smile was more an effort than an expression of pleasure and his tone was strangely languid as he said, "Lady, I do despair of even teaching you the first thing about obedience. You just plain have no knack for following instructions."

A little before dawn the Choctaws came to the clearing in the woods behind them. Josh listened intently to their exchange of astonished and angry words. Only when the sounds of their departure were all the way gone did Josh speak.

"They will track the other horse," he said dully. "They decided that whoever shot their brother left on the horse whose trail they had seen in the woods."

She felt her chest tighten with fear. "What of Jacques and Paul?" she asked. "My God, what if they search the woods and find them."

"They should be miles from here by now," Josh reminded her quietly. "When they heard that second shot they were to travel fast and far."

Not understanding the concern behind his words she laid her hand along his face. "They'll get away then," she reassured him. "You said yourself that we are not that far from the Chickasaw boundary."

His glance on her face was half amused. "But what about you, Lady? Have you thought about yourself?"

She grinned at him as bravely as she could. "We are just back where we were all those years ago, Josh. There are just the two of us on the long trail toward the Carolinas."

His response was a rueful grin. "Not just the same," he

corrected her. "You had a horse that time, if you remember, a horse you were kicking along. This time I got the kicking from the horse I cut free." He pulled up a little on her arms. "Here, help me peel this leather off my leg, Lady. I feel like my whole damned knee is nothing but a nest of splinters in there under my pants."

Chapter Forty-Three

"A nest of splinters" Josh had called his knee.

With Josh's leg laid bare in the first light of dawn, Julie studied the stained and distorted tissue that had been his sturdy muscular leg. She could feel his eye on her, waiting. She steeled herself not to betray the panic she felt at the way the splintered bone had pierced the skin, the patterning of bruised tissue where the bones nudged under the skin.

"That needs setting on a board, wouldn't you say?" he asked quietly.

She nodded and thoughtfully raised her eyes to him. "First the wound needs to be made clean," she decided aloud. "What about whiskey?"

Josh laughed. "That's a woman's way if I ever heard it. They can think of a million things to do with good whiskey without even mentioning pouring it down a man's throat."

Julie grinned at him. "I was thinking of doing a little of that, too," she admitted.

While Julie cleaned the leg with careful drops of Josh's precious whiskey, he kept his eye on her face. "Now don't tell me that doesn't hurt," she said, her voice betraying the anguish she felt at his pain.

"I've had it said of me all my life that I had a hollow leg for booze," he told her with a grin. "But if it feels like that to fill the damned thing, I'll go stone dry."

"We can't stay here too long," she told him. "The wet and cold will get to you even if the river doesn't flood in. But I hate to think of dragging you again with that leg."

"I couldn't walk," he answered. "But I might be able to hop along slow if you could stand to bear my weight."

"To where?" she asked.

"It has to be drier like you said," he answered thoughtfully. "Close to water and if possible overlooking the Trace."

"Is this Choctaw country all the way?" she asked wistfully.

He nodded his head. "But if we could get north of here even a few miles, we would be out of their regular scouting range. It would still be too far for Chickasaws to come except in a hunting party, but we'd have fewer brushes with the Choctaw by a good deal."

"It's up to you to tell me when you are ready," she told him.

There was no view of the road from the cave and through the long day that followed Julie and Josh lived in a world that came only through their ears or fell onto the surface of the river. Freshened by the rains, the forest wakened to vibrant life. Birds visited their stream and they watched the busy traffic of fishes feeding on the insects floating on fallen grasses in the swollen creek.

"I've made a decision," Josh told her softly. "I'll be ready to travel at nightfall. Not full dark, but just after the sun sets."

With his leg braced to a branch, a process that brought white lines of pain to his face, and hobbling on a stout forked stick for a crutch, Julie helped him in a slow pilgrimage across the trail and into a wide grassy meadow.

Josh had said that they would both know the place when they saw it and they did. A grove of fine old trees grew right to the meadow's edge. One of the clusters had grown so closely together that the young trees had stifled the life from the parent tree in the center. Into that open space the years had dropped dead branches and leaf litter until it was like a well, or a nest needing only to be cleared of the wood and refuse.

Josh never let a day pass without heaving himself erect on his crutches to circle the small world, sweating and cursing silently as he moved. Julie felt that she could see the flesh fall from his bones as they carefully rationed first the meat, then the hard bread, and finally the dried fruits they had borne from the Natchez village.

But the wound healed over. They spent whole days playing cards in the meadow, warmed by the sun of early spring. Julie sat cross-legged like an Indian while Josh lay at full length, his head on one hand while he taught her the fine art of never losing a hand unless you wanted to.

All notions of real time slipped away. There was nothing in their world except the trees and the high meadow. The world turned on Julie catching the first red strawberries before the birds beat her to them, on pulling the wild onions before the flavor grew too rank to swallow in spite of their hunger. Julie could not look back on her life with Antoine or think of her son. Tomorrow became a meaningless word suggesting useless dreams.

So it was that they ate bitter wild acorns together and laughed together and spent long nights wound in each other's arms. Even the possibility that she should conceive a child by Josh did not trouble Julie. This was a world of hours and days, the sparse meal lovingly shared.

Then, unaccountably, the heat came to Josh's leg and the area around the wound grew fiery red.

"This is wild," he told her when Julie felt his flaming flesh against her own bare calves. "I feel only a little more pain than I did before and yet, my God, it feels hot, hotter than any flesh in my body."

Fresh cold water from the stream laid on with careful hands not only chilled the leg, but turned it ice cold, a cold that would not be warmed even when the wrappings were removed and Julie placed her warm hands on the old healed wound. Instead the flesh shone with a faint bluish tinge that even looked cold.

Then, as Julie carefully bathed the leg with a fresh cloth a sudden rank stench filled the air and the flesh came off in her hands, exposing the rottenness of the tissue underneath.

"Jesus Christ," Josh whispered, staring at it with loathing.

Julie raised her eyes to his with a stricken look. For one long moment his face held only revulsion, then she saw his mouth twist into a determined smile and he began to laugh.

"Look at that, Lady," he shouted. "Do you know what that means? I am rotten and am dying from the inside." Then with his hands on her arms, he spoke firmly, almost threateningly, in that soft voice which had never been raised in anger at her. "Laugh with me, Lady." he said. "Come on and be a sport and laugh with me. This is funny, Lady, nothing but funny. Look at me...Josh Simmons, gambler, Indian trader, trapper, warrior, and adventurer. How does such a man die? From the inside, Lady. He gets kicked by a horse he is trying to help and rots from the inside out. Laugh with me, Lady. Laugh."

The laughter she finally summoned was a gift of her hysteria. The tears that came with the laughter streamed down both their faces and made their lips salty as they met in embrace after embrace. But when his own breath grew normal again, she pulled a little away from him.

190

"You don't have to die, Josh," she whispered. "We both know how you can be saved."

He shook his head and pulled her back into his arms. "Even if it worked it wouldn't be any good, Lady," he told her sensibly enough. "We can't last here with no proper food until the stump heals, and if we did how could a one-legged, one-eyed man and a half-teacup of girl make it through these woods to safety? Not on your life, Lady, not on my life."

"But Josh," she whispered, "I love you. I need you."

"Love me, yes," he agreed, stroking her hair. "Need me, yes. But you need the whole me, not what would be left after you tried what you are suggesting. We have no axe, no saw. I've seen that job done and I made myself a promise about it. I failed you, Lady," he finished quietly. "God knows that was not my intent."

When they had come to that meadow it had been yellow and sere from winter. Now there was a thrust of green at the roots of the matted tufts of dry grass. The masses of strawberries that crawled and tendrilled along the banks had more berries now than either she or the birds could use.

The last of the lazy geese were going north. They passed in great changing patterns of strident sound. The air smelt of hidden flowers coming to new life and the meadow birds were arguing strands for their nesting.

She smelled the stench of Josh's wound before she could even see his face. He smiled at her when she knelt and put her arms around him, but his words made no sense to her.

He told her that the fields needed plowing and begged her not to disgrace him. He called for his mother and told her that the gray hen's chicks were beginning to hatch. He chanted whole sections of the Mass in careful Latin as if it had been yesterday that he had last knelt in a church. But most of all, he called her name over and over with the warmth of a man who speaks a loved word. "Lady, Lady, Lady."

The strawberries she had gathered dried to clusters of seeds caught in small shriveled cups of green. The water was gone from the leather bag that she used to fill twice each day from the river, but she did not move from his side until the gray dawn when she realized that he had grown cold in the night beside her.

Her mind behaved strangely. There was something she needed to do but could not think what it was. The song came into her head and she hummed it happily as she stared at him

191

trying to make her mind work. But his face kept changing. He became the dwarf Titus curled in death by the hearth in Epping. He was her child Etoile gasping into silence with a face yellowed by fever.

Cold. They were all cold.

The robe that Moon Gift had made her was in the pack. She laid it gently over his coldness and the reeking stench that dizzied her head. Still singing, she knelt and kissed his lips, which felt like a smooth polished stone. Then she pulled the robe all the way up so that it covered that gentle mouth, that single eye, and walked away.

Chapter Forty-Four

On the tenth day of April 1730 two men on Indian ponies reached the cluster of birches that marked the border of the DuBois land.

Jacques DuBois stopped his horse to wait for his white-haired companion to come abreast.

"We should have gone back for them," Paul Bontemps repeated dully for the thousandth time since they mounted their horses on the Natchez Trace and rode north into the Chickasaw country.

"It was a solemn pact between Josh and me," Jacques reminded him quietly. "I had failed Josh too many times to do it that time too."

Jacques shrugged and slapped the pony on its flank. "She was the only woman I have ever loved in my life," he said quietly. "I would have died for her."

"She knew that," Paul replied. "Now the least you can do is live fully for her."

The door swung open at Paul's knock and he faced the white-haired woman who stared at him numbly. Her face broke slowly like the ice of a well-frozen pond, shattering from smooth control to helpless joy and relief. "Oh God!" she cried. "Jacques, it is you. My son, my son . . ." Then she paled. Her eyes swung to the tall slender man who approached with a strange crippled gait. She grabbed at Jacques' coat beseechingly.

Before she could ask he caught her in his arms and let her cling to him, trying to warm them both of the coldness that would come with his words.

"Maman," he said quietly. "Three of us left and we two have returned. May I present our neighbor and friend, Paul Bontemps?"

Chapter Forty-Five

The Choctaw scout named Chish-Ko heard the strange sound for many minutes before he could locate its source. It came variously, high and strong at first, then faint and wavering as if borne on a distant wind. Because it was a strange sound and because he was a man much in awe of mysteries, he moved slowly through the thick brush toward the road. What if this was some kind of ruse, a demonic Chickasaw trick to get a man to expose himself to enemy arrows?

Even after he saw where the sound was coming from, he was scarcely less mystified. From the long hair he judged her to be a woman, but if so she was scarcely larger than a healthy child. Although the trail was narrow she wove back and forth as if performing some strange dance or—he pondered this for only a minute—as if her eyes were blinded from drink.

And she was singing. The low sweet melody seemed to have no words, only a strange tune that rose and fell, repeating the same series of notes again and again.

The style of the woman's dress was Natchez, but her hair, which hung in tangled disarray to her waist, was crimped and coiling like the Frenchwomen at the settlement.

She was singing and she was dancing. He saw her graceful thin arms rise as she skipped a little like a child at play.

He watched her along the road, sometimes following and sometimes hurrying ahead that he might watch her approach. Her eyes seemed pale from this distance and sometimes he drew back in haste, thinking that she had looked directly at him through the cover of the trees. But her eyes betrayed no sign that she saw him.

With every step she took she was drawing nearer the point where some Chickasaw hunter might be watching, waiting for him to expose himself to a sneak attack. The long-standing strife that had existed between his people and the Chickasaws had flamed into the fiercest warfare in the month just past.

After the Natchez had massacred the French at Fort Rosalie, the French had taken swift and murderous steps for revenge. French soldiers led by Captain Le Sieur had led fifteen hundred Choctaw warriors on a surprise attack on the Indians still holding Fort Rosalie. It galled Chish-Ko to remember that this great force had been unable to dislodge the Natchez and had succeeded only in rescuing some twenty Frenchwomen from the people of the Sun.

After the next attack failed and a truce had finally been signed, the Natchez neglected to keep even that, slipping off in the night to make new settlements west of the Mississippi.

And all this while the Chickasaws had provided arms and warriors and refuge to the Choctaw enemies, the Natchez. When there was such hatred between tribes no death was too small. Look how some Chickasaw brave had murdered a scout only a few months ago, leaving him in a clearing with a dead horse and bear as if to suggest that the bear had killed the brave. But no bear could shoot a man in the head. Perhaps that death had begun like this, with a simple ruse of a woman singing on the open Trace. Even if they had muddled her head with drink, it was still a strange trick as long as white women brought such fine prices on the Spanish slave market. That is, of course, if they were not larded like winter bear.

He had followed her at least a mile along the trail when the sun began to set. Her steps were slower and once in a while the song faded to nothing and she walked along stiffly, as if in grief. Just as the last scarlet of the sun's setting glowed above the trees he saw her stagger and fall. When she tried to rise she got all the way up only to stagger and fall again. After that she lay on her face, unmoving in the trail.

The moon rose, turning the woman's clothing to a silvery gray. The moon was moving toward a patch of thick cloud. When it moved into that darkness, he moved with the speed for which his name had been sung in all the villages of the Choctaw.

He had the woman in his arms and was back into the woods before an arrow could be struck from a bow. He stopped, panting, to examine his prey. There was no scent of rum about her. She breathed like a person after a long fast. She was lighter than any human being he had ever lifted and she was fair of face.

Shrugging, he started back across the forest toward his village, carrying her across his shoulders as he would a fresh-killed fawn.

She knew it was a dream because she rose to it with the exhausted heaviness of unhealthy sleep. It was an astonishingly evil dream. The girl, writhing on the pallet, struggled painfully to waken but all her senses were in league against her. The dream filled her eyes and her ears and even her nostrils with its intensity.

The woman in the dream seemed to be Indian but her face was of such astonishing ugliness that the girl could not credit her own mind with its invention. Her head was flattened at the forehead, ending in a small, wizened face that was stained to a most ferocious aspect. Acrid smoke from old fires had darkened the walls of the room and the smell of the smoke started a slow rhythmic retching in the back of her throat.

But could one dream with eyes open? she asked herself, suddenly afraid.

She stared more closely at the figure squatting before the open fire in the middle of the room. This was a woman of great age whose blackened face seemed darker in contrast to the white strands of her knotted-up hair. She watched the old crone rock from one side to the other, grumbling to herself before hitching herself over to dip something from the pot with a long-handled gourd.

When the bowl was filled, the old woman braced herself with one hand on her knee to rear herself erect. There was no benevolence in her face nor any malice. She was simply a hideous old woman who seemed plagued by a painful aching in her joints. She carried the bowl of hot liquid carefully between the gnarled fingers of both hands.

As she drew near she stepped to peer into the girl's face. As she stared back, the girl saw the old woman's eyes widen and her mouth go slack. Then the old crone dropped the bowl with a shriek, and turned to flee from the room, gibbering something that the girl did not understand.

The spilled broth blazed along the girl's legs and belly. She cried out from the pain, reaching down to push away the cover which held the steaming liquid against her skin. When she found her strength unequal to this task, she sank back with a moan, tears smarting behind her eyes and a dull steady ache beginning in her head.

With her eyes closed she did not hear the man enter the room. He spoke quietly in a bastard French so heavily accented that at first she did not realize what language he was speaking.

"Mademoiselle," he repeated again and again.

She stared at him as he knelt beside her and lifted his dark hand to trace a gentle line from her throat toward her breast.

When she started to cry out, his hand covered her mouth swiftly. "Silence," he ordered gruffly. As her eyes widened under his hand and she struggled to pull free of him she saw his face darken with a sudden rage. She did not understand the word he hissed at her but his blow across her face was sufficient to bring a cry of pain to her lips. He rose and left the room in quick angry steps, without a backward look.

The old woman returned, wearing a chastened look. She dipped out the broth as she had before, this time keeping her eyes on the girl all the while. She stood a long time by the bed, spooning the broth into the air to cool it before extending the bowl with both hands.

Her order to drink was a single word that the girl did not understand. But she understood the sudden cramping in her belly as the smell of the broth filled the air about her. She lifted the bowl to her lips with trembling eagerness, not even caring that the liquid left a seared path through her throat as she drank. The old woman watched her soberly as the girl pulled the bowl from her lips and smiled her thanks.

The smile came slowly to the old crone's face but when it had come all the way, the woman was transformed. It seemed that every line in the ancient face had become a part of her good humor. Only a few scattered teeth ornamented the woman's mouth but a startling red tongue darted in and out as she nodded at the girl as if in an excess of happiness.

"She has nursed you like a babe," the man's voice spoke from the doorway. "When others would have let you die of hunger, she forced your lips apart and made you eat."

It was the same Indian man, speaking in that same miserable patois, but his manner was different.

"Tell her I thank her very much," the girl said humbly. "Thank her for her care of me."

At the sound of her voice the man's mood turned suddenly sour again. "She would have done the same for a dog or a cat," he said roughly. "She is weak in the head on such things."

Chapter Forty-Six

Chish-Ko flung himself from the cabin of his mother for what must have been the twentieth time in the past weeks. That bitch of a white squaw that he had carried home from the trail inflamed him with a fury he could not contain. He would not have given her one chance in ten even to survive, much less make his own life miserable. But his old mother seized the girl as a challenge, as she always had with the weak of the village. The old woman's passion for blowing the smallest flicker of warmth into the glowing life had certainly been fulfilled with this girl who had gained enough strength to walk about the cabin and smile with tenderness at the old woman.

But the girl's warmth seemed wholly reserved for the old woman. As he watched her body ripen into soft appealing curves and saw her thin face round to fullness, Chish found himself fighting a raging inner battle. She had only to draw near him and raise her strange yellow eyes to his face to bring a great clutch of animal hunger to his loins. He wanted to seize her roughly and at the same time have her slide in trustingly against him as a proper young squaw should do.

But she was insane. The yellow eyes that had startled his mother into such panic hid a head emptied of wit. What he first had thought was drunkenness as she reeled and danced along the Trace singing and gesturing, had been only the raving of a maddened mind.

Unless. With a gesture of irritation he thrust the thought from his mind. She could not possibly be possessed of evil spirits as the old people of the village whispered. She could not be La Glorieuse of whom the songs had been sung for so long. She was as small and weak as a hare frozen in the bush. She went from quiet sleep to a patient, smiling waking, watching his mother go about her work and greeting his advances with a blank wall of rejection.

The Glorieuse of song had been a noblewoman of the Natchez who had consorted freely with the French. This girl's French was halting and she only looked confused when he spoke to her in the words of the Natchez. Even in her childish

French, she was not quick and voluble, but tended to meet his questions with a look of bewilderment and the same sad phrase, *"Je ne sais quoi."* I do not know.

How could she know so little? She no longer sang that strange sweet song or threw her body about in childish dancing, but she answered his questions like a creature with no memory.

"What is your name?" he had asked.

"Je ne sais quoi."

"Where did you come from?"

"I do not know."

"Who are your friends? Where were you going?" All questions yielded the same quiet answer.

He fought to keep himself from seizing her and trying to choke the words from her mouth. She could not see his strained control but only the fury that resulted from it. When she withdrew from him, his own mother, seeing the terror in those golden eyes, shouted at him in their own language and bade him begone from her.

But the others in the village did not defend the yellow-eyed woman.

The shaman's eyes were hard on Chish in warning. "You have brought an evil spirit into this village," he said dourly. "It is a sleeping evil that will waken to disaster."

"A child-woman like that?" Chish scoffed at him. "A creature I can carry at a run without drawing a hard breath?"

"You know the stories as well as I," the shaman reminded him. "You know that such a yellow-eyed witch traveled all the way from the land of the Cherokee to the White Apple Village of the Natchez and then disappeared."

He waited with his eyes on Chish's face.

"So what of that story?" Chish countered.

"Did not the Natchez go wild with fury and attack the French? Where are the people of the Sun now, cursed be their spirits?"

Chish did not want to listen to the old man's harangue but even as he walked away the words battered at his understanding.

"Gone. Gone. Gone," the old man shouted after him. "The Great Sun is in chains. Tattooed Arm is a slave in New Orleans. The generations of the Natchez are bones being picked by dogs and buzzards—gone, gone, gone."

He went quietly into his mother's house to stand and watch the girl sleeping. He thought that with such a woman in his own cabin a warrior would be so great that the dances in his honor would never cease.

But when he laid his hands on her, even with gentleness, she drew away. When his mother was absent from her cabin he sat a long time watching her. When he could withhold himself no longer he drew his hand tenderly along the smooth curving line that led from her warm round breasts to her waist. Her skin was softer than the fur of any animal. He felt her stiffen beneath his touch as her eyes opened and she looked up at him. It was then that she asked the first question that had passed her lips in his hearing.

"What do you want of me?" she asked in that halting French.

He had flushed like an untried brave. Mad. What does a man want of a woman. His discomfort turned to swift anger.

"I want nothing of you," he told her brusquely. "I want you."

She had stared at him without smiling and turned her head away.

"I am here," she said simply.

He had glanced at the door, wondering when his mother might return. The thought of the smooth skin between those shapely thighs, the moist warmth within that small body, filled him with a raging passion. Pushing her garment away, he stroked her smooth belly as he loosened his own clothes. But even as he pulled the silken legs apart for entry she turned and looked up full into his face. The tenseness was gone from her muscles. She looked at him without expression, calmly, without interest. He felt the ebbing of his passion begin like a sickness in his loins.

"Not like that," he said bitterly, rising and walking away. "I don't want you like that."

If she had been the host of an evil spirit she could have owned him at that moment. She had only to smile or raise her arms to loop about his neck or stir her body toward his embrace and she would have owned him completely. But she had been the ice of winter without even the lusty combat of storm.

Before the coming of the white squaw Chish had lived with an untroubled mind. Now he found himself wishing to be let alone, to have his tobacco in his own company, to shelter his own thoughts in silence. Before the white squaw came a certain maiden of the village, a girl of nearly sixteen years, had often come to squat silently by him and smile when he

199

glanced her way. She was fair enough with an unmarked skin and her eyes were dark and languishing. He had often thought that he might make a marriage with her for she seemed gentle and affectionate and soft of tongue.

Now when she came to sit by him he wished she would go and stay at some other place. When he glanced at her she no longer smiled. Her face showed disapproval and her eyes were hard with resentment.

"Why do you stay by me if you do not like me?" he asked her crossly.

"It is not you that I dislike but that yellow-eyed Glorieuse that your mother serves as if she herself was a slave."

"The woman has been ill."

"All these weeks?" the girl challenged. "If she were such as I she would have risen and gone to the fields by now. She would bear water and rub the skins from the hominy as a woman should."

"She is not of our people," he reminded her.

The girl's dark eyes snapped at him and her voice hissed angrily. "Why do you keep her? She is maddened by evil spirits that threaten our village." She waved her arms toward the fenced enclosure where the captured prisoners of war milled behind the stockade. "She belongs in there, among the others who will be sold as slaves."

He turned away from her voice. "What business is it of yours where she stays? Why would the Spanish wish to buy a mad woman, as you say she is?"

She laughed. "The Spanish do not buy women for their cleverness of speech or wit. They buy them to warm their beds and wash their clothing. For the price of such a woman as that you could do much trading."

When he shouted angrily at her, she rose and stood to stare up at him. She was fair. He could not deny that she was fair even though her tongue was not so gentle as he had thought. As she stood there before him with her high round breasts trembling with passion and her dark eyes snapping, he was tempted to smile. Such fire as hers would indeed warm a man's bed. His mind slid to the energy of that firm young body in lovemaking, the feel of her jet black hair twisted in his hands.

"Mark my words," she hissed at him. "She will bring evil to this village and it will be your own fault. The madness behind her yellow eyes is seeping into your own mind like sickness into an old well. Get rid of her. Send her with the other slaves to market. Get rid of the yellow-eyed witch."

He turned and walked away, leaving her to stare after him. He had been dreading the long hunt he was soon to leave on. Now he wished it was nearer. He needed to be free of this village and the voices of women and shamen. He needed to be where the knowledge of that fair warm body did not press on him hourly as he moved through his day.

It was three days' travel to the land where the deer herds were feeding. The second night they made camp a buffalo was shot for potage. In the late afternoon as he and the others dressed the deer meat and waited for the food to be ready, they heard a low whine as the sky began to darken to the west and south of them. Even as they watched, coils of darkness spun across the sky, plucking now and again toward the earth like pinching fingers.

Prostrate on the ground, they watched the furious storm pass. It was followed by rain that lashed like the whips of a thousand devils. The deer floated in the sea of mire and their guns became useless without dry powder to load them. Even when they had finished dressing the meat and packed for travel, they were still a full two days of march from the village.

Word came from scouts the first day. The dark swirling from the sky had swept through three villages of their people. The bones of ancestors had been torn from the mounds and thrown about like refuse for dogs. The green fields were now scarred earth, littered with the refuse of other lands. In his own village the house of the chief had been leveled. The chief himself, struck by a piece of flying timber, lay dying in his own blood.

The shaman came forth to greet him with a solemn face. His mother had been among those killed. Even then her body was among many others on the freshly built bier where the dead lay for drying. In spite of his sorrow for his mother, Chish was impelled to ask:

"And the white squaw who was with her?"

The shaman turned his eyes as if in sadness. "She too is gone," he said. "Gone among the others."

Later, when the truth became known, Chish cursed himself as a fool. He knew the shaman not only as a priest but as a man. He knew this was not a man whose words or actions could be trusted. But the shock of his grief was too much. If even one of his friends in the village had whispered the truth about what happened in the aftermath of the storm it would not have been too late.

He had no such friend.

Only when the long funeral services were at an end and the last of the burial rites had been performed and he himself had grieved the full allotted time for the woman who had borne him did the truth come out at last.

Terrified by the coming of the storm and pained by the death and destruction that followed, many of the villagers wanted the yellow-eyed witch tortured and killed for bringing this evil to their village. It was the young girl who fancied Chish-Ko who had talked them out of this course of action.

"Do you dare have her blood on this village?" she asked the shaman. "That seems a great risk. The slave train leaves to take captives to the Spanish. Send her with the others, let her evil be visited on some place other than ours."

The nation of the Choctaw were famed for their songs as well as their singing. Many songs were sung in the seasons to follow about the warrior Chish-Ko. It was said of him that never had a warrior been so devoted to the mother who bore him and that his dark grief was a shadow on the village long after all the houses were rebuilt and new crops had grown where the storm had stripped the earth.

Chapter Forty-Seven

The sea had been remarkably calm for midspring. The Spanish ship *St. Elena* had drifted at anchor fully laden for more than a week, waiting for a wind fair enough to launch her on her course through the Gulf and up the Atlantic shoreline to St. Augustine. At the first quickening of the weather, a general sense of elation passed through the men on the ship. It was not that St. Augustine was such a desirable place to go. The little settlement on the east coast of Florida was nothing more than a military outpost for the billeting of the soldiers at Castillo San Marcos, and, of course, the seat for the Franciscan monks who served the mission there. But any change from Pensacola was for the better: the city was cursed with miserable muggy air humming with insects that considered Spanish blood the gold of the New World.

As the sails swelled and the *St. Elena* quickened her pace, the laboring sailors chanted cheerily. The sound of their joy turned like a dagger in the heart of the stout man who leaned against the rail watching the shoreline recede. Gonzales de Avila, purchasing agent for the governor of Florida, knew that returning to St. Augustine could bring him only pain and loneliness.

setting sail on the *St. Elena* for this purchasing trip he had watched as his wife Maria was lowered into the dry baked earth of this savage land. Her passing had been too great a grief for him to touch with his mind and yet he could think of nothing else.

He had watched her face grow pale and thin and her lovely expressive eyes fade to dullness. The friar who had come to administer the last rites as the bells pealed furiously in the chapel steeple had named her ailment as failure of heart.

He had been wrong to come to the New World from the first. He was not by nature a tradesman, but an artist. But it was his obsession with Maria herself that had lured him to this land. Absorbed by the witchery of her eyes, the graceful swift movements of her arms, he had been seduced to accept her dreams as his own.

Maria loved gold and music and song. She had pictured herself as a great beauty wed to a man whose talents would earn him great honor in this new land. "A mayor at least," she had said in that breathless husky voice, "or even a governor. Who knows, my dear Gonzales, how great you can be. I see it all. It is in you."

Instead of the life she dreamed of, the New World had given Maria wars with ferocious Indians and long winters when their bodies had thinned in the grip of near starvation. What children she had conceived had been born lifeless or breathed weakly a month or two before joining that small line of crosses in the graveyard in which Maria's own body was now laid.

Now he was old, nearing forty. His slender strength had moved into a heaviness about the belly and thighs. Sometimes he wakened in the night with sudden hard pains in his chest.

The wind that bellied the sails of the *St. Elena* did not stop at his doublet but pierced straight to his heart. He turned from the rail and went to his cabin with slow, tired steps.

Work. It was only through work that a man could escape his darkest thoughts. There had been a time when prayer had been a great comfort to him. When he knelt next to Maria prayer had seemed among the richest joys of life. But of late the hard floor had become painful to his knees. Instead of Maria's soft breathing beside him, he heard the voices of demons asking questions that no good Catholic dared hear on pain of mortal sin. They asked what father was this God who cursed his people with disease and painful death? How could the Holy Mary, herself a mother, permit a woman to bring forth child after child who were cold in death even as milk rose warm in Maria's breasts?

Work. Although he had gone over the accounts every day since the last of the goods was stowed away, he read the long list again.

Always the same things, blue cloth and red, pipes and combs and mirrors, bullet molds and shotguns, leaf tobacco and knives and whiskey. And slaves.

He sighed and pushed the list away. The order had been for twenty Negro slaves—men for the most part, strong, young, and free of yaws. The fortifications of the castle had already been many lifetimes in the building and still there were years left to labor.

"Bring Indians only as a last resort," he said. "As a last resort, mind you. The Crown makes it clear that it is our duty to make Christians of these barbarians and a man is poorly led to God in chains."

The governor had not added that Indians had to be paid. That was another question the demons often asked. Why didn't the love of God extend to men who were born with black skins? Why must the Indian know of God and the black men be left unsaved?

But there had been no black slaves to buy. The French on the Mississippi bid wildly against the Spanish, even for the sick and the lame.

Indians he had been offered and Indians he had bought, fearing as he did that the Adelantado might hold it against him that he could not make red men black.

He studied the list of Indians quartered below decks. The Choctaw trader had offered good strong men, warriors in their teens and mid-twenties. There were fifteen of these men and five women who were not too ugly for the people of that land.

It was the twenty-first slave who troubled his mind.

She was no Indian squaw, that one. She was young and shapely and seemingly strong. Her face was a pale flower among the stained Indian faces around her and her dark hair coiled on her neck in ringlets instead of falling in shining sheets as the Indian hair did. Her eyes, of a most peculiar gold color, stared back at him boldly but without interest.

Beside each entry the trader had written a name, along with the age and the weight of the slave. When he had asked the white woman what her name was she had shrugged that she did not know. The Choctaw slave dealer had stepped forth quickly and said she was called La Glorieuse.

"Where did she come from?" Gonzales had asked.

The Indian's face had turned crafty. "She was taken as prisoner in a just war."

Before turning in for the night Gonzales carried a lamp to the place where the slaves had been quartered. They were sleeping, twenty bulky bodies in that small space, coiled like great worms against the damp of the hold. Only the white woman sat up, with her slender back straight against the filthy wall. Her hands were crossed neatly in her lap and her small feet were hidden under the Indian skirt she wore.

The light wakened her. She stared at him without moving, those clear golden eyes steady on his face. He felt the faintest stirring of lust at the curve of her throat in the angled light. But those golden eyes destroyed his carnal thoughts. They glistened in the light. Framed by thick dark curled lashes, they stared at him without hate or resentment or even interest.

He had owned a falcon once, a yellow-eyed falcon that had ridden on his wrist for many seasons of hunting. He could still remember the grip of its claws on the leather that protected his wrist. For all those seasons it had stared at him like this woman did, without interest.

Then one morning, seemingly without cause, something evil quickened in that small feathered head. The falcon, trained for the swift murderous pursuit of its prey, had turned on a page who carried him.

Before anyone could move, the page lay screaming and writhing, with blood streaming down his cheeks from the empty sockets where his eyes had been. He wrung the falcon's neck with his own hands, feeling it throb with death as its feathers cooled.

He shuddered. She was young and strong and he had bought her from a reliable slave dealer. He hooded the lantern to extinguish the gleam of those golden eyes in the darkness.

Later that night, when the sea turned heavy and the ship tossed in the darkness, Gonzales wakened to lie stiffly in his bunk. After a while he shod himself and went down the passage to the pen below the decks.

Half the slaves were awake, moaning with terror. The rancid stink of nausea drifted like a miasma from the hold. The golden-eyed woman stared at him across the tangled mass of misery that separated them.

When he motioned her to rise, she hesitated only a moment before obeying. What a strangeness there was about this woman. Even in the distraction of their agony, the other slaves pulled aside to let her pass. She divided that sea of wailing humanity like the servant of the Lord had divided the Red Sea in his path.

When she was at the half-door he spoke to her in Spanish. Seeing no comprehension come at his words, he ordered her forward in the dialect of the Choctaw. Only as a last resort did he summon her in French.

She nodded and the guard opened the door to let her out. A great wail rose from the Indians left in the hold.

Once in his cabin, he set the lantern back into its braces and looked at her. The unconcerned patience in her face flustered him. In his faltering French, he invited her to sit down.

"They called you La Glorieuse," he began. "Is that your name?"

"To the best of my knowledge," she replied. "It is all the name I know."

"But where did you come from? Tell me about yourself."

She shook her head, the first sign of distraction he had seen her show. She brushed a loose curl from her face.

"I do not know," she told him quietly. "One day I was there in an Indian village and an old woman took gentle care of me. Then a great storm came and swept away the village and I was chained and taken to where you bought me."

"The Indians fear you," he remarked.

"I don't know why," she said candidly. "I mean them no harm."

"Are you Catholic?" he asked, his mind bolting ahead to their arrival at St. Augustine, to the questions that would rise in that village when he brought this slave woman into his house.

"I don't know," she said honestly.

Not since his first passion for Maria had the shape of a

woman's face, the curve of an arm attracted him as this woman's did. He thought he could spend the whole of the night framing questions so that he could watch her soft lips move in reply. Instead he sighed.

"It will soon be morning. We must sleep."

She seemed to sense his hesitation. "I am long among the Indians," she told him quietly. "I will be comfortable on the rug on your floor."

"You can't do that," he protested.

Her golden eyes were half amused on his face. "I heard you bargain for me," she reminded him. "I am your slave."

He tempered the sternness of his words with a smile.

"If you are a slave and obliged to obey, you sleep in the bed."

It was not the discomfort of his rude pallet that kept Gonzales awake through the calling of the watches. It was the living breath of the girl across the room from him, first tense, then slowly relaxing into the slow even rhythm of deep sleep.

Chapter Forty-Eight

When he sought privately to frame a simile for his life, Gonzales de Ávila named himself a fruiting tree. In his youth when all had been green he had known lust and love and the joy of creating beauty with the careful strokes of his brush. He had ridden like the wind and excelled in the hunt and been commended on his letters. This had been the blooming spring of his life.

With his passion for his wife Maria he had abandoned all his flowery joys and settled to bask in the clear light of God's way. He had given up hunts and games, painting and joyful idleness, to come to this new land with Maria to bear rich fruit for his King, his God, and his wife.

But even as peach leaves wither in the prime of their season his fruitfulness had been twisted from him ... by failure to excel, by the curse of childlessness, and then by death.

The heart that was once open to every nuance of color, to each vagrant bird call, closed like a fist in his chest. He shut himself off from all pleasure lest he invite loss by permitting love. He wondered that even the voices of demons had been able to speak in that withered cavern of his heart.

Was this woman a demon sent into his life to test him? As he watched her move gracefully about his cabin, straightening the small store of things he kept there, he tried to harden his heart against her. If she were indeed the Devil and caught him in her power, he would go through eternity never to see his God or Maria again.

Then she would turn suddenly with the light on her face and her beauty would stop his breath. He ached for a brush to fix that beauty onto canvas forever, not for fame, not for the eyes of other men, only for the joy of registering that perfection under the touch of his own hand.

He even knew what expression he wanted on her face. When she did not know she was being observed or when he had gone a long time without speaking, she went away into that shadowy darkness where the past lay hidden. When she listened to that secret chorus of lost songs, her face became the stuff of angels illuminated by suffering and love that challenged the work of the masters.

So it was that Gonzales de Avila took the girl called Glorieuse first into his cabin, then into his heart, and finally into his soul, forgetting all else but the joy of sharing the same space with her.

He accepted his final falling from grace when he slid into the narrow bed with her and begged her, his purchased slave, for the act of love.

He did not mind that her response was dutiful and passionless. He only breathed the sweetness of her flesh and stroked the silken mass of her hair and felt that damnation was not too great a price.

But out of his love for her came fear.

"Tell me that you are a Catholic," he insisted.

"Come now," she coaxed him. "Would you have me make up a past for you? Does it matter?"

"It matters not at all to me," he confessed. "But we are now only a few days from St. Augustine. This land may be called Florida, my dear, but it is still Spain. Spain, Gloria, the Spain that puts the knife and the torch to the heretic."

"Would you have me lie?" she asked.

"Those friars are wise men," he shook his head. "They smell carrion in a field of roses. You must tell them the truth about your memory being gone."

Even as he spoke to her, he remembered. He fished among

the boxes in his chest until he found it. When Maria was being prepared for burial, the priest had carried it to him, asking him if it should be left above her heart where he had found it. Gonzales was puzzled that he could not remember that particular piece of jewelry. He thought he knew all of his wife's treasures. Since he did not recognize it, he had replaced it with one that he had bought her himself when they were young and joyful together.

"You will wear this for me," he told the girl Gloria, holding out the tiny filigreed cross that spun and caught the light on its fine chain.

"It is beautiful," she said. "What do I do with it?"

"Wear it always, just above your heart. If someone asks what it means or where you got it, simply say that you cannot remember or do not know. But never let it leave your body. Promise."

He nodded. "It is that important to both of us."

With the tiny filigreed cross warmed by her breast and Gonzales de Avila at her side at the rail, the girl watched the Florida coast come into view.

There was an island that she was later to learn to call Anastasia. It was dotted like an ant hill with men at their labors, digging and carrying some white substance that was taken in small barques across the river.

Nearby, towering above the village like the sentinel it was designed to be, stood a great castle with its walls gleaming brilliantly in the sun. The massive walls were crowned by red watchtowers and the whole of it was reflected in the clear water of the moat that surrounded it.

Even as she stared speechless, she heard the single shot of a gun from the island they neared, reporting the approach of the ship toward the harbor. From the village buried in the fragrant trees, the church bell intoned a solemn musical welcome. Under the cover of his cape, Gonzales clasped her hand so tightly that she glanced into his face. She was startled to see unashamed tears coursing down his cheeks.

"Why do you weep, my friend?" she asked gently.

"I weep for the chill winds that whip the last leaf from the boughs of a barren tree," he said slowly, in his careful schoolboy French.

She would have reminded him that it was spring, but a sudden chill wind moved along her spine and she was silent.

Part 5

EL CASTILLO

1730

Chapter Forty-Nine

It was still early that next morning when Gonzales de Avila
sought an audience with the Adelantado Antonio Malini. The
fragrance of lemon blossoms perfumed the air.

At the warmth of the governor's greeting Gonzales
suffered a transient stab of conscience. The two men had
worked together—how long had it been now?—six years,
going on seven, since Malini had been commissioned by the
King to replace Antonio Benevidos in this coveted post at
Adelantado of Florida. In tribute to those years, the
governor's lean intense face softened with pleasure at the sight
of his visitor.

"Then you have again survived the perils of sea and land to
return to us, Gonzales," he said warmly. "Sit and tell me the
news from the west. Is Pensacola still as muggy and
bug-ridden as the outer reaches of Hell? What is happening in
the ongoing trouble between the French and the tribe of the
Natchez?"

"It is well that you ask," Gonzales said, settling into his
chair. "That paradise on the Mississippi that the French have
been so boastful about is falling to a shambles since the
massacre at Fort Rosalie."

The governor shook his head and smiled wryly. "Since we
are ourselves perched on a violent sea with the British and

211

sharks on one side and the Indians on the other, this does not sound like a happy tale to me."

"Remember that the French problem with the Natchez stems from the rapacity of white men," Gonzales reminded him quietly. "But the damage seems wholly done. The French retaliated against the Natchez with a great force of Choctaw warriors and two separate stories can be heard of what followed. The French, of course, say that the tribe is wiped out and the Suns all in slavery and that the very name of that people will die from men's tongues."

"And the other story?" the governor asked, his dark eyes bright with interest.

"The Indians themselves say that a powerful remnant of the Natchez escaped and that they are dispersed here and there among other friendly tribes. They are like lumps of yeast in a warm moist dough fomenting rebellion against the French in the camps of the Chickasaw and the Cherokee. The Indians say that even if the last Sun King dies from the earth, the French will be forced from this nation in the end."

"There would be some bitter justice in that," the governor nodded. "For treaty or no, the land that the French have been so busily colonizing was Spanish land, taken from us by stealth. Did the Indian trouble make your trading difficult?"

"Not in goods," Gonzales replied, laying his report in front of his chief. "In fact, there was more tobacco than we needed, so I was able to pick and choose among the crops. It was a good year for honey," he pointed out, "and the rest of the list was filled as usual. It was only in the matter of slaves that I was unable to fulfill your preferences."

The governor grimaced. "You say that lightly, Gonzales, but we both know that human sweat is the greatest need we have."

"I know that well," Gonzales agreed. "But the French have lost the services of the Natchez now. More plantations are being settled and every acre must be cleared of the giant cane that flanks that river. They scream for black slaves, paying ridiculous prices for men so weakened that they die in the coffle between the slave market and the plantation."

"Then how did you manage your buying?"

Gonzales laid the second report on the first. "All Indians," he admitted with apology in his voice. "But they are young and strong and, having been taken in war by the Choctaw, should submit gracefully to their fate if they are decently

212

treated. The oldest among them is still under thirty and strong of back and wit."

The governor moved his finger down the list. "And the women?"

"Fair as can be expected, and in good health." Seeing the governor's eyes pause, Gonzales went on quickly: "The last name on the list, the one with the line drawn above it is a slave I purchased with my own funds for my own use."

"La Glorieuse?" The governor looked up with knitted brows. "What kind of a name is that?"

"It seems to be French," Gonzales said quietly. The room was cool. A faint breeze stirred the papers on the desk and in the harbor beyond, the sails swelled above the barques crossing the river with their high white loads of cinchona. But still he felt the sweat begin to flow under his coat, forming irritating pools in the hollows alongside his belly. He must be calm. He must tell this tale as he had carefully memorized it. He must sound as if he held nothing back while explaining the presence of the girl Glorieuse in the house that had been Maria's.

Knowing that questions can be a spear for a man's words to swim away from, the governor laid both hands flat on the table in a gesture of open relaxation.

"She is not Indian," he began boldly, "and she speaks no Spanish. She is young, in her twenties I would say, and a girl of strange and beautiful aspect. The Indians fear her and our own sailors consider her a witch."

"A witch," the governor interrupted. "How does she answer this charge?"

Gonzales smiled. "She says simply that she does not know, she does not remember where she came from."

"Is she mad then?" the governor pressed.

Gonzales shook his head. "Not mad, but her memory has been wiped from her brain like writing from sand when the tide comes in. Coming as she did, in chains as a prisoner of the Indians, it was my own guess that she might have undergone some brutality so extreme that it shocked her mind."

"And yet she is a slave," the governor mused.

"She is a slave and she is white and a woman of gentle demeanor." He paused before resuming again in a tone of gentle reason. "When I saw her there among the savages, I felt a stab of sorrow for the many good Christian women who have been taken in war and never heard from again. Since

213

Maria is gone and I had no one to manage the woman who keeps my home, I felt that to buy her was not only charitable but wise. I have to admit that I have hopes that gentle treatment will restore her mind to her."

"Well spoken as a true worshipper of God," the governor said with a half-amused smile. "Yet you told me first that she was beautiful. Is it possible, my dear Gonzales, that your interest in this Glorieuse lies more in her tangible assets than in her immortal soul."

Gonzales grinned at his friend. "In truth, Governor, if I knew that she was both a Catholic and unmarried, I would wed that slave on the morrow. In the meantime I can do nothing but protect her until her memory returns."

"There will be vicious talk among the village women when you install someone young and fair in Maria's house."

"I depend on your understanding and support," Gonzales said candidly. "You have only to watch her to know that she is neither French Protestant trash nor a slut who should be allowed to fall into the brothels in the Indies."

"But where did this talk of witchery come from?" the governor asked, still disturbed at hearing the word aired in the bright morning light of his room.

"She is said to have a gift of almost magical healing. To the Indians this seems supernatural." He paused. "Remember De Vaca?"

The governor mused thoughtfully. "That is true. De Vaca was famed as a wizard by the Indians for the healing that he actually did in his Lord's name."

The governor rose to stretch and laid his hand on his belly. "Well done, Gonzales. And have no fear. I will make it clear to the community at large that the slave Glorieuse—for God's sake change that to a decent Spanish Gloria—is your ward." He grinned at his friend. "And I will most pompously maintain that we of the government support your noble enterprise. But I do wish to see this paragon, and I am sure my wife Pilar will be eager to do so too."

"I shall look forward to that day," Gonzales replied, taking his leave.

Chapter Fifty

Like the furtive lizards that slid among the vines that trimmed the houses of St. Augustine, the word passed swiftly from mouth to mouth of the coming of the golden-eyed woman to the house of Gonzales de Avila.

She was young. She was shapely. She was dressed like an Indian. Maria, poor dear, was barely cold in the grave. But most often of all, the word came that she was a witch.

Within the walls where Gonzales had left her, the girl sat alone.

When he had left her to this room, Gonzales had opened three chests. In his awkward French he had directed her to find clothing, "suitable for a maiden to go forth in."

She sat on her knees a long time in front of the first of the chests, turning the clothing in her hands. Festive, all very festive. The fabrics were rich and dark and felt costly.

Like a runner training for a difficult race, she forced herself to do the whole cruel exercise again. She made her mind walk backward in time. There had been the voyage through the Gulf and up the coast to this place. Before that was the long trek overland. She had ached with thirst and hunger and fallen to sleep on rough ground only to waken moaning from the scoring of the chains on her ankle. When she got clear back to the darkness of the Choctaw hut with the old woman leaning like a witch over her soup kettle, she saw nothing but darkness.

But it was a peopled darkness. By closing her eyes and staying very still, she was able to see dimly into that darkness, to glimpse faces and hear voices. And a song.

She sighed and selected a dress from the chest. It was a rich dark blue, the color of a lake at twilight when the leaves are heavy on the surrounding trees. Its sleeves came full to the elbow and from under them a ruffle of soft linen, the color of rich milk, tumbled out to swirl about her wrists. She knew that these dresses had belonged to Gonzales' wife Maria, whom he had loved with all his heart.

By the time she had dressed and drawn her hair into a great

chignon from which only a few rebellious curls insisted on escaping, she felt stifled by the house. Through the window she could see into the heart of the burgeoning orchard. Even as she stared into that sea of delicate bloom, a flash of color caught her eye. A bright bird with a hooked bill and an ornate plume lit on the branch of a tree and cocked its head to stare back at her.

Her mind registered a great tremor of shock.

She knew that bird. It had flown out of the darkness of her sealed mind to flash its bright wings at her. Without thought or will, she groped her way to the door. The bird hopped back and forth on the branch as she stared up at it. It stopped, peered at her, and scraped its bill sideways against the bark of the tree limb, keeping one eye constant on her. The voice came so softly that at first she had to hold her breath to listen. It was a man's voice, low and soft with a hint of laughter. "Lady," the voice said quietly. "Lady, Lady, Lady."

It was Josh's voice and even as she heard it, his face was printed on her mind. They had been in the swamps of the land that he called Guale.

The bird, emboldened by her attention, swaggered along the branch like a drunken sailor along the streets of Charles Town and the months of darkness were illuminated by a great white blaze of memory, Antoine's face close to hers and his blue eyes dancing. The crack of the whip at the top of the stairs and the long trek through the wilderness. Her lap was filled with dried strawberries and Josh's warm lips had turned to stone.

They were all there, but spinning, spinning in great wide circles with the wrong things coming together. Josh's song sung by a child who felt like Armand, Sophie twisting in pain in a Natchez Indian hut. And the spinning darkened her head and she stumbled back from it, crying aloud.

The young officer's errand had been to the Town House on the governor's business. What chance had taken him past the house of the agent Gonzales de Avila? Was it chance or fate? He had seen her first when she emerged from the house and the sight of her had stopped him dead with amazement. It was not Juan's habit to be unaware of a single woman's face, of a single pair of bright coquettish eyes in a wilderness like this.

And by the love of God he would not have missed this girl if she had been shrouded in a sack. She walked, unseeing, from the door and into the garden like a woman in a trance.

With her arms half lifted, fair linen fell back from shapely arms and the finest of soft white hands. Even the length of her dress failed to conceal the delicacy of her foot and the fine turn of the ankle above it.

He was still staring with astonishment when she paused beneath a tree to stare fixedly up into the branches. Her cry was strangled, as if it had been torn from her throat in great pain. With a few swift steps he was beside her to catch her as she fell.

Holding her, with that fair face so near his own, he found his own breath coming unevenly. He could not search that face enough with his eyes; the full bright lips, the brush of dark lashes against her cheek, and the scent of her flesh made him giddy.

He might have stood there forever except for the scrape of boots behind him as Gonzales approached with fear and fury blended in his face. "What is the matter?" the older man asked. "What have you done to her? What is wrong?"

Juan shrugged without releasing his burden. "I have no idea," he said honestly enough. "I was simply passing on my return to El Castillo. She walked from the house to the tree and then suddenly cried out and began to fall."

Gonzales, his suspicion overwhelmed by concern, moved jerkily. "Here. Let me take her indoors."

Her eyes fluttered open to stare first at Juan and then at Gonzales. At the sight of the older man's face, her arms went toward him in appeal and she gave a quick cry of alarm.

"Gonzales," she cried. "The bird in the tree."

Gonzales, conscious of Juan's eager eyes on the girl's face, grew suddenly frantic for what words might tumble from her lips. His fear made him crafty.

"I do not know what ails her," he told Juan. "But she is of tender size and has sustained great adventures. Would you do me the service of summoning a priest? Just in case."

The soldier stared dumbfounded at Gonzales. Of all the things that this creature summoned to his mind, the priest was the last. Yet, indeed, there was a pallor on her face again and the limpness of her delicate hands was frightening. As he backed from the room, Gonzales knelt by her side and began rubbing her wrists briskly with his own hands.

"Glorieuse, Gloria," he pleaded. "Waken to me, waken."

As her eyes opened, she moved her hand to his shoulder.

"Julie," she said swiftly. "Juliette Rivière. Oh, God, Gonzales, I know my name. I know my name."

When she paused, something in her eyes confirmed his fears.

"My name is Juliette Rivière," she whispered again. "Oh Gonzales, I want to go back home."

French. That name was truly French. The settlement at Charles Town was not a Catholic settlement but there were many French who were not heretics.

"How did you come here," he asked. "From the Indians?"

"Natchez," she said slowly. "We were at Natchez when the French there were killed."

A great relief swept over him. The French at Fort Rosalie were good Catholics, not like the Huguenots of Charles Town.

"And your husband?" he asked quietly, presuming the worst.

She shook her head and a darkness came to her eyes. "He was at Charles Town when I left. Now I do not know."

He rose, feeling a limpness strike about his knees. Married. Charles Town, that stronghold of heretics. She was a heretic Huguenot woman and married, and yet his soul was bound into her like colored strands into a tapestry.

In spite of his distress, Gonzales realized that the bells of the mission had begun to toll slowly. For the bells to toll at this hour meant only one thing. The priest was leaving the sanctuary bearing the Sacred Host to administer to the sick or dying.

He knelt by her and spoke swiftly. "Tell me, my love, do you know the fate of heretics?"

She stared at him, her eyes darkened a little by her memories of the tales of the Inquisition. Before she could reply, he went on, "Could you force yourself, just for me, to claim to be a Catholic?"

"Are you giving me that choice? Between claiming to be Catholic or death?"

"It is not I who gives you the choice," he said frantically. "It is Spain. It is my people. Choose life, Gloria, choose life for me."

Her head fell back heavily and she turned her face away. How many times had she chosen life over death when death would have been so much easier? Done this way, the choice for life was recanting. Kings had done it for lands and crowns. Queens had done it for the convenience of a marriage bed. She was neither King nor Queen nor even a strong Huguenot.

218

If she did not, she would lose all hope of ever seeing Antoine and Armand again.

"I cannot claim to be a Catholic," she told him honestly. "No priest would believe me anyway, I do not know the prayers, the simple habits of your faith. But I can always pretend that the dark curtain over my memory is still there... for a time."

He seized her hands and covered them with kisses.

"But I cannot live that or any lie forever, Gonzales."

There was no time. The bells of the mission pressed on his brain with their incessant sound. "Even a little time," he begged. "A year." Then it came to him. "In a year I shall go back to Louisiana on this trading trip. You could accompany me there. There are many French there who would help you reach your own people."

Even as he watched her consider his plan with her thoughtful golden eyes, he saw the dark gulf of his own damnation yawning before him. That darkness was lit only by eternal fire. Surely he had already lain with her, but the sin of fornication was an act of passion and could be confessed. Surely he had coveted her in his heart not caring that she was another man's wife, but this too was a sin easily whispered to a priest in confession. But to conceal her heresy, to conspire with her against the Church and the state would mean that his own confessions could only be mortal sins, stepping stones to his own damnation. But her eyes on his face were clear and golden and he remembered the taste of her mouth as she replied:

"A year, then, Gonzales, only a year."

He sensed a wariness in the priest's eyes that told him that Fray had heard of the woman in this house. He listened to her slow recital of illness with the sickness of despair. How glibly she deceived this messenger of God. How quickly she enchanted him with the purity of her face, the levelness of her eyes.

"For a moment there, it was as if a door opened into my past," she told the friar quietly. "I saw the bird that I remembered from another time. I tried to reach back into that time." She covered her face with her hands. "But it was gone, wholly gone into darkness."

The friar laid his hand on her in blessing. "Do not weep, my child," he told her gently. "All that is hidden will be revealed. Kneel and pray with me for the return of the light."

With her shoulder by his as Maria's used to be, Gonzales tried to pray. But instead he was conscious only of the scent of her hair and the softness of her flesh beneath Maria's dress.

"We will lead her back into life by degrees," the friar said gently. "It is the safety of her eternal soul that is our great concern. What does it matter about the rest? We will start as soon as you are rested from your voyage and this sad event today. We will lead you to God as a child is led, in patient instruction."

Chapter Fifty-One

Juan de Cabrillo had often heard it said that nothing cools the fever of a young man's lust like the shadow of a church spire. For himself he had not found that old adage to be true. When, after some indiscretions that would have put a lesser man's son behind bars, he had been exiled to the colonies, he discovered that the vigilance of a cluster of doddering old monks only added spice to the chase.

God, he irreverently admitted to himself, had not endowed him with a manly face and a fine body to see them always bent in prayer.

This Gospel According to Juan had earned him dueling scars and a string of half-Indian bastards along with a heightened interest in womanizing. He had become restless for his release from exile to return to the fleshpots of Europe until he caught the swooning yellow-eyed girl in Gonzales de Avila's orchard.

His own French had been too long unused. He had caught the word "bird," of course, and then "tree." At first he thought she was speaking of a "July river" but then decided it was a name. Roughly, very roughly replayed, the girl had told Gonzales that the bird in the tree had caused the past to come again . . . whatever that was supposed to mean.

It was the habit of the Adelantado to invite the officials of the village for a combined dinner and conference every Thursday night. For many months Juan had made it his careful concern that his own night without guard duty should be Thursday. While the governor and his wife Pilar had handsome suites within the castle itself, the mayor of St. Augustine had a large house in the village. The mayor's wife Catherine had a great passion for garden design in the French manner.

With the thought of the golden-eyed girl still filling his mind, Juan left the street to stray among the trees and be lost to sight in the garden of the mayor.

Catherine was waiting as usual, posed against a tree, smiling, with a single arm upraised. The pale light fell, by no accident, on the tender flesh of her inner arm. He had thought the attitude charming for all these months but suddenly it seemed forced and contrived to him, like bait in a carefully set trap.

Yet she was beautiful in the purest Spanish way. Her full red lips opened on the astonishing whiteness of small even teeth and the olive-toned curves of her cheek melted into a smooth throat that was an invitation to a man's lips. Even as she smiled at him, her full breasts half revealed by the dark mantle thrown carelessly across her chest, she spoke the same arch words that always began their trysts.

"Good evening, señor, what a surprise to meet you here."

His own response was always an amused, "I do hope I did not startle you, my lady. I was only enjoying the beauty of your garden."

As always, before the words had left his lips she slipped into his arms, fitting the lush curves of her body against his own. To his astonishment, he felt none of the usual surge of rising passion as his lips met hers.

And she chattered, a stream of bright whimsical talk that his mind never registered, and raised her eyes to him again and again in a formalized dance of invitation. Only when she had led him into the small private room where they had shared so many evenings did she finally turn to him with petulance in her voice.

"You have not said three words past your greeting to me tonight, my love. What in the world is on your mind?"

"Only you," he said automatically, reaching for her.

"Terse, terse, that's all you are." She was suddenly sulky. The gown she had begun to loosen was snatched back across her breasts.

The flash of anger in her dark eyes caught his fancy. He forcefully seized her and spun her around against him so that she might have no doubt of what passion her round body had roused in him.

221

"If you wish to talk, you should send for the priest," he told her, pressing her down on the narrow pallet.

Why hadn't he noticed before that there was a certain roughness to her flesh around the knees or that under the finely chiseled nose a faint line of hair suggested a coming darkness?

In the drowsy content after lovemaking, she turned again to chatter.

"I thought you would be full of stories of your fine adventure today," she said archly.

He forced his body to remain relaxed. "What fine adventure was that?"

She half rose and laughed down at him. "You fraud. Do you intend to tell me that you chance on a swooning maiden and race for a priest every day of the year?"

"Oh, that. You mean the girl at the agent's house," he said in a deprecating tone. "I happened to be the only person passing."

"But you must admit it was something out of the ordinary," she insisted. "Tell me about her. The whole village is agog with the story."

"I probably know less than anyone," he admitted. "I simply heard a cry as I passed the orchard, saw this woman spinning into a faint, and deposited her in Gonzales' house. God knows what I would have done with her if he had not come back from El Castillo at the right moment. I had no idea even where she belonged. Who is she, anyway?

"He bought her on his trading trip to Pensacola. She had been captured by Indians and was offered for sale by the Choctaws. Gonzales bought her."

He was startled enough to rise and stare at her. "Then she is a slave to Gonzales?"

Catherine frowned a little and shook her head. "Who knows what is truth in this village of babblers? But I had it from Margarita that Gonzales, compassionate of her plight, brought her here that she might be healed."

"Then she is ill?" Juan pressed.

"Not in the ordinary sense," she said thoughtfully. "Some dread experience seems to have shocked her memory into leaving her.

"She is Spanish then?" he asked with surprise, remembering her swift soft prattle in French.

"No, she seems to be French. They guess that she might

222

have been captured during the massacre of those people and carried away into slavery."

Juan's mind turned again to the girl's breathless outpouring of French as he was letting himself out of Gonzales' house. His silence was not welcome.

"Enough of that," Catherine said softly. "You seem much exhausted by your small act of gallantry. Is she then such a great burden that she has sapped the strength from this great body of yours?"

"On the contrary," he said softly, sliding his arm about her. "She is lighter than a pillow and no larger than a half-grown child."

"And pretty?" she goaded.

"Her eyes are a clear surprising gold," he said, conscious of the flame of jealousy that would dart out at him at the least suggestion that he thought the girl beautiful.

"Ahhh," she said quietly. "Then that is why the women are all whispering that she is a witch."

His body stiffened in spite of himself. "A witch! Mother of God, where did that story start? A lovely young girl, helpless among savages, is brought into this kettle of tongues and at once burned as a witch."

"Oh, lovely is she and helpless? Why didn't you say that from the first? I had heard nothing more than that she had bewitched the governor and Gonzales with her strange golden eyes."

"Oh, Catherine," he scolded with disgust. "Don't be such a shrew. She is lovely and she has strange golden eyes, but surely you must know that it is her plight that has earned her the sympathy of these men.

She laughed softly, her breath crushed by his sudden weight. "I will not worry then," she told him. "I have many talismen against witches."

He wondered about her remark as he wound his way back through the village toward the fort. At some point during the last few minutes of their lovemaking he had realized that indeed he was not where he wished to be. He knew better than most men when an affair was over and he had long ago learned that the way to end any such relationship was sharply, without warning or explanation.

But his mind did not stay on Catherine. So the girl and her old man had told the priest that her memory had not returned. Why? Had he mistaken that tumble of French words? Yet why would they lie to the priest? What possible motive would they have?

Chapter Fifty-Two

"Flowers," Gonzales explained to himself. "It is the flower of womanhood that draws the traffic of bees to a simple house." For the rooms were again visited by constant guests who livened their evenings with talk and laughter that spilled into the shadows of the orchard outside.

The difference now was that no other satin skirts swayed through the rooms. The women of the village made a point of shunning "the yellow-eyed slave" so that the guests in the house of Gonzales were all men.

Juan had come the day following Gloria's swooning, bearing a bouquet of flowers and his own flowery hopes that the señorita's health was much improved.

Gonzales, tensely listening from across the room, thought miserably that he had never seen the man so charming, so filled with subtle wit or so attractively attired. Juan's French, although scarcely less stumbling than his own, was larded with fancy phrases and flattery that brought blushes to the cheeks of Julie... whom Gonzales stubbornly continued to call Gloria. He had always resented the young Juan. It seemed unfair to him that the renegade sons of the nobility should be shunted off on the shoulders of the colonies to live down their disgraces. Such scions had money beyond measure and dominated their companies with a careful disdain that was demoralizing to less fortunate young men struggling to make their names in this hard world. Juan was worse than any of the young brats whom Gonzales had seen come and go. The whispers of his dalliance with women of the village, decent married women whose heads he had turned with flattery and gifts, made him sensitive to every chance remark the young man made. When Maria was alive and well, he had gone so far as to reproach his wife for encouraging the young man who hung so eagerly on her every word and glance.

The Adelantado, bearing apologies from his wife Pilar who had a continuing problem with her legs, came often to sit and enjoy the girl's graceful talk.

224

A strange weakness of spirit came over Julie after her memory returned. She was content to let the days flow over her like warmed water. Always in the back of her mind was the promise that Gonzales had made to her, that when he went again on his annual journey to French territory, he would take her along. She dared not question that, once united with some of her countrymen, somehow she would be able to get back to her family in the Carolinas.

But the thought of going home held private terrors that only grew worse as time slipped by. Try as she would to erase her memories of Antoine's final brutality, the scene kept returning to her mind. What if Marta had truly won? What of Antoine, unable to pull himself from the morass of drunkenness and debt, was truly lost to her? And Armand.

She was forced, in this calm existence in the shadow of El Castillo, to concentrate on Gonzales and her daily routine to keep her mind from spinning off into depression.

Being attentive to Gonzales was no burden. In fact, when he left on his short trading trips with the inland Indians, she missed him sorely. Although unable to return the breathless passion that he felt for her, Julie responded with gentle affection to the lovemaking of this devout man whose heart she had so inadvertently ensnared.

They dined together, talking of music and art and the doings of the village. When he told her, almost shyly, his great desire to paint her portrait she was delighted to pose long hours while he stared and dabbed at the canvas that was to be, he humbly explained, his "Gloria forever."

But while she enjoyed the company of Gonzales and his friend the governor, she dreaded the calls of the young officer Juan de Cabrillo. The silkiness of his tongue and the ill-concealed roguery of his eyes frightened her. She sensed Gonzales' discomfort when the man was in their home and tried to tell herself that his flattery and gallantry concealed a lustful passion.

But fortunately there were few excuses that Juan could find to invade their privacy. She spent long hours with Fray Jacobo under whose tutelage both her knowledge of and resistance to the Catholic faith grew steadily. She was impressed by his diligence and the simplicity of his life. She watched him grieve over the sick and mourn the dying until, little by little, she was drawn into his work to the point where she functioned as his assistant among the sick Indians of the village.

225

To any who would listen, Fray Jacobo sang her praises. "She is an angel with the children," he told the governor. "She seems to know what brew will ease, whose spirits can be lifted by a smile or gesture." Both to the governor and to Gonzales, he insisted that she most certainly had been a good Catholic in her earlier life.

"She learns her Latin so swiftly that the language of the Mass must be buried in the darkness of her scarred mind. And there is the cross she wears," he added triumphantly. "When I saw the gold cross that never leaves her breast I knew that she was indeed a child of the faith."

Julie, when told of his words, shook her head sadly. "I bleed to deceive him even if it is to save my life," she told Gonzales. "It was my own father who insisted that I be tutored in Latin, believing a girl should have all the skills that a young man was taught."

"I have never known a Protestant heretic before you," Gonzales said soberly, not realizing that she would find humor in the phrase.

"And I have only known one artist before you, Gonzales de Avila," she laughed softly.

"I am no artist," he confessed. "I am a man who loves to paint. An artist is a man whose hand is inspired by God."

Knowing that the year he had promised her flew in days and weeks, not hours, Gonzales labored with great haste on the portrait set on an easel in the room that had been Maria's. He had posed her in a gown of Maria's that was the same gold as her eyes, wearing that distant half-smile that she had worn so constantly during the days when her memory was lost.

"The look is not the same," he told himself ruefully. Only when he could persuade her to talk of her old life did that look of yearning visit her fair face.

"Tell me about the artist you knew," he urged.

"He was an apprentice in London," she mused. "I was young and lived in the house of my governess's sister. By the fire in the evening, Mark Hatter worked, not painting like you in oils, but sketching simple drawings with pen or charcoal."

"And where is this Mark Hatter now?" he prodded.

She shook her head sadly. "I wish I knew, Gonzales. After it was too late for me to stop him or even thank him I learned that he had spent a handsome inheritance sending me to the Carolinas to join my family."

He laid down his brush and smiled at her. "He is well paid," he said quietly. "The greatest joy of life is to serve those you love."

Quick tears came to her eyes. She jumped from the chair to put her arms around him. "You are so dear, Gonzales, so dear and so pure of heart. I owe you so much."

He held her close with a gentleness that wrung her heart. When she pulled away to smile at him she was pained to see the brightness of tears on his cheeks.

"Are you all right, my dear?" she asked quickly. "Is something wrong?"

He forced a quick bright smile and patted her arm.

"Like a bull," he laughed. "It is only that I must leave on another of those Indian trading trips when my selfish wish is never to leave your side."

Chapter Fifty-Three

The unexpected arrival of the ship bearing the King's auditor delighted Antonio Mallini. Because the visit, necessitated by small repairs to the ship, was not an official one, it would provide Mallini and his wife Pilar the opportunity to spend some private time with their old friend. Having given orders for a very special small dinner to be prepared for Friday evening, the Adelantado canceled his ordinary Thursday night dinner with the village officials and arranged for his and Pilar's evening meal to be served in her apartment.

"Do you remember, my dear, that I told you that Gonzales has returned to his early love of painting since the girl Gloria came?" At his wife's nod, he went on with enthusiasm. "If one had any doubt of that man's feeling about the girl, he need only see the portrait he has done of her.

"Has he painted her as beautiful as she actually is?" Pilar asked, having been charmed by the girl when Gonzales brought her to call at El Castillo.

"The likeness is remarkable," her husband assured her. "He has posed her in an informal sitting position that shows her fine head rising from that perfect throat like a lily on a stem. I would not have thought it possible for Gonzales to love another woman as much as he did Maria, but I was wrong. His passion for Gloria has literally melted her image on that canvas." He sighed. "Poor fellow. It is time again for him to be off into the territory of the Seminoles, a trip he must necessarily take with fear and trembling."

Pilar glanced up at him in surprise. "Is there some trouble brewing with those people?" she asked in amazement.

"It is not his work that concerns him," the governor laughed. "It is his beloved Gloria that he is worried about."

"I don't know what you mean," his wife protested. "What possible harm can come to her in our village?"

"You must remember that when he first brought her here he told me quite openly that if he knew her to be a Catholic and unmarried he would wed her at once. Well, now she is well on her way to becoming a good Catholic, better than many who were born in the faith if we are to believe Fray Jacobo, but her marital status is still unsettled."

His wife shook her head in irritation. "Then nothing has been changed. Why should he be fearful?"

"Ah, my dear. You have been too long imprisoned in this room with your illness. You have forgotten what life is like outside your sheltered apartment. There is not a man stationed here who has not assessed the beauty of that girl and yearned for the privilege of her favors."

"He should simply forbid anyone to go near her," Pilar said flatly. "What business has a rake like that Juan with a sweet young girl like Gloria? Why does Gonzales permit it?"

"How can he forbid it?" her husband countered. "She is not wed to him nor even betrothed, nor can she be until her marital status is known."

"It's not fair," she said crossly. "Juan is too much skilled in intrigue, he is totally without morals. That man—God only knows how many of the creole babes toddling about this village are the results of his lust."

Her husband laughed. "God would need the help of a saint or two to keep the tally on that. But you yourself, my dear, have been known to hold your head at its most becoming angle and smile very mysteriously when Juan leans over your hand."

She grinned at him. "He is charming. He is the Devil in satin breeches and a man of no scruples."

Laughing, he leaned to hold her close. "Your forthrightness commends you, Pilar, but that is not a truth to ease Gonzales' mind."

She clung to him, suddenly thoughtful. "Why does this talk

make me think of the mayor's wife Catherine?"

"I would guess her response would be more fury than fear," Mallini laughed. "She is not only a beautiful creature, but also a woman of singular emotional strength."

"She is a bitch and a shrew," his wife said matter-of-factly.

"You have reported some rather spicy things about her," he conceded.

"And I have not told you the half of it," Pilar said tartly. "I have kept many of her adventures from you because I fear that knowing how roundly a man was being cuckolded might change your attitude toward the poor fellow. She is truly a bitch and a shrew."

His laugh rang merrily as he threw her own words back at her. "My dear, I am certainly pleased to see that you are not too old to get a quick fit of jealousy when I say kind things about another woman."

Unlike the Adelantado Mallini, Catherine's husband the mayor had been selected for his post not because of valor at war or skill in diplomacy but on the strength of his father's fortune. The same convenient marriages that had widened his family's holdings and kept his name powerful through the whole of Spain had diluted the nobility of his blood until there was little left to endow his fourth son. He was a man conspicuously short of neck with a broad, pitted nose. It was considered fortunate that his weak vision made it unlikely that he ever drew comparisons between himself and other men.

That Thursday, the hour grew late and still Alfonzo, the satin of his breeches straining the seams against his thighs, sprawled in a chair, filling his glass still another time from the decanter of sherry at his side.

Finally, unable to restrain herself any longer, Catherine turned to him with a feigned look of astonishment. "Alfonzo, my dear, are you sure you have time for more wine? Shouldn't you be dressing for dinner with the governor and your council?"

He grinned at her. "I have been waiting for you to ask. I have a small surprise for you. Tonight I will not leave you, my sweet. Instead we will have a quiet dinner together, perhaps some extra wine and a few little games later, eh?"

"What a good surprise," she lied softly. "But to what do I owe this pleasure? Don't tell me that the governor is not well. It is rare for him to change his routine like this."

He shook his head. "Not that man, he has the strength of a legion. No, the ship of the King's auditor is beyond the bar,

229

being repaired in some small way. Mallini and the man spent the long day together and will dine together on the morrow."

"This is astonishing," Catherine said with real disappointment in her tone. "The governor always holds that great fete, with a dinner and dance to honor his visits. Does that mean we will not have this party to attend?"

Her husband laughed. "There will still be the great party, Catherine, don't fret your pretty head about that. I dread telling you this because I know it will begin a great huzzah of new clothes for you, even though it is still many weeks away. The auditor is scheduled to check accounts here after a stop in the islands. That will be the state visit."

Soothed by his explanation, she fell into silence. Green. She would wear a rich emerald green that would pick up the lights in the emerald necklace that had been Alfonzo's mother's. She would have only weak tea and a biscuit at noonday for the coming weeks so that her waist might shrink to a handspan.

But in the meantime it was Thursday and Juan would be coming to stand alone in the garden.

A weakness came over her as she thought of Juan. The past weeks had taken a great toll of patience from her. She refused to admit that what he had insisted was "bad luck" had anything to do with the yellow-eyed bitch at the agent's house. But she and Juan had not been together since the girl's arrival.

"I can read your mind," her husband interrupted her thoughts smugly. "You have already chosen what color to wear for the coming party."

"How can it be, Alfonzo, that I am not able to hide my tiniest thought from you?"

"Because your husband is not a stupid man, Catherine," he told her. "Come, let's walk through your remarkable garden until dinner is served." He tucked her hand under his arm with a leer. "I will read your mind under those flowering trees and your thoughts of love will only further inflame my desire for you."

I am going to be sick, she told herself silently as she let him lead her along the paths with his hand moist on hers. Could he read the relief that flowed along her limbs when they reached the end of the garden and only a startled parakeet showed himself among the flowering trees?

230

Chapter Fifty-Four

During the weeks of Julie's residence in St. Augustine, Fray Jacobo increasingly valued her work with the ailing Indians of the village and at Fort Moosa, a settlement that lay a few miles north of El Castillo. It was not that her healing skills were so sensational, the good friar admitted that to himself, because many of the country simples of the area were unknown to her. But the Indians believed in her. The friar himself had long observed that more fevers had been cooled by belief than by the Peruvian bark that the governor imported at so great a cost.

He tried to make no demands on her time when her mentor was in residence, asking her to accompany him to Fort Moosa only when Gonzales was away on his trading trips and he felt that the days might hang heavy on the girl's hands anyway.

That same Thursday that found the governor dining alone with his wife and Catherine forced to do the same with her husband the Mayor, Julie, Fray Jacobo, and two of other clerics were still far from the walls of St. Augustine at sunset.

Julie laughed at the friar's concern. "I am no flower that closes its face at the passing of the sun," she reminded him.

"But won't the Indian woman you call Dolores be concerned and possibly raise an alarm when you don't arrive for your evening meal?"

"I am a light eater," Julie told him. "Dolores is aging and tires easily. When Gonzales is away I simply have her leave out fruit and cheeses and go to her quarters when she is ready."

The moon was high when they arrived at the house. Fray Jacobo cast a careful look about the shadowy outer room before taking his leave with the others.

As she closed the door behind him Julie fought off a sense of apprehension. She smiled at her own nervousness. Somehow the priest had managed to infect the rooms of the house with his unreasonable fears.

She stirred the coals to life and set water to heat on the freshly laid fire. With only the light from the hearth and the shafts of moonlight that dappled the window, she slipped off her dress and the lace-trimmed camisole and pantaloons she had gotten from Maria's trunk.

The air felt clean and refreshing on her body. She stretched and wistfully clasped her shoulders with her hands. It was at times like this, when she was totally alone, that Antoine came back most strongly to her mind.

How many times had she slid out of her clothing to move with passion into his arms? How many days? How many nights?

It was as she reached for her night robe that a movement in the shadows froze her with terror. Clutching the robe in front of her nakedness, she whispered fiercely, "Dolores, Gonzales, who is there?"

He stepped from the shadows of Maria's room, a giant figure moving swiftly in the half-light. She would have cried out, but his hand was too swift against her mouth.

"Do not cry out, my dear," he said softly. "Do not raise an alarm you will regret."

She knew his voice at once and clawed at his hand on her face. Juan de Cabrillo. He was mad to come here like this. She struggled to free herself of him, to cover her shameful nakedness and escape his hold. Instead his free arm held her in a vise as the water began to chuckle in a slow bubble that announced its readiness for her bath.

"Do not fight, my dove," the voice coaxed, as gentle as a caress. "I did not come to hurt you but to love you."

How long they struggled there she had no idea. But within moments she heard, with pure horror, the first hollow clang of the mission bell. The Church she had so evilly deceived was to take its revenge on her.

She felt the rush of laughter through Juan's chest. Even as the bell continued its heavy tolling, the sound reverberating through the dark room, he began to laugh aloud uproariously.

"See how God serves those of great passion," he crowed, holding her at arm's length. "Now cry out if you wish, my sweet. Scream and call alarm in every language you know and not even the Devil himself will hear your voice."

With her lips freed, she attacked him with every insult in her vocabulary. "Bastard," she screamed. "Monster. Leave off from me or I will kill you."

He shut her lips with his own even as his firm young body forced the stiffness of his passion into her belly.

"Not until I have my fill of you," he whispered. "Don't tell me that a fat old man has filled that cup of yours with satisfaction. I will drive the memory of his sagging belly from your mind forever."

Exhausted by his weight and the fierce struggle she had so uselessly made against him, she stared at him helplessly.

"You beast," she hissed. "You rotten lecherous beast, do you think you can get away with this? Don't you know I will immediately tell Gonzales—Yes, even the governor himself, what you have done to me?"

Drawing himself a little away without releasing his hold on her, he smiled winningly at her. "And what do you think they will do to me?" he asked softly, cradling her breast in his hand and leaning to catch the nipple in his teeth.

"Chain you," she spat at him. "Chain you and flog you like the beast you are. I don't give a damn what they do as long as you hate it as much as I hate the touch of you. You are nothing but a miserable skulking animal."

He grinned at her quizzically. "I really regret that my French is not up to all the nuances of your insults, but I am sure that I am getting the general idea."

The damned bells continued to toll. Too much time had elapsed. Where had the priest taken the Host? If it was to an outlying village she was doomed to spend the night with his taunting face above hers, with his moist hard body paining her flesh. But if, please God, the communicant was only in the village or the hospital, the bells would stop and he would hear an alarm that he would not soon forget.

"How tight your smooth body turns of a sudden," he teased. "Have you thought of some new plan? Are you thinking of some way to protect this poor ravished maiden?"

He paused as the clapper struck the bell for the last time. Even as she drew her breath to scream, he whispered softly, "What is your plan, Julie? What now, Julie Rivière?"

His tone was no louder than a whisper but it stopped her breath in her throat.

At the expression on her face, he laughed softly and drew her close. "You may keep secrets from your priest, my little dove, and you may conspire with old Gonzales to deceive the Church and the governor and even the governor's wife who is a lady of no mean wit, but I know. I know."

Trying to pull free of his grasp but with her lips silent, Julie's mind raced wildly. How did he know? What was she to do?

"Julie Rivière," he mused quietly. "I was here, you know,

233

when your memory returned. I heard the words even though it took me long hours to put them together right. You have been damnably clever about not remembering your past, but I saw it come to you, remember? Juliette Rivière, no virgin, no widow, only a passionate woman waiting for the love of Juan de Cabrillo."

"No," she said abruptly. "I will not be your doxy. Better I would confess to Fray Jacobo that I am wed and Protestant and let them do what they will."

"Protestant too?" His eyebrows raised in mock dismay. "Aren't we free with our confessions all of a sudden?"

"I will scream," she warned as he slid his mouth down her belly until his tongue forced itself into the moist matting between her thighs.

"Julie," his voice warned as he clapped his hand tight against her face. "Before you take desperate steps there is something more that you should know." Sliding his fingers about her throat he caught the fine gold chain that held the cross that Gonzales had fastened there.

"If you will not behave prettily to save yourself, what will you do for that old man?"

She was confused by the quiet threat in his voice.

"Perhaps he could survive the disgrace of having been duped by a heretic bitch, but could he survive knowing where this trinket of yours came from? Do you know?"

She stared at that fine open face that hid a devil's mind. "I don't know what you mean," she stammered. "What are you saying?"

"Gonzales gave you this cross, didn't he?" he asked.

At her nod, he smiled. "He had to. It belonged to his wife Maria. I know because I gave it to her when the two of us made love together, even as you and I have tonight."

His voice was droning on, bragging how he had had a hundred of the trinkets made by a smith in the Indies, how it amused him to walk the streets of the village seeing whores and squaws and the wives of the townsmen alike wearing this memento of his passing fancy. But his words meant nothing.

She could only see Gonzales' gentle face. She could see heartbreak in his eyes. My God. My God. She had not lived all this time with Gonzales without knowing that his dead wife Maria stood, in his mind, only slightly below the angels, and that only because she had trucked with so common a mortal as himself. Maria was the single rock that moored him.

"You lie," she whispered. "He wouldn't believe you."

"It would be easy enough to establish," he shrugged. "It might even spread my local fame before I shake this miserable place from my boots. I could even name the other fair necks that have earned the prize. It is like the mark of Cain: once seen, never to be forgotten."

There was a sickness in the fury that rose in her breast. Her eyes narrowed as she glared at him.

He dressed with efficient dispatch, his eyes amused on her face. Still numbed, she saw him salute her mockingly from the door.

"Until next time, my little Protestant whore."

Chapter Fifty-Five

Pilar Mallini trembled with excitement as her maid put the finishing touches to her hair.

"Oh please do hurry," she fretted. "I want you to be absolutely through and ready to leave the instant the governor arrives."

"There is only this last curl," the girl protested, turning her mistress's fine fair hair over the comb to fall in a spiral ringlet.

Let her wonder, Pilar told herself triumphantly. Let them all wonder what excitement has been rising in my heart all these weeks. It was her own secret, her very own.

Sure enough, the discreet sound of his knock at the door was answered by the maid, who bowed only slightly at him before scurrying away.

"What's chasing her?" he asked, staring curiously after the girl.

"I told her to leave when you arrived, my dear," his wife smiled. "I wanted us to share our morning coffee in perfect privacy for once."

He smiled and bent over to kiss her cheek. "I must confess that you look especially ravishing this morning. With your eyes sparkling like that, a stranger who did not know you might think that there was some mischief afoot."

She laughed merrily, tilting a stream of rich dark coffee into his cup. "But you know me better than that, don't you?"

"I wish I could say I did," he admitted warily.

"You must remember that this is the day that I entertain the wives of the officers from the fort and the town."

He nodded and gingerly tested the heat of his cup against his lip. "I do, indeed, but the prospect of spending the morning with that gaggle of giggling geese has never put such a sparkle in your eyes before."

"True, true," she agreed, unable to stand the suspense any longer. "I had a surprise for them and I wanted to show it to you first."

"Surprise," he mused. "A new sweet to serve with their drinks? A gown that has been stitched privately behind my back? A game!" he decided.

"None of those," she shook her head. "This is the kind of surprise that you have to cover your eyes for, as we did when we were children."

"It was a game then," he decided triumphantly, covering his eyes and beginning to count aloud.

Even as her husband blocked his eyes, Pilar slid silently from her chair. Moving with only the slightest hesitation, and that because she was on tiptoe, she crossed the room. She plucked a flower from the vase and assumed a stiff pose to wait while he droned on, "... eight ... nine ... ten."

She watched him stiffen with astonishment as he stared at the empty chair, then at the cane by its side without which she had not been able to walk for so many months. His face, when he turned to her, was slack-jawed with astonishment. With a laugh she threw the flower into the air and crossed the room to embrace him while he was still struggling out of his chair.

"My dear," he cried. "My very dear. What miracle is this?"

She shook her head and twirled on one toe, swinging against him so that he had to catch her in his arms.

"Healed," she said. "Altogether healed and the clean flesh growing back pink and springing to the touch."

"Let me see it," he asked eagerly.

Standing on one foot, she braced herself against his shoulder and slid the slipper off to expose the new pink flesh forming on the sole of her foot.

"Pilar, Pilar," he sighed, leading her back to her chair with his arm tight about her. "What joy this is. Coffee, indeed! We should be toasting this day with the finest wine."

"The one thing you have not asked is how it came about," she reminded him.

He snorted. "I presumed that that bumbler Jacobo, having

236

tried every bit of nonsense he had ever heard, finally stumbled onto the proper cure."

She shook her head and leaned toward him. "La Glorieuse. The girl Gloria," she whispered.

"No, my dear, she did not come here to treat me without your knowing of it. But after we had received her that day along with Gonzales and Fray Jacobo, she asked the good friar why one so young and healthy had been confined to bed so long. He told her of the ulcer that had formed after the insect bite and how helpless he had been to cure it."

"And she prescribed a cure?"

"Not at once. I gather she was shy about suggesting anything after all the talk of her sorcery has been bandied about. But she kept it in her mind for a few days before asking the friar if he had ever heard of the cure for ulcers that the Indian people of Louisiana use. It seems that they bind the wound with crushed ground ivy. After several days they apply the balm that comes from the liquidambar tree. It worked. Not overnight of course, but it has been three weeks and you can see how healed it is."

He shook his head. "That woman is wise beyond her years."

"But not her beauty," his wife said. "You may even tell me that she is beautiful and I will not pout."

"She is becoming a sort of a legend among our people, I fear," her husband said soberly. "I had forgotten what a chatterer our good friend the auditor is. Do you remember how we both raved on to him about her beauty and her healing powers, that night the three of us dined alone and there was little news to keep the talk going? And how I compared the portrait of her to a Titian?"

She giggled at the remembrance.

"That is all coming home to roost. An emissary from Spain was in my office yesterday telling me that the stories are being reported at court in Spain."

He was at the door when he turned with a thoughtful frown. "What do you think, my dear? Would it be better if you were simply to spring your surprise on your lady friends and not tell how this miracle came about? There has been so much evil talk about this girl that I hate to feed the fires of it."

Her face fell with disappointment before she agreed with a sigh. "I am sure you are right, though it is a much better story the way it actually happened. But I certainly wish no more anxiety for her than those snobbish bitches have already given her."

Within an hour the room was filled with women milling about and eying one another's costumes, exchanging inquiries on the health of children seen the day before and discussing which new styles were current in Europe. When the last guest had settled to her needlework, Pilar, with the cane by her side, said brightly, "My goodness what a goose I am. I have a hoop of silk work that I meant to attend to this morning."

Even as the ladies looked around to see where it was, in order to carry it to her, she was on her feet and across the room to retrieve it for herself.

Later she was to admit to her husband that the excitement of their cries of astonishment and congratulation were almost worth the months she had been injured.

What she did not confess to her husband was how badly she had behaved when the mayor's wife Catherine stayed on after the others had left. Catherine, curled and scented with musk like a courtesan, lingered a moment to plead a short private audience with Pilar.

"I am always delighted to talk to you, Catherine," Pilar said with forced cordiality. "What is on your mind?"

The woman smiled, her teeth brilliant against her carmined lips and her eyes careful of Pilar's face. "It is nothing really important," she said softly. "But I think so much about our dear friend Maria. Since you were her friend too, I wondered how you feel about all this...."

"All this?" Pilar asked.

Catherine waved her expressive hands. "Oh, the yellow-eyed slave there at Maria's house, the persistent rumors of her witchcraft. No women ever go there, you know."

Pilar had to bite her lip to keep silent. There was no point in reminding Catherine that Maria had been much less than a dear friend to the mayor's wife when she died. For six months at least before Maria's death she would not speak to or about Catherine. When her name was mentioned Pilar had seen quick tears come to Maria's eyes.

"Are you suggesting that something is amiss when my husband and the friar and other officers from the fort pay calls on Gonzales at his home?"

"Oh, no, not the Adelantado and the friar," Catherine protested. "But it is whispered..."

Pilar shook her head. "I do not deal in whispers, Catherine.

As far as any of us knows the girl is unmarried. Any single man who wishes has a right to pay court to her as long as her guardian Gonzales does not object. Are there married men going to visit her, Catherine, or is it only Juan de Cabrillo?"

Catherine, caught off guard, flushed a deep crimson.

"The slave's suitors are none of my concern," she said brusquely. "But the talk of miracles, this business of magic healing, it flies in the face of my faith."

Pilar studied her thoughtfully, idly tapping the freshly healed foot on the carpet. "It occurs to me that the tales of miraculous healing by Señorita Gloria are carried more by the doctors and the priests than by any others."

"What about Gonzales himself?" Catherine pressed. "He has grown lean and gray since she came. His face, once so smiling, is always wreathed in thoughtful concern."

The words took Pilar aback. Because of her long confinement she had seen Gonzales only once since his return from the long trip to Louisiana and Pensacola.

"It would be my guess that his thoughtful concern is for the welfare of his ward," Pilar said primly. "Naturally he has a high concern for her religious instruction and the return of her knowledge of her former life."

Catherine was flushed from her inability to infect Pilar with her concern. She shrugged. "Very well, I just felt that being walled in as you have been, you might wish to know how the wind blows in the town."

"The wind blows over back fences as it blows in all towns," Pilar replied quietly. "And as in all other towns, those talkers might better be advised to tend to their husbands and children. If the same amount of energy were spent in the home as is spent in the garden, this would be a happier place."

Catherine's eyes narrowed at Pilar's words. Almost alone among the women of the village, Catherine had remained childless.

"I hope you are right," Catherine said, rising. "But it would be embarrassing for you if the woman were proved to be a witch."

Pilar looked up at her guest. Catherine was wearing a rich deep brown that set off the glowing amber of her skin. Her neck was festooned with strung amber beads among which was a single fine thread of gold chain. As Catherine dipped her skirts to bow to Pilar, the governor's wife saw the tiny filigreed gold cross nestled between her ample breasts.

"I have always been led to understand that the flesh of

witches is burned by coming into contact with a cross," Pilar said mildly. "As a matter of fact, Señorita Gloria wears a cross at her breast exactly like the one you have there. I noticed it especially when she knelt to greet me at a recent visit."

Pilar was astonished to see the color drain from her guest's face. Her hand flew to her throat as she caught the chain between her fingers. "She can't. It isn't possible."

"Oh, but she does," Pilar said mildly. "I remember thinking when I saw it that it was a strange thing that a girl wearing such a dainty cross would be accused of witchcraft by anyone." She rose and laid her hand on Catherine's arm. "But thank you anyway for your concern for me. Come, I will walk you to the door. Let's talk about the festive party that is coming nearer by the day. As always I shall strive to be the most beautiful woman there, but as always you will put me in your shadow."

Elaborate compliments had always been the one sure way of capturing Catherine's attention. This time the ruse did not work. As she bowed again at the door, Pilar realized that Catherine's fingers were still woven in the gold chain and that her face was ashen beneath suddenly dulled eyes.

Chapter Fifty-Six

It had seemed like spring when Julie first came to St. Augustine. The blooming orchards had persuaded her of that. Only as the months passed and the orchards completed their life cycles of blossom, fruit, and seed did she realize that her sense of time, which had abandoned her in the nest by the meadow with Josh, had never returned.

Too many other things pressed in on her consciousness to leave time for idle questions of what month it was or how many more months must pass before Gonzales returned her to her people. Fort Moosa, the colony of mixed Indians and runaway slaves from the Carolina plantations, was struck by an epidemic of swamp fever that kept the bell in the mission tolling day and night for weeks. Gonzales, who seemed to be aging before her very eyes, left on his Indian trading journeys to return thinner and more exhausted with each excursion.

"I was altogether too portly in the first place," he told her when she fussed over him with almost motherly concern.

"I hate the trips as much as you do," Julie confessed, standing in the circle of his arms. Guilt came with her words. She did miss his gentle company but it was more anguish over Juan's demanding visitations that made her follow his train to the walls of the village, fighting back her tears of frustration.

She begged Fray Jacobo to let her spend those nights when Gonzales was away working the late shift in the hospital. The good friar, innocent of her need, refused flatly, insisting that her strength must be saved for the return of her memory and for the good works they did together when the sun was high.

Caught between her need to protect Gonzales from the truth about his dead wife and the revulsion she felt when Juan's handsome face appeared in her rooms, she grew so distraught that even to summon a smile for Gonzales became a labor of love.

Each time that Juan managed to catch her defenseless he seemed to grow more frantic in his need for her. His compliments and flirting turned to fury at her lack of response so that, in the end, he took his way with her brutally, always threatening her with exposure as a heretic and the inevitable heartbreak of Gonzales. But still he refused to believe that this woman who obsessed him would not one day turn to him with eagerness and longing. "In time," he told her, smiling wisely. "In time you will cry for what you now pretend not to enjoy."

The ship bearing the King's auditor continued to be plagued by problems, putting in at this port and that as it fell behind its assigned schedule. During all those weeks of delay Pilar, moving about with her old happy celerity, carried on a lively controversy with her husband about the girl she called Señorita Gloria.

"You have to figure out some way she can come to the party," Pilar insisted.

"But my dear," he repeated patiently, "one does not invite a slave, regardless of her charm and culture, to a party in honor of the King's representative."

"I say that you are being hopelessly stuffy," she pouted. "I want her there with Gonzales and Fray Jacobo and the few really fine people in this miserable outpost."

He stared at her thoughtfully. "You may have the answer there. Perhaps she can come, simply dressed, and sit at a table with Fray Jacobo and the other Franciscans and refrain from dancing or taking any real part in the festivities."

"Absolutely not," she said flatly, stamping her foot at him.

As a slow wind wears away stone, she smoothed his resistance to her wish. "Very well," he finally sighed. "Ask her to come as the ward of the agent Gonzales. But for God's sake find her something to wear that was not Maria's."

Julie, terrified at the summons, followed the awestruck soldier who had been sent to usher her to the governor's wife's chambers. Only when she saw Pilar's radiant face did she begin to hope that the summons did not represent a death knell for her.

"Come, my dear," Pilar bubbled. "Come and sit here by me. We have an exciting thing to do."

When she saw Julie's eye stray to her foot, Pilar laughed merrily. "Did the good friar tell you that your remedy for the ulcer worked like magic?"

Julie grinned in spite of herself, the dimple coming into her cheek. "I am so glad. I hesitated to ask but I am thrilled that it worked so well."

"Tell me, my dear, how can you be so wise in healing and in the other skills that Fray Jacobo tells me of."

Julie, pained as always when forced to be devious with someone she liked, spoke softly. "If I could tell you that, I would be able to tell you the whole story of my life."

Pilar shrugged. "As a woman of faith, I am schooled in mysteries." Then she laughed. "And as a woman of other parts, I am also schooled in fashion. Let me tell you the delicious news. You and Gonzales, you as his ward, have been invited to the long-postponed party for the King's auditor. I get to help you plan your dress for that festive occasion."

Before Julie had time to recover from her astonishment, Pilar chattered on. "It has to be a gown that the ladies of the village have never seen."

Julie laughed softly at that observation as Pilar rose and threw open the lid of a great decorated trunk.

"Nothing that I own now would possibly fit a tiny thing like you, but I have not always been this voluptuous. When I was married at the tender age of twelve . . ." She laughed at Julie's astonished expression and delved into the trunk as she continued, "I have never been brave enough to ask if it was my beauty or my dowry that hastened my marriage, but I was in truth still a child. And this was my wedding dress."

Julie gasped as the dress unfolded before her. It might once have been white but the years had given the fabric the soft sheen of ivory. The deeply cut neckline was trimmed with a single row of handsome golden trumpets that proceeded to march down the bodice in a double line. Around the hem of the dress a line of small golden birds flew, carrying a ribbon of tiny pearls in their beaks. The undergarment, designed to explode under the sleeves and the full upper skirt in a mass of pleated ruffles, was in the finest cloth-of-gold studded with single hand-sewn pearls.

Julie was still dumb with astonishment as Pilar frowned at her. "There is so little time to be sure that it fits perfectly. Tell me, is Gonzales at home or away with his Indians?"

"He is away from home," Julie said. "He is not expected until tomorrow evening, if then."

"Marvelous," Pilar exclaimed. "This couldn't be better. This is the night when my husband dines with all the tedious men who run the government of the village. It takes one whole evening a week to listen to all their bragging and whimpering, but he is a patient man. We shall have a light dinner together here while they bore one another down there. The fitting woman will be here very early and you can be home before Gonzales can possibly make his way back. Isn't that a good plan?"

"It is too much," Julie said, tears behind her voice.

"Nonsense, I will hear none of that," Pilar said briskly. "I shall dance at that party, my dear Gloria. I had thought that I was doomed to an early grave from that wound."

The moon rose over the silken sea early that night, so early that the sun still hung low in the west. Gonzales saw the moon rise and sighed.

A numbness in his left arm had been plaguing him all the day. He held the reins in his right hand, keeping his left arm bent protectively across his chest. The air was heavy, making each breath an effort. He had brought on this fatigue by trying to rush his schedule in order to be with his Gloria.

The walls of Fort Moosa were just beyond. It would be kinder to both men and animals to stop. But like him, many of them might prefer to push on those last few miles to their own beds.

The soldier cantered up to his side with a question in his eyes. "What do you say, señor?" he asked hopefully.

Gonzales grinned at him. "Oh, hell, let's go on in. We will be at the town gates by ten, if not before."

Chapter Fifty-Seven

With her husband safely off for his regular Thursday night dinner at El Castillo, Catherine ranged the rooms of the house, picking up one thing only to lay it down again and begin her pacing again. The early moon dusted the leaves of her garden with silver. Early. It was too early. Still she could barely restrain herself from walking that path to the special tree where she would meet Juan. Pray God he would be there. This time he had almost promised.

She had humiliated herself by seeking him out, one week on a village street and just a day ago by going on a trumped-up errand to El Castillo where she knew she would encounter him among his fellows.

"Do you believe I am staying away by choice?" he had asked, his eyes warm on her face.

"Does that mean I can expect you?" she had asked, swallowing her pride, keeping her tone light lest others overhear.

"If you want to," his voice had been noncommittal but there had been other soldiers walking toward them.

What should she think? She had lied to herself for a long time, months now. She had taken his excuses, one at a time, like bitter pills, swallowed them entire. Not until Pilar had put it into words so impudently had she faced the fact that Juan might really be paying court to the yellow-eyed witch.

But Juan. Pilar had to be wrong. It must not be true that he had given the yellow-eyed slave a cross like the one he had presented to her with such flattering words the night of their first tryst. Pilar was only jealous enough to be baiting her.

It was senseless to torture herself. If Juan had not already come, he could find her waiting as he had for all those months before the yellow-eyed slave came.

In time the dampness of the night air set her bones to chilling. Something had happened to keep him away again. She would not think of how attentive he had been to Maria in those last weeks of their affair when he had already begun to meet Catherine herself in the shadows of the garden.

It was as she stared at the moon over the empty garden that she thought of how she might put her mind to rest.

How easy it would be. She would simply walk by Gonzales' house and, seeing a light, stop in. She would not even have to go abroad on the street but could follow the paths through the garden that she and Maria had used before their friendship was severed over Juan de Cabrillo. Catherine pushed from her mind the haunting idea that the loss of Juan's love had caused Maria's death.

Once at the door of Gonzales' house, Catherine paused. It was too still. Not even the hum of an insect sounded in the garden, yet a lamp shone through the window. Straightening her back, she rapped softly on the door. To her astonishment, it swung open. She stood a long time staring into the room before she summoned the courage to call out.

"Gonzales," she called brightly. "Gonzales."

Her voice seemed to reverberate through the rooms. Her eyes studied the room swiftly.

Not even the dour old Indian woman that Maria had named Dolores for her solemnity was about. They must have stepped out, she decided, Gonzales and his woman. She sneered. Would such a creature be invited to dine at the house of Gonzales friends? Not likely.

More than anything she needed to see what was so rudely draped in the room beyond. Could that covering conceal some evidence of the woman's sorcery? A devil's altar would be all that would be needed to turn Pilar's mind to reason.

After listening carefully and peering up and down the geography of the place, Catherine, without changing the position of the half-open door, stepped inside. With swift steps she crossed the room and the hall and lifted the dark drapery and revealed the portrait.

The richly colored oils glistened in the light from the room beyond. She gasped and stepped back with the drapery loose in her hand as the eyes of the girl in the picture stared at her with a mute wistful appeal.

Everything about the woman was appealing, the curve of the wrist, the delicate throat, but it was her eyes that set Catherine's heart pounding. My God, this was a work of pure art. Having seen the girl only from a distance and then hurrying along beside Fray Jacobo with a covered head, she was not prepared for the lush magnificence of the thickly curled hair, the appealing perfection of that face. And there, between the white rounded breasts half exposed by the gown

245

Catherine recognized as one of Maria's, hung the filigreed gold cross, the cross that only Juan could have given her.

She gasped from the shock as she heard the scrape of a foot at the door. She whirled, her heart in her mouth.

"Gonzales," she cried. "My goodness, you startled me."

His face made it plain that he was no less surprised than she.

"Catherine," he said, "I didn't expect..." Then his eyes narrowed with concern. "Where is Gloria? Why are you here?"

"I don't know where she is. I was passing and thought I would call on you. The door was ajar. I came in fearing something had gone wrong."

After staring at her in a distracted way, he pushed past her to search the other rooms. He looked dreadful. There was an ashen color to his face and in the lamp's glow his lips had a bluish tinge.

"Dolores," he gasped before plunging out the door toward the quarters where the Indian woman slept.

Wakened so abruptly, the old woman's eyes could not manage the light that Gonzales carried. She held the flat of her hand in front of her face as if expecting a blow.

Her stumbling Spanish was unmistakable. "A soldier," she said. "She went off with a soldier."

"When?" Gonzales shouted at her.

"Long time," the woman mumbled. "Long time now."

"Then you weren't here?" Catherine asked.

He stared at her almost stupidly. "I was off north in Indian country," he said with some difficulty. "I was not even expected tonight. Where can she be?"

Gonzales had sunk into a chair as if she were not there. His head was almost on his chest as he continued to talk aloud to himself, as if to reassure himself. "She was needed," he said. "She was needed and they sent a soldier from the fort to fetch her. Fray Jacobo sent for her."

The fury of Juan's betrayal flamed in Catherine's throat like bile. The old fool. He had been cuckolded by Juan until Juan tired of the pious Maria with her constant fears of hellfire. Now he was being cuckolded again with his precious slave and making excuses for the filthy little tramp.

"Don't be such a fool, Gonzales," she sneered. "You were gone and not expected and she went off with a lover. I would bet on Juan de Cabrillo, who will lay any tramp he can get down."

"You lie," he gasped. "You lie about Gloria and Juan. But you would think of that, wouldn't you? What a strumpet you are, Catherine. But other women are not like you. Other women have grace ... purity."

"Grace and purity," she scoffed at him. "All right, you double-horned old fool. I can prove quickly enough who the strumpet is. Look at that picture ... look at it."

Confused, Gonzales rose and turned toward the portrait he had so lovingly painted, stroke by stroke.

"Look at it," she was shrieking. "She is wearing Juan de Cabrillo's sign."

Gonzales stared at the painting, helpless with confusion.

"The cross, you old fool," she spat at him. "That little gold cross that Juan gives to all the women who sleep with him ... the prize, at the close of the first tryst."

Something in the way his eyes fixed on her, frightened her. He was trying to speak but could not. Instead his lips moved thickly and soundlessly and his face turned ashen as he groped for the arm of the chair to support himself.

It was strange what he finally said. "Maria," he choked with astonishment, "Maria. Maria."

The sound of his fall reverberated in the room. Catherine stared at him in horror. What could she do? How could she send for a priest and explain her presence here?

But if she left ...

Her limbs trembled with terror as she backed out the door and pulled it shut behind her. She lost her way twice, having to retrace her steps to get to the safety of her own garden. Once there, she fled to her room and curled into a large chair, helplessly trembling. She tried to pray but the only words she could think of were not words that could protect her from what she had seen. And done.

Chapter Fifty-Eight

Pilar watched from the chaise as the seamstress adjusted the pale ivory gown on the girl Gloria. Magnificent, she thought with satisfaction. A low chuckle of laughter rose in her throat. This girl would outshine everyone at the party like a full moon fades a skyful of stars. Secure in her own husband's love, Pilar saw no threat in the lovely girl who turned to the nudges of the seamstress with calm patience.

The girl looked round at her, that swift dimple coming in her cheek as she smiled. "You sound very happy, señora," she said softly.

"It is you who make me happy," Pilar admitted. "I like sitting here and pretending that I was as lovely as you when I wore that dress."

"I am sure you were," Julie replied sincerely. This warmhearted Spanish woman had attracted her at their first meeting. After she had spent many hours with her, the pleasant supper of the evening before, a few hands of cards later, and now this early morning time, Pilar had wholly won her heart.

Pilar clapped her hands softly with excitement. "What a party this will be, my dear, a glorious party."

Julie had not time to reply before an urgent rapping sounded at the door. When it was opened, Julie could see the governor standing outside with Fray Jacobo at his side.

"May we come in?" the governor's voice sounded strange and strained as he addressed the careful words to his wife.

Why were they all looking at her so strangely? The governor's handsome face was seamed with concern and even Fray Jacobo whose every mood Julie knew by now, seemed terribly doleful and a little distraught as he turned his hat in his stubby hands.

After what seemed a long and careful glance at the others, Fray Jacobo stepped forward. "Gonzales," he said quietly. "Our dear friend and fellow in Christ . . ." Julie did not hear the rest of his words. She did not need to. The dawn returned to her, the sounds of that very dawn when the bell in the mission church had begun to toll and toll and toll without ceasing.

"Gonzales," she whispered because she knew.

"Oh my God," she heard Pilar moan. "What happened? Oh, please tell me—not the Indians . . ."

Fray Jacobo shook his head. "A failure of the heart," he said quietly. "The Indian woman Dolores came wailing to my quarters a little after dawn."

He had begun to answer Pilar but as he spoke his eyes turned to Julie. She knew it was her heart that he was speaking to. "Apparently the train returned from the trip early. She found him on the floor between the rooms. He had not even changed his clothing from the road."

248

"Then he was already gone?" Pilar cried. "Without . . . without anything?"

"He was still breathing when I got there. He received the final rites. There was no time for confession. He called on the spirit of his wife Maria and for La Glorieuse. He asked my promise that she would be lovingly cared for."

The friar's words seemed to be coming from a great distance away. Julie had known he was ill. She had known in her inner heart that he was ill and that she had been too distracted by her own problems to help him.

He had tried to save her and been foiled by death.

"We will pray for Gonzales de Avila," the friar was saying quietly.

She did not speak as she knelt with the folds of the ivory satin around her, spilling the cloth of gold on the floor. The words came easily, the dignified Latin words that she had learned first from her father and which this gentle priest had imbued with a new meaning.

"We will take care of you, my pet," Pilar said with her arm about Julie's shoulder. "You will be safe with us always."

"*Siempre*," Pilar had said. When Julie's expression betrayed that her still clumsy Spanish did not include that word, Pilar resorted to her simple French, in which they had communicated all the time they had been together. "*Pour toujours*," she said softly. Forever.

A sickness of spirit settled on Julie, an apathy that made it easy for them to do with her what they willed. The clothing she had worn and the picture, still unfinished, were brought to a pleasant room in El Castillo near Pilar's own quarters. Nothing mattered. With the death of this great good friend had come the death of her own hopes. With a dead spirit, she stared at the sea and watched the gulls weave sunset beyond the cinchona walls. She did not even turn away when Juan de Cabrillo fell into step with her as she took her solitary evening promenade.

"You don't understand what I am saying," he insisted stubbornly. "I do not intend to lose you ever. I made a great mistake, the greatest of my life. Too late I discovered that it was not your body that had trapped me. I love you, Julie. I want you for my own and I shall have you."

"I do not intend to lose you," he repeated as she walked away and closed the door on the emptiness of his voice.

249

Chapter Fifty-Nine

To keep the flowers fresh on the grave of her dear friend and protector Gonzales, Julie walked daily through the village and past the mission church to the cemetery. After she placed a fragrant wreath of lemon blossoms on his heart, Julie would walk thoughtfully among the graves, reading the Spanish tombstones, pronouncing the melodic names out loud to herself. Using the dates on the headstones to calculate the ages of the interred at their deaths, she realized that life in this place was frailer than the foam that crusted the beach outside the sea wall.

There was Gonzales himself, dead at thirty-seven. His Maria had been thirty-three and their many children sleeping there seemed to have been brought to life only to be snuffed out like so many candle flames.

And this was where she too would end. Never again would she run across a room to throw herself into Antoine's arms nor see the face of her child Armand. Like Josh, she had gambled and lost. She almost envied Josh under the fur robe beside the Natchez Trace. At least no man would stand and read his name and dates without understanding anything of his life.

Pilar's soft reassurance was constant. "We love you, my dear. We want you always. You are needed and wanted in this place."

"Needed and wanted," Fray Jacobo echoed. "And loved by all you serve."

The party for the King's auditor at which Julie was to have worn the ivory and gold dress was a somber event because so many of the guests were mourning Gonzales, whose hard work and gentle manners had won him the admiration of the community. Julie herself was not expected to attend and only met the auditor privately when he came with the governor and Pilar to her rooms to convey his condolences and admire the painting that Gonzalez had so nearly finished.

She accepted all this as her life, the life of a lonely desperate woman, far from the people she cherished, living a false and traitorous lie.

It was Pilar, eyes flashing with anger, her movements too swift for grace, who shattered Julie's hard-won peace.

"They cannot do this," she shouted at Julie. "It is simply not fair. What fools men are. They jest and chuckle at the gossip of women and yet they cannot let a thought into their heads without opening their mouths and braying it to the world like great stupid asses. Natter, natter, natter! Fools! Idiots!"

Julie could not repress her chuckle at Pilar's colorful fury. "What has this breed of men done to throw you into such a state?"

"They have ruined my plans," she shouted, stamping her foot angrily. "That stupid auditor has gone the length of this empire, blatting, blatting like spring freshet. He has made you famous, my dear. He has said that your portrait is more beautiful than anything from the brush of Titian. He has painted your mysterious background, your piety and beauty on such a scale that you are considered the most fascinating woman in the Spanish world. Not in St. Augustine, mind you, not in the colonies, but the world. He has ruined everything with his big mouth."

Her fury suddenly melted into tears as she seized Julie by the shoulders and began to weep.

"Whatever are you talking about, Pilar?" Julie begged. "I can make no sense from your words."

"Spain," her friend said unhappily from against her shoulder. "He has been ordered to take you to Spain. At the express command of King Philip himself and Queen Elizabeth."

Julie pulled herself a little away to stare into her friend's tear-stained face.

"I have never had a woman friend in all my life before," Pilar whimpered piteously. "How can they take you away from me?"

"Spain," Julie breathed in disbelief. "Why should I go to Spain? What good will it serve?"

"It will please the King," Pilar said bitterly. "But the King would not have known to be pleased by you if the auditor had not noised you about like the blabbermouth he is."

"Spain," Julie repeated, the enormity of the thought dulling her mind.

"Well, he is actually a French king you know, even though he sits on the throne of Spain. His own grandfather was Louis XIV who was called the Sun King. It intrigues him that you speak French, it intrigues him that you are artful in healing. It intrigues him that you have no remembrance of your past yet have learned the prayers of our Church like a genius. I think he simply wants you as an ornament to his court. I want you for my friend."

"No, no, Pilar," Julie said softly. "I cannot leave here. I cannot go to Spain."

There was triumph in her friend's voice as Julie's tears began to flow. "I told him," she said bitterly. "I told my husband clearly that you did not want to go."

"Beg him," Julie pleaded, "coax him. Tell him you want me here. Tell him I want to be here.

Pilar sighed. "Don't you think I have done all that? Don't you think I exhausted every trick in my bag before I even came to you with this? He told me that he would give me the sun and the moon and seven peacocks that sang like larks, but only if King Philip had not asked for them first."

"Pilar," she said suddenly. "What if I told you that my memory has returned. That I know who I am and where I was from and that I was French indeed but a Huguenot. And that I have a husband and child . . ."

Pilar stared at her openmouthed and then began to laugh. "Oh Gloria, Gloria, you are such a treasure. Is it any wonder that I weep to lose you? Why stop halfway? Why not have ten children and all of them strong sons who fought against Spain in Queen Anne's War?"

"But Pilar," Julie said seriously, "I am telling you this. My name is Julie Rivière."

"That's very good," Pilar said with a twinkle. "But the name of Rivière is well known in France. I am sure that our King who was born at Versailles, knows many of your kinsmen among his court. It is no use, Glorieuse. I am to lose you. When the ship leaves to join the convoy in a brief two weeks you are to be aboard. They will not even let me keep the picture to remember you by. You are lost to me. Lost."

Julie watched the days pass as Pilar raged between tears and fury and tears and grief.

What had become of the Julie Duvall who had set out in a night of storm to London to save herself? Where was the Julie Duvall Rivière who had left husband and child to try to save her family from ruin? Gone. There was no place she could run. There was no Margaret, no Josh to lend a helping hand. Yet once she was aboard that great Spanish ship her fate was wholly sealed. She would never see Antoine Rivière again.

When the sun had already set but the faintest glimmer of

light still illuminated the harbor beyond the sea walls, Julie walked out alone and listened to the crash of the tide against the earth. She clasped herself tightly against the chill that settled in her bones at the very name of Spain. The small sails of the barques were pointed shadows in the darkness, but the galleon that was to bear her south to Havana to join with the rest of the convoy had a great carved square face and a network of rigging like a forest reaching for the sky.

As the trunk was beginning to fill, Pilar had turned and taken Julie in her arms with a frightened face. "Remember all that stuff you made up that day about your name and the husband and being a heretic? Please, my love, don't ever say such things in Spain, not even in jest. There is little humor in my country or our Church. Their ways of testing for truth can be monstrous even to a believer's eyes. They do not confer such swift and dignified death as was given to Gonzales, but torture and the rack."

"I will hold my jests," Julie promised, shivering a little as she spoke.

She was at the door of her apartment, to sleep in that safe haven for the last time, when Juan came suddenly from the shadows of the hallway.

"They think that they have won," he said in rapid, clipped words. "I have sworn to you that I will not lose you and I do not swear light oaths. Remember this, Julie. You will not go to Spain. You belong to me."

She sighed and turned away.

"*Bonne chance*, Juan," she said quietly. She did not mean for the words to sound as patronizing as they did. Who was she to make sport of losers?

Part 6

BATTERY JOHN

1730

Chapter Sixty

Once before Julie had braced herself against the rail to stare at the fortress of San Marco and the village of St. Augustine huddled in its shadows. But that time Gonzales had stood at her side, pointing out the spires of the mission church and where his own housetop showed through the trees. Now Gonzales slept with his Maria and the man at her side was a certain Captain Rudolfo to whose care she had been gallantly committed by the governor himself.

Events had come full circle in her life. The last time she had stared at the towers of San Marco with dread. A similar heaviness of heart stirred in her as she watched them recede. So little had changed. Bands of dark laborers still toiled on Anastasia Island, mining the cochina for the castle eternally under construction. Identical barques moved heavily across the strait to cluster in the inlet south of the castle.

Although still unable to express herself fluently in Spanish, her friend Pilar had taught her to understand almost everything said to her in that flowing musical tongue.

"You are blessed, señorita," Captain Rudolfo said quietly, "to have friends well positioned."

She glanced at him, thinking this a strange way to express himself, but she nodded in agreement. "I am indeed fortunate to have the governor and his wife as my friends."

She felt the wind catch a strand of her hair and saw him

follow it with his eyes. He was young and sturdy with a strong aquiline face and thick glossy hair. But there was a strange hidden expression about his mouth that concerned her. She would not, at first meeting, select Captain Rudolfo as a man to trust.

"You are indeed," he replied. "But that was not what I was speaking of."

"We seem to be sailing south," she suggested, as much to change the subject as for any other reason.

"Almost due south," he confirmed, "in order to meet with the rest of the convoy in Havana."

"I had heard of the convoy before," she said. "I was only surprised when I saw this galleon. It seems great and strong enough to cross any ocean alone."

"And indeed it would be," he agreed, "if it were not for the pirates that prey on these seas."

"Pirates," she sighed. "Always pirates."

He chuckled softly. "Oh they call themselves by more names that that: privateers, buccaneers. They are as thick as sharks in these waters. There was a time that such ships as this tried the lonely crossing, but we have learned. Now the pirates must be bold enough to face a whole flotilla to threaten us."

"Then there are no pirates between here and Havana?" she asked.

He laughed. "Pirates are only after what they can easily sell or use as money. They have little interest in what is shipped out of Florida. They are after the gold and silver and gemstones that come from the southern ports. As a matter of fact, you and that carefully stored painting are the most precious cargo I have ever carried from this port."

In the days that followed all her contacts with the captain had this same unsatisfactory air about them. His gaze was too intent and knowing. His enigmatic comments suggested some special understanding that lay between them.

What was more natural for a man than to inquire of a lady's health? Yet when she replied that she was well and comfortable, his response was a conspiratorial smile. "Your well-being is gold in my coffers, señorita," he said cryptically. She dreaded the long elaborate evening meals that she shared with him and the quartermaster, a solemn man whose eyes seldom rose from his plate.

She sometimes wondered if the quartermaster's taciturn

256

manner was forced on him by lack of opportunity, for the captain was a man of many words, most of them boastful. She learned that his was the finest cook in the entire Spanish fleet, that the wife he had left in Seville was famed throughout the region for her beauty and charm. Then, one by one, he began to tell her, at tedious length, of the battles he had fought with audacious skill.

Fortunately she was at least able to avoid him during the days. With her silent Indian companion, she spent long hours watching the dolphins play about the ship in dancing circles.

But evening came inevitably, with dinner served on gold-rimmed china that the captain said was from his wife's dowry. At least he had not exaggerated the skill of his cook. As pitiful as she found the plight of the sea turtles, she was unable to resist the rich salty turtle soup laced with fine Spanish sherry.

They were halfway through one such meal when the captain of the watch rapped on the door to report that he had heard another vessel approaching.

Captain Rudolfo studied the man without the least sign of distress. "Are you sure that it was a boat and not just the slapping of sea water against our own prow?"

The man flushed at this suggestion of his own inexperience, then nodded. "It is an unmistakable sound, sir."

The quartermaster's eyes moved from the officer to the captain with a puzzled frown. Julie saw him thrust his own napkin aside and lay his silver on his plate preparatory to rising, but the captain smiled at him patiently.

"Finish your meal, friend. The sea brings strange noises at night. Go and hark a little longer and then tell us what you hear."

"I will go and check it out with him," he said flatly.

Unaccountably this remark seemed to irritate the captain. "What foolishness is this?" he asked, raising his voice. "Oars at night on these deserted waters? Sit and finish your food."

"Is that an order, sir?" the quartermaster asked, pausing half out of his chair.

The captain shook his head, still showing his annoyance. "For God's sake no, man. Do as you please. But the señorita and I will not insult this fine meal by chasing a suspicious-sounding wave, will we, my dear?"

Julie felt that the two men had barely left the room before the quartermaster returned, his usually bland face tight with

257

concern. "There is indeed a boat, sir," he said tersely. "The sound is clearly the rattling of oars in locks and the slip of water falling from raised oars."

When the captain only stared at him thoughtfully, the quartermaster's tone grew even more urgent. "I ordered the second mate to hail the craft but no answer came in return. But there is a boat, sir, and it draws very near."

The captain sighed, elevated his brows at Julie, and rose. He moved with extraordinary leisure, wiping his hands and taking a deep draft of the chilled white wine before pushing his chair into place and bowing at her.

With her taste for the meal suddenly gone, Julie listened only a minute to the heavy tread from above before pushing her own plate aside. Pulling her shawl from the back of her chair, she crept up the stairs far enough to see the deck at eye level. She had no more reached a comfortable place on the stairs than she heard the sudden crackle of small-arms fire very near.

The blaze from the firing blinded her for a moment, but almost at once she saw that a boat had drawn alongside and she heard the muffled voices of men and a clambering on a ladder whose hook had been thrown on the deck. The first mate was shouting a call to arms and men were plunging toward the steerage shouting for cutlasses. It was too late. Frozen there in the darkness, Julie watched dark shapes swarming over the sides of the ship, heard the tumult of shouting and cursing, the fire of pistols. Acrid smoke filled the air as grenades exploded on the deck and on the stairs to the steerage.

As she fled to her quarters, she found the Indian girl already hysterical from the din. Her high screaming wail battered Julie's ears. Seizing the girl to comfort her, Julie held her tightly as dreadful sounds of scuffling and gunfire sounded from above. Then with horror, she heard conversation just outside her door and recognized Captain Rudolfo's voice speaking with insulting calm.

"I tell you, man, here is what you came for. This is the only bounty we carry." Even as he spoke, he flung her door open.

The man staring at her from the doorway was of medium height and coloring. He would have been quite an ordinary, even an attractive man, if it were not for the ridiculous attire he wore. Perhaps it was her own fear that almost made her laugh at the ludicrous appearance he made. His clothing was the gaudiest imaginable, dark breeches trimmed with pale blue braid over knee boots, a gold blouse with ornate sleeves and a bright scarlet sash about his trim waist into which were stuck daggers and a brace of pistols. Her laughter died in her throat when she realized that the sword in his hand was red with blood.

At the sight of her and the cringing Indian girl he let out a curse and turned on Captain Rudolfo.

"What filthy rotten trick is this, you miserable Spanish dog?" Turning, he whipped the dagger from his belt and plunged it through the captain's shoulder, pinning him to the door.

The captain, his face dead white, moaned, "But it is she, the one who was promised."

"What is this blithering idiot trying to tell me? And for God's sake don't give me any heathen Spanish prattle."

English. My God, the pirate was English with a taint of the west country in his speech.

"I don't know," Julie whispered.

"Speak up, woman," he shouted furiously. "What is this craven beast slobbering about?"

"I don't know," Julie fairly screamed at him as she fought to keep herself on her feet.

A look of astonishment crossed his face. "English, is it?" Then with a change of demeanor too swift for Julie to believe, he turned his eyes on the captain. Tugging the dagger from where it was embedded in the lintel of the door, he laid the flat of his hand against Captain Rudolfo's forehead, pressing his head back against the wood as he held the blade of the dagger at the wounded man's throat.

"Out with it, you sniveler, what's this about the English bird?"

In a voice choking with pain and terror, Captain Rudolfo spilled a stream of almost incoherent Spanish.

"Ransom," she heard. "Five hundred pounds in Spanish gold. Juan de Cabrillo."

At her gasp, the pirate turned to her. "Do you ken this heathen babble?" he asked. "If he can't speak so a body can understand we might as well split his babbling throat."

"Bastard," she breathed at Captain Rudolfo. "I understand well enough."

"So that's why you didn't heed the mate's alarm? So that's why you made no defense of this ship? You dirty rotten bandit. You sold me to Juan de Cabrillo. God in Heaven, can that man's money buy everything in the world?"

259

The pirate stared from her to the captain, who continued to babble and whine under the dagger's edge. Then the pirate began to chuckle softly.

"Is that how you read it then? Did he sell you to a man you already know?"

"I am not to be sold," Julie said furiously. "I was being taken to Spain. The governor himself put me under this beast's protection. But you made a deal, didn't you, you made a rotten stinking deal with that puffed-up young cad. Now I understand Juan's veiled remarks, now I even understand your own veiled hints. You thought this was another ship, didn't you? A ship disguised as a pirate craft that was to take me and the picture into the hands of that lecher?"

The pirate, without loosening his threat on Captain Rudolfo, was rocking with laughter.

"Up, up," he shouted to the captain. "Arms up and march and never mind that you bleed like a pig. You are fortunate that there is blood left in you at all." Dragging Julie from the Indian girl's grasp, he herded them both up the stairs.

"Hey, John," he yelled. "God's blood, we have a prize."

The huge man at the prow, who had been superintending the loading of the supplies, turned to stare at them.

"Eh, Darby? A prize, is it? It's only a woman as I see it from here."

A thin dark pirate stopped abreast of them and peered into Julie's face with a leer. "Strip her," he ordered. "There may be more than meets the eye."

"Keep your filthy hands off, Bartram," the man at her side said warningly. "This one is worth five hundred pounds to the right buyer. The captain himself has the deal set for us. We wasted our powder when we boarded this tub, John. He was waiting for pirates. This craven bastard here."

Across the deck Julie saw the quartermaster stare at Captain Rudolfo with blank astonishment.

The tall man called John had sauntered to Julie's side to stare down at her thoughtfully. Wearing clothes even more flamboyant than those of the man at her side, he was a giant of a man, heavy of bone as well as flesh.

"What would ye have us do with this sniveler, you hearties?" he bellowed to the Spanish crew. "He sold you all out at once, he did." He struck the captain on his wounded shoulder. "There's a little blood here for bait, shall we throw him to the sharks?"

The quartermaster stepped forward and spoke softly in

awkward, heavily accented English. "A better fate might be to put him in our hands. Believe me, we can make a case to His Honor the Governor for this trick."

"And a good joke that would be, to take the master to his own port in chains. And if I was to set you adrift now, with the rest of you breathing, would you be fair enough to tell me what other bounty you conceal that I not have to tear the ship from end to end to find it."

"You have already our cargo in hand," the quartermaster admitted. "The foodstuffs for the flotilla, and the woman and the picture for the King himself."

The big man turned to his mates. "See that the picture is brought along with the rest. If it is good enough for the French king who holds the Spanish throne, I can probably use it too."

Julie did not witness the remaining humiliation of the captain and his men. She was lifted and taken aboard the pirate sloop with her trunks, fuming silently.

"I will be damned," she promised herself. "I will be damned if any man delivers me to that treacherous Juan de Cabrillo."

At the sound of rending wood she glanced back at the ship to see its mainmast falling with a great crash to the axes of the pirates, leaving the ship adrift with the crew in its hold.

The lean pirate at her side was in her face again, the same leering man who had reached for her on deck. "You are fair," he conceded with his rotten teeth steaming into her face. "A kiss maybe, just a quick kiss to earn my friendship."

"Keep your stinking mouth off the bird," a voice shouted from behind them. "The prize belongs to all of us and Battery John ain't going to take kindly to your mauling her, Bartram."

Battery John. Julie, leaning away from the miserable Bartram at her side, cringed. So that was who the giant was. She suddenly saw Marta's face, there in Sophie's elegant living room, talking with verve about Battery John.

"No wild-eyed beginner," she had said. "A mentor rules him, some wise head that controls him and his fleet with an iron hand."

Chapter Sixty-One

Once aboard the pirate ship, Julie was thrust into a dark cabin and left alone. The room seemed to have no locks, for she heard the rough scraping of something being hauled across the floor to be set against the door outside to prevent her fleeing. The man who thus imprisoned her was the pirate who had come to her cabin with Captain Rudolfo in tow. She had heard Battery John call him Darby, and later she was to learn that he was the quartermaster of the pirate ship known as *The Black Dog*. As she had guessed from his accent, he was a Welshman, and his full name was Darby Dray.

Once over the shock of the bloody scene on the embattled deck of the galleon, she found her fury returning. That monster Juan de Cabrillo. How had she failed to guess what was in his devious conniving mind? All the pieces of the puzzle had been there before her eyes, even the warning voices that had told her of his wealth and arrogance.

"Everything in this New World is to be bought for gold," Gonzales had told her from the first.

And Fray Jacobo's quiet complaint: "It is of no help to the labor of the Lord that ruthless young men are exiled here to do penance for their carnal sins."

And, of course, Juan's own words as he gloated over her: "I will have you, you know. I will not lose you."

But what Pilar's anguished tears and Juan's wild plotting had failed to accomplish, Battery John had done with a longboat rowed quietly under cover of darkness and a few grenades tossed into the confusion of an unarmed Spanish crew. She would not go to Spain.

But she must not let Battery John release her into Juan's hands at any price.

Her mind, as exhausted as her body, refused to work cleverly. Instead of turning to her plight she found herself thinking wistfully of the half-eaten meal she had abandoned at Captain Rudolfo's table. Hunger and fatigue overcame her will to wrestle with her problem. She sat on the floor of the cabin and leaned against the bunk, laying her head back to rest.

"By God, I nearly stepped on you." The voice wakened her rudely. Holding the lantern, Battery John looked down at her, his face in half-shadow as she stared up at the great bulk of his body, his widespread legs, and the stained blade of a dagger glinting in his belt.

"Up with you, wench," he ordered. "You are not a dog to sleep on the damp of a floor like that."

Struggling for balance in the swaying ship, Julie got to her feet to stand, wavering a little, before him.

"Aye, you're not half big, are you?" he asked, peering into her face. "That makes you a poor bargain by the pound. But you are fair. Very fair. And the King of Spain wanted you. Was this for mischief you've done or mischief that he means to do?"

"He was curious," Julie said resignedly. "I had been sold as a slave by an Indian trader and I had no memory of how I came there."

"An Indian trader, an Englishwoman like you with a tongue of speech clearer than Herself even?"

His odd expression caught Julie's mind but before she could speak, he yawned widely and scratched his great belly with a rough clawing motion. "It's been a long day for the lot of us," he said. "And not even for five hundred pounds in Spanish gold will I give up me bed to you. However ..." He turned to a round-topped chest that Julie had noticed in her groping survey of the room. With a flick of his hand he threw out a great goosedown coverlet and a wad of some fabric. "A clever woman like you could make a decent pallet of these, I ween. Lay down and sleep, miss, it be a long way to home."

"I wanted to talk to you about that," Julie said quickly.

Without even loosening the laces of his boots, he let his great body down on the bunk with a groan, blowing out the lamp as he did.

"It will damned well wait for day," he said. "If there's one thing I can't abide in a wench it is a chittery mouth when a man is ready for sleep."

She stood a long minute with the comforter and the fabric at her feet. She could capture him, she thought suddenly in a wild flight of fancy. She could seize the dagger at his belt and hold him hostage.

"If you are hatching some plot in that feathery head of yours, be warned, woman. We are far at sea and there are two

263

hundred of us to your one. Now let out your damned laces and get some decent sleep."

She couldn't resist a grin. The crafty old rascal. He had read her mind as surely as if she had shouted her thoughts to him across the room. She knelt and spread out the comforter, covered with the fabric which felt sleek and soft to her hands.

Sliding in between the layers of fabric she fought a sudden urge to laughter. The little sleep she had taken against the edge of his bunk had marvelously refreshed her mind. Curled in the smooth fabric, she began to plot. If a woman were to be bought for a certain price, what did the seller care who bought the goods? It was the gold he was after. Hugging her shoulders in her arms she thought of Antoine. Was it possible, or was her wild plan only a desperate night scheme that would be riddled with holes when she faced it with the morning?

Chapter Sixty-Two

The boy was sitting against the door of the cabin, his arms looped lightly about his knees, staring at her. His hair was shaggy above a pointed face dominated by bright dark eyes that stared fixedly at her own.

Rising on an elbow, Julie pushed the curls back from her face and smiled at him.

"And who might you be?" she asked softly.

His face was determinedly serious. "I'm called Ned," he said curtly. "You ready to eat?"

"I will be," she replied, pulling herself to a sitting position. As she rose she really saw the fabric she had slept in for the first time. Her eyes widened in disbelief. This was the finest Oriental silk in a deep green shade, shot through with a thread of pure gold. This then was the stuff that Battery John had said that a clever woman might make a bed of. Looking up to see the boy's sober eyes still fixed on her face, she laughed softly. "So you are a pirate too, Ned, a boy of such tender years."

She had struck a sore point. His face reddened as he leaped to his feet to stand as tall as possible against the door.

"I am no wise a babe as you can see," he said huffily. "I'm rising eleven come Michaelmas."

"And how long have you been at sea, Ned?" she asked, rising and folding the priceless silk on top of the coverlet.

"Coming up two years," he calculated.

"And always a pirate?" she asked.

"Oh no," he said hastily. "I was pressed by the pirates. I have an honest paper from Battery John himself to show that I was took off the coast of Madagascar a year hence."

"And before that?" she asked.

His face grew suddenly sullen. "Why drive these questions at me head? I was to watch over you and get you fed. Nobody said you was to be a white-wigged judge making me spill me guts when there's been nothing put in me belly this day."

She laughed softly. "I am no judge, Ned. I am only curious because I have a son of my own."

"And is he of my years?" he asked.

She shook her head. "Nothing so grandly grown as you." She paused as the thought of the child Armand brought a cold plunge of loneliness to her.

"I was pressed by His Majesty's Navy in Liverpool," he told her in a sudden burst of confidence. "To serve King George himself."

"Taken from your family by His Majesty's men?" she asked.

Again, that ruddiness visited his face. "Not exact like that," he admitted. "My own folks left me off, they did, and my aunt was no wise fond of another hungry one underfoot. Her husband carried me off to Liverpool and left me there. I stayed clear of the press gangs for a month or two."

"But what does a—" She paused from delicacy. "What does a very young man like you do on His Majesty's ships?"

"Well, they 'come cabin boys sometimes," he said. "But I was a powder monkey meself. I've a fast pair of legs for all that they be thin. There was none on that ship who could get a powder cartridge from the gunner's mate and into the salt box and up to the guns as quick as I." His face turned crafty. "If I was to tell them that you was hungry then the both of us could eat."

"I'm hungry," Julie told him in honesty.

Warmed by a good breakfast, Ned grew more talkative. Julie listened idly, grateful for anything to distract her from the restlessness she felt to put her case before the captain. She must speak to Battery John before he sailed this craft to where the ransom money was to be paid by Juan de Cabrillo's agent, whoever that was.

"Do you think I could talk with the captain?" she asked Ned when the long morning finally passed and he had rung the bell for a lunch to be brought to them.

"If he wills," Ned said casually.

The man who took Julie's message was back quickly. He was a rough young seaman with bold eyes and an engaging grin.

"The captain says to tell you he will chitter with you when he is damned good and ready, that there's nothing he can't stand like a wench that chitters when a man is about his work."

"I just need to know where we're going," she insisted.

He laughed. "Knowing where *The Black Dog* is going would be worth a dagger through your throat, lady," he chuckled "There's no better-kept secret in these waters than where Battery John moves."

She felt immense relief when she finally heard the scrape of Battery John's foot at the door. As Ned was sent away for the night, she looked up eagerly at the big pirate.

"I understand that you've been plaguing everyone to talk to me this daylong," he said, glaring fiercely at her.

Flaring a little at his words, she answered tartly, "I only asked once, sir, which is hardly a plague to any man."

Instead of taking offense, he looked at her sharply, a new hesitation in his glance as he studied her face and then her form. He turned away with a sort of low snort and dropped himself on the side of the bed.

"All right, chitter a little if it gladdens your heart. But make it fast before I have a mind to sleep." He eyed her sitting primly on her chair. "I'm not a man of iron, you know. I am flesh and hot blood like the others above. But I mean to take no chance on Herself getting her claws into me over you."

Herself. She mused at the strange expression again. Somehow the thought of a woman who had this great giant of a man so intimidated was more fearsome to her than Battery himself.

"Chitter," he shouted, annoyed by her silence.

"It's not chittering that I am about," Julie said quickly. "I want to ask what you are going to do with me."

He laughed and reached for his pipe. "It's the same song all the day," he said mildly. "The goats in the pens, the chicks flipping up there in the spray, even the turtles all want to know what I am going to do with them. What I damned please, is the answer, wench. They and you will know when I am ready. There are two hundred of us counting a piece of you as our

266

prize. What else in hell would a man do with a yellow-eyed wench?

"And don't be giving me them looks about my language," he added crossly after a minute. "If Herself can swallow the heat of my words, then a bloody prize taken at sea can do it without any silly simpering."

His words irritated her. "I'm not given to simpering," she said to him fiercely. "And as for your language, I couldn't give a damn about that either. It is only who buys me that is my concern. For this money you call ransom is nothing but a black-hearted bounder buying a free woman for a whore."

He moved restlessly on the bed, stabbing at his pipe with a broad thick finger. "There's a piece of business you should be told, miss, for your own sake. I am no man of iron as I told you before. But I have a weakness for strong-willed women, like Herself even. You keep your damned mouth low and mealy around me or you'll be fishing your petticoats out of your throat before you know what hit you. You're warned, wench, warned."

"It is only that I hate and despise the man who made that kidnap plan," she said, careful to keep her voice gentle.

"You think the world is full of such fools?" he snorted.

She swallowed her ire with effort. "I have a husband . . ." she began.

His shout of laughter interrupted her. "Show me a man who will ransom his wife with gold and I will show you a man with a cock for a wit."

"And what of the picture?"

Gonzales was suddenly in her mind, his glance moving from the easel to her face and back with the golden Florida sun streaming across the floor.

She shrugged. "That is a piece of canvas stretched out with oil smeared on it. It would bring a good price from someone who had a yen for something bright to liven a wall."

He stared at her a long time without speaking. When she stirred, he raised his hand against her. "Keep your trap shut. If there is anything I can't abide it is a wench who chitters when a man is thinking something out."

She waited for a long time. He rose and filled a cupful of rum and handed it to her. He filled one for himself and tossed it off neat and refilled it before finally rising and yanking at the bell cord.

When the seamen appeared at the door, Battery John spoke to him briskly. "Tell the pilot we aim to change course.

Aim for one stop, he'll know what port, to unload cargo, and then home."

"You're not a cabbage that will rot in a week," he said mildly. "You're alive, ain't you? This is a trick I need to talk with Herself about. We'll sell the picture right off but hold you. If you be worth that much to a fucking Spaniard, who knows what you might bring in a careful sale?"

She did not speak, but he must have read the despair in her face. "Face up, there," he said a little more gently. "You ain't out there where the crew could make a punching board of you for their pleasure. You're fed regular and you sleep dry. Now stop that eternal chittering and let a man sleep."

When the dark had settled into the cabin and she had slid in between the layers of green silk, he spoke again. "And for God's sake, don't snore. A man needs his rest after such thinking as all that."

Chapter Sixty-Three

When she had been a prisoner at Newgate all those years earlier, she had noted the obsession that pent-up men have with time. If they were so lucky as to have a knife, they scored the wall where they slept. Lacking a knife, they would keep a soft stick and notch it daily with their teeth to mark the day's passing. She wished she had started such a rude tally when she was first taken aboard *The Black Dog*.

After the first two weeks Battery John, struck by her paleness, took her for grumbling walks about the deck at night, "to keep her legs in trim."

All the other excitement of the voyage came in the sounds of voices from above, sounds and reports and sometimes some comment from Battery himself when he heaved into his bunk, sodden for sleep.

"Something afoot" was how he generally referred to the tumult that came muffled through the wood of the cabin. That "something afoot" could vary from taking a small prize that chanced in their path to mistaking a British patrol boat for a craft more vulnerable to attack. With the din of that battle deafening her even below stairs, Julie could not believe that

The Black Dog could escape unscathed. But by midnight Battery John lurched into the cabin with a gray wasted look on his usually ruddy face.

"By God, that was a near one," he told her, collapsing on his bunk with a great groan.

"What happened?" Julie asked.

He raised himself on his elbow with an aggrieved look. "That cheating son-of-a-bitch was running a set of flags without the sign of the King's business in there anywhere. We was on him before Darby, with his lively eyes, noted that the cannons were coming out of hiding like thorns on a goddamned Scots thistle. If the *Dog* here was not the fastest four-rigger in these seas we'd be marching in chains right now."

Julie giggled inwardly at his indignation. Too many times she had seen him issue from the locker in this very room the flags of whatever nation seemed safest when approaching a prey.

"And what flag were you flying, sir?" she asked sweetly.

"Damned impudent bitch," he stormed at her. "You'd be as dead as any if the English had a single man in that crew as well paid as all of mine. And you know better than to chitter at me like that...."

Julie's strongest temptation to "try something," as Battery John called it, came when the ship was at anchor unloading cargo.

She had thought that she had thoroughly earned Ned's friendship until they stopped in that port. The boy turned suddenly sullen, glaring at her from across the room, muttering under his breath and sighing heavily whenever she spoke to him.

"My, haven't you turned into a grump," she grinned at him as they shared a cold lunch which the cook had prepared and sent along with their breakfast so that he might be ashore for the day.

"You," he said fiercely. "If it were not for you, I'd be ashore myself, buying a little and selling a little, and ..." he paused, "just fooling around."

"I'm safe here," she teased him. "Go on, give it a try."

He glared at her. "You heard the captain yourself. If I so much as put my nose out to smell the air or let you near a weapon while we're in port, I will be listening without ears for the rest of my days."

"Where would I go?" she asked. "What would I do? We

must be beyond the bar, how could I manage a boat by myself?"

"Hear that," he scoffed. "You do think you are a wise one, don't you now? You'll have to get up earlier than that to fool me. Any woman who knows enough to figure us beyond the bar can figure how to get herself across it."

"And it wouldn't be even the captain after me either," he added. "I'd take a lash or three from every man aboard, seeing that you belong to the all of us."

Once they were at sea again, Julie sensed that they were moving south. The air was sweeter and the stars seemed to have shifted position in the satin sky. Just when she thought that indeed this journey would be endless, one late afternoon she heard a cry from above.

"Land. Land, ho!"

That night she was kept below deck. Pleading with Battery John for the briefest walk in the outside air, he snapped at her shortly.

"Ah," he snorted, "so you would like to see the place, would you? So that one day you could describe it careful like and lead in the King's patrol on old Battery John. Not on your life, wench. It is chancy enough to bring you here at all."

Whatever mysterious place this was, it was clearly home to the crew. At noon the next day the sounds of jubilation were constant. A drum and a horn of some kind made music above the sounds of jigs being danced on deck and the raucous laughter of celebrating men. When she heard the dropping of the anchor, she knew her days of grace were over.

Ned had come in that morning natty in a fresh shirt and knee hose of the same pattern.

"This will be the end of it," he told her solemnly. "I'm to stand here while the captain and the men go ashore for a bit and then he'll come back for you."

"Why is that?" Julie asked in amazement. "Why can't we just go ashore with them and have it done with?"

Ned's eyes twinkled as he grinned at her. "The captain has been doing a little worrying about you. I heard him and the first mate chewing it over. He thinks it would be easier if he was to tell Herself about you before she sees you, about the ransom and all, so that she would take you for the lady you are instead of suspecting him of some hanky-panky."

"But surely she would just listen."

"Herself is not best known for her listening," Ned said quietly.

After the longboats had taken the men ashore, the ship became uncomfortably quiet. The craft seemed to chatter quietly to itself, a screech in the pulleys and a stirring among the rope, and the undeniable skitter of rats in the hold.

When they finally heard the nudge of a boat against the ship's side and the slap of the ladder, Ned could barely contain his pleasure. He had the door open before the footsteps reached the stairs.

Julie saw him as soon as Ned did and her gasp of astonishment was a copy of his own.

"Bartram," Ned said "Is it you then? I thought the captain..."

Bartram braced himself at the top of the stairs, his face flushed and weaving unsteadily above them. The stench of rum suddenly fouled the air in the passage as he spoke.

"That was the plan but he changed it over. He sent me out to stay with your lady friend here so you could take the skiff back and be with the others."

Ned shook his head. "No," he said thoughtfully.

Bartram, his eyes cold with fury, forced a laugh. "No, is it? Since when is a snivelling cabin boy able to say that to an able seaman? Is this the way you have been brought up to treat your elders and betters? Now get your skinny ass out into that boat before I undertake your education for myself."

"No, sir," Ned repeated, his voice quavering. As he spoke she felt the boy's hand inching furtively toward the dagger at his belt.

Bartram, as unsteadied as he was by drink, was too trained in combat to miss the move. He abandoned all pretense. With a cry of rage, he dove for the boy. Skipping aside from him, Ned lost his footing and fell, the dagger clattering away on the wooden floor.

In his lunge at the boy Bartram had left the stairwell unguarded for that one unexpected moment.

Sweeping the dagger from the floor, Julie slid past them up the stairs and onto the deck.

She stared about in dismay. She had never seen this ship in the light of day. Antoine's tutelage along the docks at Charles Town had not prepared her for a hybrid such as this. She had known from Battery John's words that *The Black Dog* was a four-rigger but this was a strange one, a stripped ship with a strange sleek hull. In the open space beneath the fo'c'sle deck stood a rude galley with space only along the side for extra cannons.

She heard Bartram even before he appeared at the top of the stairs. She prayed that he would not sense her presence there above him. She was dimly conscious of shouting coming from the land beyond, but she was acutely aware of Bartram's fuzzy drunk voice, low again and properly wheedling as he topped the stairs and stared about, searching for her. He was calling out to her in a strange sing-song whine. "Come out, little lady, there's no fear. Just come and show thyself, for there's only the two of us now. Come like the good bitch that you are. I mean to find you," he warned. "I mean to find you and claim my share. A fool's bastard trick it was to treat you like a prize. That bloody John, keeping you all these weeks for his own use. Well, by God, it's my turn now and I'll be damned if I am robbed again."

When he fell silent she knew that he had seen her. Worse than that, he was able to come in from behind and block her escape, leaving her only the railing over the sea as an exit. She scrambled backward along the railing, the dagger stiff in her hand.

"You're mad," she told him. "Battery John will kill you for this."

"So what's a single share?" he leered at her. "After he's took his own over and again."

His knees were deeply bent, like a fighter's. He was so near the deep rich scent of the rum was in her face. She fought back a scream for fear the suddenness of it would startle him into jumping on her as he had on Ned.

With a sudden shift he reached across the cannon and caught her by the shoulder. The dagger in her raised hand barely caught the flesh of his lower arm but the spurt of his own blood made him jerk away with the better part of her blouse in his hand.

"Bitch," he screamed. "Would you cut me? By God, I'll make you bleed for that."

His hands were suddenly tight on her wrists and she fell with his weight on her. Rolling along the deck, they struggled for the dagger. Then catching her arm in a twist, he was able to rock it free of her grasp.

The explosion sounded so close to her head that Julie felt its impact in her veriest bones. The sudden limpness of Bartram's body crushed the wind from her. From under his dead weight she stared up into the terrified face of young Ned. The pistol held in both the boy's hands still smoked in the clear light. She felt a great exhalation come from Bartram's lungs as she fought herself free of his body.

Stripped of her dress, with only the fine sheer petticoat between herself and nakedness, she stared at the blood dripping down her front into a pool on the floor.

Before Julie could even stammer her thanks, the boy laid the pistol down, lifted his voluminous blouse over his head and thrust it at her, his eyes still averted.

"Cover your nakedness," he said hoarsely. "For God's sake, cover your nakedness."

Julie tugged at the shirt, her trembling hands unable to cope with the great mass of fabric. Even as she wrestled with the shirt she heard the bump of a boat alongside and loud voices shouting questions and curses.

Ned let up a great wail as he turned to Battery John whose face was livid with rage as he stared at the dead seaman on the deck. "I tried, sir, oh God, I tried, but there wasn't any other way but to kill the bastard."

Battery John stared first at the boy and then at Julie with the blood streaming down her front under the half-donned shirt.

"Goddamned goat," he snorted. Then, with a gesture that Julie could hardly believe, he reached for the boy and touseled his hair with a gentle hand. "You done good, Ned boy. God only knows how he sneaked off with that skiff for his mischief. He lost no more than he deserved to be stealing from his buddies."

Then turning to Julie, he howled in fury: "For God's sake make yourself decent, wench. Herself is waiting to see you."

Chapter Sixty-Four

At first glance the island they were approaching was only a mass of deep green banded by a gleaming sandy beach studded with driftwood. Here and there on the horizon, palm trees rose against the deep intense blue of the tropic sky.

When the rowers pulled suddenly to the right, Julie saw an almost hidden estuary that led inward toward the heart of the island. The flash of bright birds and the chattering of apes accompanied their passage down the wide clear stream whose banks were here and there touched by trailing flowered vines. At the next bend the camp was revealed, an untidy mass of rough tents and thatched shelters of tattered sailcloth seeming to extend forever on the glistening sand. Only one wooden building among the lot boasted windows and doors. Julie stared in disbelief at the disorder.

A troop of tattered children raced among the grownups, weaving in and out among the barrels and abandoned oars. In their wake scrambled a mixed pack of goats and dogs, adding barking and bleating to the general uproar of the place. Over a giant fire a dressed goat turned on a spit, sending great clouds of garlic-scented smoke into the air.

"Now what do you think of that?" Battery John asked with unmistakable pride in his tone. "Some village, that one, eh?"

When the boat touched on the sand, Ned was first out to offer Julie his hand. A roar of laughter rose as she stepped out only to sink knee deep in the muck.

Then she heard the voice, a woman's voice screaming with the frenzy of a Cockney fishwife. The tone was imperative even though the phrases were not what would ordinarily rise to a lady's lips.

"Give the lady a hand, you sons of bitches," she screamed in fury. "Help her before I lay the lot of you stiff as cod salt."

That voice brought a clutch of sudden anguish to Julie. How long had it been since she had heard such a Cockney voice, warm with laughter, strident in fury and gentle in confidence. Her Ellie, the dearest woman friend of her life, had spoken in such an accent, even to the remarkable choice of words. But her own Ellie was long dead and the memory of that loss filled her eyes to brimming as she raised them to see who was shouting.

She was coming at a dead run, a small girl whose round generous breasts strained against laces that barely contained them. Still vilifying the hapless men who had gathered about Julie to obey the command to lift her bodily from the sand, the woman streamed tears from dark eyes as she approached the shore.

Julie gasped, her strength leaving her. Unheeding, she let the shirt fall awry, exposing her half-bared torso to the hearty and open admiration of the watching crowd on the beach. This was a dream, she told herself numbly, staring at the woman's familiar face, the cloud of untidy dark hair falling

274

free as she ran, the tip-tilted nose that gave the face the pertness of a curious child.

"Ellie," she whispered, "my God, it is Ellie." The woman running at her, screaming blasphemy at every step, could be no one but Ellie. But even as she gaped, the memory of her last glimpse of Ellie darkened her mind, Ellie being dragged from her side and condemned to certain death on the deck of a sinking ship.

Then she was there, beating the men aside with pummeling fists.

Julie wept with joy as Ellie's firm arms circled her and the apple-red cheeks pressed against her own and Ellie rocked her back and forth, half laughing and half crying.

All the time she was muttering, "Sacred Jesus, what a trick."

Suddenly loosing her hold on Julie, Ellie pulled back to peer into her face with that broad gamine grin that Julie remembered so well. Then, pulling away, she set off at a run.

Julie watched as Ellie crossed the sand in a run that was interspersed with quick flying leaps like a kid goat. When she approached Battery John she threw herself into his arms, barely giving him a chance to reach out and catch her. She buried her head against his ludicrous coat for a moment, then, seizing him by both ears, she tugged his face down and kissed him heartily on the mouth to the chuckling delight of his watching crewmen.

"Thankee, thankee," she crooned, "how did you ever manage to do it?"

Understanding came slowly to Battery John's broad face, and with it came a glint of mischief.

"We always try to please Herself here, don't we, mates? Even if her pleasure comes as the courtesy of the King, Philip Five, as you might say. If it's good enough for the King of Spain, it should just about work for Herself here."

Followed by a seaman bearing her trunk, Ellie led Julie to the single wooden house among the tents on the littered beach. Ellie moved easily among the nanny goats trailing their young and the children and pups tumbling about her feet. Although Ellie never ceased her chatter, her words were such a jumble of hysterical joy and expletives of disbelief that Julie could glean no sense from them. She only smiled and nodded and tried to absorb with her mind the miracle of seeing Ellie again, alive and well and lusty of spirit, as always.

Once inside the door of the house, Julie stopped with a cry

275

of astonishment. Ellie fell silent at her side, watching almost shyly as Julie's eyes moved about the interior of the room. Beneath her feet glowed the rich gleaming colors of fine Persian rugs. On tables of fine carved teak stood elaborate brass lamps and the rough unfinished wooden walls were covered with tapestry such as she had not seen even in the public rooms of El Castillo.

"My God, Ellie," she breathed. "What masterpieces you have here."

Ellie tugged at her lip. "Pretty, ain't they? Himself brought them to me, John Himself."

Something in her words caught at Ellie's mind. Battery John in the cabin that first day saying she was even smaller than Herself.

Ned standing guard on her while Battery John went to shore to explain her presence to Herself (who was not much good at listening).

"Ellie," she giggled. "Are you Herself?"

After the briefest moment of astonishment, Ellie tightened her shoulders and giggled. "It's wot he has always called me, you see. So that band of robbers does it too. Sort of a pet name, you might say."

Julie caught her friend in a tight hug. "I would say that Himself has done himself proud."

"That rope swings both ways," Ellie said softly. "And as to that great bloke," she said briskly, "I must be off to him now lest he get in a great pet over not being proper greeted. I've whistled a hot tub for you, knowning what a thing you got about soap and water. You make youself comfy and we'll be having some eats after a bit." She paused and clasped her hands rapturously. "God knows what I will be asked to pay for this day, but I swear by Jesus I won't haggle over the price."

She was all the way out the door before she stuck her head back in with a gamine grin of triumph. "They stole you, Himself said, right from under the nose of that Spanish king. Didn't I always tell you that stolen is better than bought. Didn't I, though?"

With her hair piled high, Julie lazed dreamily in the tub of hot water. From the beach below the house she heard the piping of a jig and occasional shouts of raucous laughter, the chattering of apes and dogs, and the sound of some stringed instrument played sweetly. Delicious smells of cooking food tightened her stomach.

276

Not until it was on her lips did she realize that she was humming Josh's song. How long had it been since her inner heart had been warmed and safe enough for that song to spring from her lips?

Yet she was in a pirate camp, hidden somewhere in the southern seas surrounded by hundreds of Battery John's cutthroat crew. There was a ransom on her head that John's men would not relinquish easily, if at all. Yet she knew within herself that she was safe. She was still humming lazily over her dressing when Ellie thrust her head in to announce that if she didn't get a move on Himself was threatening to come in and bring her out himself. "And that," Ellie added, eying her friend with appreciation, "could be done over my own dead body."

Chapter Sixty-Five

Julie did not at once recognize the man who leaped to his feet as she entered the room where the table had been laid. But as he came quickly to escort her to her seat, she realized that the well-tailored gentleman in the dark suit with the ivory ruffled shirt was the quartermaster, Darby Dray.

"Forgive me, Mr. Dray," she dimpled at him as she took her seat across from Ellie. "I wouldn't ever have known you in those clothes from afar."

Darby Dray grinned broadly. "To tell the truth, it is rather a lark to dress up in all that nonsensical garb for a boarding, though I do find myself more comfortable passing as myself."

Ellie answered Julie's question before it could be put.

"There's a good deal of the pirate business that is just trimmings," she said wisely. "It throws them off somewhat when the men are dressed like madmen."

Julie laughed wryly. "There was little enough fear in our captain when you boarded our ship. Not a weapon was fired," she explained to Ellie. "The mate was roaring about below looking for the arms chest, which the captain had thoughtfully locked up. Our own quartermaster was going wild with concern while the captain chewed quietly in his cabin with the face of a well-fed cat."

"He'll be well enough fed once they make port and his officers and men make claim against him," Battery John laughed. "He'll be tasting cold steel instead of such stuff as he is said to serve on that galleon."

"Then he really was expecting a different ship," Ellie said. "What other ship was this?"

Julie shook her head. "I have no idea. I only gleaned from the captain's stammering that this devious plan had been made. I was to leave St. Augustine for Havana, where our ship was to join a great convoy for Spain. He and Juan de Cabrillo had hatched this plot that I should be kidnapped from the ship before we reached Havana."

"And someone was to deliver you and the picture for a half million in Spanish gold for his pains." Battery John looked thoughtful. "'Tis a shame to let that fine prize go when we have the bird right here in our own cage, don't you think, me love?" His eyes strayed thoughtfully to Julie as he spoke.

"Be shut on that," Ellie laughed, slapping him sharply on the arm. "She'll be believing your bullshit and be scared again."

"It is a shame," Julie agreed eagerly enough. "There's nothing I would rather see than that lecherous Juan de Cabrillo lose his money and his quarry both at once. But on this trackless ocean—"

"Trackless indeed," Ellie laughed. "There's a lot I've learned about this great tub of a sea in these years, my friend. During the last days of our voyage out from England, Himself was circling the craft, keeping it in his glasses, trying to decide if the prizes aboard would be worth the fighting. Then the storm came."

Julie leaned forward eagerly. "Tell me, Ellie. How did you manage to survive? The last I saw as my own boat was pushed off was that captain throwing you back among the prisoned passengers who seemed doomed to go down with the ship."

"And indeed they were and indeed most of them did," Ellie nodded. Then she grinned rakishly. "But I was never a one to be trapped, you know. When I saw the lay of the land there, so to speak, that the bastard was fierce mad at me for leading him on falsely, I thought I would take my chances on the broad sea rather than with a narrow man such as he."

"You jumped," Julie cried, amazed.

"Not before skinning off most of her clothes," Battery John put in with a grin. "Safety before decency, that's Herself for you."

278

"You think I was to be dragged to the bottom of the sea by that great wad of wool?" Ellie asked. "There was barrels and timbers floating all about and I just hied meself onto one, not even hollering when the sea licked at my face. But I kicked. Good Lord in Heaven, did I ever kick."

"She was fair out of her head by the next morning when we drew near to see what had been left adrift. She was paddling along like a cur dog, singing some bawdy song in her shivvies and laughing fit to kill at her own music."

"I was not out of my head," Ellie protested with flashing eyes. "I was merely singing to keep my spirits up."

"Spirits indeed," Battery John scoffed. "And you was calling me 'your honor' and bowing and scraping and telling me you was an innocent girl and too sickly to stand trial."

Julie giggled as Ellie shot him a reproachful look. "Well, maybe I was a mite giddy from the sun, but out of my wits I was not."

"Well, the years have been good to you both," Darby Dray said, gallantly tipping a flow of red wine into Julie's glass. "But there is still a problem with the crew."

"Damn the greedy bastards," Battery John grumbled. "There was no thought of a prize when we boarded that ship. We was hungry and had not enough water to make port, that was the size of the hope."

"I agree with Darby here," Ellie said. "You named them a prize and they have been counting it in their heads this long time. Look at Bartram there, may the Devil roast his kidneys, his thoughts were those of the other men, only more drunken and scheming."

Ellie looked at Julie piercingly. "Himself tells me that other ransom than the Spaniard's might be paid for you. Tell me how that can be."

Julie laid her fork on her plate, the bite of food stopping suddenly in her throat. "Those were words out of great fear and bravado," she confessed. "I have been gone so long. Who knows what has happened in Charles Town since I left?"

Ellie leaned to pat her friend's hand. "Never you mind. One way or another we'll settle the men by some other means other than making a whore of milady here."

"You say that . . ." John said in a worried tone.

"God in Heaven!" Ellie exploded at him. "There's more ways to raise a half a million in gold than you've thought of this day yet."

Darby Dray roused from his silence at her words. "Beg

your pardon, John," he said softly. "As first man to board, it being my job as quartermaster, I took a careful look around the ship."

"Great provisions," John broke in. "They were great provisions and we all commend you."

"The liberties I took in the captain's cabin included my tucking his private box in under my arm."

A redness started at Battery John's neck and his cheeks puffed threateningly. "What is this I am hearing, Darby Dray? Have you taken to private thieving to keep a just share from the rest of us?"

"Good God, no, man," Darby said quietly with a withering look. "I only thought he might have some word about the movement of Spanish ships among his papers that might be useful to us in days to come."

John nodded, mollified.

"It was from that box that I drew the sailing instructions to meet the man who would take delivery of the girl here. And alongside was a letter that I think must be offered with her that the bearer be paid." He drew it forth.

"The instructions were simple sailing directions with the name and address of a man at the end. This is written in some heathen tongue that I do not read. I speak many languages but can only read English."

"Jesus," Battery John groaned. "Herself and I are hard put to read past our own names in English alone. What about you there?"

Julie sighed. "I learned to speak Spanish, but even as Mr. Dray here, I am not sure I can decipher it in writing." She took the document and stared at it only a second before giving a little cry. "This is not written in Spanish, it is in French. How can that be, Juan himself was barely able to speak French."

Ellie leaned forward with interest. "Why should a Spaniard be sending a message writ in French?"

Julie was too busy reading to reply. By the time her eyes had moved down the page, her face was aflame with fury.

"Read it to us," Battery John shouted. "Keep us on no pikestaffs."

Julie pressed her lips together unhappily for a moment, and then began:

"My dear friend,
"I am again engaged in a great adventure and again I

wish to presume on our long and glorious friendship. If the phasing of this language seems strange, it is because I am using a scribe due to my insufficiency in your own elegant tongue and I wish no eyes other than ours to peruse this missive.

The ruse runs like this. The bearer of this letter has with him a companion that he has obtained at my order. Please pay him from the accounts you manage in my name the sum of five hundred pounds in gold. This must be paid only for the delivery of the living creature in good health, if not spirits.

The period of my exile is almost over. By the first of this coming year I will join you and pay amply for your kindness to my ward. Do take caution in the handling of this yellow-eyed bitch since she is as wild and clever as she is beautiful.

"My gratitude in advance, Juan de Cabrillo."

"Bitch is it?" Ellie cried furiously. "That miserable scum of a Spanish kennel. His day will come."

Before Battery John could respond, Darby Dray spoke softly. "Martinique," he said softly. "The sailing instructions were for Martinique. If this friend of Cabrillo's has access to a private account of the Spaniard's there, this will be easy to accomplish. Just easy...one of the lighter ships..."

Julie stared in amazement at the man's complex gentle face. He was serious. He meant to deliver her to this agent of Juan's. Even Ellie's mouth hung agape at Darby's thoughtful musings.

Dray was oblivious to them both. He leaned back thoughtfully in his chair and studied the tapestry on the opposite wall.

His chair scraped as he rose and left the room without a word to any of them.

"What the devil is he up to?" Ellie asked with a trace of irritation in her voice.

Battery John shrugged. "Who's to know? But mind you, if it is stewing in that man's head it will come up a rich brew. Better brains were never set in a Welshman's skull than those of Darby Dray."

His gentle attitude toward his quartermaster did not survive Dray's return.

Battery John leaned forward in his chair and bellowed.

"What in the name of God has gotten into you, Dray? What kind of a trick is it to bring a beast to a table like this, with the ladies yet?"

"Hush, man," Darby said quietly. "Use your eyes instead of your lungs for a change."

Julie, stunned by what stood in the door, found herself drawn from her chair as if by magic strings.

The animal remained by Dray's side with an alert, aristocratic expression on her face. Not more than two feet in height, she was gracefully shaped, the pure whiteness of her coat patterned with well-defined spots of a reddish liver color. Her large attentive eyes, which studied the people in the room, were rimmed with deep brown like a woman who has been carefully made up.

"A plum pudding dog, she is," Ellie said. "And what a beauty."

"A coach dog," Julie breathed.

"Beautiful," Julie sighed, memories of the coach dogs of London and Middlesex filling her mind. "Whose is she? How did she come here?"

"She belongs to a man named Moggedly Ben," Darby said quietly. "She was among the prizes he took from a ship that was headed for Boston."

"Lift the lantern," Darby ordered. "Look at her eyes." In the full light of the lantern, the eyes of the bitch shone a clear golden yellow.

"Well, son of a bitch," John said heavily.

"No, my friend," Darby said quietly, motioning the dog to be at ease. "This is the bitch herself, if you will pardon the joke. And what a fine-blooded one she is. Suppose she were delivered to a certain man in Martinique. Delivered by small craft in a fancy cage made especially for herself. Suppose she was wearing such ornaments as a—well perhaps, a ruby collar or a chain decked with fine topaz that matched her eyes. Is it possible that we could convince this Frenchman that his old friend had bought a companion as priceless as she was clever and beautiful?"

Chapter Sixty-Six

While the swiftest of the pirate sloops was being carefully disguised for the journey to Martinique, one of the ship's carpenters constructed a wooden pen for the Dalmatian that was in the words of Ellie, "fittin' for the Lord Mayor himself should he get into hot water with his wife." Because the fooling of the Spaniard was such royal sport, few of the pirates wanted to be left out of the game. Julie did not at first understand what the smith had done when he brought the delicately designed copper plate for her to admire. It was three or four inches in length and its outside rim was finished in curls and tendrils as beautiful as a piece of jewelry.

" 'Tis a name plate," he explained. "And if you have a proper name for the beast, it will be 'graved on there in a nonce."

Darby Dray turned to Julie with a frown. "What was the name inscribed on the picture that your friend Gonzales painted?"

"Gloria," she told him. "He had shortened it from La Glorieuse."

But once the sloop moved down the estuary and into the wide sea on its mission, Battery John grew sullen and morose.

"It's Darby he's fretting over," Ellie confided to Julie. "They've been the best of friends from the first. And there's many a slip of the noose from Himself's own head that only Darby Dray could have managed. He has a nose for a lie that catches it in the wind blowing away. If you ever think of hiding somewhat from Darby, you may as well try to hide your father's name from your mother. He is a wizard for sure."

She paused and stared wistfully at Julie with her head cocked to one side like a wistful parakeet. "You must know that it will be Darby who will take you to Charles Town once he's back with the booty. That is, if you still want to go."

"If I still want to go!" Julie exclaimed. "Oh, Ellie, don't you realize that with the turning of the year I shall have been gone from Antoine and my son for a full two years? Do you realize how long two years is in the life of a child?"

"It only seems longer when you are small like that," Ellie protested, leaning forward intently. "And what do you know of what you will be going back to after all this time? Do you have any idea at all?"

Julie shook her head. Oh God, if Ellie only knew how many times she had pondered those questions. While Ellie drank and bawdied and made love to her great Battery John, Julie languished all alone, aching for Antoine with all the passion of her earliest love for him. For the first time she really appreciated Sophie's great fear that when Paul returned he would not find her pleasing. Did Antoine still have tenderness for her after her bold escapade down the Natchez Trace? She knew nothing, nothing at all. It might be that he would pass her on the street and not recognize her, much less find her demeanor dear to him. But how could she say these things to Ellie? She simply laid her hand on Ellie's knee and said, "You don't understand."

Ellie, as always nervous with tenderness, leaped to her feet and began pacing back and forth. "Don't know. Don't understand. You've not learned a single bloody thing in all this time, begging your pardon. A perfect booby you've stayed in spite of your fine head that gathers cobwebs where life is concerned. Because I am a tramp should I have no heart? No grief and fear when Himself is out there on the seas with that band of cutthroats, the whole of the Spanish fleet and the King's Patrol besides peering through glasses to lay a shot of cannon across him?"

"It's not that, Ellie," Julie protested. "Antoine is my husband."

"And who has the gall to say that you are more married to him than Himself and I are?" the woman challenged fiercely.

"The words mean something," Julie insisted tiredly.

"Which words?" Ellie challenged. "Tell me what words make any difference."

Strangely, Julie could suddenly hear the birds in Sophie's garden as she heard the words of the marriage ceremony.

"Until death do you part," Julie repeated aloud.

"Death, is it?" Ellie cried triumphantly. "Well, if that is all that bothers you, we are more married than the mayor of Boston town and his broad-bottomed spouse."

She waggled her finger in Julie's face triumphantly. "I have swore that if any man draws blood from Himself, I will in person slice him to ribbons; and Himself has sworn the same by me. There's death-do-you-part, that's what it is. And if it be that he turns from me to any other woman, I have swore to kill him in his boots; and he has swore the same by me. That's real marriage," she ended triumphantly.

Battery John's fears turned out to be unfounded. Darby Dray returned with the gold on a fair wind.

"Then the trick went without a hitch?" Ellie asked.

"The man was somewhat astonished when I brought the beast forth," he admitted. "But then he had no idea what to expect. The polished crate and that loop of topaz went a long way toward making the business look sound. Just as I left he asked why Juan had resorted to all the secrecy and padding about. Why had he not had the beast delivered in St. Augustine into his own care for these few months?"

"And what did you say to such reasonable questions?" Ellie asked, bouncing with delight at his tale.

"I made a great mystery of it," Darby grinned, "hemming and hawing and having him pull it out of me a little at a time."

"Drag what?" Battery John asked impatiently. "What did he manage to drag out of you a little at a time?"

Darby's eyebrows rose with innocence. "That the creature had been especially sought and desired by the French king who sits on the throne of Spain. The man laughed a great deal at that, swearing it was like his friend Juan to pay dear for something that another man had picked as his own, be it bitch or bedmate. And now, if you are ready," he turned to Julie, "we should set our sights next on the port of Charles Town."

"On *The Black Dog*?" Julie asked.

Battery John howled. "Not on your life or mine. That city has a battery of guns that have cut more pirate timber than any man can pile in a lifetime. Nosiree. You will set out with Darby himself in a small proper craft where he will leave you with a friend of mine in that city."

"A friend in Charles Town?" Julie asked.

"You have a face as clear as water. Nay, this is not a man that you would be apt to know from the social wingdings of that town. But he's a sharp man with a good wit who can be trusted for all that his father was a murdering scoundrel and a lusty old wretch. Fourteen wives he had," he added a sly leer at Ellie. "Fourteen wives and never a one knew the other was waiting for the same set of breeches. God knows how many babes he set along this coast, that William Teach, but this son of his is the best of the crop."

"There are some of his crop that would be better off for the sword that set his own head free," Ellie grumbled, glaring at Battery John. "That thieving, conniving wench, for instance."

"Enough of this woman chittering," John said, rising to slide his hand along her hip. "There's nothing I can abide less than a woman who chitters when her proper position is on her backside."

Darby Dray, his keen eyes on Julie's face, nodded at her reassuringly. "You will be safe with this man. For all that he is Blackbeard's son, he is a good man and a true friend to the two of them. And therefore to you. As I am," he added quietly.

Chapter Sixty-Seven

To Darby Dray the journey to Charles Town was much too brief. Yet it held enough time for him to make an astonishing discovery about himself.

He wanted the woman that the Spanish called Gloria and Herself called friend.

It was not that another man had considered her favors worth a fortune, even though he had held that fortune in his own hand. It was not that the coming of this woman had revealed new and astonishing depths in Ellie Titus, the power behind Battery John. It was not even the wildly romantic story of her life which, at Ellie's telling had endowed this girl with the quality of a legend. It was not, he insisted to himself, her beauty, though he could watch forever the motions of those well-formed lips or the change of expression in those shadowed golden eyes.

None of this, damn it, but all of it. And more. It was the essential woman whose unique spirit flowed like an underground river, springing forth now in bubbling laughter and then with the cold steady force of conviction. But always some power moved within this calm alluring package, promising the fullness of life like a brook at winter's end.

That was it, he decided at hopeless length. To have this woman would be to have perpetual spring in your life. To have known her and not to have her was to waken to a lifetime of winter.

"You are thoughtful, Mr. Dray," she said quietly from his side.

He smiled ruefully at her. "I am regretting the end of this voyage we have shared," he admitted. "I know this coast almost too well. From the patterns of birds swinging about us and the pull of the currents, I know we are nearing your home. Very soon you will see a land shadow against the sea and it will be Charles Town."

"Do you know what instructions Battery John gave me for our arrival in Charles Town?"

She looked up at him. "Not altogether," she admitted. "I simply presumed, I guess." She smiled, creasing her cheek with that quick dimple. "I guess that between the two of them, Herself and Himself, they set me up proper."

He laughed at her teasing and nodded. "Down to the details of your dress. It was Ellie who insisted that you be garbed as a widow for this trip. And when we go ashore you are to be veiled so that no man can see your face. She has some fixed idea that a woman in weeds has a wall of safety built about her."

Julie giggled softly. "Ellie has been variously schooled," she told him quietly.

"So we are to go together, you in your veils and me in my proper business garb, to make contact with our old friend in Charles Town. He will welcome us as he welcomes all friends of Battery John and Herself, but mind you, their names must never be spoken. Not even John. He is 'our mutual friend' and as such we must always refer to him."

"But I am not to leave you until I am assured that you are safe with your husband and family," he went on.

"But what if, by chance, we cannot find my husband or family?" Although her tone was level, he knew how much it cost her even to suggest this possibility.

He smiled at her, striving to appear reassuring. "I shall tell you what John said when I made such a suggestion. He slammed his great fist on the table and bellowed at me, 'Use your wits, man. Use your bloody wits to see that she is set up in style or I'll have your head on a pikestaff.'"

She turned and smiled warmly as she looked at him. What did she see, he wondered. Did she still remember their first meeting in the cabin of the Spanish ship when she had been near laughter at the ludicrous clothing he had donned for the boarding? Or did she see him as he was now in the sober garb

287

of a businessman with his thick dark hair brushed close to be ready to don a gentleman's wig upon landing? Did she sense the yearning he felt for her, the conflict that assailed him at the thought of leaving, never to see her again?

Whatever she saw startled her enough that her eyes moved swiftly away from his and she caught some ribbons from her belt in her hand and began to tug at them anxiously.

"You are an extraordinary man, Mr. Dray. And I have much enjoyed my time with you. I must also tell you that there are no words to tell you how much I appreciate your kindness to me and your wit and cleverness in dealing with the problems I had when we first met."

"I have done naught that did not delight me," he admitted.

Even as he spoke he heard the faint intake of her breath and felt her body tense against the rail, leaning forward so that the ribbons waved and curled in the breeze.

He watched her eyes seek the landmarks, the curve of the Battery, the steeples of churches reaching skyward from among the clustered houses. When a veering of the wind brought a faint music of church bells, he felt her shudder and drop her eyes.

"I am afraid," she said.

"All will be well," he said quietly, wishing in his heart that such sentiments could be as easily achieved as mouthed.

It was when she dropped her veil to hide her lovely face that he felt the first painful tug of loss. Her fingers were like ice as he helped her into the small boat and then onto the wharf. She stood unsteadily before slipping her arm in his.

"Where are we now, Mr. Dray?" she asked after they had walked a little way.

"This is called Bay Street," he replied. "We are only a little way from the Battery."

"This street seems very quiet for this hour," she said after a moment.

"I was thinking the same," he admitted. For indeed, the street was near deserted with only a passing slave walking along at a swift pace, his face bent to his chest.

As he paused at the door of the warehouse he motioned the boy following with her trunk to draw nearer.

"We have arrived, my dear," he said quietly. "One moment and I will see if our friend is about."

At the opening of the door the man at the desk looked up from his accounts. Darby grinned broadly. "God in Heaven," he said. "At least in this place nothing is changed." Barrels and coils of rope and stacks of paper were everywhere. An open bottle of rum shared space with a crusty inkwell on the desk as the man behind it paused, stared, and then rose with the dripping pen in his hand.

"Darby," he cried. "Darby Dray for the love of God. What ill wind blows you to Charles Town? Come in, man, come in."

Then, seeing the veiled woman behind him, he paused and stared. "What is it, man, speak up."

Darby felt the pressure of her hand on his arm as if she had received a shock of some sort. He was turning to her when her hand left his arm to lift the veil from her face.

Later, when he tried to describe the scene to John and Herself, he found he did not have the words to tell how startling it was, or what a great tension sparkled in the room as the two of them stared at each other.

Weston, his eyes never leaving Julie, caught at the edge of his desk with outstretched hands. His mouth tightened into a strange round O and he emitted a slow painful rush of air like a man who has been hit in the gut with the broad side of a blade.

Darby, unable to restrain himself, began to chuckle.

"I presume from this that the two of you have met before."

The mockery in his tone broke the spell. The girl, with a quick amused glance at Darby, began to laugh too. Then she moved toward Ethan Weston with both hands extended. "Forgive me, Mr. Weston," she said with laughter in her voice. "It must be a shock after so long."

He grasped her hands and clung to them. "From the dead," he said stonily, then turning to Darby, he shouted, "God damn you man, stop that snickering. Gone, she's been gone for years, given up for dead. What is a man to think?"

"They thought me dead then," Julie mused, her hands still pinned in Weston's grip.

"Not for a long time," he amended. "Not until the others returned, your cousin Jacques DuBois and Paul Bontemps."

It seemed to Darby Dray that a sudden sun lit the room.

"Returned," she repeated in a whisper. Then, leaning toward Weston with her eyes sparkling, she asked, "Tell me. Sophie and Paul, they are together then."

"Tony," Weston said. "You want to be hearing of Tony."

At her nod, Weston tugged at his coat, as if thinking how best to tell her. "The *Sojourner* was finished to sail," he said quietly. "Three times she has gone and three times comes home with such profits as your husband dreamed of. Now there is another ship in the line, and a pretty one she is too."

Dray, as he watched her face, felt the full loss of his hopes drained away in her rapt expression.

"He seated a place on the Ashley," Weston went on, choosing his words carefully.

"Alone?" she asked.

He glanced at her, startled. "Well, not alone, you might say. The Scotswoman Mrs. MacRae is there as housekeeper and there is the boy always at her side. Great strong lad, your son," he said, suddenly smiling. "A handful for old Tony, but they do well."

Darby saw her waver and caught her arm. "Good God, Weston," he blustered. "What kind of dung heap have you here that there is not a place for a lady to catch her ease? And tea. I would say that a spot of tea would help about now."

Julie clung to him for support, but the radiance in her face almost blinded him.

"Oh, no tea, thank you, sir. I want to go home." She was suddenly pleading. "Nothing else, nothing else. I just want to go home."

As if relieved to be free of the room, Weston reached for his coat and shouted up his servant. "As soon done as said," he told her. "We'll pop you in a carriage and take to the road . . ." He paused.

"God help me, I have the wit of a bung hole. Your coming like this threw it clean from my mind. There's fever here, yellow jack. Hardly a soul has stayed in town and the countryside not much better. Because of the babe, Madame Bontemps took your son and the Scotswoman too, and went north for safety.

"North?" she asked. "Philadelphia? Babe . . . what babe?"

Weston howled. "You'll be another two years catching up. Paul and his missus had a fine sprout of a boy some months ago. A great bouncer of a child, he is too, like your own Armand." Then he smiled at her. "You'll be honored to find that they named him Julius, that being the closest they could get to your name in a handle for a boy."

The sound of the carriage at the door set Weston to springing about again.

"Come now, let's get that gear stowed. Tony will be half wild at what time we have wasted." He paused. "Coming along, Darby?"

"Our mutual friend would not have it otherwise," Dray said quietly.

Weston froze to stare at him and then Julie. "That's how it is, then. I had not the wit to wonder."

"That's how it is," Dray replied, holding the man's eyes with his own.

"And Herself?" he asked delicately.

"As charming as ever," Julie put in quietly. "You see Mr. Weston, Herself and I are life-long friends."

Dray watched Weston's astonishment turn to laughter.

"Tony told me once not to underestimate that golden-eyed wife of his. I made that mistake. And so did Marta."

"Marta?" Darby asked.

"It will all be told," Weston laughed, opening the carriage door for him. "In time, man, in time."

Darby settled back in the seat beside Julie. So Blackbeard's daughter had tangled with this one. And lost, if he was to guess from Weston's laughing face. He stole a glance at the fair face beside his in the rumbling carriage.

He wasn't even surprised, now that he thought on it. He felt a sort of fatherly pride. By God, he wasn't even surprised.

Chapter Sixty-Eight

With her hands clasped together in her lap, Julie felt pools of damp form in her palms. She had told Darby Dray she was afraid. That had been the truth when she said it. Now she was terrified. Was this terror her own mind's way of warning her against what was coming? Knowing, simply knowing that the swaying motion of the carriage was taking her nearer to Antoine gave her a sense of helpless falling, a reeling of her senses out of control at the passion that his very name roused in her.

She roused from her reverie with a start. "Forgive me," she told her companions. "I was quite rudely buried in my own thoughts."

"How could it be otherwise?" Ethan Weston asked. "And we are very close to the place now. I have a sense that you will approve of the house and grounds. Tony drew the plans during the first voyage of the *Sojurner*, as an act of faith, you might say. The building was begun at once when the trip turned to success. He was ever a one for doodling one design or another on what should be built."

"Ever," Julie repeated quietly, remembering the finely drawn maps in the gamekeeper's hut in Epping, the plans for Sophie's new kitchen house that he had drawn, along with a colliery, after the great fire.

Although she strained to see, the house was at first only a dark shape behind the outspread arms of a giant live oak tree. Then the carriage turned smartly into the drive and drew to a stop before a porch trimmed with pilasters. Lamps at each side of the door flooded the wide porch with a golden light that gleamed on the bald pate of the black man who responded to Weston's tug at the bell rope.

"Mr. Weston, sir," Julie heard the man cry, with delight in his tone. "How nice to see you. Come in, sir, come in."

Weston's words were muffled but the man's nodding could be seen clearly from the carriage.

"Yes, indeed, sir. He's having his ride around the place. Every night, sir, just a brisk ride before he settles in for the night. Will you be staying?"

At Weston's reply, Julie saw the old man strain to peer at the carriage. His voice cracked a little with uncertainty.

"Why, I am sure the master will be glad to see any friend you brought. Just come on in now."

"Why do I want to hide?" Julie asked Darby Dray at her side, fingering the veil that lay across her shoulders.

"Probably because you don't want your arrival shouted at your husband by a hysterical servant," he replied with a chuckle in his voice.

She laughed softly in agreement, the veil still loose in her hands. "You are so delightfully reasonable," she told him.

"You are so delightful," he said quietly with no trace of lightness in his voice.

Julie studied the man at her side. He was her friend, a wise gentle man who had been her friend over and over in the weeks past. To bid him farewell brought a sudden sadness to her.

"Mr. Dray," she said softly. "Darby, may I tell you that I shall miss you?"

"I admit to being terribly pleased to think that you might," he replied. "Just remember, my dear, that all of us... our mutual friends and myself are at your call... always."

Before she could reply, he went on: "A message to Weston would bring us on the speed of wind."

Perhaps it was her fear that made her maudlin, but she realized that tears had formed behind her eyes. She heard the scrape of Weston's steps returning to the carriage as the black man, stiff against the light, waited at the open door.

"All joy to you, Darby Dray," she said, lifting her lips to press a kiss against his cheek. "All joy and my gratitude forever."

He had not meant to catch her into his arms but there she was. With fragrance of her hair against his face and the softness of her cheek against his, he groaned, "I am a madman, a creature of no wit at all."

She pulled back to stare at him, startled.

"Don't you see, my dear?" he asked with a rueful smile. "I could have bought that picture of you from my mates as easily as the art dealer did. Then I would have had you near me forever."

She giggled as Weston leaned into the carriage.

She paused, her hands in her lap. Then she raised her eyes to Ethan Weston. "Would it be too ungracious for me to ask that you not wait?"

"But my lady," Darby said swiftly.

"It's a rather delicate time, Darby," Weston added. "Even as rough a man as I can see this as a delicate time."

"Please, Darby," she pleaded.

"If that is your wish," he conceded with a sigh.

"It is my wish," she replied. Then after brushing his cheek with her lips, she dropped the veil over her face and moved down the path, conscious of the nervous servant at the door.

"Please, ma'am," he said warily. "Can I offer you something? Tea perhaps, or a glass of the port that the master keeps for those who call? Sherry?"

She shook her head.

"It might be an hour or more," he warned. "He rides late and long when the young master is away."

She hesitated. "I have never seen his new house," she said quietly. "Do you suppose I could just wander about and look at it while I wait?"

His eyes never stopped probing. "Oh yes, ma'am, that would be fine. He's mighty proud of this house of his that he drew himself. Come now, I'll show you around."

She shook her head firmly. "I would rather just take a candle and wander about by myself."

"If you is sure?" he said doubtfully.

"I am sure," she said firmly.

Only when the man had retreated into the back of the house did she raise the veil that darkened her view. With slow careful steps she wandered through the rooms. This house had been lovingly built. The high ceilings, which gleamed at the passage of her candle, were patterned with a bas-relief of swirling flowers. Deep fireplaces flanked by long windows adorned the living and dining rooms and to the left of the entry hall she recognized a large book-lined room as Antoine's study. She stood a long time staring at the neat desk, at the heavy footstool by the fireside chair that still bore the imprint of his foot. His books. His pipes.

She fled from the intimacy of his presence to the rooms above the wide stairs. It was easy to see which was the master bedroom. The massive bed dominating the room was hung with fine curtains drawn tightly shut. The room was lived in—there was no doubt of that from the array of toiletries on the tall dresser. The half-open closet door revealed a man's clothing hung and folded on neat shelves. Compulsively she crossed the room to open the other closet.

She gasped as she held up the candle. There, in neat rows, were her own slippers, sorted by color, her folded shawls, her dresses carefully wrapped. She strained to see the shelf above where a linen-covered series of round lumps piqued her curiosity. Bonnets, her own bonnets, their ribbons faded by time and their feathers pressed down by the dust covers.

She fled from the room, just reaching the top of the stairs when she heard the scrape of shoes at the door.

She stood there, the candle flickering in her hand. She wanted more than anything to run away, but she was frozen to the spot, watching as the great door swung inward and Antoine stepped into the hall.

He stood deliberately, the way he always had, with his long legs set well apart and his head bent a little as if in concentration as he pensively slid the gloves from his hands, one finger at a time. The servant was nowhere to be seen, but Antoine did not seem to miss him. He shrugged off his riding coat and laid it next to his crop on the polished hall table. Then he turned and glanced up the stairs.

She felt her heart stop in her throat as he stared at her.

He looked quizzically at her a long time, his head cocked as if waiting. She could not move or speak.

Then, when it seemed that her heart would burst if he did not speak, he turned and started toward the door of his study.

He almost stumbled over the sea chest. He stared at it curiously a moment, then called:

"Jacob."

The old man came at once, chattering with apology. "You came so silent," the old man said. "I meant to hear you come."

Antoine shook his words away. "What trunk is this?" he asked.

"A lady, sir," the old man was contrite. "I was to tell you the minute you came in, but you came so silent. Mr. Weston, sir, she said she was a friend of yours who would wait."

She watched him turn and walk woodenly back to the bottom of the stairs. He looked at her directly this time, his eyes steady on her own.

There was no change of expression in his face. He simply stared at her. She felt his eyes travel from her face to her hair and down the length of her body and back again to her face. There was not even a glimmer of recognition in his gaze.

Something inside her seemed to break. The worst nightmares of her return had been fulfilled. With a strangled cry, she covered her face with her hand and turned to flee, not caring where she went as long as she escaped the cold measuring gaze of that closed face.

Even in the dark she recognized that the room she had entered must be Armand's. The bed she flung herself across smelled faintly of horses. The dark cover was rough against her face and as she fought back the tears, she felt a wooden soldier fall against her from where he had been propped against the pillow.

Chapter Sixty-Nine

The carriage had barely turned from the drive of Antoine Rivière's house when Darby Dray called to the driver to stop.

Weston stared at him in astonishment. "What are you doing?" he challenged.

"I want the carriage stopped here," Darby said firmly. "I am going back."

"Good God, man," Weston exploded. "What for? You know that she wants to meet him alone."

Darby shook his head as he gathered his cloak and stepped

from the carriage. "Not all the way back. But I mean to stand there in the shadows of the trees and see that man return. Who knows? This could be the night that his mount stumbles and breaks the rider's neck. Or bandits be abroad. Or footpads."

Weston laughed softly and leaped down to join Darby.

Darby watched a candle move from room to room in the darkened lower story of the house, wondering what hand carried it.

"What was this bit about Marta that you hinted at?" he asked, self-conscious under Weston's studious gaze. Even as he asked, he saw the candle reappear in an upper window.

"That Tony is a great giant of a man of unusually handsome appearance," Weston said. "Marta had her eye on him from the first glance she had of him. When she wasn't able to get his attention with her ordinary womanly wiles, she offered to lend him unsecured money for this shipbuilding business he wanted to start. You should have seen her fume. He stayed cool as a trout even when she had him tied to her in debt. She hated that little wife of his with real passion; the cool lady way Julie has makes a bitch like Marta feel the dirt crawl on the flesh."

Darby glanced at his friend in astonishment. He had known these two people a long time. In spite of their differences, Ethan and Marta had been as close as any brother and sister he had encountered in his life. To hear Weston refer to Marta as a bitch opened an entirely new door in that house.

Weston shrugged. "To make long into short, she got worried about her money and set off to find some way to secure her loan. She found that Tony's old father in France was near death and that Antoine's snake of a brother was trying to get his hands on the estate."

"But wouldn't Antoine stand to inherit?" Darby asked.

"He had left home and shaken the dust long before," Weston laughed. "When all hell broke loose here, the hurricane wiping out the building already done and Tony's favorite child being taken by yellow jack, Marta closed in for the kill."

"What could she do?"

"Foreclose," Weston replied. "And she threatened to. With Tony behind bars, the child would go to that sick brother who had promised her the money if he got hold of the kid."

"The boy was all that stood between this Emile and the estate."

"Well, for God's sake, go on and tell me what happened."

"Ugly," Weston said quietly. "Marta braced Tony with all

296

this when he was already almost dead drunk. He fell on Julie and beat her to within an inch. My own theory is that he thought it was Marta he was using his boots on, but the little one was damned lucky to get away as I hear it."

At Darby's waiting glance, Weston shrugged. "Only after a little more than a year had passed and Julie's cousin Jacques wandered home with Tony's brother-in-law in tow, did anyone even know where she had gone. There was even talk here that Tony had killed her and she had been secretly buried. But it was agreed that she was dead in fact ...somewhere on the trail they call Natchez."

"You never did say what happened with Marta and the debt," Darby reminded him.

Weston grinned in the dark and spat into the matted leaves at his side. "Do you think I was about to let that bitch of a pirate's spawn ruin a pair like Tony and Julie? Let's just say that Tony was offered the money to pay her off by a near friend."

"Oh, guess who the near friend was," Darby laughed.

The candle had stayed in one room for a long time.

"Speaking of bitches," Darby said quietly, "I have the greatest new story that even concerns this little golden-eyed Julie. How about a rich Spaniard scion who gets the hots for a golden-eyed girl and has her kidnapped from the King of Spain?"

The candle was gone.

Darby held up his hand for silence. They could not see the horse, but his breathing and stamping carried in the cool night air.

He looked like a giant coming out of the shadows into the light of the porch. He was tall and fair in a leather riding coat, slapping a crop against his right thigh. His boots scraped on the porch as he opened the door, then closed it behind him with a dull thud.

"The King of Spain?" Weston asked, after a minute.

"Later," Darby said, his voice suddenly rough.

As the carriage picked up speed on the road back toward Charles Town, Darby stared morosely at the passing blackness.

"It's winter, Ethan," he said dully after a time.

Ethan shrugged. "Spring is never long coming to this place."

"It's winter," Darby repeated heavily. "Winter from now on out...all the way."

Chapter Seventy

Antoine Rivière stood a long time staring at the top of the stairs where the figure had appeared only a few seconds before. It had taken him a long time to get used to Julie's appearing suddenly from nowhere to stand cool and contained and incredibly graceful, those golden eyes holding him like a vise.

At first his mind had not accepted the tricks that his eyes played on him. He had run stumbling through brush, through sodden rice fields, even down the winding streets of Charles Town pursuing that phantom, calling her name, pleading. Always it ended the same way, the rough dark ridges of tree bark meeting his hand where he had seen the silk of her gown, the suddenness of a brick wall where her dark hair had caught the light.

Between each of these appearances he had gone over again in his mind the indignities he had visited on this woman whom he loved. Every small battle, every large engagement of their long war of wills over Sophie came back to him. His deceptions, his failure to support her during the loss of their Etoile, his final hideous assault on her ... they all haunted his sleepless nights.

Wraith or woman, he needed to make peace with her. He wanted to let her know that he was a changed man. He could feel the pain of his disciplined change like a thorn in his hip at every step, but, by God, he had changed. He had sworn to do penance and penance he had done and was doing hourly. He had even humbled himself to make peace with her cousin Jacques DuBois, peace which had remarkably changed in the months past to a wary, watchful friendship.

For a time, while the building of the house was in progress, she had been gone from him. It was as if the sturdy frame of the house, every room of which was designed with her in mind, had somehow managed to wall her away.

When she had returned, as mysteriously as she had left, she came sometimes in the garden behind the wall, sometimes standing quietly by the fire in his study when he raised his head from reading.

But this time it was different. She had not faded from his sight slowly like a fog being stirred by the wind. Instead she had turned and fled so that he imagined he heard the sharp beat of frantic heels on the floor of the upper hall.

But even this was easy to explain, he told himself stubbornly. There was the sea chest on the floor and Jacob's stumbled explanation that Weston had left a woman at the house...an old friend, he had said.

But what friend could it be that he had probably scared out of her wits? It could not be Marta. Since that night that he had nearly killed Julie, thinking her to be the gypsy wench, the woman had not dared to show her face.

He stared at the small trunk for a clue. It was an ordinary enough chest by any standards, wooden, bound with bands of decorated metal. He bent and tugged at the lock, only to have it resist his force. Only as he got a candle to examine the lock did he see that a row of letters had been carefully etched onto the metal band beneath the lock.

The letters had been done with exquisite care, but were so small that it taxed his eyes to make them out in the poor light. He made them out slowly, one at a time: J. RIVIÈRE. His hand holding the candle trembled, spilling a droplet of burning wax on his wrist.

Julie he whispered. Julie Rivière."

He bounded the steps three at a time like a madman. He slammed from room to room seeking her. When he opened the last door, the one to Armand's room, he saw the small figure twist on the bed, twist and struggle upright to turn and stare at him.

"Julie," he suggested softly. She was Julie. She *had* to be Julie returned from the dead, bearing a salt-stained sea chest with a Spanish-style hasp.

But still she didn't speak. He watched her slide to the edge of the bed, one small slipper groping for the floor until she stood scarcely taller than a child...smaller even than he remembered, a waif of a child-woman whose perfect face, damped by tears, pleaded with him silently from its frame of shadowy hair.

His own voice deserted him. He moved toward her slowly, searching the darkness for a sign. Now she would disappear. Now he would see only the moving curtains, stirred by his own breath.

But this time the figure did not melt or fade or even turn and run. It stood stiffly, and as he neared, the mouth—it was always a sober mouth when she appeared to him—moved hesitantly and she spoke.

"Antoine," she said. "It is me, Julie."

Not since the day she had disappeared had he held a woman in his arms. He reached for her awkwardly.

"Here," he said gently. "No more tears." Disengaging her arms, he leaned over and lifted her in his arms to carry her to the room he had so lovingly planned for her. With his free arm, he threw the curtain aside and set her down. The last of the candle guttered in its wax. He tore it from the socket and set a new one in its place.

With tears clinging still to her dark lashes, she leaned toward him. "Oh, my love," she sighed, her mouth curling in a smile. "I have been gone so long . . . so very long from you."

"Forever," he said, still at her feet. "You have been gone forever."

She shook her head and reached out to him. "No grave, my love, no grave."

He started to talk again, ignoring her outstretched arms and frowning as if his life depended on the words that poured from his mouth. On and on he talked while Julie listened in horror. Why was he going on like this? Why was he groveling with apology? Good God, he had not even taken her into his arms except to set her here on this great bed to make this elaborate and unreal confession. *Mea culpa*. She heard Fray Jacobo's words. *Mea culpa*, I am guilty. He was so bewitched by his own litany that he could not see that she was frantic to feel his arms about her, his lips on her own.

She had to break the spell. She stared at him, wanting to cry out, "Why are you talking, Antoine Rivière? Why do you ply me with words when our lips have not even met? Have I fought my way through hell to this place to return to conversation?" She reached out and laid her hand along his cheek only to have him start restlessly and rise to pace across the room.

"I must talk to you, Julie," he insisted. "My God, the words I have already said to you have streamed through my mind so many times that I know them by rote. Guilt—can you imagine how it has been to love with guilt like mine? And the anger at myself. Anger that I drove you to such desperate adventures,

300

I, who treated you worse than a cur. I have done penance a hundred ways, Julie, and I still am not clean. I have become a monk from contrition. How can I ever make it up to you, my dearest, for all the pain I have caused you?"

She stared at him thoughtfully. The tormented creature in her husband's skin repelled her. She wanted to cry out, "It is over. It is done. We are together." But the heaviness in his face warned her that whatever flame of guilt burned in him could not be dampened by words.

She slid forward and smiled up at him. "Antoine," she beseeched, "I have just ended a long journey. I am tired, thirsty, and hungry. Could I perhaps change from these dreary weeds and have some wine and bread and then we could talk?" Startled, he stared at her. "Oh, my dear, of course. What was I thinking of? What would you like?"

She sighed silently at his instant subjection. I will run away again, she told herself recklessly. I will not have this great man of passion licking my hands like a dog.

"Don't bring me anything," she said. "Just find a little wine and cheese and I will join you."

Even as his footsteps sounded on the stairs, she ran to the closet. She pawed desperately among the clothes. Good God, she did not even remember her own things!

She threw aside one garment after another as too staid or too heavy. Finally she found it, the sheer gown that Sophie had ordered for her wedding so many years ago. The peignoir that matched it must be there somewhere, too.

With the widow's garments tossed away and the peignoir still across the chair, she stood with her head thrown back, tugging the brush through her hair which was curled tighter than usual by the salt spray of her journey.

Distracted by her haste, she did not hear his careful steps on the stair. Clad only in the sheer chemise, she turned to see him enter the room carrying a tray laden with a decanter of wine, cheese, and some biscuits. And a single glass.

His eyes touched her body and darted away. That marvelous bold glance that used to trace the fullness of her high breasts and the curve of her rounded thighs slid away as he moved toward the table. She followed him, leaving the peignoir. If this was to be a struggle of mind against body, she was on body's side.

"Come, Julie," he said solicitously. "You are tired. You must have something to eat and drink."

She felt herself stiffen with something like fury. "I am certainly thirsty," she told him briskly. "And hungry, but I am not cold."

She watched him fill the single goblet halfway.

He lifted it carefully by the stem and held it out to her.

"You will not drink a toast to my safe return?" she asked.

"I have not drunk a drop since the day you left," he replied.

"But then, you had nothing to celebrate," she said brightly. As he hesitated, she smiled at him warmly. "For heaven's sake, Antoine, a sip is all I ask."

Since he was still holding the glass, she lifted the bottle.

She clinked the bottle merrily against his goblet and took a deep draught from the neck of the bottle.

"Now I propose a toast to the years we have had and the good years remaining." She tilted the bottle to her lips again and drank from it, eyeing him all the while.

At least his expression had changed from that sanctimonious look. She thought she would define his new one as wary.

"Just one more toast," she said blandly. "It is to that bright star that brought us together."

He nodded and lifted the goblet one more time. It did not seem to Julie that the level in the glass had changed at all while the bottle was now less than half full. With her words still in the air, she stood up abruptly and slid off her shoulder strap to reveal her naked torso and the star-shaped scar beneath her breast.

Antoine flushed and said, "Julie, what in hell are you doing?"

But his tone was not good manly anger but indignation. Indignation, Julie told herself angrily, is only a pious excuse for passion.

"I am celebrating, Antoine," she said quietly. "I am celebrating my return to the only man I have ever loved with all my life."

"I am unworthy of your love, Julie. I can only remember how I used your passion to my own ends, how ruthlessly I exploited your love."

"Hell's fire," she said suddenly, feeling the wine like a ruddy strength in her veins. "It is over, Antoine. It is over and I am home again and we are alive ... do you know what it means to be alive in this dangerous world? Your ships lie in the harbor, your son is safe in Philadelphia, and I want to celebrate." She lifted the bottle to find that it was empty.

302

He sat stolidly without looking at her. As she watched him she realized that he was wavering.

"Would one of you please get me more wine?" she finally asked.

They both shook their heads and she saw them start to rise.

"Very well," she said. "I can damned well find it for myself."

"Come back here," he shouted. "Where are you going? Jacob."

She looked down at the stairs that spun crazily before her. "To hell with Jacob," she called back. "A cat can look at a king, you know." Then it struck her. It was a saint that he wanted her to be.

"And Jacob can look at the saint. And a horse can look..." It turned into a song in her mind, not Josh's song, tender and haunting, but one of Ellie's tunes, Ellie who had asked her what she would do if she came back home and didn't like Antoine.

Still gripping the bannister, she began to jig, pirate-style, on the stairs in her sheer chemise.

"Oh bring me a bawdy and spill me some rum
For the sea is welling full
And I need a cunt for my cock for to rest
And a bottle of rum for to pull."

She heard him coming but she could not move fast enough to get away. The stairway was rising and falling wildly before her and she laughed to see it writhe like great coils of rope swinging free of belaying pins.

She heard the muffled banging of a door deep in the house and thought of Jacob. She heard a muffled curse behind her and knew it was Antoine.

He bore her, wrestling and cursing, back upstairs and laid her on the big bed in the master bedroom.

"For God's sake, woman," he said furiously, glaring down at her. "What are you trying to do?"

"Antoine, my darling," she said sadly, "I was trying to seduce you. But I am afraid that I have forgotten how."

The wine closed over her in a red wave. She hiccoughed and passed out.

303

Chapter Seventy-One

Antoine had never slept in the grand bed he had ordered for the master bedroom of the house on the river. The bed itself was made of finest native cyprus, polished and finished so that the convolutions of the grain made a delicate traced pattern of a sweet light color. The mattress was stuffed with French goose down since the local people found that geese only drew the foxes and the wolves from the forests to their barnyards. The captain of the *Sojourner* had been given the privilege of purchasing the coverlet, having only been told that the color must be a pale soft blue and the texture as soft as the face of a new child.

But he had never slept in the bed. The bed was to be saved for the day when Julie, restored to him by the miracle of his faith alone, would begin with him a marriage based on a higher, purer plane.

And now she lay in that great bed, her ripe mouth open in drunken sleep and her body, God help him, loosely abandoned like a soft doll thrown away by a careless child. Self-control over carnal lust, he discovered, was easiest when not tempted.

There was a cot in the room across the hall where he usually slept alone for the few hours he found rest. He pulled a coverlet from it and slouched in the chair across the room from Julie, ready in case she should call to him in the night.

What demon possessed her that she could down an entire bottle of wine? If it were not so sad, it might be funny, that small delicate woman lifting the bottle to her lips like a raucous bandit. She was overtired and excited beyond reason at returning to her home.

A soft snore stopped his musing. He considered pulling the curtain aside to watch her but thought better of it. His resistance to her carnal appeal was almost unbearable without any further testing.

Finally he slept. The sound that wakened him startled him into remembering. It was weeping. Slow heavy sobs filled the room. He leaped to his feet, still dazed from sleep, and pulled the curtain aside. She was still sleeping even as the tears slipped from under her closed lids to stain the bed linen. As he watched, she stirred in her sleep, her arms curling out helplessly. "Antoine," she moaned softly, "my love, my love."

How many times had she turned to him at night for such comforting? "Comfort," he told himself, slipping off his breeches and sliding into the bed beside her.

Time slid away from him. He was in the dark room of the gamekeeper's cottage in Epping with Titus in his cranny down the hall. The girl had wakened screaming and thrown herself from her fevered bed with dreams of fire.

He had lain beside her that night too, reining in his passion because of her fevered state, lain in innocence until she turned to him in the agony of a dream. Then he had taken her, virgin that she was, in a great storm of lust. But that was another time, another Antoine Rivière.

As he sweated with the force of his memory, she stirred in her sleep and pressed her warmth against him. When he tried to pull away she only clung tighter with a small cry of alarm.

She smelled of wine, a rich fruity flavor that only tantalized his own lips. When she fell back a little, he pressed his lips on hers, exploring the forgotten sweetness of her mouth. After that there was no stopping the beast in him. He threw himself between her thighs in an agony of desire. She rose to him, thrusting her roundness against him as the rhythm of their passion rose to the final peak of fulfillment. He groaned at the release of his seed into that responsive body. Then, as she fell limp in his arms, he felt that low vibration of laughter begin to well from deep within her. Her laughter sounded soft and clear in the dark room.

"Antoine, Antoine," she said in a hushed whisper. "I am home. I am home.

Since the habits of many weeks and months were not easy to break, Antoine often tried to speak to her of guilt and repentance in the days that followed. Once when Paul and Jacques were in the room and he began his miserable monologue, Julie crossed the room and casually lifted a full bottle of wine and stared at him. He did not explain his spontaneous laughter at her pose but dropped his lecture and fell back into his usual easy banter.

Once while dining with her aunt Anne-Louise, Julie heard the familiar refrain begin. She kicked him fiercely under the table while smiling brightly at his startled, pained glance.

But delicious as Julie found their shared time, she yearned to see the child Armand. Antoine obtained daily reports of new cases of yellow fever in Charles Town.

"Soon," he promised her. "Soon we will get a message from Sophie and they will all come flying home."

"I cannot wait," she confessed. "After you it was always Armand that I dreamed of."

But many of their hours were spent in happy reunion with Paul Bontemps and Jacques. By the time they were free to pay a call on Ethan Weston, Darby Dray was gone, having left a message to Julie for Weston to deliver. It read:

Dear Lady,
Thank you again for the pleasure of your company. Do remember that your need is my dearest privilege. All blessings on your life. •

It was simply signed with two gracefully swirling *D*'s. Touched by his simple words, she tucked the card in among the Spanish clothes that Pilar had so carefully packed for her. Already that part of her life was fading in the brilliance of her newfound joy with Antoine. Already she thought of herself first as Antoine's wife and Armand's mother and then, as herself. Together they eagerly awaited the message that would announce the return of the family from Philadelphia.

The message, when it came, was not delivered in the normal style, by a paid messenger. Instead it came when Paul Bontemps banged on the great door of the river house while a December moon swung toward dawn.

A lathered horse drooped in the drive as Antoine, hastily trousered with little to cut the chill, took the message from his brother-in law's hand.

Watching the two men from the stairs, Julie felt a surge of rebellion. Something was wrong, something was terribly wrong. She read it in their faces, in the drawn look of Paul's eyes.

Then Antoine turned to her and took her hands in his. "I am sure that Sophie is needlessly upset," he said quietly. "You know how women can be when they still have a child at breast."

"Stop that," Julie ordered. "Tell me what is wrong."

"She says—" His voice failed and he had to begin again.

"Sophie has sent a message saying that Armand—"

The note was there beside him. Julie pulled her hand away and seized it. The words flashed like quick lights against her mind. "Worry" . . . "Come at once" . . . "Armand . . . disappeared."

Part 7

SHADOWS

1730-31

Chapter Seventy-Two

Her first reaction had been anger. Knowing Armand as she did, his aunt Sophie thought he had willfully wandered away. It was like him, she said to herself, for he was a headstrong boy who did not hesitate to disobey instructions that displeased him. But it was a bitterly cold day with patches of ice lying in the low places of the street.

But he had insisted on coming along, even though Sophie had warned him that she would spend a long time in the shops and that his feet would surely dance with cold on the Philadelphia streets.

"Trump will miss me if I don't go to Mr. Hatter's silver shop with you," Armand had protested, his handsome face drawn into a pout.

"For heaven's sake, who is Trump?" their hostess Mignonette had laughed. "Surely you don't mean that great wheezing pump of a dog that waddles around the smith's shop?"

"He is my friend," Armand claimed defensively. "He's old and fat and half blind but he likes me to pet him."

Sophie, realizing how much the boy missed his own dogs, how empty his days were of childish fun, relented at last and let him come with her and Sally.

Quite casually she had mentioned to Mignonette that while she was in Philadelphia she wished to shop for some silver pieces for her tables, adding that now that Paul was safely back home, they meant to entertain more often.

"How lucky you are, Sophie," Mignonette said. "For many finer crafts we have to go to Boston or New York, but the finest silversmith I ever saw is right here in town."

She jumped to her feet and selected a key from the ring she always wore at her waist. "This must seem very self-important," Mignonette had explained when Sophie first looked at the great loop of keys. "It may not even be necessary, but my maid, Dodie—" Her voice had dropped to a whisper. "She's a darling girl and a quick learner but she did not come to the colonies by choice. She chose emigrating over Newgate and her offense had been stealing. I keep all my fine things under lock and key as much for her sake as mine."

Unlocking a large cabinet built into the wall of the dining room, Mignonette drew out a cloth-wrapped bundle and returned to Sophie's side. As she did so, she chattered on about Mark Hatter, whom she referred to as "Philadelphia's own artist."

"Not only is he an artist in silver, designing articles to the smallest whim of his customers, but he is a collector too. You should see that house of his. He and that miserable pug dog and a deaf old crone of a housekeeper live among paintings and sculpture that would make a museum-keeper green with envy."

"He must be a man of great wealth," Sophie observed.

Mignonette nodded as she unwrapped the silver. "And he is a self-made man too, the most eligible young bachelor in this city."

Sophie turned the piece in her hands in disbelief. She had never seen a creamer more elegantly shaped. Her hand reveled in the feel of the polished silver, the curved delicacy of the handle and three small curved legs.

"How marvelous it would be to possess some of his fine work," Sophie said wistfully.

"You must go and talk to him about what you want. You will like him as well as his work."

"But you say he is so busy," Sophie hesitated, her eyes suddenly wistful. "You cannot imagine how hard it is for me to stay away from Paul even in the joy of your company. I must leave for Charles Town the first day it is safe."

Mignonette laid her hand on Sophie's arm. "It is so marvelous to have your dear Paul the same as raised from the dead. I would be the same if I had been apart from my Jean. But let me send a note to Mr. Hatter in my own hand. I shall

310

appeal to the romance in his soul and tell him of the fever that has driven you and your little family up here. I am sure that he will make time for you. He is such a man."

Now Sophie rose and paced the room again. If only she had not coveted her friend's lovely silver and begun the first of her many trips to Mark Hatter's shop. Even Armand had been enchanted with the place. The first time they went he talked her into buying him a charming silver whistle.

But Armand had accompanied her only to learn that the dog Trump had been left at home because the cold weather made him lame. When he grew restless and wished to go out and watch the crowds passing in the street, Sophie had reluctantly permitted it, certain that he would not long forsake the warmth of the shop for the chill winds.

When she had first glanced through the window and not seen his bright hat, she thought him temporarily out of view and sent the girl Sally to check.

"He's gone," the girl reported glumly. "He is nowhere. Just simply gone."

"Ridiculous," Sophie protested. "He can only be a few steps away, go and call him lustily."

Mark Hatter called his apprentice Seth to go and help Sally with the search. Unable to concentrate on the design they were discussing, Sophie apologized to Mark Hatter for the interruption.

"He is such a mischief, that boy," she told him. "But he is so dear to me. I must locate him before my head will work at all again."

As he piled the sheets of design together, Mark Hatter smiled with understanding. How charming he was, Sophie mused. And such a large man to have such delicacy in his hands. She guessed him to be as tall as Antoine but with large heavy bones that produced immense hands.

"I feel some responsibility that the child strayed away," he admitted. "He plays so happily with old Trump. I wish I had thought to bring the beast today in spite of the weather."

She would have protested his leaving his work on her account but he gave her no chance. Once they were both dressed for the street they saw Sally coming toward them, still searchingly darting her eyes from side to side. From the other direction came the apprentice Seth, bearing no better news than Sally's.

The whole business seemed to turn to madness at that moment.

When his own inquiries along the street yielded nothing,

Mr. Hatter, his hand supportive under her arm, took Sophie to report to the authorities.

The man studied Sophie. "Any mark or sign on the body?" Sophie's heart sunk at the question so that she was only able to shake her head helplessly. It was Mr. Hatter who mentioned the whistle.

"He was carrying that whistle of his, wasn't he?" he asked Sophie. "It is silver," he explained at her nod. "On a fine chain of the same material. Four bells like tiny sleigh bells are mounted on the post and at the end was set a polished tip of coral."

"His initials are engraved on it," Sophie reminded him.

Mr. Hatter nodded. "And my own sign, a joined MH is on the stem near the coral end where the initials ADR are found."

The man assured Mr. Hatter that a search would be launched at once, then turned to Sophie. "Do not fret your head, dear lady. This is not a city of thieves and bandits. The boy has wandered afield, I'll be bound, and you might expect him home in time for tea."

Sophie had accepted his assurances with numb civility. How could he know what she herself knew—that a person could walk through the door of a house as Julie had done, never to be heard from again.

Mark Hatter too, had said that Armand would be home by teatime. As winter darkness sifted into the streets, pushed back by only torches and lanterns, no knock came at the door. Teatime came and went but Sophie was unconscious of the maid Dodie's eyes on her in compassion as she held her infant son, chilled by the enormity of her fear.

Mignonette's husband Jean, a man of good repute and some influence in the city, cast out a great net of inquiry among his friends and acquaintances. Servants were sent running to every home in the city where the child Armand had been taken as a guest—to the home of old Madame Saint-Leger who was an intimate of Sophie's own parents, to the family DeBarre where Julie's aunt Anne-Louise was a frequent visitor when she was in from the Carolinas.

Where was he, where could he be? Oh God, let him not be cold or hungry or ill-treated by rough men. Terror and contrition alternated in her heart. How badly she had spoiled him. Let him not be arrogant wherever he was, let him be appealing and gentle so that strange hearts might be concerned for his well-being.

Yet she knew that the child had to be held against his will if

312

he were not painfully hurt. He had so quickly learned his way to here and there, and although too young to read, had memorized the names of streets and where their friends lived. How could she have failed Antoine so miserably? In a space of time no longer than a minute, she had failed her brother and her dead friend Julie.

"Just one day," her host Jean pleaded the next morning. "Wait just one day before sending them the news. The boy will be found, he must be found. What an agony to launch those men on an arduous winter journey here for nought but to find the child safe at their arrival."

Sophie burst into helpless tears. "I cannot wait. I at least owe them that, having failed so miserably in the other."

Chapter Seventy-Three

Mark Hatter forced the thought of the red-headed nephew of Madame Bontemps from his mind. Darkness filled the shop to be pushed back only a little by extra candles that Seth lit as it neared five o'clock. How could this be? The day was surely no darker than other winter days in Philadelphia. It was the lost child, he finally conceded to himself, laying his pen aside to stare into the bleak frozen street beyond his window.

The plight of the boy had laid a shadow on his mind. He had been astonished to learn that the child was not Madame Bontemps' son. The obvious intimacy between them and the startling resemblance in their hair color had led him to this natural conclusion. But then, he knew nothing of this lady except that she and her children had sought refuge with his patrons while yellow fever raged in Charles Town. But no matter whose child he was, his sudden disappearance was appalling.

While the boy was no weakling, he was of tender age. Many times as he had played on the floor of the shop Mark had felt himself drawn to the strong-willed little fellow. Very sure of himself, he was, talking away to Trump in a low steady chatter as if the wheezing old dog were catching every word that he said.

From the chatter Mark himself knew the boy to be a child

313

of the fields and trees. Armand had spoken to Trump about his pony, whose name was Steed, and of a great white cat who nested in the stable to bring forth spotted kittens.

"You may come and chase the great cat if you will," the child had told Trump in a burst of generosity. "If it hurts you to run, I shall even put her on a rope for you. But you must not run after the dappled kittens, for they are small and fearful."

Now it was the red-headed boy himself who must be small and fearful abroad in the dark cold of this strange city.

Startled by a tentative sound at his elbow, he turned to see his apprentice Seth watching him hopefully.

"Good Lord, Seth," Mark Hatter cried, pushing his work aside. "It's well past time for tea and here I am sitting and dreaming." He fished in his pocket for coins. "Trip around the corner and get some fresh loaves for us. Have the monger fill them with oysters on the way back. And mind that he drops some of the pepper sauce onto each one." He grinned at the boy.

Mark watched at the window as the young man beat a swift course down the street. He had been at the point of launching into a great tale that would have bored Seth as like as not.

What was Seth now, nineteen? He himself had been older, in his mid-twenties, when the only woman he had ever loved had disappeared mysteriously in an instant as this boy Armand had done.

Never before or since had a woman meant to him what she had, coming mysteriously into the home of his protector, living there among the loutish lot of them like a flower blooming in a kennel. Mark sighed into the emptiness of the shop. When the girl had disappeared he himself had made a plan to find her. He had set up a great conspiracy among the apprentices, naming a grand prize of money for one who could lead him to where she was hidden.

It had worked though it took all the money he had to get her to safety.

Now there was money beyond what he could spend and nowhere to spend it. A man could only eat so much and drink so much and even buy so many fine paintings unless he wished to exchange his fine brick house for a cold museum. After that, all became dross.

Seth, struggling with his packages at the door, roused him from his reverie. Swinging the door wide, he grinned at the lad.

314

The boy set down his things to clap his hands over his ears. "It is a night to freeze blood," he admitted, turning to the pouring of the tea.

While his master was sunk in thought, Seth ate prodigiously, careful that the juice of the plump oysters not spill on his only shirt. He was startled by the sudden sound of his master's voice.

"Cold though it may be, Seth," Mark Hatter said thoughtfully, "I have a guinea for your hand if you will run me three errands this night."

"A guinea, sir?" Seth repeated in delight.

As was his way, Mark Hatter smiled swiftly. "It is surely worth that much to have your blood frozen. First I would have you go to Master Burrough's art gallery—you know the place, you have collected pictures for me there. Ask for the master himself and take my apologies. Tell him that a matter of great import prevents my coming by this evening as promised. Ask him to hold the new paintings but a day or two more before hanging them out for the people of the town to pick and choose among them."

"And the second one, sir?" Seth nodded.

His master was frowning now. "Go to wherever the most 'prentices of the city gather . . . never mind what trades. There are always such places where there is music and cheap ale and a great gathering of young people. Go there and make it known that a boy has been lost that matters to your master. Tell them that a reward is out for the lad. Tell them there is a week's wages for any information about him at all. Tell them there is a month's wages if one can be led to the child himself . . . alive and unharmed. Oh, and be sure, Seth, to describe the whistle, for it is the only one just like that in the world as far as I know, having designed it myself."

Seth's eyes flew wide with greed.

"The third is simply a delivery. I will write a note for you to deliver to Madame Bontemps. I wish her to know my great distress about the loss of the child from our very doorsill here. I want her to know the reward has been posted. It might give her some small ray of hope."

Later, after making the rounds of the art gallery, the home where the red-headed Frenchwoman was visiting, and all the taverns he knew about in town, Seth chose a place to stop where he was not known that he might sit over his own pint in peace.

315

With the second pint before him, he was still brooding on the maid named Dodie who had admitted him to the Frenchman's house.

"Is this somewhat about the missing boy?"

He had nodded and explained that his master had announced a reward and how generous it was.

Her lips had formed an O with a faint exhalation of breath. Never had he seen a mouth so kissable as that. Then she asked if he might stay until she returned.

"You are a nice fellow," she told him, smiling with her head a little to one side, looking more shy than she sounded.

"Tell me about that reward again and the whistle," she urged.

He was glad to do it and glad to have her round cheeks resting on her hands like that as she listened.

Her smile had been so gleaming, showing small white teeth.

As she watched from the door she had called after him, her breath a fine cloud in the air: "You'll come back, won't you?"

One way or another he would get back, he promised himself. Something must have come over him to attract such a pigeon as that without his even putting his mind to it at the first.

Chapter Seventy-Four

By the coming of dawn, their plans were complete. Even though one of his own ships lay in the harbor, Antoine insisted that they make the journey north by land.

"I must have a sense of motion toward a search for Armand," Antoine explained. "A calm day at sea would drive me from my mind. To go by land is slow and hard but at least one can keep moving."

Paul, having returned to his own plantation after his night visit, arrived at dawn, haggard of face but calm.

"With your indulgence," Paul said. "I have made plans to come along with you."

"'That is generous of you..." Antoine began.

"Not generous," Paul corrected him, "just realistic. Has it occurred to you that Sophie does not even know of Julie's return? Although my wife is a creature of great strength, she is still tired from the birth of the child. The shock of Armand's disappearance, no matter how brief, can only be a greater drain on her under those circumstances. And then," he smiled warmly at Julie, "we will all be together at last."

"But we can take no time to wait for you to ready yourself," Antoine said bluntly. "The chests are being loaded to leave within the hour."

Paul nodded. "I ordered the packing of my own when I returned to the plantation earlier. They will be ready to load as we pass the house on that road."

In the days and nights that followed, Julie was grateful for the distraction of Paul's companionship in the carriage that went north, always north toward Philadelphia. The travel itself was numbing, miles of bone-bruising roads broken only by brief snatches of rest caught at inns where hastily prepared meals were indifferently served to these travelers who pressed so ruthlessly for speed.

It was as if he appointed himself the social manager for the two morose people who shared the carriage with him. It was Paul who pointed out the changing scenery, discussing the growing of tobacco with Antoine, pondering aloud whether that crop, no matter how wasteful it was of the soil, might not be a better basis for a plantation than rice. He regaled Julie with the gossip of the town, delighting her with the news that Dr. Jonathan Marlow had married a lovely young lady from Newport and was even now building a home for her upriver. And he spoke much about his son Charles with whom he had corresponded often but whom he still had not seen since his return from the Natchez.

"Tell me, dear Julie," he asked. "You know that son of mine better than I do myself. How would you say that he would fall in love?"

Julie felt a grin tug at her mouth. "Charles in love? Why, Paul, he is a child. In love indeed."

"Love does not look at clocks or calendars," Paul chided her. "I myself was miserably in love with Sophie by the time I was twelve...a condition," he added with a grin, "which has not abated with time."

"Charles in love," Julie said thoughtfully, grateful to have such a happy thought to which to turn her tortured mind. She thought of Charles as she had first met him, a fatherless child. How had he been then with the things he loved? "Fiercely protective, for one," she finally said aloud. "Endlessly gentle but as protective as a lion with its cubs. And terribly romantic about weakness."

"I would not like to be the person standing between that young man and what he loved," Antoine put in quietly.

Paul glanced at his brother-in-law with surprise. "You both have such an advantage over me in your knowledge of the lad. But I thought when he was an infant that he would be a gentle type of man."

"Gentle, yes," he agreed. "But he is firm, very firm. He is not a man easily dissuaded from his goals, not easily discouraged. He clings to his own mind over anyone's resistance. But what put this strange question in your mind?"

Paul shrugged. "A father's fancy, perhaps. I just have a gut feeling that something beside his work at the University is keeping him in France. Did he come to see his long-lost father? As joyful as he was at the news, did he come to see his new brother Julius when the child was born? His letters show no lessening of love for us and I could think of nothing but love that would bind him so tightly to that place."

"His grandfather is seriously ill," Julie reminded him. "Perhaps that has affected his decision."

"My father has been saying that for many years, always dying and writing a new will only to revive and play the whole drama again," Antoine snorted. "He has long made his impending death a tool for handling people. And in any case, my father is in Paris and Charles is forty miles away in Caen."

Paul looked at Antoine thoughtfully. "Perhaps it is the tone of Charles' letters that has softened me toward your father. Perhaps it is my own experiences of the past years. But in any event, I find myself thinking of old Charles Rivière with pity instead of hate, bereft of his favorite children and caught between a warring son and a discontented wife as he is."

"Beware of your pity, Paul," Antoine said tersely. "Men like my father are most dangerous when you lower your guard against them. Look at that hideous thing he did to the young Austrian girl. Can you imagine an innocent girl brought to marriage by a monstrous pervert like my brother Emile? Can you see any hand in that marriage but my father's?"

"Perhaps not," Paul agreed, "but the old man might have

hoped that she would reform him from his madness and bring heirs to the Rivière line."

"Perhaps Emile loves her," Julie put in softly, having been sufficiently surprised by the news of the union that took place in her absence to feel that true love must have motivated this great change in a brother-in-law she did not know.

Antoine moved restlessly in his seat. "Emile knows only lust, even as his father before him did. He lusts for young fops who pander to his bestiality until he tires of them and throws them away."

"But she sounds so lovely from what Paul has said of her."

"Charles indeed thinks she is a gem," Paul agreed. "He has had only the gentlest things to say of her, even adding that his grandfather delighted in her presence."

"She came with rich land and a good dower," Antoine reminded him. "My father would enjoy the company of the Devil if he brought the deed to Hell with him."

With the inns so few and the accomodations so primitive, Antoine's towering impatience proved to be a great asset. There were no relaxed evenings over dinners nor whole nights slept in warm beds, but he was able to produce service where none was available. He was able to obtain what provender there was and a bed to tumble into by the sheer driving force of his fury and insistence.

The muddy roads of the Carolinas gave way to the frozen ruts of Virginia and still the carriage clattered on. Paul had drifted to sleep, his head rolling slightly against the cushions at his back. Antoine slid his arm around Julie's waist and lifted her face to his with his free hand.

"We will find our son, Julie," he told her. "Believe with me."

At the pleading tone of his voice she felt a silent cry rise inside herself. "Believe for me," he added as they clung to each other on the endless road north.

The winter that battered against their carriage swept through the even streets of Philadelphia with unaccustomed fury. Snow turned the fields of the country west of town to a vast, blanketed brilliance that melted under the passage of traffic only to freeze again and lock carriage wheels in blocks of ice. Pillars of icicles clawed downward from the roofs, masking the brick faces of the houses behind veils of crystal.

319

But no storm raged any more violently than the waves of guilt and anguish in Sophie Bontemps' heart as the days passed and the search for Armand yielded nothing. She went from terror to grief and on to moody silence. Unable to sleep, her slender body wasted to skeletal thinness and dark shadows rimmed her once lovely eyes.

"She has become one of the living dead," her friend Mignonette wailed. "We must do something for her, Jean, anything."

Jean took his wife gently into his arms. "Name it, my dear," he told her defeatedly. "Name what we can do and I will set at it at once. There is not an officer in this city who is not actively searching for the child. There is not a street in this city on which an appeal has not been cried. Even the handsome rewards which your friend the silversmith offered still remain unclaimed. The problem is that there is no logic in the child's disappearance. He had no property on him worth a thief's time except that single toy which could be had for the breaking of a slender chain."

She shook her head. "Logic, you talk of logic and I only know that his father and uncle must even now be drawing near to see their child. Oh God, how I dread to face them."

"The child's father," Jean mused aloud, "what sort of a man is he? Could he have enemies who would seize a child for reasons of revenge?"

Mignonette braced her arms and stared up at him. "What an odd idea, Jean," she said with shock in her voice. Then she shook her head. "I knew him as a child, of course, but have only heard stories since."

"Stories?" he asked quickly. "What stories?"

Mignonette shook her head. "He did not come to the colonies with Sophie and Paul, you know. He was in England. It was there that he met the girl he later married here in the colonies." Again she shook her head. "How can there be anything there? The Rivière family is a fine old family in France. You know le Comte, a crusty old man and known to be ruthless, but of good blood. And the girl Antoine married is a niece of Anne-Louise DuBois whom you have always liked."

Her husband shook his head. "I just find myself always coming back to one question. The streets of any city are full of children racing and sledding and escaping the eyes of their guardians. I notice them all the time since this happened. And I always find myself faced with the same question: Why was

320

this particular child chosen? What do you really know of these people?"

Chapter Seventy-Five

The house that Jean provided for his wife Mignonette was considered palatial by Philadelphia standards, even when first built. While planning the great rooms and halls with generous quarters for servants, Jean had imagined that one day their children would tumble on the wide stairs or curl up in the generous cushions of the window seats to stare out at their world.

Although these children did not come, Fortune smiled on Jean and Mignonette in so many other ways they grew comfortable in the role of host and hostess, using their vast, elegant house and well-trained servants to provide hospitality to an almost endless stream of relatives and friends.

So it was that Sophie Bontemps, her infant son Julius, and her nephew Armand Rivière had spent a pleasant, pampered month with Jean and Mignonette, while waiting for the pestilence to leave Charles Town.

Not all of the members of the staff were equally pleased by the extended stay of Madame's old friend Sophie. The cook, Nabby Barnes, was delighted, because young Armand had a prodigious appetite and was exuberant in his praise for her skill.

The rest of the staff, having little contact with the guests, were indifferent as to who came and went. But the principal maid, Dodie, found her work doubled by the five strangers since the Scotswoman Mrs. MacRae and the Negro Sally had come with the party. Mrs. MacRae's efforts to corral the lively Armand were hampered by the time she spent helping Sally with the new infant, who was fretful and demanding. The parties and teas for the guests, the extra laundry to be seen and sorted had set Dodie's teeth on edge against the visitors.

It was the boy who bothered her the most. How pampered he was, with always more money in his pocket than she had left over at the end of a month. His every wish was expressed as a command and he had that horrid silver whistle that he blew at odd times, sending a body into shrieks of surprise.

But when the child so mysteriously disappeared, not even Dodie dared to say anything too positive about his absence.

"This place has gone from a circus to a tomb," she complained to Nabby. "When he was here the place was a bleeding madhouse and now it's as still as a burying ground."

"He was a healthy boy and shut in too much," Nabby said sadly, looking up from her dough. "He had some fire to let out at his age. God hold him wherever he is."

"He's probably melting snow without fire instead of keeping this place in a turmoil all the time," Dodie suggested. "But there's still the little one with one or the other end of him going all the time. It's a fresh stack of bibs or nappies ever time a body moves."

"That's good for you to notice," Nabby warned her. "The way you carry on you'll be having one of them yourself to wipe one of these days."

"What kind of a thing is that to say?" Dodie challenged her. "Just because I have a fellow of me own and you have none, you have to be foulmouthed about my Barney."

"I've no use for sailors such as he is," Nabby told her. "Not only are they gone more than they're here, but that one has a look that makes me nervous."

"Any hot-blooded man would make you nervous," Dodie snapped. "Spinster that you be."

"Spinster I may well be," Nabby said tartly, "but you don't find me short of ribbons because I made a loan of every cent I made for some fellow to swill rum."

Dodie slammed from the kitchen, knowing that one retort would lead to another until she wanted to ram the old hen's head into her own stewpot. And it was like Nabby to put her tongue on a sore point. The whole time she'd been walking out with Barney he had been asking her for a bit of money whenever they were together, but those loans never seemed to get repaid. They went for rum or gambling, she was sure.

And she had thought him so grand when they met, big like he was and fresh of face with a smart tongue. But the glister was fading off. She was even beginning to doubt the future he spelled out for himself, how he would one day have a carriage and a brick house and live like a king. He seemed no richer for that dream than when they met, while she herself never had two coins to jingle in her own pocket.

Even now he was beginning to hint about what little gift of

money Madame Bontemps might slip in her pocket when she finally took her crew back South. Him and his lucky break!

Her steps slowed on the stairs. The silversmith had made such a fine offer of reward. She had told Barney about it right off, wondering if Barney might not be able to locate the clue that the others had all missed.

Mignonette, piled in her pillows, stirred her morning tea thoughtfully. In spite of herself, her husband's words kept coming back to her. "What do you really know of these people?"

With Sophie it was easy enough, they had been girls together in France. As always when she thought of those days, her eyes turned misty. How delicious it had been to be young with the excitement of a whole life spread before her. How she and Sophie had whispered by the hour in Sophie's fine bedroom suite.

"Love," Mignonette laughed softly in the empty room. Love in those days had nothing to do with fidelity or marriage or the bearing of children. Love was the scent of flowers and the thrill of young men's eager attention.

But love had turned to pain for Sophie. Charles Rivière had fought the betrothal to Paul Bontemps, uneasy about the wildness of the young man. When Paul had gambled himself into prison with his own father rejecting him, le Comte Rivière had canceled the betrothal and tried to force Sophie into a profitable marriage. Only through the bravado of young Antoine had Paul been ransomed and he and Sophie made free to start their life in the Carolina's.

How fortunate she had been to marry a man like Jean whom she loved and whose wise head had turned a modest inheritance into a handsome estate. So what was she doing lying abed when he had given her a question she could not answer? She pulled on a robe and went to her escritoire. Who in Philadelphia would be full of French gossip? She needed to pump someone of the French colony.

She formed the letters of her note carefully, knowing that the shape and size of each stroke of her penmanship would be as carefully examined as the paper on which it was written. Once sealed, she rang for Dodie to deliver it by a fast messenger.

Only when she was fully dressed did she go to call on her guest Sophie. Sophie's cheek felt slack against her own, like the flesh of an old ill woman. Plumping herself at Sophie's feet, she smiled hopefully up into her face. "Come, my love," she fretted. "I worry about your never leaving this room. I have written the family Saint-Leger telling them we will drop by this afternoon. You will accompany me, won't you?"

Sophie's large eyes turned to her sadly. "I could not possibly, Mignonette. I cannot behave in a social manner with that child on my mind." The warning of tears gathered in her eyes and Mignonette patted her hand.

"What a bore I am," Mignonette cried. "See? I have made you cry. Stay where you are comfortable. I shall not be long."

The reply to her note, as she expected, included an invitation to tea. All day Mignonette wondered who might be among the old women gathered at that table. Feeling much the hypocrite, she wrapped herself in her fur cape and set the matching hat in place.

"This is for a good cause," she told her face in the mirror, a sweet guileless-looking face becomingly trimmed by the softness of white mink. Even as she spoke, she heard Jean's mocking laughter.

"More evil has been wrought in the name of good causes than the Devil has time to reward."

The Saint-Leger money had been made in the shipping of grains and wheat. Those great golden piles of harvest had been transformed inside this house into silver and fine porcelain, hand-turned wood, and rugs so thickly piled that Mignonette felt like a young doe struggling in deep grass as she crossed the room.

How delighted they were to see her, she realized guiltily. The eyes of the old women bored into her openly, sniffing for some gossip to liven another group, another tea. And she would give it to them, she decided deviously. I shall feed them a tidbit at a time as long as they keep squawking out things I want to learn.

She told them of Sophie's weak appetite and how thin she had grown from the loss of the child. Then she added, "What anguish it would give her mother to see her so ill."

The old woman Eugénie seemed to have some problem with balance. She wove back and forth in her chair. Her hand, straying to her cup, trembled so that the amber fluid swayed dangerously near the rim.

When she nodded, the pearled wattles swayed. "Indeed Bérénice would be interested no doubt, but it would be her father who would be dismayed. Bérénice herself has little concern for any of her children except the youngest son, Emile. He has been her pet from the first, the pet and her treasure." Her throat rattled on a bit after her voice fell silent.

Her daughter spoke with some embarrassment. "Perhaps Bérénice will find pleasure in Emile's young wife. Sometimes mothers resent the marriages of sons, but this was such a good marriage."

"For him maybe," the old crone broke in. "For the girl herself it must be hell on earth. What does young Charles say of the new bride?"

There was something in the tone of the question that ran up a flag of danger in Mignonette's mind. Why would Charles Bontemps' opinion of his aunt matter? Why, he was scarcely more than a child for all that Sophie had sent him to France for early tutoring.

"He speaks of her as a lovely and charming person," Mignonette framed her reply carefully. "But then he has always been a very amiable boy."

The old woman reached for a cake and finally got it into her trembling grasp. "It is natural that he be so pleased. At his age the very fire of their blood blinds them to a woman's flaws."

At Mignonette's puzzled look, her daughter laughed softly. "Mother corresponds with Bérénice, among others, and is always one letter ahead of anyone else on French news. She is referring to the fact that the betrothal arrangements were made by a go-between. Not until the marriage was confirmed did they know that the girl has quite a hopeless stammer."

"Poor child," Mignonette said swiftly.

"It is doubtful that the flaw will be visited on children," the old woman said slyly, "given Emile as he is."

Mignonette felt herself flush. Granted, she had come for what gossip she could glean, but she did not wish to engage in one of those delicate conversations about perversion that women of great years seem to find so tantalizing. "Well, they have only been married a little over a year," she said blithely.

"But look at Antoine," the old woman crowed. "He and his notorious yellow-eyed wife made up for time that others had left over. Tell us about her, and Paul and the Indians..."

By careful direction she led the talk back to Antoine himself, though she was to learn little that was new from them. Their words swung in and out of the Rivière family tree until she felt quite giddy. Pleading concern for her ailing guest at home, she took an early departure, sitting in the carriage with her face buried in her muff to rid her head of the stench of heavy perfume from the overwarm room she had left.

She had ruined her afternoon, chattered like a magpie, and what had she learned?

Nothing.

Le Comte was a ruthless and shrewd tyrant. Bérénice was an old shrew. Antoine was a daredevil. And hadn't Sophie asked for her punishment by marrying against her parents' wishes?

Mignonette growled softly into her muff.

Bitches, bitches, bitches the lot of them. If it was thus that they described their friends, she would pick the position of enemy gratefully. And she was no wiser about the child. No wiser.

Chapter Seventy-Six

Seth was able to think of little else but Dodie. Never in his brief life had he enjoyed quite so heady a sense of importance as he had felt when she leaned across the narrow table watching him draw a picture of the whistle that Armand had carried with him. "I have seen it often enough, God knows," she told him, "but for the life of me I can't remember how it looked."

It was a joy to draw for her. She leaned so close with her round fair breasts fairly bursting toward him. Even the shapes of her arms propped there supporting her bright face had set him squirming.

One day he would take a girl like that for his own. Oh, not the way he had taken the sailor's wench that first and only time, not in a whispered, giggling fury, terrified at the least creak of a board lest it be the father coming back for his pipe or whatever. Not with the smell of stale mutton long cooked and rat dung in the corners. There was such a thing as marrying in which a lad could do what he wished and be patted on the back by the father instead of clapped into jail. And given some money to boot. The thought of marriage, of always returning to sweet waiting thighs between fresh sheets, was enough to send him into ecstasy.

He watched Mark Hatter eagerly working. The smallest piece that the red-haired Frenchwoman had ordered was a porringer, and his master made it first. It was not even a full-sized porringer but a dish that one would feed a babe from. She had told him the pattern she wanted on it, small grains with wispy heads like rice because that was what they grew on their place down there...then the initials JB in swirling letters. When the baby porringer was finished and set on the shelf, Seth grew nervous.

"You finished that in such haste I thought you might be meaning to take it right over to the lady," he told his master.

Mark Hatter raised his eyes to Seth thoughtfully. "I promised to hasten the work," he explained. "But it never occurred to me to take the order over piecemeal."

Seth shrugged. "I guess I was just thinking about that Madame Bontemps being so distressed, thinking maybe seeing it might be a little cheering."

"Very thoughtful. It is for her own infant son as I understand it, a boy of only a few months. I'll just wrap it up and take it over as you suggested."

Seth's heart tumbled. Fine lot of good it would do him. With the weather being so cold and his master not being a very social man, it had never occurred to him that Mark Hatter might deliver the piece himself. But even as he watched, his master raised his eyes to the clock and measured the trip against the coming of night. Then, with immense relief, Seth saw his rueful nod.

"I'll have to make a cold errand of this for you, Seth, and put a little extra for a pint with it." He wrapped the silver in pale blue muslin as he spoke. "As much as I'd like to give my greeting to my friends there, I have stalled that art dealer Burroughs off as long as I can. If I don't get over to see that new batch of paintings, he will put them out on display. And who is to blame him?"

Seth's heart was beating immoderately. By damn, it had worked. With the help of that weasel of an art dealer who had never been known to press a coin on a lad, he had got another chance at Dodie.

Then his master frowned again. "You are sure you don't mind the trip in the cold, Seth? I don't want to be punishing you for such a charitable thought."

Seth controlled the jig that his feet wanted to dance, and set his mouth in a sober line. "Not for a lady in such grief, sir," he said. "not for such a one as that would I mind."

327

Mark felt no such joy of anticipation at his coming errand. He brewed some hyssop tea and finished the last of the broken shortbread cakes left in an old tin. He was forced to deal with Burroughs simply because there was no other art dealer about, but he secretly despised the man. Burroughs was civil to the point of groveling and had a look in his eye that made Mark wary. But Burroughs occasionally produced a painting worth buying. Business, Mark sighed. You do learn to accommodate in business.

The street was in half-shadow as he stepped out among the other bundled-up souls hastening toward their family fires. In an hour or so the clear stars of winter would appear in the sky, but the world seemed bleak and emptied of light as he rapped at the door of the gallery.

Burroughs obviously had not expected him. The man's usually elaborate wig had been replaced by a dark knitted cap and the dealer's footsteps were silent as he padded ahead of Mark in capacious felt slippers that gave him the appearance of an underfed elf.

"I kept holding these because I hated to put them out without your having first chance," the man babbled as he led Mark into the back of the shop. "Come on back, they're in the regular place. Masterpieces, some of them, I am sure, but I hated to let them into the market and have you wish for them later."

"I appreciate that," Mark mumbled, following along the unheated hall that led to the big unfinished room where the newest acquisitions always waited before being put on display.

After fussing with the candles and drawing up a chair for Mark to get the best light, Burroughs chuckled. "Your own private showing, eh? Just set you there. A glass of Madeira?"

Mark shook his head. "No thank you. I'll just give them a glance-over and be on my way."

"Glance-over," the man laughed. "not when you see these beauties."

In truth it was an ordinary lot and not at all worth his brisk walk through the cold. But even if there had been a gem among them, Mark would have carefully hidden his response lest the price be doubled by the flicker of a lash.

Burroughs, his excitement rising with each canvas he

undraped, was clearly disappointed when he had reached the last.

"Sorry, Burroughs," Mark sighed, rising. "I do appreciate your giving me the first look." Why did only the most ordinary or inept English paintings ever reach these shores? Were there no dreaming eyes with clever hands rising from the soil of this new land? "And that's all of them?" he asked idly, edging forward to rise.

"Well," the man hesitated. "There was a portrait but you always say you have no interest in them. And anyway it's Spanish."

Mark reared to his feet with a grimace. "Right you are, Burroughs. I like my people live and lively."

Burroughs laughed. "Well, this face is lively enough, but it's an unknown, unsigned piece. The artist must be a strange one...to paint this lady Gloria with eyes the color of burnished gold."

Mark paused. Then he laughed shortly. Strange it may seem to Burroughs, but the only girl he had ever loved had such eyes. He had known her as Sukey only to find her name to be Julie Duvall. But Gloria?

"If this painting is about I might glance at it," he said idly.

Burroughs shrugged and pulled a large canvas from the dark beyond the lamp. He did not even bother to whisk the cover off with his usual flair. He simply uncovered the piece and set it into the full glare of the light. As he turned he saw his client's eyes fix in a glazed way on the painting and heard the quick unmistakable intake of breath that spelled money.

"But lovely, isn't it?" he recovered quickly. "Look at the brushwork...the color."

"Be quiet, man," Mark Hatter said in a fierce low voice.

It was she...Julie Duvall to the living breath. The years had ripened the incredible beauty of her girlhood into seductive womanliness. Her hair, still dense and swirling with life, held the light around that perfect face. The expression tugged at his heart. She was not smiling but the strange golden eyes held his with a hungry yearning and a promise of coming laughter.

"Magnificent, no?" Burroughs was shouting at him, almost dancing with glee.

"Where did you get this?" Mark asked, not caring that he interrupted the man in mid-sentence.

"Spain," came the quick reply.

Burroughs' eyes slid away as his voice turned plaintive. "You know better than that, Mr. Hatter. How can I run my business and go popping off to where these paintings are done? I meant to say it looks painted in Spain—the clothing, you see, and that comb in the hair and the name—"

"And no name for the artist?" Mark pressed.

"Unsigned," Mr. Burroughs sighed.

"How much?" Mark asked.

In his gut Burroughs knew that Mark Hatter would pay whatever price he put on that painting and for that reason he sweated mightily at the terse question. Mark Hatter was a free man with money at his command. If he felt that Burroughs took an advantage he had only to hop off to Boston or New York where there were other dealers happy to take his silver. The trick was to name the price that was quite a lot more than he had hoped for and not quite enough to irritate his best patron.

"Ten pounds Pennsylvania," he said boldly all in a breath.

Mark swung his eyes from the painting to the dark man who suddenly cringed under his glance. Mark himself knew well how much silver ten pounds Pennsylvania would buy. He also knew how much wheat and barley it would purchase and that it was a fair price for a healthy young female slave. Then he laughed.

"This will be a story for you to make your rounds with, Mr. Burroughs," he laughed. "That the fool Mark Hatter bought an unfinished portrait by an unknown artist for ten pounds of good Pennsylvania currency which you probably got off a pirate trader for a bottle of good Madeira or a dose of mercury for his rotten disease. But that is what you asked and that is what I am willing to pay. Please wrap it against the wind. I'll take it with me."

"The night is chill," Burroughs protested. "It's large and of heavy stuff. I can send it around on the morrow."

"As you said yourself, the artist is possibly dead. In that case there will be no other. I take it with me. Who knows but that this place might burn down in the night."

"God forbid," Burroughs stammered, wrapping the painting awkwardly as he spoke.

Never had the streets of Philadelphia been so smooth to Mark Hatter's tread nor the distance home easier to traverse. His heart sang. He was in heaven. She lived. But where did she live? Was it Spain as Burroughs guessed or in the Catholic

330

jungles of southern America where the Spanish converted the blood of slaves into bars of silver and gold?

It did not matter. Too long ago he had felt that she was beyond any dream he might nourish. But she lived and this image of her would light the days of his life as long as he breathed.

Ten pounds. Little did that weasel Burroughs realize what a chance he had lost in naming that bid.

Chapter Seventy-Seven

It was almost full dark by the time Seth circled the road-soiled carriage in the street and went around to the back door to deliver the porringer.

She liked him well, that Dodie did. It was as clear as a fresh dip of spring water caught in the hand. She smiled like the sun at morning when she saw who it was that rapped at the door. She hung on his arm as she led him in, leaning so close that the bulge of her bountiful breasts pressed against his arm.

"Sit now," she coaxed. "It will be a while before anyone gets back to us." She smiled excitedly into his face. "I have a great burning to tell the news. They came today, the mum and the dad of the little boy that was spirited away from your shop those many weeks ago now. All the way from Charles Town they came, and scarcely a stop on the way from the look of them and their carriage. And the husband of the red-headed one, Madame Bontemps, is with them too. Gar, what excitement."

"But the lad who was lost has no mother," Seth interrupted. I heard Madame Bontemps herself say that again and again when she and the master were raising the great cry over him being lost. She kept calling him a poor motherless boy and ways like that."

Dodie nodded eagerly. "That's what I was fixing to tell you. The carriage came pell and mell all muddy and the two men came in. After a great whispering and talking they brought the mother in from where she had been waiting lest she startle Madame Bontemps who had thought her dead of

331

Indians. The mistress went up and brought Madame Bontemps down, poor frail thing like a dead person on stalk legs.

"The boy's mother ran into her arms like a child herself. Little bit of a woman she is, French with a name like our Julia only said soft in the French way. Her eyes are the strangest I have ever seen in a face. It has been like a stage play this day and me getting to watch it all from a high-priced seat."

She nodded vigorously. "And all the while the little bounder is probably froze in the mud of the river beyond there."

"Don't say that," Seth protested. "He wasn't a bad sort, that boy."

"That shows what you know." She tossed her head tartly but showed her teeth in a bright smile as she did. "It wasn't you that he pinched and teased and blew that whistle at like he was the Lord high mighty hisself. Spoiled little bounder, he was, and so I will name him, but not hard to look at. Like yourself," she said softly. "Like yourself that is not hard to look at, not at all."

He felt the red rise to his face and the dreaded thickening in his breeches as she leaned against him playfully. She leaped away quickly as her mistress swung through the door already calling.

Then the woman spoke briskly. "Dodie, get water up to the blue room for Mr. and Mrs. Rivière and pull Nabby out to fix supper for them, just something cold will be fine but with the best wine. Oh, you," she said, turning to Seth. "Wait right here and I will be back in a minute."

Staring after her into the room beyond, he saw a great number of people all at once. He saw them quickly as the door hit and stalled and then swung shut slowly. They seemed to be caught in the light of a forest of candles. There were two tall men, one with proper fair hair and the other with hair that gleamed white in the light. Between them, her hand resting on the blond man's arm, was a woman such as his mind could hardly credit. She was simply, even dowdily dressed in comparison to her hostess, but her face was a picture of what a face should be. As she glanced at him, her lips half apart as if she were startled, he saw that her eyes were as pure a gold as a fresh-clipped coin.

As the door swung shut Dodie thumped him fiercely on the arm. "And what was you doing staring at the quality like that?" she challenged, then giggled and looped her arm in his. "I didn't mean that, you know. It's just that it ain't civil to gape the way you was. Unless you should choose to gape at me," she added in a soft whisper.

Then her voice dropped quickly to an urgent tone. "She'll be back with your money in a minute. Take it and thank her and all, but don't really leave. Hang outside a minute until I can get back to you. I have a something for you," she added. "A something that you might find very interesting."

When she joined him in the cold outside the door, she slipped a whistle into his hand.

"A friend of mine looked at the drawing you made for me," she confided. "Then when he saw this one he grabbed it up. What do you think?"

Seth stared at the whistle in his hand.

"God in Heaven," he breathed. "Your friend may have a good pot of money coming to his hand. Where did he get it? How can he be reached?"

"Show it to the smith first," she cautioned. "He don't want to be involved unless it is the proper whistle for sure."

Then she did that casual thing that she had done earlier, looping her arms about his neck loosely, but this time she did not merely peer into his face. She planted her firm lips on his. And even as their lips touched, hers lost their firmness and turned to a miraculous softness that he fell into like drowning just as her mistress called urgently from within.

"Dodie, Dodie..." Then they heard her grumbling. "Where has that little bitch gotten to?"

"A real lady, that one," Dodie giggled, pulling herself from his arms with a wink. "Later, love."

He was halfway to his own quarters when he realized what the whistle might mean. God in Heaven. It might be a sign from the boy, the first break that had come at all.

He turned and started back toward his master's house. It was not that late yet. The master had sent him off early, before tea even, and he should be through with the weasel at the art gallery by this time.

There were lights on in both the front and the back of his master's big brick house. Seth tugged the bell rope a second time hard before the old woman came grumbling, her lantern high that she might see his face before the door was all the way open.

"Seth," he shouted at her, remembering from before that she was deafer in one ear than the other though he could never recall which was which.

Although Seth had been in that room several times before, he was never able to believe what he saw. The hearth fire crackled with a great fiery warmth as the dog Trump, his head between his paws, stared up at him. All about the room were hung giant paintings whose colors leaped at him from the canvas, a ship whose sails swelled so believably that a man could smell salt spray just standing there, a river, his own river the Susquehanna, smooth as glass beneath the scull of a single fisherman.

Mark Hatter rose, laying his book aside with a smile.

"A whistle," Seth said quickly. "I was handed this whistle and thought you best see it yourself."

Frowning, Mark Hatter turned into the light with the whistle between his fingers. As his master bent to the trinket, Seth continued his study of the room. There was a new painting over the hearth itself. He was stepping toward it with his mouth agape as his master turned back to him. "Another copy, Seth," he said dully. "Much the cleverest one yet, but still the work of someone making a go for the reward money." His voice stopped and his tone turned almost irritated. "What has gotten into you? What are you staring at?"

Seth shook his head like a man besotted. "I just can't believe it myself, sir. The lady there." He pointed to the new painting, the one above the hearth. "You see, sir, I only just saw that lady this afternoon. Right before I come here when I was taking the silver for Madame Bontemps. Has to be. There's no two such faces or such eyes."

"You saw her? The lady in that painting?"

Seth, terrified, nodded vigorously. "She's the mother Dodie said. She's the mother of the lad who was stolen away. They thought she was dead but she's alive all right, as I saw her myself!"

"Tell me her name," Mark Hatter ordered, his eyes suddenly flat on Seth's face.

"Rivers or something like that," Seth stammered. "Something like Julia, Dodie said . . . Juleee, sort of in the French way. And she is the mother of the boy himself. God help her, with him gone and not even this whistle being the right one."

Chapter Seventy-Eight

Having let Mark Hatter have his pick of the new selection of pictures, Burroughs set about to dispose of the others in his normal fashion. Handbills were printed and distributed throughout the city announcing the day of the exhibit.

There had, of course, been no other sales in the class with the sale he had made to Mark Hatter. He wished he could get that damned picture out of his mind, to forget the incredible beauty of those weird golden eyes staring at him wistfully from under the cloud of dark hair. But most of all he wished he could recall that fatal moment when he had said "ten pounds" only to know within a split second that if he had said a hundred the sale would have gone the same. And then Hatter had pricked him with that remark. He had tossed off that remark about getting the picture from pirates as casually as if he knew it was a fact and not just a lucky guess.

Sure, he bought from pirates, Burroughs told himself defensively, but who didn't? Maybe there were a few Quaker diehards who would never put their honest money into a pirate's profit, but hadn't Frederick Philips traded with the pirates straight down and then died in his bed as one of the richest men in New York? And what of the Governor of New York, old Fletcher who was so cozy with the pirate Tom Tew that he gave him a gold watch?

And he had turned a tidy profit on the lot. He surveyed the remaining stock hopelessly. His best hope on the hunting picture had been old Dame Rigg who was big on that tally-ho type of thing and had a squint eye besides. But even her squint eye was sound enough to spot something amiss with the horses in that one. And the grouse would end as firewood. He sighed and lifted his lantern to shuffle up and throw the night bolt on the front of his shop.

The man standing silently inside the door was fair-sized, a well-dressed man with the finest velvet to his coat and a cape over his arm lined with beaver. He gave a sense of command all out of proportion to his size.

"Forgive me if I startled you, Mr. Burroughs," the stranger

said quietly. "I am looking for a picture and was directed here."

Burroughs had a quick ear for a phrase. It had long been an axiom with him that if a man calls your name and does not give his own, a man should be wary.

"Yes sir," Mr. Burroughs said pleasantly, summoning his exhibit-worn smile. "My shelves are near bare from a most successful exhibit here this week . . . Mr. . . . ?"

The stranger smiled amiably and took his hand with a bow. "We haven't met before," he said as if that were all the name that Burroughs required. "I was sent to you by an acquaintance who told me that you had a new selection of pictures to market."

Burroughs could not explain his own reluctance to proceed with the man. If it had not been for the obvious quality of the man's attire and his aristocratic manner, he would at once have said there wasn't a picture left in the house and bade him a good night. But as cupidity always had the upper hand over caution in his life, he nodded.

"Some old and some new," he said. "And some in between."

"I am looking for a portrait," the man said quietly. "It is a rather unusual portrait, the head and torso of a young woman, very handsome . . ."

Burroughs felt his heart sink. He knew before the man continued his careful description what picture he sought. When he closed with the name "Gloria," adding that the painting was unsigned, Burroughs shook his head.

"I had such a picture, but it is gone."

"Gone?" The man's eyebrows revealed his extreme incredulity. "But I was told when you obtained the picture, sir—"

"Things move very fast here," Burroughs lied. "This is a city of people of great culture."

"May I ask what price it brought?" the gentleman asked quietly.

"Twenty pounds Pennsylvania," Burroughs lied calmly, not really knowing why he did it.

"Only twenty," the man sighed. "That is really too bad." He pulled a heavy money bag from his pocket. "I had expected to pay twice that at least. At the very least," he added significantly.

He turned as if to leave, then paused. "Perhaps I could speak to the new owner of the painting. Perhaps he would

336

enjoy such a rapid return on his investment in art."

"Oh, no, no," Burroughs said hastily. "He is not of this city."

"I thought you told me that it was the gentry of this city who kept your shelves so bare," the man reminded him calmly.

"Here and about," Burroughs said unhappily, wishing the man gone.

"Perhaps I could make you my agent," the stranger suggested thoughtfully. "If you were to...retrieve this painting for me, I would be more than happy to pay twice the full purchase price plus a generous commission for your services."

"Oh, but that's not possible," Burroughs protested, thinking at once of how a man might gain entry to the handsome brick house that Mark Hatter used as a combination home and museum.

"I meant that you might buy it back for me," the stranger suggested softly as if he had read Burroughs' mind.

That was enough. It was more than enough. Burroughs fitted his fingers together to give some rigidity to his arms which seemed suddenly as limp as his spirit. "The painting is gone," he said flatly. "Totally gone with no hope of recall. Since it is past my closing time, I will bid you good-night...Mr.?"

Again the hint was ignored but this time the stranger bowed stiffly at his words and stepped toward the door. "I appreciate your cooperation," he said quietly.

Then he was gone.

Burroughs locked the door securely after him, then unbolted it again and peered down the street. The man must have come on foot because there was neither the sound of a horse nor a carriage in the crisp night air. He shrugged. Twice twenty pounds and a generous commission. This was a game of some kind. Hatter had sent the man to catch him in a trick.

Instead of his usual pot of tea, Burroughs carried a fresh bottle of Madeira to his account table and partook of it freely while he totted his earnings for the day. By the time the figures were all reconciled, the bottle stood at only a third full. By the time the moneys had been counted and locked away, there was scarely a drop of the liquid left. It was then that it occurred to him that possibly Mark Hatter had not been as fond of the portrait as he had thought. It further occurred to him that if he offered the silversmith twenty pounds for the picture and was successful, this commission, on top of what he had already disposed of would make his purchase of the paintings he had bought from the pirate market in North Carolina one of the more profitable ventures of his career.

By the time he had thought this all through, he had replaced his wig and his slippers and set out toward the handsome brick house that Mark Hatter called home.

The old woman who answered his ring pretended deafness. Burroughs was obliged to shout his name at her until her master emerged from an inner room chuckling at the furor.

Hatter, clad in a comfortable smoking jacket, stood in the hallway without inviting him in.

"What brings you here at this hour?" the silversmith asked, looking at him with a curious intentness. Only then did Burroughs realize that in his haste to dress he had set his wig a little awry and that the buttons on his coat were unevenly fastened.

"The picture I sold you . . ." Burroughs began. "I came to see if you would consider selling it back to me?"

He saw the look of astonishment on Hatter's face, followed by a sudden grin. "No, sir," he said firmly, "I am very satisfied with the purchase, even at the price I paid," he added with a wicked gleam in his eyes.

"If it was the price," Burroughs said, "if it was the price that bothered you, I would be willing to offer you twice."

At this Mark Hatter laughed merrily, and slapped him on the shoulder in a most unsteadying way. "That was indeed a good bottle you have been nipping from, Mr. Burroughs. Best you go home and sleep it all off. But when you wake, sir, my answer will be the same. I cannot think what inducement would persuade me to part with this particular painting, but it is not money."

The door had been soundly closed before Burroughs realized how thoroughly he had failed.

He turned and made his way unsteadily down the walk. He was past the house, hunched into his muffler against the wind at his face when he thought he glimpsed something from the corner of one eye. A chronic fear of footpads made him whirl his head about.

Nothing. Only the stirring of a stripped tree against an ice-coated fence. And shadows, a street of weaving shadows, swaying from the approach of the watchman and his lantern.

Chapter Seventy-Nine

With the door closed behind Burroughs, Mark returned to his study to stand a long time smiling at the wistful face of the girl in the painting.

"You have changed my life again," he told her, smiling. "Where is the Mark Hatter who was first at the drafting board in the morning and the last to lock his shop windows against the night? He has changed to a sluggard who wishes nothing better than to spend all his days staring moon-eyed at your image."

But the peaceful joy that came into the room with the hanging of the portrait had been dispelled by Seth's blurted insistence that he had seen this same woman, in the flesh, in the parlor of his patron across town. He had grilled the apprentice unmercifully without the boy wavering from his claim. As a matter of fact, the more he asked Seth to describe that glimpse of the stranger who was the child's mother, the more convinced Mark was that the boy had been absolutely correct.

She was small, Seth said. How well Mark remembered that the top of her gleaming head had come only to his shoulder and how she angled her bright face upward when she spoke to him.

She had been standing with her hand on a tall man's arm, yet Seth said it did not look as if she were leaning on anyone. Instead she stood very straight, like a river reed, lithe and dainty and independent. It was so that Mark had seen her pass along the streets of London at Margaret's side, in a drab cape and hat but like a queen.

And then that creature Burroughs came, thick-tongued with drink, trying to make another pound or two from some other patron by reclaiming the picture. The man would be hanging pictures in Hell before he got this one back, Mark told himself firmly. She is mine, mine to keep, all that I will ever have ... or need ... in the way of a companion.

And yet ...

Why had it made him so restless to think that she might be

rising and going to slumber in that great house across town? Why did the thought that she was the red-headed boy's mother change the boy's disappearance from a brooding mystery to a biting tragedy? Did she weep? Did she walk the floors in that quick, almost soundless tread that he remembered from her days in London? Did she stop and draw her fine hands back from her face so that those irrepressible curls danced back across her forehead in tumbling rebellion?

She grieved. He knew that she grieved and grief grew in him at this knowledge. On this night, as on so many others since Seth told his startling story, Mark went under cover of darkness to pass the house where she stayed. The house was no grander than his own, yet with its many windows lit against the night it seemed more imposing by far. When, here and there, a shaft of light streamed from an uncurtained window, the light seemed more golden, more warm and throbbing with life.

From the shadows he stared at the house, trying to guess which window hid her sleeping, where she dined. Perhaps she did not dine. Perhaps she also, as it was rumored of the boy's aunt, refused food and sleep in grief for the lost child.

During his apprenticeship in London, then through the whole of his indenture in these colonies, he had promised himself that he would be rich. He would be rich and possibly even famous. He would go to her then in fine velvet clothes and a graceful carriage such as the white and gold ones she used to stare at so wistfully in London, and he would ask her hand in marriage. That sort of thing happened in the colonies, they said. A 'prentice could indeed marry a noblewoman if there was money enough and the wanting.

But when he had been free to search for her she was gone. In Charles Town, they said, but the folk of Charles Town had never heard of a girl named Duvall, there was no family named Duvall anywhere about.

It had been a 'prentice's dream which had died at his coming of age.

But now she breathed behind the elegant windows of that house as far out of reach as she had been that first day she stood in the open door of Margaret's kitchen.

"There's a great honor in being given love," Margaret had told him gently. "But there is also a great privilege in being able to give to someone you love."

Once before he had known that fulfillment. What wouldn't he give now to be able to ease her heart's strain again? The boy

340

must be found. New avenues must be sought, new efforts must be launched. The boy must be returned to her. To give that joy to her would be the greatest privilege of all. But how?

As he had on nights past, Mark pondered the question relentlessly on his way home, scarce heeding where his feet fell or what other night traveler walked the streets.

And so it was that he came to his own door, sorting out the key so as not to waken the old woman, when the stranger separated himself from the shadows.

Mark was quick to turn and assume an attitude for defense if such were needed. But the man held out both hands, palm up. His voice was quiet for all the authority that rang in his tone.

"Do not be alarmed," the stranger said, moving into the light. "I only wish to have a word with you in private."

"Do I know you?" Mark asked, still a little wary at the suddenness of the man's appearance.

"Not yet," the man replied with a hint of humor in his voice. "Not yet..."

Chapter Eighty

Later, when he looked back on that evening, Mark was astonished that he had even granted the man an audience. He remembered glancing into the darkness for fear this stranger had henchmen ready to spring out on the opening of his door. He remembered telling the man firmly that the hour was late and that he would be delighted to talk with him at his place of business on the following day.

At this, the man's face lightened with amusement. "But my dear sir," he said quietly, "since I do not know your name, nor the nature of your occupation, much less where you keep these business hours, that would be quite impossible. I am requesting such a few minutes of your time that your rest could hardly be damaged by their loss."

"Since you admit that we are strangers and you have no business with me, why don't you go on about your own affairs like a good fellow," Mark suggested, beginning to lose patience.

"Oh, but I do have business with you," the man corrected him. "I wish to discuss a painting you recently acquired."

Mark eyed him, sure at once what painting he referred to.

"The painting is not for sale," Mark's tone was firm. "I told Mr. Burroughs that very clearly and will happily tell him the same when he is sobered enough to listen with more grace. Now, if you please..."

The stranger's grin was unmistakable as he shook his head. "Please do not think that I come from Mr. Burroughs. He would, in fact, be terribly incensed to know that I was here. I deliberately baited his greed to get him to lead me to where the painting was."

"The picture is not for sale," Mark repeated, not to be distracted by the man's charm.

"You are sure which picture I mean?" the stranger asked.

"I believe so," Mark replied. "The Spanish portrait of a girl called Gloria."

The stranger nodded. "And you are able to tell me positively that there is no consideration that you would accept for this picture?"

Before Mark could even speak, the stranger went on in that same, almost ironic tone. "There are other considerations than money, you know. What a rare man you must be to insist that you would not part with a simple piece of oiled canvas for any consideration in this world."

But it was not the cold of the night or the stranger's exceptional manner that finally induced Mark to unlock the door and invite him in. It was the sudden faint realization that flickered in Mark's mind, the knowledge that there was, indeed, one thing that he cherished more than the picture itself. The thought was so exciting to Mark that his hand rattled awkwardly at his own lock.

Mark was not surprised when the guest only paused in the doorway before walking directly to the painting.

"You have seen this work before, then?" Mark asked.

"I had it in my possession and let it go."

Without asking, Mark poured two glasses of port for himself and his guest. "From the way you look at the work I would say that letting it go was an act of singular carelessness."

The stranger turned and saluted Mark with his glass before laughing softly. "That is an understatement. I am called Darby Dray. And your name, sir?"

"Mark Hatter," the smith replied, finding himself suddenly

amused. "It strikes me as remarkable that my name is apparently as meaningless to you as yours is to me."

"It is never necessary for men to have more than one thing in common," Darby replied. "But I do wish to comment that your taste in port is as flawless as your taste in art."

"Good taste is an accident of opportunity," Mark replied.

A strange circling conversation followed. The golden-eyed woman in the painting was never mentioned and yet she dominated the thoughts and words of both men. Only after his glass had been refilled did Darby Dray return to his discussion of "considerations."

"Tell me, Mr. Hatter," he said quietly. "We seem to have a cleverly balanced game here. While we are equally matched in our desire to possess that painting, we are similarly unconcerned about what its cost is to us. This is a rare balance."

Mark nodded agreement.

"You might as well have spoken your thought aloud," Darby Dray said. "The difference in that balance is that you have the picture and I do not. My problem, then, is to discover what there is in this world that you desire enough to give up the painting."

When Mark remained silent, Darby nodded with satisfaction. "Your silence implies that there is such a consideration, Mr. Hatter. That is the first hope that you have given me."

Mark grinned. "My silence only implied that I was impressed that you felt that you could supply any desire that I might express."

Darby laughed softly. "That was hardly a humble suggestion, was it? But then I do not delude myself that I am a humble man."

"If I were to tell you that I know where the woman in that picture is at this very moment, would you seek her out?" Mark asked.

Setting down his empty glass, Darby replied without a moment of hesitation, "No."

"Would you like to explain that?" Mark asked.

"It doesn't seem necessary," Darby told him. "From your tone I infer that you yourself have that information and yet you cling to this picture rather than the real person. We are both bargaining for second best because the first is not ours to claim."

"Given that, do you really think that I have a price to set on the painting?"

Darby studied him. "Yes I do. And I admit to a most damnable curiosity to hear what it is."

With the moment at hand, Mark's nerve almost failed him.

"There is a missing child," he said quietly. "He is a lad of very tender years who disappeared from the streets of this city some weeks ago. In spite of the most careful and diligent searches not even the whisper of a clue to his fate has been heard. If you could locate that child, I would release the painting to you."

"Was this your child?" Darby asked.

Mark shook his head.

"And what if the child be found dead?"

"That will matter greatly to those who cherish him but not to our agreement," Mark decided aloud.

"I will need access to all that can be learned of this child, his parents, his situation..."

"All that is known will be made available to you."

"Shall we begin with the child's name?" Darby asked.

Mark turned that he might see the light on Darby's face as he spoke. "His name is Armand," he said quietly. "He is the son of Antoine and Julie Rivière."

The stricken look that crossed Darby's face, the sudden movement of his eyes to meet the gaze of the woman in the portrait, caused a sudden lurch in Mark's stomach. He and this man were indeed in what Darby had called an equal situation.

"There's only one more thing," Mark added quietly. "It is understood between us that if I should succeed in finding the child before you do, the picture stays where it hangs."

On his feet now, Darby stretched out his hand in agreement. Then that sly, satiric smile crossed his face again.

"God in Heaven, Mark Hatter. If anyone had told me that I would meet such a man as you through that serpent Burroughs, I would have laughed him off the deck."

"The devil take my rest," Mark said with enthusiasm. "Get your coat off and settle down. Let's get to the job of work here."

"I intend to own that portrait," Darby reminded him.

"I hope you can, Darby Dray," Mark said earnestly. "I hope to God that you can."

Chapter Eighty-One

After the frantic pace of their trip to Philadelphia, Julie and Antoine found the frustration of the search for their son maddening. For a solid week Antoine had thrown the force of his incredible energy into the pursuit only to find the city a cold wall with no crevice, no clue anywhere.

From the window of the room that she and Antoine shared, Julie stared into the wintry garden behind her host's house. Drear. Cold and dead and drear.

At least the men found errands to take during the long days, following leads, conferring with officials of the city, and generally busying their hours. Sophie and Julie, with the fretful baby Julius, could only survive the passing moments one by one.

A week and three days had passed when Julie, drawing a deep, determined breath, proposed to her sister-in-law that she and Paul and the baby go back to Charles Town.

"Home?" Sophie cried, instant tears springing to her eyes. "With Armand still missing? Leaving you here?"

"Home," Julie nodded sternly. "There is a break in the weather that you should seize upon. Paul has the rice crop to get in," she paused. "As well as doing what he can to help Antoine with the business of his shipping. The four of us can do no more than two of us. Do it, Sophie," she urged. "Persuade Paul that even Antoine would be more relaxed, more free in his mind for this search if he knew that his affairs down there were in good hands."

Sophie hesitated, her eyes pained on Julie's face.

"Can you forgive me?" she asked for the millionth time. "Can you ever forgive me, Julie?"

"No," Julie said firmly, going to sit down near Sophie. "I cannot forgive you because there is nothing to forgive. When we know where Armand is and how he went, then we can look for fault, if fault there be. But the fault is not yours, Sophie. Don't you realize that I would have done exactly the same? If I had been in the shop of a silversmith and a child was restless and wished to stand without, I would have let him go."

345

Sophie would have turned away to weeping again, but Julie leaped to her feet.

"We will not ask them, we will tell them," she decided aloud. "I shall go this minute and tell Maggie MacRae to start packing the baby's things to travel. Would you like to talk to Mignonette, or should I?"

"I should," Sophie said. Then to Julie's delight, a faint glow of color came to her sister-in-law's cheeks. "But will there be a ship going that way? What if we cannot get passage?"

Julie laughed at her. "There will be ships and you will get passage. But for now, go and seek out Mignonette and make your own plans to be gone. And be firm," she warned. "That dear Mignonette is a lonely creature and would keep us all forever if she had her way."

"Lonely creature," those had been her own words. Julie stared at the garden. Those words had come unbidden to her lips. Yet Mignonette had her husband Jean even as she herself had Antoine. Why was a woman without a child a creature to be pitied?

As she watched, Julie saw a dark figure come briskly along the back of the garden and stop beyond the wall. He was a young man and strong from the shape of his shoulders beneath a rough blue coat. When he lit his pipe, the flare of the fire showed a strong face with eyebrows that cocked up sharply, almost joining above his nose. "An interesting face," she decided. "Not handsome but interesting."

She had idly begun to wonder of his business there when she saw the small figure of a woman, completely wrapped in a great dark shawl, run across the garden toward him.

Then she was in his arms. As she stretched up into his embrace Julie recognized Dodie, the bright-faced maid from the house. Knowing it was rude but not caring, Julie watched the two young people. After a long and passionate kiss, they stood with their arms around each other, talking earnestly. Then she saw Dodie draw something from her pocket and hand it to the man. He leaned to kiss her again before Dodie came flying back toward the house.

She had turned from the window with a sigh when Antoine opened the door. His touch on her hand was gentle but his face was quizzical.

"I presume that it was you who decided that Paul and Sophie must pack off for home?"

When she nodded, he tightened his arm around her. "I have

346

been trying to get Paul to listen to me on this for days now. You are right, Julie. This is our vigil, and ours alone."

Turning from her, he walked to the window to stare out just as she had. Julie felt some burden heavying his step, making his usually graceful stride awkward and choppy. She drew a glass of sack from the decanter that Mignonette kept filled on the desk. Sliding her arm around his waist, she handed him the drink.

"You have something else to say to me?"

He looked down at her soberly and touched the sack to his lips. "I would to God you could guess my words as well as you have guessed my nervousness about speaking them," he said crossly.

"We need to set a time ourselves," she said quietly.

He stared at her as if thinking to soften the firmness of her voice with his glance. He finally dropped his eyes. "We need to name a day," he agreed, his voice heavy with defeat.

She clung to him, feeling the hammering of his heart pressed against her own, conscious of the great strength in the arms that held her so close, of the flames of impatience that were burning away his gentleness and humor.

"One more week after Paul and Sophie sail," she suggested quietly.

"Ten days." he bargained.

"Ten days," she agreed. She felt the fingers of her hands flat against his back. Ten days, like the ten fingers of her hands. Ten days before the hands opened and let Armand slip away from them in defeat. In that moment, the numbness left her and the same driving impatience that fueled Antoine flooded into her mind.

Pulling herself from his arms, she straightened briskly.

"I will go and make certain that Maggie MacRae is managing to get the baby's things properly packed," she told him. "We must not let Sophie soften on her resolve."

He looked at her, his eyes a little wistful.

"There is a great strength within that soft alluring body of yours, good wife," he said sadly.

"Would you have it otherwise?" she asked from the door.

"On occasion," he admitted. "But not now."

The whirlwind preparations for Sophie and Paul's departure brought Julie into much contact with the house-maid Dodie. Julie's first impression of the girl was that her pretty face hid a greedy little strumpet. Fearful that her inner thoughts had somehow been guessed by the girl, Julie went out of her way to court the girl's friendship. By the time the trunks and barrels were off on the boat with Sophie and Paul, a saucy but tentative rapport existed between the two of them.

She discovered the girl to have wit along with her tart tongue, and a pert charm that she was wholly aware of. Julie had chanced into the kitchen when the silversmith's apprentice had delivered the last of the pieces that Sophie ordered. She saw at once from his calf-eyed look what was afoot. She also noted that as Dodie passed with the silver, she swung her skirts to display the neat turn of her ankle to his eager eye.

Afterward Julie teased her. "It is clear that you have that young man's heart in your pocket," she told Dodie.

Dodie bloomed with a sudden pleased grin. "Oh, indeed!"

"As if you didn't know," Julie scoffed.

Dodie giggled. "It's known to happen between a man and a maid," she said airily.

Remembering the garden scene she'd glimpsed from the window, Julie grinned. "How about two men and a maid?"

The girl's startled face turned a little cross. "And what would you be meaning by that?" she challenged.

Julie laughed. "Dodie, Dodie," she chided her, "my window overlooks the garden and the back fence."

The dawn of understanding brought quick color to the girl's cheeks. "Two men and a maid then," she corrected herself with a shrug.

Julie felt the girl's eyes thoughtful on her. "And how would you choose between a sailor and a 'prentice?" she asked.

Julie laughed. "The only sailors I ever heard of making a real living for themselves did it by piracy or some thieving trickery or another. On the other hand, a smith like that boy has great expectations. Your own mistress told me that his master came to this land indentured and now has a business and a fine house and great fame besides." Julie dimpled at her. "Pirates may be more exciting but they do tend to lose their heads young."

Dodie went pensively back to her work. It was as if the yellow-eyed woman was a witch, as friendly and cheerful as she was. The way she had seen into Dodie's own mind was amazing. Madame Bontemps had been no farther than the wharf on her way home when there was Barney at the fence seeking her kisses and a loan of a few shillings.

When Dodie told him that she had no money, he grew right irate. "You mean that bitch put all that work on you with her kids and all and never gave you a bit of change as a thanks?" he asked indignantly. "What kind of folks are these? You ain't holding out on old Barney, is you?"

The way he had said that, as if the money, if there was any, was proper his own, made her cross and bold. She didn't even tell him about the note the lady slipped in her apron pocket instead. She stopped halfway up the stair to try to puzzle out what she meant by it:

Dear Dodie,
My words cannot express my appreciation for your kindness to me and my party these weeks past. At first I thought to leave a gift of money as I did to the others on the staff, but I changed my mind. Money is too quickly gone with no memory of its passing. I have arranged for a surprise for you which will be along in short order. Please know that it comes with love and gratitude from all of us.

She had signed it with her name and the phrase, "With all good wishes for your life."

Tucking the note back into her pocket, Dodie tossed her head. He had only been waiting for another stake from her, like the time he got her to get the 'prentice to draw the whistle for him.

Aye, and how fierce he had been when the 'prentice gave the whistle back saying it was a fraud. Only then did she realize that Barney had put up the money to have the trinket made to win the reward by foolery even though he knew no more of the lost boy than any other roisterer in the taverns along that waterfront.

But she found the thought of a coming surprise a warming one. Even as she found the friendship of the boy's mother to be a bright pleasure in her days.

Unable to express her sympathy to one so far above her, Dodie tried to distract Madame Rivière in the days after the others left. She reported on the carter who was kicked "into Tuesday next" by his own horse when he leaned in front of the beast to pick a coin from the cobbles. She told of the goodwife who had found a lost ring in a turnip she was carving for stew. It was natural enough, a few days after the others were gone, that she should tell the woman about the new man who had been prowling about the riverfront making inquiries of a lost boy.

"He's a man no one has seen until just lately," she explained. "He is a raggle-taggle, my friend says, for all that he seems to have change to buy a round for all that will talk to him."

"Then what is so strange about this man?" the lady had asked.

"He claims to be on an errand for a great house," Dodie explained. "He claims there is fortune for a certain boy if he can be located. He meets every ship and talks with every sailorman."

At the woman's thoughtful look, Dodie chattered on. "My friend Barney says that probably your husband is paying for his time."

The lady shook her head. "We have hired no one to tell such a story," she said positively. "It is a different boy."

"That's what I told Barney," Dodie said. "But he'll have none of that. The man describes the selfsame clothes even to the red hair and the silver whistle. It is your lad that this man seeks, Barney swears it."

"But he has no leads," the woman said. "Even as we have none."

"He spends all his days down there listening and watching," Dodie said. "It only takes one right lead, you know."

"I wish him Godspeed," the woman told her, raising those golden eyes to her with a defeated look. "The days pass swiftly toward the time we have to leave. And there is nothing. Nothing."

Dodie, chastened by the pain in Madame Rivière's face, descended the stairs sadly, little guessing that even at that moment, the unraveling of the mystery was as near as an impatient hand raised to rap at the kitchen door.

Chapter Eighty-Two

Never before in his nineteen years had Seth been under such a strain as in the days just past. Oh, he had been privy to secrets before and kept them or betrayed them as his spirit moved him, but the order to his master for the silver bracelet had been the most exciting piece of information that had ever come his way.

He had carried the note to the shop himself after making the final delivery of the silver for Madame Bontemps, carried it straight to his master's hand without ever even wondering what the carefully sealed folds of paper contained. When his master broke the seal and read it, he looked up with an amazed expression.

"Would you look at this now, Seth? Just when my faith in human nature hits the lowest point, something like this always comes along. This note, with the money enclosed, is from Madame Bontemps, written just as she left for the Carolinas.

"It opens with a flattering paragraph or two about the work that I will skip over—oh yes . . . here. 'There is a lovely young maid in this house who has served us all so tirelessly and cheerfully that I feel a special need to thank her. I have noticed that while she seems to love pretty things, she has none of her own. Please use the enclosed money to design a silver bracelet for her. I thought perhaps of something with ribbons on a plate surrounding her name in delicate letters, the kind of womanly design you do so well.'"

His master looked up with a smile. "She goes on to say that her hostess will supply more funds if the amount is not correct. But say that isn't a rare thing for a lady in great grief to think to do!"

"Does she tell the girl's name?" Seth asked, almost interrupting his master's flow of words.

Mark Hatter looked up in surprise at Seth's tone which sent the apprentice into an agony of blushing. "Why yes, she does," he replied wryly. "Else how would I know what letters to inscribe among those ribbons? Do I gather from your hasty words that you have guessed the name?"

"I had thought of a girl there," Seth confessed, his face still flaming with color.

"That's interesting. I am sure you are right." With that, his master refolded the note and set it away.

Unable to control his fury and impatience, he turned to march away, not caring that his footsteps sounded like the stamping of a giant. He was bare half the room away before gales of laughter swept over him.

"Come back here, you young fool. Can't you tell when you are being joshed? I'll tell you the name quick enough, but mind it is a deep secret. The girl is not to guess a hint of it until the bauble is put into her hand."

Seth turned, waiting a little sheepishly after his show of spleen.

"Tell me the name you want it to be," his master said.

"Dodie, sir," Seth said very low.

"The same," his master smiled. "And by God's beard I will have you in stocks if you let this out before time."

"On my word," Seth promised, his chest splitting with joy. "Oh my God, what a great crying and laughing it will be for her, sir. A great giggling and admiring and then tears all over."

And now the days had passed and the silver bracelet with its attached note was in his hand. He hoped that the sour-faced cook was not about and that Dodie herself would be the one to answer the rap that he laid on the panels of the door in a sharp staccato rhythm.

And his luck held good. The fire blazed cheerily and a bubbling pot gave off the rich scent of chowder as Dodie peered out and then threw the door wide. The cook was at her work but after a disgruntled look, she turned away unheeding.

"Well," Dodie smiled, one hand on a hip in that way that threw her body into a fair imbalance, twisting the slender waist a little and exposing the flesh of her arm where her sleeve fell back. "If it isn't himself wandering about in the cold like a gypsy."

She was all smiles and within the minute had him in on a seat with a cup of hot tea before him. Then she sat across from him the way she had at the first, with her fair round arms supporting her face and her eyes on his own.

"What is the news from the world?" she asked.

He was still dumb. Should he hand her the bracelet at once or relish this homely scene as long as he could? And what news would he possibly have to hold the intent gaze of those bright eyes?

"One day and another," he said. "The master keeps to his home a good deal more lately so that I have much responsibility at the shop."

"What fine trade must come there," she said thoughtfully. "Such ladies and their men of high station."

"Indeed there are, but there are others too." He paused and because the happening was so fresh on his mind, he went on and told her about it. "Just this afternoon a man of strange appearance came to the shop. A raggle-taggle he was for sure

352

and I watched a little that he not mean the master harm. But the master has no feel for such and sent me down the road on an errand."

"A raggle-taggle man?" she asked, leaning forward. "And what business would such a man have with a fine silversmith?"

Seth hesitated. "Not silver," he admitted. "For I saw no order on the table when I came back. But the master was agitated when I returned. Before I caught my breath he scratched a note for your mistress and sent me along here."

She was so near that the scent of her flesh was stronger in his head than his steaming tea. "But I needed to come this day anyway," he confessed, "to give you this." He simply knew the time when it came and pulled the package from his coat to lay before her.

She stared at it and then at his face before undoing the bindings. As the circlet of delicate silver fell into her hands she stared at it dumbly. He had been wrong, he decided. There was to be no screaming and leaping about. She held the bracelet in her hand, turning it to the light as if it was to explode like an egg any minute. Then she saw the polished plate and read her own name there. Her face fell slack and she looked up at him, gripping the bracelet tight in her hand. Her eyes were brimming with tears.

"Here, Dodie, take the note that goes with and read it."

"I cannot," she whimpered. "I cannot see to read for this silliness in my eyes." As she spoke she wiped tears from them with the back of her hand.

"'For the arm of dear Dodie,' the note says," Seth read aloud. "'For her kindness to a lost child and his family.' It is signed Sophie Bontemps."

It was then that the wailing began. She let out such a shriek that Seth was at once on his feet and could hear cries and running from the room beyond.

He had seized her, trying to still her wailing when the door burst open and the golden-eyed woman and the tall fair giant stood in the doorway with the mistress of the house at their side.

"What in the name of God is going on?" the mistress cried almost crossly.

"It is mine," Dodie cried. "Look at it. It is mine!"

It was Madame Rivière who broke the spell. Her merry laugh suddenly filled the room. Seizing Dodie in her arms, she dimpled over the maid's shoulder at Seth.

"Dodie, Dodie, don't take on so," she pleaded. "Show your mistress the bracelet. Show it to me. I only heard of it when Sophie planned to have it made."

Even the tall giant was smiling by the time Dodie raised her arm with the silver loop around it. Only when their shouts had given way to laughter and Dodie's tears to a marvelous secret smile did he remember the other package.

"Forgive me, madame," he told the mistress of the house. "My master said to put this into your hand." She glanced at him curiously as she took it, but in truth he was not paying that much attention to her. Instead he watched Dodie, who had fallen into something like a trance, turning her arm this way and that so that the light changed on the delicate loop about it.

It was the gasp that caught his attention, the gasp and a strangled cry. As he watched, the madame's face turned strange and she groped as if falling. The tall man caught her as she swooned, holding her as easily as if she were a doll. He heard a faint musical clattering on the floor and the sound of bells.

It was Seth himself who lifted the object from the floor to stare at it openmouthed.

"Is this then the whistle?" the tall man asked.

"The right one," Seth stammered, his heart suddenly thick in his throat. "The only right one."

Chapter Eighty-Three

The words of the apprentice, as softly as they were spoken, still sent a shudder through Julie's entire body. She felt herself reeling physically so that she had to reach out to brace herself against the lintel of the door. Antoine did not meet her eyes. Mignonette, whose swoon had been as brief as it was sudden, stirred against his chest and she cried out even as her eyes fluttered open.

"This whistle—my God, it is Armand's whistle." She whirled from Antoine to face the apprentice. "Where did you get this?" she asked fiercely. "Where did it come from?"

Seth stepped backward from her, stammering, "My master. He sent it, with this paper."

She saw Antoine's eyes move swiftly down the lines of

script. A faint frown came to his brow as his eyes moved to the top of the page to read the note again.

Then wordlessly, without meeting her eyes, he handed the open sheet to her.

There was no salutation. This was a terse paragraph written in a bold, clear flowing hand. It passed her mind fleetingly that she had seen such handwriting before but she had no idea where or when.

"The man who had this whistle tells of stealing the red-haired boy. He has been questioned at great length without altering his story in any particular. The only hope for locating the child seems to lie in having this story fall on different ears. Send such listeners to the Stag Horn Tavern this evening. God willing, someone will understand the significance of his tale."

"My God, I must be off at once," Antoine said, turning toward the door.

Julie was blocking his way. "I must go too," she said as he neared her.

"What foolishness is this?" he challenged her. "What business have you at a waterfront tavern like that?"

"He is my son," she cried, incredulous at his tone.

"Good God, woman," Antoine exploded at her. "Even if the child himself were there—which it seems from this that he is not—you would not even know him. He was only a babe when you deserted him to plunge off into the wilderness."

Julie felt her cheeks flame with humiliation, but it was the injustice in his words that brought the fire to her tongue.

"I have as much business in that tavern as I had in the wilderness," she said coldly. "The same business, I might add."

She saw him freeze where he stood and stare at her as if she were suddenly strange to him. His eyes turned cold as she met his gaze. The shocked watchers in the room stayed so still that the fire on the hearth was suddenly loud and hissing.

"Very well, madame," he said in an icy tone. "Do as you damned well please since that is your particular style."

Not since the days in Charles Town when their disagreements over Sophie had led them to quarrels and harsh words had she endured such public shame from his lips. She felt the stiffness move along her spine as she stared back at him, refusing to betray by a single sign the impact that his words had on her. She only nodded and turned to collect her clothing.

"I wish Jean were here," she heard Mignonette wail as she

355

went. "Jean should be along with you, just in case."

She also heard the acid on Antoine's tongue as he replied, "Be at ease, madame. Madame Rivière obviously considers herself equal to any challenge that this, or any situation might offer."

It was clear to Julie at that moment that Antoine intended to be as unpleasant as possible. Declining the offer of a carriage, he strode off into the darkening street at that swift pace that was native to his size and strength. Julie, hastening along behind him, grew quickly breathless with her feet pained by the rough icy street. Not even when she stumbled and almost fell did he slow his pace or offer his arm to her.

It was thus that they passed through the city toward the riverfront. Her face flamed at the curious glances she felt as she hurried after the tall stalking man, sometimes barely keeping him in sight at the busier thoroughfares where she was loath to force herself through rudely as he did.

He only slowed his pace a little as they turned onto a mean narrow street directly on the wharf. Knots of curious sailors followed in her wake, insulting her with crude comments. The air choked her, dank rancid air smelling of tar and smoke and stale fish mingled into a stench that burned her throat. The place she followed him seemed more alley than street at last, slick underfoot with hubbub all about them, voices raised in drunken song that wove in about the mocking and jeering whistles that greeted her passing.

The sign was hanging unevenly by a rusted chain so that the beast's face stared down at them drunkenly. The stench of ale and soured food and rum spilled from the door as Antoine pulled to a stop.

The place was darkened by the same oily smoke that hung in dense clouds above a scene so crowded and various that her eyes couldn't absorb it all at once. It was a soup of humanity, men and women and lean dogs stirred together in a dense hideous potion. A raucous shriek sounded near her as a parrot lunged from his owner's shoulder only to be thrown, fluttering and protesting, when he reached the length of the leather that tethered him.

It was from the midst of this confusion that a single calm face emerged, a plain, almost anonymous face whose dark eyes caught hers and held them compellingly. He was the same and yet so different that she barely believed it was he. His beard was short but rough and disreputable-looking, his

356

clothes the raggle-taggle of the prideless poor, carelessly donned and soiled upon stain.

A sober gentleness in his expression held her glance as she moved toward him. Remembering his kindness, the tenderness she felt toward him sent a weakness along her legs as he drew near.

"Darby," she whispered softly. "My God, Darby, it is you."

Instead of stopping, he continued to walk casually past her. Antoine, unconscious of her encounter, continued to frown from the doorway, looking about the room in indecision. When Darby was just past her she heard his soft voice.

"Is that the father?"

"Aye," she replied without turning to meet his eyes.

"Then the two of you do as I say. Order a drink and drift to the rear of this room. You will find a stair. At the top, veer left and enter. Be silent and wait."

As Darby drifted on past her, Julie turned and sought Antoine's eyes. She motioned him to come and for a horrifying moment saw him almost refuse. Then he was there, his eyes cold on her face.

"Would you have a pint pulled for me?" she said firmly. "It is a thirsty enough night."

His eyebrows rose and he shrugged, but he turned away to return with two brimming mugs. He let her move away a few feet before he decided to follow. She heard his steps behind her as she ascended the narrow dark stair.

At the landing she paused to see the door to the left a little ajar. Laying her finger on her lips to caution Antoine to silence, she entered the room.

She could not imagine being tired enough to lay her head on the covers of that bed nor to sit on the rude bench against the wall. A single rank candle snorted from a hook on the wall and what had once been a window was now only a rude opening boarded over with evil-looking rags stuffed in the crevices between the wood.

At Antoine's questioning glance she shrugged and repeated the symbol for silence. At once she realized why silence was needed. Between this cubicle and the room beyond was a slapdash wall made of boards hastily laid one above the other. Between the slats she could see narrow strips of light and hear the slow uneven slap of something soft against wood. Cards. Someone was playing cards in the room beyond.

As the key rattled in the lock of the room beyond the wall she heard the scrape of a chair.

The voice began at once, an almost whining complaint.

"Jesus, man. It took you long enough. Wot's for it now? A little food maybe? Some grog?"

Then it was Darby Dray speaking, that soft voice calm and assuring. "All the food you want and all the grog your belly can hold. Only first I will hear the story one more time."

The man cursed and slammed something on the table. "God in Heaven, man, I might as well be a fucking parrot. How many times have I said it over to you? Once did I change?"

"This is the last time," Darby said calmly. "Have I told you that before? Never. But now I do. There was the clink of metal coins. "Here is half the price we agreed on. The rest will be there beside it when you have told the story one more time. If there are questions from my friends you will answer them. If they have no questions, you can take the money and begone."

"Not half soon enough," the man grumbled. "From the very start?" The question was pleading.

"From the very start," Darby insisted firmly.

"There was this gent. And no, by God, I did not ever ask his name. He told me as how a boy had been snatched and taken from his own mother's bosom and spirited away. This was in Boston. He said that the boy was being kept on the river outside of Charles Town in the sticks down there. All I was to do was snatch the boy back and deliver him without questions and I would be paid."

"I was three weeks in Charles Town and I saw the boy but was never able to get near. There was always an old white lady or a young one or wot looked to be his pap. Then he was gone, by ship to this place, and I left the message for the gent as I had been told to do. He said I should meet him here."

"In this town?" Darby pressed.

"Hell, man, in this very dive. He took me to where the boy was being kept, same boy, same red hair. I was to watch. To keep me eyes on that kid day or night until the chance came."

"How long did this go on?"

"A month mebbe, more or less. I tole you how the days slipped off from me, waiting like that."

"Very well," Darby said quietly. "Then one day the boy came out of the silversmith's shop by himself."

"I run up to him pretending I had lost my dog. When he said no, he hadn't seen any such, I showed much pain and asked if he would help me find it, it being little and the day cold. We went along looking for only a couple of storefronts and then there was this alley and I bagged him."

"Bagged him?" Darby pressed quietly.

"Good Lord, man, slipped a bag over his head and took him under me arm to me quarters."

"And how long did you keep him there?"

"Only three days, thank God, him being a ruddy little bastard always giving me a lot of mouth and trying to give me the slip besides. We went on ship as father and son with me claiming him to be sickly and in danger from sea air so that none might pry that I kept him in the cabin. Famous little liar he was, telling me he had never been snatched from his ma and didn't even have a ma as a matter of fact because she had been kilt by Indians."

"And your destination was France?" Darby asked.

"Some place called Ruin. And it all went as the gent said it would do. Our small boat was met and pulled ashore by a great broad man with legs like a stork. I held the little beggar until I got him right inside that carriage."

"Describe the carriage," Darby said quietly.

"Big one, the biggest one I ever saw with a crest blazed on the side, red with an angle of blue across and a tree and some animal in the divided parts."

"And the people," Darby urged.

"There was a driver tricked up in an ape suit and a footman the same only fancier, up in back. The man with the barrel shape that helped the boat in was there trying to help me make the little beggar get into the carriage. But he wanted none of either of us so that I had to pin his arms and thrust him right in there that he might be held down."

"So you saw who was in the carriage," Darby suggested.

The man groaned. "Hell, man, I don't even like thinking on that part. It was Death, or a man so like to Death that he could pose for a graveyard cutting. That white hair standing apart from his head and skin stretched on bones. But rich he was with great claw hands gripping the gold handles of a cane."

"No names were spoken?" Darby asked.

"No."

"Describe the crest on the carriage for me again," Darby said. As the man's voice droned on Julie was conscious that something in the room was changed. Glancing over, she saw that Antoine had abandoned his listening position and sat with his head buried in his hands. His breath came convulsively. Oh God, how she wanted to reach out to him, but something stayed her hand.

They heard the passage of the talker along the hall outside and his steps on the stairs. Julie went to the door at Darby's discreet knock.

She reached her hands to his cheeks and touched them tenderly before leaning into his grasp. "Darby, Darby, my great good friend, how can we thank you? How did you know?"

She felt Darby meeting Antoine's eyes over her head. She saw his arm reach out and realized with stunned relief that Antoine had accepted this proffered sign of friendship.

"Darby Dray, at your service, sir," Darby told Antoine. "Does that story make any sense to the two of you?"

"Only to me," Antoine said quietly. "The man with Death's skull for a face is my father."

He looked at Julie and the sober-faced man with his arm companionably about his wife's shoulder. "I will not ask you how or in what manner you two have become friends, Darby Dray," he said, "but I thank God for that day. And this one."

In that grimy room the three of them talked a long time. They talked of payment for Darby's work and he soberly insisted that he was better paid than they knew. They asked what thing they could do to thank him for the great service he had done and he smiled at Julie, saying he had already been thanked beyond his highest hope.

Then he paused. "May I ask what course you will take?" he inquired after a moment.

"Go to France," Antoine said forcefully.

At Darby's slight frown, Julie leaned toward him. "Knowing what magic you have done for our mutual friends, Darby, and having seen you perform one such miracle myself, what would you do?"

He stared at the floor thoughtfully before speaking. "First of all I would seal all lips that know that you have learned where the boy has been taken. Then," he looked up at Antoine, "only then would I go to France. Once there I would remember that this plan was carefully made and nursed over a long time. Whoever holds that child will not easily let go of what was so difficult to obtain. By going in with your hand showing you can lose again, and this time perhaps forever. Neither a strong impetuous body or a wily careful mind can achieve your end. They must be joined together." He shrugged, spread his hand wide and rose. "I do not consider it politic that we leave this room together. I shall leave and in a little while, please follow."

"Darby," Julie cried, rising to catch his hand.

He closed her hand in both of his and smiled. "My best regards to young Armand," he said simply. "When the three of you are together again."

She stood and listened to his steps on the stairs. When the room had been silent of that sound for several minutes, Antoine rose with a sigh. He offered her his arm.

"Shall we go, good wife?" he asked quietly.

As she slid her hand inside his arm, she felt hot tears form behind her eyes.

So now she had become his good wife again. She had been transformed, by an accident of success, from a shrew who could be publicly humiliated at will to something treasured. She might have lied to herself that the sickness of spirit she felt came from the nauseating air of the room through which they passed. She did not bother to try to fool herself even on this. Nor did she care that her bruised feet stumbled on the rough cobbles of the street as she pulled her arm away and walked apart from him on the way home.

Part 8

THE CHOOSING

1731

Chapter Eighty-Four

The second ship of Antoine's fleet, which had been built and launched into service while Julie was in the West, had been christened *Etoile de Mer*. Somehow Antoine had managed to channel his agony over the loss of his daughter and his guilt and confusion over his wife's disappearance into the building of this rugged craft from whose prow stretched the figure of a child with curls spinning back from the wind and a smile so gentle that the sight of it stopped all passersby when the ship swung at anchor.

With a red velvet bonnet pulled tightly over her curls and her cheeks whipped by the wind to the same color, Julie buried her hands in a fur-lined muff to watch the final loading of the ship. Antoine seemed to be everywhere at once, his great long legs moving him from one end of the ship to the other in giant strides. She felt strangely removed from him. It was almost fortunate that the past weeks had been too full for even the smallest sharing between them. They had functioned as two industrious strangers bound in a common cause—this desperate journey to find the lost child.

The screeching of the winches and the flapping of the sails almost drowned out the squealing of the fat stoat who skated on his hooves in his deckside pen beside the chickens who clucked with dismay at the ship's lurching motion. Julie, watching the harbor fade to a dark blur, fought back unreasonable tears.

In that bedlam of sound she did not hear Antoine approach. As she felt his hand at her waist she glanced up at him. He did not meet her eyes. Instead, he stared intently at the land they were leaving, leaning a little that his words would not be whipped away from her hearing.

"I need to talk to you, Julie," he said, his tone sober to the point of severity.

She nodded, feeling her chest tighten with dread within the loop of his arm.

He shook his head impatiently. "No," he said, "not here. Your clothes are wet from the spray. Come below. I have put this off too long already."

Once below, her head spun with questions as she removed her damp outer clothing and stowed it to dry. By the time she was through, Antoine had arranged two small chairs by the cabin table and set out a decanter of Madeira with two glasses.

"This Darby Dray," he finally began. "A strange man, he is a good friend to you."

"To both of us," Julie suggested quietly.

He nodded and stared at her vacantly. "Perhaps he is a better friend to me than he knows," he agreed. "He set my head to spinning with his counsel and from that churning I have found myself come to a new place . . . with you, Julie."

Julie realized that his sober calmness was only a frail pose as he sprang to his feet and began pacing back and forth across the narrow space of the cabin.

"Goddamnit, Julie, we have made an utter mess of this marriage so far. How can that be?" As he turned to her with the question, his handsome face was tight with emotion. "How can two people whose love is as powerful as ours manage to mess up their lives so thoroughly? Look at us, a man and a woman clearly designed by God to be joined, and yet we keep flying apart in pain and agony. It can't go on, Julie, lest one day we lose all in one such fatal misstep. I am telling you that it is through, the two of us have to start all over again at the beginning, as if we had never met, and do this thing right."

"What do you propose, Antoine?" she asked, impressed by the single-mindedness of his appeal.

Seizing his chair, he drew it near to face her, leaning almost knee to knee with her as he began to speak rapidly and almost incoherently. With his clear bright eyes intent on hers, he spilled out the frustrations and anguish and pain of the years past, running their lives past her mind like a swift panorama . . . the ecstasy of their first love at Epping, their separation and final reunion, the turmoil of the years that brought Etoile and then Armand and, after Etoile's death, her long absence and his mindless grief.

"Don't you see what kind of tale I am telling, Julie? It is the story of two stallions each with his head set on his own path? I plunged into what I wished with no thought of your own dreams and aspirations. You made great monumental decisions and proceeded to act on them as if I were a pawn in your apron pocket. You cannot make a team of two wild beasts wrangling in harness, Julie. A team, Julie, we have to make a team of ourselves or we will lose this last desperate gamble along with the rest."

His voice suddenly lost its ferocity. "And there is more than that, Julie. We have been scarred by my jealousy, pain, and abuse. We have been scarred by your readiness to pull apart from me and become unreachable behind those cold golden eyes. I want something better for us, a joining without scars, a tender joining where casual words do not fall on old wounds and make our souls flinch."

"You cannot wipe out the past," Julie reminded him softly, aching at the pain in his voice.

"You are right," he agreed, "but we can start again, as a team. God knows, I never thought to say these words to you or any woman, but Julie, you are my equal and I am yours. We must pledge to live and love and work together as equals." He stopped suddenly and stared at her expectantly.

Conscious of his waiting glance, Julie felt suddenly helpless. She lifted her arms and laid them lightly across his shoulders.

"My love, my love," she sighed. "I agree with you wholly, but how do we begin, how do we start?"

"We start now," he said fiercely. "Today. This urgency may seem strange with the width of the sea between ourselves and France, but believe me, the journey we are on now, this crossing of the ocean, is the easiest part of what we are setting out to do. It was your—our friend Darby Dray who turned my mind to this. We only know that Armand was delivered to an old man in the Rivière coach. That at least assures us that he did not start in Emile's hands. But where is Armand now, Julie? With my parents? That is unlikely. My father is a count who maintains a large and gossipy household where nothing

365

stays hidden for long. Also, Sophie's son Charles must be back and forth from the University at Caen. Would my father risk those two cousins coming together to have Charles learn that Armand is a prisoner in France?"

He shook his head distractedly. "God, how I have been troubled with questions these past weeks. My father has money and position, Julie, and in France that means power. We come without power, without access to information, without friends in any real sense. Yet we must discover where our child is, get him into our own hands and bring him home. Do you realize what a challenge this is?"

"I hadn't until now," she confessed.

He shook his head. "I have asked myself how to meet these challenges a million times, but I find no answers. I have no gift for such strategy. My natural approach is to force myself in boldly and openly, just the course that your friend Darby Dray so wisely advised against. The two of us, Julie, while we have this time must weld ourselves together and come up with a plan that will outwit my father who is an old fox, as well as my brother who might more aptly be named a serpent. If it were Emile alone we were fighting, the answer might even be easier, for it is always easier to subvert the ends of an evil man than a good one. There are more ways to buy a man like Emile than the treasury of France knows of, but with my father it is different. He does not hold the boy for his value but for his life. We must free him for his own life."

Julie stared at him thoughtfully. "A plan, a strategy," she murmured, wishing that Darby Dray were there to make three of them about that decanter of wine.

He leaned down and pressed his lips gently against her forehead. "I am the great bull who would attack the world with force and speed, Julie. You must restrain me, you must approach this problem with the same cleverness with which you approached the problem of bringing back Paul Bontemps from the living dead. You must be general and I will be lieutenant. I hope you will not find me a hard pupil."

A panic seized her. He had overstated her cleverness by far. What she had achieved had come about not by her own wit, but from the love that others bore her: Mark Hatter, back in London so long ago, Josh, Jacques DuBois, Gonzales, Darby Dray. She would have stopped the words but she was too distraught: "Those things were done because of people who loved me."

His eyes changed a little but he did not refute her

statement. "What we have to do here must be done by you, Julie, and by one who loves you. Are you saying that my love is insuffecent to your need?"

She clasped his arms tightly. "Oh no, my love, not that. It is only that I know nothing of this place, these people, I am dismayed at the magnitude of your trust."

"What I know is wholly at your command. We need a plan. You must come up with a plan. Armand's life depends on it."

"You don't really mean he is in danger of losing his life," she said.

"It is possible," he admitted. "I would not put the death of a child past my brother Emile if such a child stood between him and the inheritance he seeks. But it is that other sense of the word life that I really had in mind. He must have the days of his life, Julie, even as you and I have had them in the colonies. He must be free to choose what he is to be and do with his manhood, not pressed into a stale mold chosen by an old man desperate for an heir."

"Or his father?" Julie asked quietly, her heart quickening at her own bravado in framing the question. "What if it is his own father who chooses the mold to press him into?"

He shook his head. "I am past all that," he said quietly. "The weeks just ended have been fraught with examination of myself, too. When I heard Paul Bontemps speak gently of my father and his own, when I hear Paul able to give freedom even to his son Charles in spite of his loathing for the Old World, I saw things anew. Believe me, Julie, I will not fight again to make Armand's life for him or even his fortune. I will simply fight for his right to make that choice for himself."

"Even if that choice be France and the title?"

He didn't even try to hide the look of pain that crossed his face. "I know you are thinking that it seems that Sophie's son Charles has made the choice that way, choosing the Old World over the New. Yes, Julie," he sighed as he spoke, "if that is his decision, I would also fight for that."

"We still have each other," he reminded her, touching her cheek and letting his hand stray down to cup the fullness of her breast. "We have each other and our love."

As he spoke the ship bucked on the waves, sending the decanter sliding along the tabletop. He seized it even as Julie caught the glasses. "And we have these goddamned ships, if they can manage to keep the ocean under them in these swells."

He braced himself as he opened the decanter. "Hold

there," he said. "I would propose a toast to the new Julie and Antoine, team, instead of two wild stallions bucking in their braces."

She smiled as the wine warmed her throat. "And to a plan," she added, lifting her glass to his again.

"To a devilish plan," he whispered, his eyes warm and smiling on her own. "By the yellow-eyed devil who owns my soul," he added softly.

Chapter Eighty-Five

It was Julie's idea that they should quietly get in touch with Sophie's son Charles before they went on to Paris.

"Ridiculous," Antoine exploded. "Why should we counsel with a boy on a man's business?"

"Because he is here," Julie said reasonably. "He is our friend as well as being privy to the household of your father."

When she continued to try to make him listen, he continued to outshout her gentle reasoning, turning her arguments away with furious denials. Exhausted from combating his every word, she finally slammed her fist down on the table, making the china dishes dance at the force of her blow.

"All right," she said. "Close your mouth and listen to me for one full minute. Did you consider yourself merely a boy when you robbed your father to ransom Paul out of prison? Were you a 'mere lad' when you arranged Sophie's elopement and made your own escape to London to earn back the money to repay your father? How old were you, Antoine, when you took Sophie's life and your own into your own hands?"

His expression had turned from shock to anger at her tone but as she continued to shout at him, his frown was lost in a deep throaty chuckle. Crossing the room, he pulled her from the chair into his arms, burying his face in her hair. "Vixen, vixen," he sighed. "You have won again. I was seventeen years of age. God in Heaven, I was seventeen even as Charles will be within the month. I cede to you. But even if we seek out Charles, how can he be of help?"

"We can find out what he knows," she murmured against his chest. "Even if he knows nothing, he will at least know what is going on. He might even have an idea where the child is secreted if he is not with your parents."

He nodded, holding her close. "Very well, my love, we will go first to Caen." Even as he spoke, his free hand loosened her blouse, freeing her breasts to his lips. "You have won fairly again, my love. Tell me that the victor has a tender prize for my wounded manhood."

She giggled as his lips moved from her throat to her breast, filling her with shivers of anticipation. How could this blaze of passion for him still rise with such tumult after so long? The chill of the ship's cabin disappeared in the flame of her desire for him.

Even as he lifted her onto the bed she felt the softening of her body for his touch. What richness came with time. She rose to his smooth hard body with a throbbing joy.

That was the first but not the last of their battles about the strategy in France. That was the first but not the last truce confirmed by lovemaking in the rolling bunk of the *Etoile de Mer*. By the time the longboat delivered the two of them, along with their baggage, to the docks at Caen, Julie felt strangely like a bride again, invigorated, with her senses sharpened to a new and exciting consciousness of all about her. It was indeed a new beginning and she tightened her hand on Antoine's thigh under the lap robe as the boat nudged the dock.

"Are you ready, *ma générale*?" he asked, smiling down at her.

She could only nod. The tenderness in his handsome face filled her throat with a sudden rush of joyful tears.

The castle built by William the Conqueror dominated the city. What portion of the sky the castle did not claim was usurped by the two massive abbeys which flanked the hill. The town itself seemed to be a miserable place of shallow hopes. Houses stood empty everywhere, with storefronts boarded against the ill-kempt streets.

Once installed in the inn under Julie's maiden name of Duvall (another hard battle fought and won in the cabin of the *Etoile de Mer*), Antoine's impatience could not be stayed until morning.

"If you must send a message to young Charles, let me do it," Julie insisted. "Who knows what stranger here might know your face? It is unlikely that he will remember my name, but it

369

is a rare seventeen-year-old whose curiosity will not compel him to attend a lady at night in a public inn."

"You are truly a devil," Antoine groaned. "But let me at least write the note that is enclosed."

"And risk his carelessness in leaving it about?" she asked.

He reluctantly ceded her the rude table that was all the room supplied as a desk. "Get it done, then," he ordered. "While I send for a messenger from the innkeeper. God, what a tyrant hides under those silken petticoats!"

With the messenger dispatched, they dined on lamb as delicate as Antoine had promised. Tiny succulent potatoes swam in the faintly salty gravy and Julie was barely able to breathe from the tightness of her laces by the time the plates were removed. She twirled the stem of her wineglass between her fingers impatiently. "What keeps him?" she asked when the two of them were finishing their second bottle of wine. "Do you suppose we made a mistake by coming here at all? That innkeeper didn't send an unreliable messenger, did he?"

Antoine laughed merrily. "You have more questions than I have answers. I may remind you of this night the next time you call me down for being impatient."

A pale moon had swung over the abbey when the soft tap finally sounded on the door. Antoine rose, then drew back into the shadows for Julie to respond. A single lamp lit the room from behind, throwing her own face into darkness but revealing the strong handsome face of the young man whose bulk filled the hallway outside the door.

"My God, *tante*," the young man cried, catching her in his arms. "How can this be? I thought you long dead. Papa wrote..."

"You might well have thought me dead, you wretch," Julie interrupted. "But you also thought I was another woman ...someone younger and more handsome, I am sure. Confess it. If ever I have seen a man's face ripe for a tryst it was yours."

As Charles flushed, Antoine came out of the shadows and seized his nephew's hand. "Don't let this golden-eyed wench bully you. We are here on clandestine business. That is why we sent your message in a strange name with such a cryptic note."

"Secret business?" Charles asked, studying his uncle's face with frowning interest. "I pray that nothing is awry."

"Come and sit," Antoine urged. "Julie and I have a problem and have come to seek your help."

370

Watching the men was a revelation to Julie. Charles was indeed now a full man, although still endowed with the lithe slenderness of his youth. As he plied Antoine with questions about his parents, the plantation, and the new brother he had never seen, Julie saw in his face first a glimpse of Paul Bontemps, and then the shadow of Sophie's smile. But it was Charles himself, a strong, articulate, even firm-minded young man who filled her with delight. When Antoine had explained the nature of their business, Charles seemed doubtful.

"Then you have heard nothing?" Antoine pressed.

Charles paused, stroking his face thoughtfully with his long slender hands. "Nothing," he said finally. "And yet ..."

He shrugged and waved his hands in a gesture of futility. "Nothing really at all. But in the past, ever since I have been here in France, I have been to see Grandpère at least every fortnight.

"You must know that he and I have become fast friends since I came over here. Maman was still alone and while I did not want for any real need, I never had the extra money that the other students had. It was Grandpère who sent a serving man to wait on me and he used to send his carriage for me on holidays and other times in between. He made me the gift of a fine horse that I could never have bought, much less kept boarded without his assistance. Yet for the past month or so he has neither sent for me nor written to urge that I ride over to Paris to visit him."

"No word at all?" Antoine said thoughtfully.

"There was some word," Charles revised. "I wrote him a letter inquiring of his health and relaying my hope his failure to communicate with me did not mean that his health had failed further. He replied at once, claiming that business affairs had kept him too busy to enjoy my company."

He looked at Antoine shyly. "He is a fine old man, Uncle Tony. I know that you and Mother had much trouble with him when you were young, but to me he is a fine, proud old man who suffers greatly from pain and loneliness."

Antoine's words were almost a growl. "Lonely enough to steal an heir from the bosom of his own parents?" he asked.

"He thought Aunt Julie dead even as we all did," Charles pointed out. "He might have thought that his establishment in Paris offered more for a motherless child than a home in the colonies with my mother who has this new babe to absorb her interest."

"Are you defending my father for kidnapping my son?"

Antoine asked, his voice deepening with challenge.

Julie was astonished to see young Charles hold his uncle's gaze boldly until it was Antoine himself who looked away.

"Very well, Charles," Antoine said quietly. "I did not come to do combat with you but to enlist your help. Tell us, if you will, how matters stand in my father's house."

Charles' face grew thoughtful and sober. He stared at them unhappily. "I do not have the same love for my grandmother that I do for my grandfather," he admitted. "She is wary of me, as if she suspects I visit for reasons other than friendship and family bonds. She is a vain, foolish old woman whose head can be completely turned by false flattery."

"Emile's?" Antoine asked.

Charles could not conceal the distaste he felt at the mention of his other uncle's name. He nodded. "Uncle Emile is a very sick man, a sick and dangerous man. His passion for money and power is only exceeded by his lust for self-gratification."

"Tell me of his wife," Antoine interrupted.

"My uncle Emile is richly blessed in his wife," he said simply.

"Oh come now, Charles," Antoine laughed. "Describe this blessing to us. Is she fair? Is she amiable? Does she appeal to a man's senses? Is she worthy of bearing heirs for the house of le Comte de la Rivière?"

"She is as fair as any woman in France," he said steadily. "She has a difference in her fairness even as Aunt Julie has, that kind of fairness that once seen is never forgotten. Her eyes are like the eyes of a young fawn, wide-set, rounded, and terribly vulnerable. She is slender and delicately shaped and not given to idle chatter. But her silences are warm and inviting. As for children . . ."

Antoine raised his hand. "Never mind that, we are not speaking of children here. But that is not to say that Emile might not try to breed normally no matter how little taste he has for it. Does he treat her well?"

Julie watched Charles' struggle for control and knew the answer that the young man was too well trained to speak. "She is not that kind of woman who is given to complaints," he said finally. Then, as if unable to bear the tension of the conversation, he said abruptly, "Tell me, Uncle Tony, what can I do? What steps can I take? I waited very late to come because I wanted my own man freed and settled to his own affairs for the night."

"Then your man is a local sort with a tongue for gossip," Antoine said.

"I used to have such a one," Charles said, "but only a few months ago Grandpère sent this new man to serve me. He is the youngest son of Grandpère's own man Henri, who has apparently been with the old man forever. The boy's name is Michel and has been a fine, amiable companion in these few months he has been with me."

"Good Lord," Antoine cried. "I remember Henri's son as well as his daughter. They are certainly more than grown by now. The son was my own age and the daughter but a few months younger."

"But this is another son," Charles put in. "Henri has told me the story again and again of how his wife Jeanne was taken to childbed at near forty and delivered of this son before she died. He is the apple of his father's eyes, that Michel."

"Yet he has sent him off to Caen to serve you?" Antoine asked.

Charles laughed. "Michel is very young and so handsome as to be almost beautiful. I got the idea from Grandpère that he had been in some sort of trouble or another, a wench I would guess from his fine body and winning eyes. But he is abroad tonight on his own mischief and I do need to return myself before he hies himself home to become curious. Is there something you wish of me?"

"We had thought of paying a simple visit to your grandparents, Charles," Julie said. "Not mentioning that Armand was even missing, making as if we had left the colonies before the event took place. We thought perhaps that we might be able to tell from their response if it was indeed Antoine's father and the man Henri who met the kidnapper in the coach at Rouen."

Charles stared pensively at his uncle for a long time.

"Grandpère is very fond of Emile's wife Anne," he said quietly. "It is her custom to spend a couple of afternoons a week with either Grandmère and her little coterie of women, or in playing chess with Grandpère."

"Then you think an interview could be arranged with this girl Anne without Emile being apprized of it?"

"He spends little time at his own hearth," Charles said curtly. "They reside in a manor house on the Normandy estate between here and Paris, and his coach is ever racing along the city road."

"What would be the earliest time?" Julie asked hopefully.

"Within a day or two at most," Charles guessed aloud. "For all that Michel is a great strapping lad, he goes home to Paris every few days with my consent. If we should seize on his passing we three might be able to see Anne at her home with none the wiser, lest Michel be inclined to carry tales to his father. Do you still ride, Aunt Julie?"

At her nod, he looked pleased. "That would be the way. Three of us on fast horses would be there and return within a long day ... with time to spare."

Charles rose, again reminding Julie of Paul by the proportions of his tall slender frame.

"We will wait word from you." Antoine said, rising with him. "And thank God for you, Charles, at this time which finds us in great need of friends."

Charles' smile was rueful. "Let us save that until the end is achieved, Uncle. Grandpère's power has not diminished with his strength."

When Antoine had returned from seeing Charles to the head of the stairs, he turned to Julie with a quizzical smile. "Did you hear what I heard behind that young man's words?" he asked.

"That Charles is hopelessly in love with Emile's wife, this Anne from Austria?" she asked.

"That is a dangerous game he plays," Antoine said quietly. "The only thing more dangerous about Emile than his affection is his enmity."

Chapter Eighty-Six

Seven weeks had passed since Henri Vannay had accompanied his master le Comte to Rouen to receive the boy Armand Rivière from the hands of his abductor. As negatively as Henri had viewed the whole venture at the first, he found when he had an opportunity to visit the child in his hiding place that his heart rose in his throat like a bird filled with song.

What a fine boy he was for all his swift temper and tart tongue! Not even Henri's own sons had taken to the falcon with such skill at a tender age, nor mounted a pony better with legs still rounded from babyhood. An the old Count, unable to visit the child himself, gave him free rein to report on the child's charm and wit, his good nature and playfulness.

374

"Do you see him coming to love France?" the old man always asked hopefully.

Henri, dreading to see the disappointment in the old man's eyes, could only reply, "He holds Margot very dear, sir. And he asks less often when his papa will arrive to take him home."

"Time," the old man always said. "Children forget with time. And as he does the papers are being drawn for his inheritance and the custody being arranged. I shall die in peace, Henri, I shall die with my lands and name going to a worthy heir, a hope I have not cherished since Antoine turned to such a viper in my bosom these long years ago."

When le Comte, with the doors carefully sealed against idle ears, had first broached his plan to Henri, his man had stared at him in sad astonishment.

"Steal Antoine's son?" Henri had repeated in horror. "Take the child from his proper father in the colonies and bring him to France?"

"Am I not his proper grandfather?" the old man had challenged him. "The child is a Rivière. His mother went off into the wilderness for God knows what reason and has been lost to him. I little thought that my wife's gossipy friends in Philadelphia would be of such unwitting service to me, but at least I am kept abreast with the affairs of that madman son of mine, Antoine.

"Remember how you cherish your own son Michel, Henri. Do not bedevil me for searching for an heir in my great age. What chance have I?"

Henri did not have it in his heart to mention le Comte's living son, Emile, whom the old man referred to only as "my wife's son." The mere mention of that simpering profligate was enough to throw the old man into a fit of fever.

And how shrewd of the old man it was to mention Henri's own son Michel. For indeed, Henri cherished his youngest son with all his heart. And when it had become obvious that Emile Rivière had become attracted to the young boy's vibrant beauty, it was the old man himself who had arranged for the boy to go into service with Sophie's son, the young Charles, in Caen that the boy be removed from Emile's notice.

"He will not be gone that far from you, Henri," the old man had assured him. "And just let him roll a few of those Norman wenches in the hay and he will be the first to spit in the face of the likes of my wife's son."

"There is always the boy Charles," Henri had told the old

375

man when the plan was first discussed.

The Count had nodded. "There is an heir I would be proud to pass this title to," he agreed. "I even had such hopes, as you well know. But with the return of that reckless Paul Bontemps from the dead, I had no more hopes for that. You remember that proud young buck, Henri. Can you imagine his letting his own son take another man's name and heritage over the Bontemps name?"

Henri had had to agree with his master, for the words rang true.

"So I shall steal the boy and bring him to France," the old man had insisted, "and you will help me."

Sick at the thought, Henri could do naught but listen to the conspiratorial whisper. "But I cannot bring Antoine's son here to Paris," the old man said. "Bérénice, in her addled senility, keeps nothing from her son. God knows what he would do to keep the inheritance from falling into hands other than his own."

"Then where would the child go? Where could he be kept?" Henri had asked.

"Tell me about your daughter Margot," the old man had said.

Henri's jaws had dropped. "Margot?" he asked dumbly. What did his widowed daughter Margot have to do with this affair?

"Margot," the old man repeated. "That girl of yours whose husband was lost four or five years ago with the Duke's forces. How does she fare?"

"Not well," Henri admitted. "There was little money and no property. But she has a situation of sorts, in a banker's house here in Paris. They are not fancy or noble people."

"Does she live in with her employers?"

Henri nodded. "In the garret room supplied."

"Henri, you know that cottage on the estate in Normandy that is unused? It is only an hour's drive from here more or less, with three rooms and a garden plot and a shed for two horses."

Henri had nodded. "I know the one."

"Would Margot like that cottage for her own? Would she like to be given that dwelling place and the privilege of the garden and a small allowance for all the days that remain to her?"

"My God, sir," Henri had exploded. "That would be a gift from heaven." Then he paused. "For what price?"

"The care of the child Armand Rivière," the old man

whispered. "He is not a babe that will take all of her time. He is a finely grown lad, according to reports, and she would not have him forever either, only until such time that I can bring my legal affairs into order and arrange for his safety and win the boy's heart to the France that will be his home."

Henri nodded numbly, torn between his dismay at the evil of his master's plan and the temptation of a father who loved his daughter well.

"She is kindly to children, is she not?" the old man asked.

"She is Jeanne's child, sir, she could be no other way," Henri came back quickly. "It was she, child that she was, who undertook to raise young Michel when her mother joined the saints. But what if the child hungered for home? What if he will not stay?"

"Oh, he will stay," the old man assured him. "He will only know what tale we tell him. We shall tell him of how we paid ransom to free him from his captor. He will be told that we have sent a message and in time his own father will come for him."

"But sir . . ." Henri protested.

The old man had smiled with arched brows. "Is that so mortal a lie, Henri? Surely you must confess that if the father knew where he was, he would be on the first ship that passed."

"There is only the consideration that the great house on that same estate is occupied by your wife's son and his own wife Anne . . . very near."

The old man shook his head. "The master of that estate is never caught in his own fields while there are new dens of sin opening daily in Paris. And the wife Anne, poor creature, cringes in the garden dreading the arrival of her beast. And even if he were to come upon Margot and the child while on the hunt? She has the different name of her marriage, and a child by a mother's apron is a child and no more."

Henri passed the gamekeeper's cottage, waving cheerily to the wife who was sweeping the stoop with a broom as tall as herself.

But this visit was unlike those joyous ones that had come before. Sure enough, the boy leaped from the floor to run to greet him, letting himself be caught and thrown as high in the air as the roof of the cottage would allow. And sure enough, the scent of rich lamb stew and of fresh baked bread filled the air. But at the first glimpse of his daughter, his own smile faded.

377

Her face was puffy from weeping and her dark eyes so full of sadness that she looked as she had the day that the report had come of her own man's falling on the field of battle.

As Henri set the boy on the floor, Armand grinned up at him. "You have brought me a trinket because I see it there in your belt."

"Indeed, I have, young man," Henri said jovially. "Now you must go off in the other room and learn to use it well so that I can be proud of you. I need to have a word with Margot."

The boy seized the top with a shout, then hesitated, his eyes on Margot. "You be kind to her, Henri," he said sternly. "You be kind and don't make her cry, she has not felt happy all this day."

"I will be kind to her," Henri promised, patting the boy's rump as he trotted away.

Henri saw the tears well in his daughter's eyes as he looked at her questioningly. She covered her face with her apron for a long moment until she mustered spirit to speak.

"Oh Papa, Papa," she said in a tear-choked voice, kept low that the child not hear from the next room. "I would have my tongue cut from my mouth before telling you this. I would I had died before I spoke to you today."

"Come, Margot," he patted her awkwardly. "Whatever plagues you, it cannot be so sad as you say. The boy is well, the sun shines, whatever mood is upon you will pass away."

"Michel," she croaked.

"Michel?" he stared at her. What could have happened to his precious son? "Michel is in Caen serving the young master," he reminded her.

"Oh, but he is not," she gasped. "He was here, here in these woods just this night past."

"In these woods?" her words set such a chill on Henri's heart that he struggled to keep his voice down. "Stop that bleating, my girl, and tell me what nonsense you are talking."

"The child was sleeping," she said, "and the night was dark. When I heard a sound I rose and went to watch from the shadows. At first I thought they were lovers, a lad and a maid, someone from the village walking out together on the sly.

"But as they passed into the moonlight in the clearing, arms about each other, I saw it to be two men. And Father, one of them was my brother Michel."

"You lie," he hissed. "Your eyes were dim with sleep."

She shook her head.

"And there in the clearing they embraced, as a lad and a maid might, Papa. Then I saw Michel mount his horse, the black one with the white blaze and the one white foot that Monsieur le Comte bought him and he had shown me so proudly."

"And then what?"

She covered her face again. "Then Michel leaned from his horse and kissed the other man, full on the lips, for a long time."

"Describe the man," Henri said icily.

"Tall," she said slowly. "And very thin with pale white hair and a coat that stuck out in back like an evening coat, very stiff."

"Do you know le Comte's son, Emile Rivière?"

"He was pointed out to me once in Paris, a long time ago."

"Was this the same man?"

She could not answer but her father groaned softly at the movement of her head.

"Did they see you watching?"

"Michel didn't," she said quickly. "But the tall man came from the clearing before I gained my senses. I fled inside the door and latched it tight. But he came and banged against the door and shouted so threateningly that I was afraid that he would waken the child."

"So you opened the door."

"He asked my name and what business I had on his property. I told him my name which meant nothing to him, and told him that I was here at the behest of his father, Monsieur le Comte. When he saw the child standing in his nightshirt staring at the light, he asked if it was my child. I claimed him even as the boy ran and put his head in my skirt from the fury in the man's voice."

Henri buried his head in his hands with a groan.

Chapter Eighty-Seven

One day passed and then two. Caged in that mean room at the inn waiting for word from young Charles, Antoine grew hourly more restive. Julie, terrified lest he lose heart with this careful enterprise and go plunging off in his violent way, tried every trick she knew of to help him pass the hours.

They played at cards until the games palled and they turned to gambling.

On the third day Antoine reached for the cards as soon as their breakfast things were cleared away. His glance at her was clearly wicked.

"Don't think that I have missed your tricks, Julie Rivière," he told her softly. "I have been enrapt in conversation, lured into bed, and made a fool of at gaming as slickly as I have ever seen such tricks pulled. A great star was lost to whoredom when you settled to this one man."

She grinned at him slyly. "And a great whoremonger was pulled from the streets when you wed me, Antoine Rivière. Another night like the last one and I should be unable to sit a horse as far as your brother's house though he live only a mile away instead of many as Charles says."

Her jest disappeared into his scowl. "God in Heaven, what is keeping that boy? Why does he not simply leave his man and take off with us? Is he a weakling that he must hang on the whim of a common valet?"

"Perhaps he fears that the boy is a spy," Julie suggested. "Although he states that the boy is drawn on these excursions by homesickness, perhaps he suspects other motives for the boy's running back and forth to Paris as he does."

"In that case, I might swallow my ire," Antoine conceded. "But what could be luring the boy and why?"

Julie shrugged and smiled at him. "It is your family, my pet. But I have a niggling concern that there is more to this lad Michel than passes Charles' tongue. I do not think he really likes the valet."

"Ridiculous," Antoine snorted. "You heard him boast of the boy's fine appearance and his amiability."

Julie shrugged and began to lay the cards out for patience. She moved a three onto a black four without replying.

"Here," he said, taking the cards away from her. "We are going to play a new game. For every trick you lose, you have to remove a garment."

"And you?" she asked as he shuffled the cards in a smooth stream.

"I will make the same pledge," he told her, "but I shall warn you. I do not intend to freeze in this dreary room."

By making his own choice of what he must remove,

Antoine found himself shoeless and shirtless when the rapping came at the door.

Julie, hastily pulling her shawl around her, called from the inside of the panel before undoing the lock.

"It is I, Charles," the welcome reply came "It is time."

"Michel was quite forward about leaving," Charles said. "I simply found a note waiting when I returned from my tutor's. He said that his father had sent for him by messenger and he would return as soon as possible."

"And you have horses?" Antoine asked, finishing dressing.

"Ready at the door," Charles replied.

It seemed to Julie that hours had passed before Charles reined in at a stream to water the horses and turned to Antoine with a note of apology in his voice.

"I have not been wholly candid with you, Uncle Tony," the young man said. "I am not welcome at my uncle's house."

"So?" Antoine asked, careful not to let his eyes stray to Julie's face.

"I have decided that it would be better, just in case the master be in residence or the servants be gossips, to ask you and Tante Julie to approach the house alone."

"And what would we say? How would we announce ourselves?" Julie asked.

The young man flushed deeply. "Announce yourselves as M. and Mme. D'Amour. I am quite sure that the mistress of the house would receive you under those names."

"Suggest that you would like to see her gardens," Charles went on. "They are really quite famous and it will occasion no surprise. I shall be waiting in the garden for our conversation."

"And what if my brother be in residence?" Antoine asked.

Charles paused with a concerned look. "Do you think you could possibly approach the house alone, Tante Julie? It would be safer by far."

Julie, caught off guard, felt a moment of panic before stiffening her spine. "I see no problem with that," she replied without even a glance at Antoine.

It took a uniformed servant a long time to reply to the repeated tolling of the bell. It took even longer for Julie to be ushered into a large graceful room to wait for the mistress of the house.

She was not astonished that Emile's wife Anne received her alone, without an attendant. What did astonish her was the girl

381

herself, who stood in the door staring at her with wary eyes. Julie's heart went out to her. This was no woman at all, but only a lovely and wounded child.

The girl entered the room and closed the door firmly behind her. Her hair was a tawny wheat color arranged casually with loops of shining curls falling on her slender young shoulders. Her eyes, even as Charles had said, were like those of a fawn, set wide apart and very large—gray, vulnerable eyes whose great dark pupils suggested fear. But the delicate jeweled hand that toyed with the fan was without tremor.

She watched the girl moisten her lips carefully twice before she spoke. "You...you...you wish to see me, ma...madame."

Julie groaned inwardly. God in Heaven, this beautiful child had a stammer. She saw a hint of color rise in the girl's face as she waited.

"Let me explain this intrusion," she said swiftly. "My nephew, M. D'Amour has been unstinting in his praise of your garden. Since I was passing, he suggested that you might not mind my imposing on your hospitality to see the design..."

"Your nephew," the girl repeated carefully, watchful of each syllable that she might not stumble over the sounds.

"Yes, from the Abbey," Julie lied, trying to think of a safe way to indicate that she was from Charles.

"Of course," the girl said, "at Caen." But the flush came to her face again as she spoke.

The maid who answered the ringing of the bell went at once for a cloak and bonnet for her mistress.

The girl did not speak for many minutes after they left the house. She was a consummate actress, Julie decided. If any eyes watched from the house they would have seen two women pause at a winter bed planted with bulbs for a spring wakening, then at a fountain whose stream was silent from the cold, and finally at a row of young linden trees bedded in some rich evergreen shrubs.

Only when they were out of sight of the house did the girl abandon the careful slow walk of a guide and walk briskly to a latticed summerhouse which stood at the center of a great wheel of evergreen beds.

In spite of the dimness of the light filtering through the lattice, the enclosed space of the summerhouse seemed ablaze with radiance as Anne raised her eyes to Charles with puzzlement.

He did not touch her except to lift her hand to his lips in a stiffly formal greeting. "Your health, Madame Rivière," he said tenderly. "I would like you to meet my aunt Julie Rivière and my uncle Antoine, from the colonies," he said stiffly.

Her eyes flew to his with a shocked gasp. "*Mais non!*"

Charles smiled at her. "But yes, dear Anne. My aunt has been miraculously saved from the doom we all heard of. She and my uncle are here on a secret errand."

As Charles explained to Anne about the disappearance of the child Armand and their own fears, Julie saw Antoine carefully watching the girl. Like herself, he was obviously enchanted by this lovely young creature and his knowledge of her plight brought a blazing fury to his eyes.

"Anne, my dear," he said. "Do not worry how the words come out, just tell us. Have you heard anything? Seen anything?"

At this she nodded. "Maman is very restless," she said. "But then she often is. She says that Papa is up to something." She stopped and grinned shyly at Charles. "But then she always thinks that too."

"But more than usual?" Charles asked.

She nodded. "A few weeks ago Papa made a two-day journey attended only by Henri. She could not find where he went and she speaks of that a lot, fretfully. He has his lawyers there a great deal and their coming always make her angry. And she says that he simply must fire Henri."

"What has Henri done to her?" Charles asked.

She shook her pretty head, making the tawny curls dance. "She says that Henri takes advantage of him now that he has become a doddering old fool. Henri goes away and leaves Papa alone very often...he is lazy and sly, Maman says."

"Where does he go on these absences?" Antoine asked.

She shook her head that she did not know.

"Where is your husband now?" Charles asked.

Her eyes darkened. "Away," she said. "The servants said he left this morning very early. Last night there was a great screaming very late. From his words to his man I gathered that he was angry at Papa. Something about Monsieur le Comte taking rights that were not his own to claim anymore."

The girl grew increasingly nervous. "I fear someone will come to look for me," she explained.

Julie rose. "Thank you, my dear. Let us walk back before you have any trouble on our account."

Sick at heart, Julie cantered down the drive and onto the road where she knew Charles and Antoine were waiting. Julie shivered to have the darkness of that great house behind her. A lark rose from the roadside field, singing as she drew abreast Charles' horse.

"How old is Anne, Charles?" she asked quietly.

His eyes were expressive on her face. "She will be fifteen in the spring, Tante Julie."

The lark's song was finished. From the woods beside the road that wound through the great estate Julie heard a small child's voice raised in play and a young woman's laughter. She felt the grayness of the sky sift into her heart.

"Was any purpose served by this?" Charles asked quietly.

"We know that it must have been Antoine's father and Henri who took the child from his captor at Rouen, as we thought," Julie replied. "We know that the child is being kept out of Paris but somewhere near, to judge by Henri's absences."

"I hope for more," Charles said glumly.

"We simply take the next step," Julie shrugged. "We visit Paris and beard the old pirate in his den."

From Charles' soft chuckle she knew he had not minded her disrespect to the old man whom Anne called "Papa."

Chapter Eighty-Eight

"They will both know that I didn't compose this letter," Antoine said crossly as he copied the careful note that Julie had written for him to send to his parents.

"Is it that my style is womanly?" she asked, grinning at his discomfiture.

"Civil," Antoine corrected her. "They hardly expect me to be this civil. Listen to this: 'Being in France on business concerning my shipping company, I would be greatly honored if you and my mother would receive me and my wife

384

Juliette for a brief call before we embark for the colonies.' Good God in Heaven, do those sound like the words of a son who left with half his father's fortune in his pouch and a runaway sister in tow?"

Julie caressed his shoulder. "Come now, Antoine. We have both learned in hard schools that the past must bury its own dead."

They had withdrawn to Rouen, partly to conceal their contact with Charles and partly to improve their accommodations which were threatening to force Antoine into open assault on the innkeeper. So it was to Rouen that the message came back from Paris with astonishing promptness. A terse note stated only that M. and Mme. Charles Rivière would be delighted to receive M. and Mme. Antoine Rivière at their earliest convenience.

"Cool," Julie commented, reading the note over again.

"Cold," Antoine corrected her acidly. "As soon as you select a gown we will be off."

She stared at him in astonishment. She hadn't even thought of that. How long had it been since she had really concentrated on her attire? Living closely with Antoine certainly did not encourage this kind of vanity. "The more attractive a garment, the quicker I wish it off that smooth body," he told her quite honestly. Now she would not be dressing for a lover's eyes but rather for the careful scrutiny of the woman of a great Paris house. She selected and laid back and chose again until Antoine was in a rage of impatience.

"God in Heaven, put on anything," he shouted. "If there is nothing in the chest to wear, then we will have something made."

"And take all that time? Never!" she retorted. It was only then that she remembered the ivory gown in the very bottom of the sea chest, the gown that Pilar had fitted to her for the party for the King's auditor . . . the gown she had never worn because of the untimely death of Gonzales de Avila.

She held the fabric lovingly in her hands as Antoine knelt beside her. Drawing the dress from its wrappings, he whistled softly. "There is something I have not seen." Then the sudden edge of jealousy turned in his voice. "And what admirer presented this trinket to you, this fortune in hand-sewn gold and fine pearls?"

"Her name was Pilar," Julie said quietly. "It had been her wedding dress and she had it fitted to my size."

"And for whose eyes did you wear it?" he asked, only slightly mollified by her soft answer.

"Only hers and the seamstress," she replied. "The festive event for which it was fitted was canceled because of the death of a dear old friend of mine."

His eyes held hers a long time before dropping again to the silken fabric in his hand. "I hear the scrape of a shovel as the past buries its dead," he said with resignation. "Wear the dress now for me and the court of my parents. What it may lack in current French vogue will be more than made up for in its magnificence."

Trembling on the arm of her husband, Julie was ushered into the massive room of the great house in Paris. Braced for the whole family in concert, Julie was amazed to see that the room held only the old Count and his manservant Henri, whom she recognized at once from the description she had first heard in the upstairs room of a riverfront tavern in Philadelphia.

The old man, wearing the face of Death she had been prepared for, took Julie's hands in his own yellowed claws. His eyes searched her face silently for a long time.

"You seem to have sustained no visible damage from your great adventure in the West," he said coldly.

"I was blessed with good fortune," Julie replied, meeting his gaze squarely.

He growled fiercely and glanced at Antoine, stiff behind her. "And where is this red-haired son of yours that your sister describes with such boundless praise?"

"He accompanied his Aunt Sophie to Philadelphia to escape the yellow fever in Charles Town," Julie told him calmly. "Along with his nurse and the baby Julius."

"It is remarkable that a mother would have the heart to go so far from her son after being away from him for such a long time," the old man commented.

"It seems to me that it would be even more remarkable for her to expose him to the perils of a long sea voyage in the chill of winter, sire," she replied calmly, her eyes still bold on his face.

In spite of Charles and Antoine's words, Julie was not prepared for the woman who swept into the room. She was spare in weight in spite of her years, and moved with a restless urgency in her step.

Her face was powdered so heavily that no color of flesh

386

remained. Upon the discontented furrows that lined her cheeks were pasted a variety of ornamental patches and her brows which had been pulled to a high thin curve were stained a dark vermilion to match the ornate wig which dropped coquettish curls on her seamed neck.

She was a harridan, Julie thought without wishing to. On the streets of any city she would have been pursued by rowdy boys and stoned as a whore, but here in this room she moved with a true belief that she was magnificent, and wore a cold smile of superiority on her painted mouth.

"This, then, is our famous Juliette Duvall," Bérénice said, offering her hand to Julie. "That name is not unknown in France."

"She is now Juliette Rivière," the old Count corrected her. "A name that is also not unknown in France."

Julie was conscious of Emile at his mother's side, but found it hard to raise her eyes to his. He had the same spare height as his brother Antoine, but a powdered wig concealed his natural hair and the jaded face beneath its curls bore no resemblance to that of the man whose hand rested reassuringly on her arm. Why had she always thought of Emile as young? He was an old man, older by far in appearance than Antoine. The decadence in his face turned her stomach as he bent over her hand. She barely restrained her gasp as the ruffles at his cuff fell back to reveal a raw but characteristic wound like those she had learned to recognize long ago in London in her work at Margaret's side.

Later she could not even remember what she had said to Emile or he to her. She was only conscious that as she stared at that flesh at his wrist she had seen Anne, his wife, in her flowering innocence, and known with anguish that this terrified young child had been wed, not only to a decadent man but a syphilitic.

Never had Julie been in a room of such opulence. Yet the gleam of polished furniture, the delicate rendering of the bas-relief walls, the sumptuousness of velvet draperies stood in sharp contrast to the tension in the room. In spite of the sumptuous repast set out for their pleasure and the priceless wines breathing in open decanters, Julie was only conscious that she was in a camp of open war.

"Since we are a family who have been so long apart," Bérénice said from behind her fan. "I believe that all the servants should be sent away."

"Henri stays," the old man said firmly without glancing at

387

his wife. "My health is so poor," he added to Julie as an aside, "that I often need help with potions. Only Henri can be trusted."

The fluttering of his wife's fan expressed annoyance, but nothing more was said. The strange formal conversation moved like a court dance, a question followed by a circumspect reply. Sophie's health and the beauty of her new child, Paul's miraculous return from his Indian bondage, and Antoine's shipping business were at once brought up and dispensed with while Julie felt the old man's eyes on her own face, watchful and curious.

As Henri served wine and cakes, Emile stirred impatiently in his chair, but it was the old woman whose restlessness was most apparent. She seemed to be concealing some inner excitement that could not be stilled. She twitched this way and that in her chair like a child whose undergarments are binding. More than once Julie saw her lean forward with glittering eyes only to clamp her mouth determinedly and hold a purposeful silence. What was on this woman's mind? What possible thought or question compelled her to such strangely frantic behavior?

The old Count's strength was obviously taxed by this meeting. Julie gratefully felt their hour drawing to a close when Antoine's mother suddenly turned to them.

"And where did you sail from to come here?" she asked.

"My ships are based in Charles Town," Antoine replied, evading her question neatly.

"Good God, woman, where does it matter where they have sailed from or been on that savage coast?" her husband broke in. "They are here and we are delighted to meet our son's wife and the lovely mother of our grandson."

"That is precisely why I ask," Bérénice went on with a triumphant glance. "I have a natural interest in my own grandsons. How old is young Armand now, five, going on six?"

At Julie's nod, the woman pulled her face into a strange expression as she struggled to remove something from the sleeve of her dress. The old woman's hand shook wildly as it brought a sheet of crisp paper into view.

"I have constrained myself with only the greatest effort," she announced. "But I received a letter today from my dear friend in Philadelphia . . ."

"Good God, Bénénice," the old man said hastily. "We have no interest in the gossip of those old crones of yours. Save it to

388

chatter over with your hens upstairs."

Her eyes were evil on him. "Antoine and his wife will be interested in this even if you are not, and dear Emile, too, who came too late to hear the news. They report that the child Armand has been stolen from under the nose of that careless Sophie . . . that a great search has been launched with rewards offered and the message sent to his parents in the Carolinas."

Everything happened far too fast.

The old man gasped and then began to bellow at his wife. Antoine clutched Julie with a deadly grip, but it was Emile who caught Julie's own eye and held it. The man stood a long moment with a dumb look on his faded face. Then his eyes narrowed and he leaned forward, a strange intensity glittering in his eyes.

"A child of five or six?" he said slowly. "A red-headed boy of about five or six?" The softness of his tone was deceptive, like the smoothness of an adder moving silkily through green grass. Even as she forced her eyes from him she saw the servant Henri, his face pale with terror, move toward the door and leave silently without even meeting his master's eyes.

"That is impossible," Antoine was saying. "How could our child be missing? He is safe with his aunt Sophie who is devoted to the boy."

"Stupid woman chatter," the old man was protesting, "anything to raise a clatter of tongues. These are his parents, you old fool! If the child were missing, wouldn't they be searching for him?" But even as he spoke, Julie saw his eyes watchful on Antoine's face.

"The letter, madame," Antoine said, holding Julie tightly in the circle of his arm. "I would see the letter, please."

It was Emile who stepped forward swiftly and took the letter from his mother to hand to Antoine. Then he turned and caught the old woman close, whispering to her urgently. The old man's eyes went from one to the other of them and then sought Henri. "Where has that man gone?" he asked plaintively.

"Probably for some dosage or another," his wife said testily. She raised her hand to her head. "I must beg leave to be excused myself, all this shock has been quite too much . . ."

"Come with me, Maman," Emile pleaded, taking her arm. "I need you, my dear. You must help me break this dire news to my wife who tends to grow emotional even over trifles."

Then they were gone and the old man fell back with a groan. "God knows how I have survived that woman this long.

389

Where has Henri got to? You must pay no attention to anything your mother says, Antoine, letter or no. You know how she is."

Julie felt genuine concern at the loss of color from the old man's face. She would have sped to him if Henri had not entered the room at that instant. Something in the valet's carriage had changed. He no longer seemed a potbellied old servant on thin stork legs but a man of power and dignity. He was carrying a tumbler of water in unshaking hands. As she watched, he poured a powder into the glass, stirred it briskly and handed it to his master.

"Will it be all right?" the old man asked, lifting the mixture to his lips in his claws.

Henri's glance on his master's face seemed to be strangely serene. "Everything will be all right," he said with surety.

Chapter Eighty-Nine

Since neither Julie nor Antoine trusted the privacy of the room to which they were assigned, they clung together, speaking only in whispers.

"Who is that woman in Philadelphia who wrote the letter?" Julie asked. "I had no idea that your family had such links to the colonies."

"Some old crone, even as my father said," Antoine shrugged. "I should have known that my mother would figure out a way to gossip even though an ocean lay between her ear and the mouth of a friend. Who needs spies while my mother can lift a pen?"

"I am frightened all over again for Armand," Julie confessed. "I didn't like the way Henri shot out and then came back assuring your father that all was well."

"I felt the same," Antoine sighed. "But what could he have done in that brief five minutes? It is perfectly obvious that the child is not here or my mother would have ferreted it out by now."

"He must be in Paris then," Julie concluded, "and Henri made arrangements to have him moved."

"It's still too fast. This is a big estate. Unless there was someone right here on the grounds that he could reach, he didn't have time, Julie. My God, if we only had friends here, within this house."

"I loathe your brother," Julie said suddenly. "The expression on his face when your mother made that announcement turned my stomach even as much as it confused me."

"I didn't even glance at Emile," Antoine admitted. "I was too busy trying to make a proper response with my father watching me like a hawk does a hare."

"He looked ..." Julie paused, then shook her head. "I know this makes no sense, but he looked as if he had a sudden and exhilarating flash of understanding."

"That worries me, Julie," Antoine said quietly.

"It worries me too," Julie admitted, clinging to him. There was defeat in her voice. "We have to find our baby, Antoine. We have to find Armand."

Shielded by his arms, Julie did not at first realize that the sound level in the house had changed. She did not hear the muffled sound of scurrying feet in the carpeted hall outside their room or the voices raised in alarm in the hallway at the foot of the wide staircase.

But Antoine raised his head and listened intently. "What in hell is going on?" he asked, setting Julie away from him to stride to the door.

He was halfway down the stairs with Julie behind him when the wide door opened to admit the first of the two bodies that were to be carried into the great house of Charles Rivière. A clot of figures surrounded the men bearing the draped form. The face that looked up at Antoine was blanched and sickly in the blaze of the great crystal chandelier.

"Who is that? What has happened?" Antoine called, hastening down the stairs.

The man with the pale face swallowed convulsively before he could reply. He was in dark livery which was stained with dark streaks of mud and blood. "An accident," the man finally stammered. "Your mother, sir. Your brother."

"Accident?" Antoine challenged, even as the second draped body was carried past the great light.

"The carriage," the man said. "It was passing along the Normandy road at great speed when the axle broke. At great speed," he added.

"My father," Antoine breathed, remembering.

The old man, unable to accept the news in his exhausted

391

state, had lapsed into unconsciousness. As Julie followed Antoine into the room she saw Henri lift the old man in his arms like a sleeping child.

"It is probably just as well," Henri told Antoine calmly. "He will be better able to face it when he comes back to himself."

"But my God, what happened? What really happened?" Antoine pressed.

"Your brother was fierce on horses, sir," Henri said calmly. "The carriage was on its way to his own home, a road he felt he knew too well. When the axle broke, there was no hope for anyone aboard."

He raised his eyes to Julie in the doorway. She could not believe the complete serenity in the man's eyes in the midst of such tragedy. "If you will excuse me, madame," he said quietly, "I will put Monsieur le Comte into his own bed. The doctor has been summoned."

Chapter Ninety

The old man was not to regain consciousness for three days. Henri would not leave his side. From the moment the doctor arrived, a lonely vigil was kept by the old man's bed with Henri sleeping like a great spider in a side chair. As the old man slept, the house filled with people. There were arrangements to be made, investigations to be launched, and questions to be answered. Antoine was suddenly thrust into this place of authority.

It was Antoine who summoned the authorities, made arrangements for the laying out of the dead, and dispatched messengers to Bérénice's principal friends and to young Charles Bontemps in Caen.

"As to my brother's widow," Antoine told the examiner, "my wife Julie and I will leave immediately to bear the news to her."

"For God's sake, be careful," the stablemaster warned as he ordered the second carriage to be brought around. "I would have sworn that nothing could break on that great carriage. We keep it in perfect condition, sir." He blanched as he studied Antoine's face.

"Accidents happen," Antoine reassured him. "They tell me it was traveling at great speed."

There were lanterns still moving alongside the road where the great carriage had overturned only a mile or two from the drive that led to Emile's house. The driver did not pause as he passed but kept his eyes on the road ahead even as Julie forced herself to do.

This time the carriage rolled directly to the door and Antoine, with Julie at his side, pulled on the bell rope of the house that had been Emile's last earthly residence.

The man who responded shook his head. "Madame is not in," he reported.

"But where is she?" Antoine pressed. "I must see her at once."

Startled by the tone, the man hesitated. "I believe she may be in the garden," he said. "She went out carrying a cape and bonnet."

"We will seek her there," Antoine told him. "Never mind coming, we know the garden."

Leaving the man still staring in the open doorway, Antoine and Julie started along the path that led to the summerhouse. They were startled when they passed the row of lindens to see Anne, her head slightly bowed and her hands in her lap, sitting pensively on a bench.

The girl raised her head with a start, then stared at Julie a moment before rising.

Anne had to struggle for speech. "For—forgive me, dear Julie," she said, catching Julie's hand in her own. "I did not hear you. Thank God, you have come. And Tony," she added. It touched Julie to realize that this child said "Tony" with some of the same affection that came to Charles's voice at his uncle's name.

"We come on an errand of great importance," Antoine said. "Here, perhaps you should sit there where you were."

The girl's eyes shadowed with fear and she looked helplessly from one of them to the other.

The reality of the death truly struck Julie only at that moment. They were dead, Emile and Bérénice were dead, and yet the realization brought a surge of joy to her for the liberation the event brought to this lovely child. Wordless, she took the girl's hands and drew her down beside her on the bench.

"There has been a great disaster," Antoine said levelly, standing stiff and tall above them. "A coach was overturned."

393

Even as the girl's eyes widened with horror, Antoine continued evenly, without emotion in his voice. "Your husband and his mother both perished in the accident."

Julie watched the girl struggle for understanding. She saw her fail. She felt the child tear her hands from her own clasp. Leaping to her feet, she began to run like a frightened animal, running toward the woods that hid the summerhouse.

Her voice was a plaintive desperate wail. "Charles," she called. "Oh, Charles, Charles."

After a stunned moment, Julie and Antoine followed, seeing her swerve among the bushes on the winding path. Then, just before she reached the opening where the summerhouse stood, they saw a figure step from the shadows, pause, and run to meet her.

Julie felt Antoine's hand catch her arm to stop her. Anne, looking more child than woman, hurled herself into Charles' arms. Julie saw his head bend over her bonnet, pressing her tightly against him with an anguished expression on his face. He raised his face to theirs almost angrily. "What has happened? What is going on?"

Antoine had called him a child. There was no child in this Charles as he heard the news of his grandmother and uncle's deaths. He only held the trembling girl closer, stroking her slender back with gentle hands as he nodded.

"God has moved in a singular way," he said quietly.

Even in that dimness Julie saw Antoine's eyes move to meet her own. The God had been named Henri. They both knew it even though no word had passed between them. A man can weaken an axle in five minutes and return to a drawing room unruffled and serene. A man with such murderous hate as Henri obviously bore for Emile could do this, knowing what route a carriage would take and how fiercely a man had his horses used. But why had he done it? For hate alone? Why at that moment when Emile was setting off with his mother to tell Anne . . . to tell Anne what? It made no sense. But the God had been spidery-legged and bore the name of Henri, she knew that.

"Thank God you are here, Charles," Julie said softly, seeing the girl's frantic sobbing begin to subside in his arms.

To her astonishment, Anne pulled free of Charles' embrace at her words. Even with her face stained with tears, she was beautiful, beautiful and tender like a freshly washed flower.

"I had sent for him," she stammered. "I never did that before but I sent for him."

Charles nodded. "Why, my love? I was terrified when the message came. You could not have known of this—"

She shook her head. "It was something else. Something I want to show you—all of you. Come..."

As Charles hesitated, she took his hand and tugged him along. "Oh please come, all of you." She started toward the woods.

"But my dear," Antoine said. "Perhaps we should go to the house. You have had a great shock..."

She stood stock still with Charles' hand in her own and shook her head. "I...I have to say this, now to you. I am glad. I am glad they are dead. I am free. Dear God, I am free." She shuddered as she spoke and the tone of urgency came back into her voice. "Come, you must all come with me, into the woods."

"A lantern," Antoine insisted. "Let me go for a lantern at the house."

She shook her head. "I know the woods like my hand. I have spent many hours here, and there is the moon."

They wound their way along woodland paths, startling hares from their nighttime feeding. A hawk clattered from his high perch to protest their passing, and still Anne led the others on.

The gamekeeper's evening fire perfumed the woods, but Anne led them on to where a small cottage with an attached shed stood in a dark clearing.

"I remember this cottage," Antoine said suddenly. "I used to come here as a boy. It was never lived in."

"Now it is," Anne said. She raised her hand to rap at the door but Charles was too quick for her. His tap was firm without being bold, and he waited a long time before repeating it.

A woman's voice came, low with fright. "Who goes?"

"Madame Rivière," Charles replied. "With friends."

"I have a right to be here," the woman protested. "Monsieur le Comte himself has given me the right. Go to Monsieur le Comte. I have a right."

"We do not challenge your right," Charles said calmly. "We only wish to speak to you a moment. Open the door. No harm will come to you."

"Wait a minute," she called. Julie heard a rustling and whispering from within. When the door swung open, a plump young woman, breathing hard, faced them with terrified eyes.

"My God!" Antoine whooped. "If it isn't Margot!" He seized her in boisterous embrace. "How many years, you saucy little wretch. Julie, this is Henri's daughter Margot—"

"Tony," she cried, her face wreathed with smiles. Then seeing the others, she drew back in fear again. "I have done nothing, Tony. Monsieur le Comte your father sent me here."

It was Anne who first stepped inside the door with a new authority. She looked about the room. Julie, following her eyes, observed the neatness of the large room, still fragrant from a recently prepared meal, saw the distaff set by the low chair near the fire and a pot of porridge on the hob. Then on the round rug before the hearth she saw the small bow and a handful of arrows, a whistle carved of a willow bough, and a red top lying on its side.

"The child," Anne said carefully. "Where is the child?"

An unreasonable hope stirred in Julie's breast and she felt Antoine's hand grab at her arm. She could not speak, she couldn't possibly ask the question that burned in her mind.

"The child," Anne repeated firmly. "We wish to see the child."

The door to the room beyond was opening slowly, a crack at a time. Then it was banged all the way open as a child leaped out into the light, his nightshirt flapping behind him and his crown of bobbing red curls shining in the light from the fire.

"Papa!" he screamed. "Oh Papa, Papa! You have come for me, just like Grandpère said you would."

Margot groaned as Antoine caught the child in his arms and held him close. Julie's own legs grew suddenly weak beneath her. She stared at the lovely child pressed against Antoine's breast. How big he was, how beautifully shaped. His fine strong legs wound about his father as he buried that riot of curls in his father's neck.

Antoine's voice choked as he spoke. "Indeed I have come for you, you little beast, and your maman too."

She could see the child stiffen in Antoine's arms. Then he pulled back to stare into his father's face. "Maman too? What do you mean?"

"Look about you," his father ordered.

The boy craned his neck and stared at each of them in turn: Anne, Charles, then Julie.

"Hello, Armand," she said softly, fearful to move lest the spell of that moment be broken.

After frowning at his father's face a moment, the boy

wriggled free of his father's arms and felt for the floor with one bare foot. He walked toward Julie slowly, studying her intently as he came.

"Then you are not dead of Indians," he said soberly.

She shook her head, unable to speak.

"You stayed a long time," he accused her.

She only nodded again and knelt that they might be the same height.

"I can shoot a bow and arrow as good as any Indian," he told her boastfully. "Henri has taught me."

At her father's name, Margot began suddenly to wail and threw her apron over her head. Anne moved to her and touched her arm. "How came you by this child?" she asked.

"Monsieur le Comte and my father," Margot sniffled. "I meant no harm. I love the child."

Anne nodded. "D-d-don't cry now," she pleaded. "No harm will come to you from this. I am the mistress of this land now. You are safe."

"You?" Margot asked, dropping her apron to stare.

"I am the widow of Emile Rivière," Anne said quietly.

"Widow," Margot repeated hoarsely. "Oh my God, my God—my father. It was my father, wasn't it? Oh God protect him, my father."

Antoine stepped forward quickly and grasped Margot by both shoulders. "Listen to me, Margot, and listen well. A carriage axle broke—an accident, do you understand? The carriage was overturned and Emile and his mother and a driver killed. Do you understand? It was an accident." Then he paused. "Tell me only one thing, Margot. Was it Michel, your brother?"

She nodded numbly. "Oh God," she groaned.

Charles and Anne stared at them puzzled. "She is overwrought," Antoine told them, "terribly overwrought, as you see. Because there was bad blood between her father and Emile. We will keep this little scene among ourselves, lest there be talk?"

Julie felt the small hand imperious on her own. "Maman," he said crossly. "Don't stand there, make Margot feel better. I love her. She is my friend."

Maman. The word sang in Julie's mind as she turned to the pudgy little woman whose eyes still streamed tears. Pulling a linen handkerchief from her sleeve, she handed it to Margot with a smile.

397

"I owe you much for your loving care of my child," she told her.

"You won't take him away from me?" Margot asked, her face suddenly alive with panic.

Antoine laid his arm across Julie's shoulders. "This is the general," he told Margot soberly. "Her wish is our command. And for now her command is surely that we all pack up and get back to Paris tonight. The old man will need us when he wakens."

Chapter Ninety-One

Weeks passed as Julie despaired of the Count's ever recovering his wits again. He drifted in and out of the coma, rallying only to sink again into a dream world peopled by phantoms.

He was unconscious at the time of the funeral masses held for his wife Bérénice and "her" son Emile. He lay unknowing as his great house throbbed with the voices and life of his generations, Julie, Antoine, young Charles, and the lovely young widow Anne who had closed her own house to join the others in Paris until her required period of mourning be past. But most of all he missed the knowledge that Armand, his red curls bouncing, was sliding down the great bannisters of his house, chasing the swans on the ponds in the garden, and being hauled from mire to bath by the constantly amiable Margot.

The young people, drawn close by tragedy and time, became fast friends as well as family. Even Anne, always hesitant to speak because of her impediment, became free enough to talk a little of the home she had left in Austria and to tell how her lonely walks in the woods had led her to discover the red-haired boy whom she hoped would be the lost child so earnestly sought.

When morning came again to his mind as well as his chambers, the Count found Henri, thinned by his vigil, and Julie, radiant with happiness, staring soberly into his face.

"Was it a dream?" the old man asked quietly.

"It was no dream," Julie told him.

"Bérénice?" he asked, almost timidly.

At Julie's nod, the old man turned his face away. "There was a good time. Early, there was a good time..." Then his voice trailed off.

"And her son too," Julie added so that he need not ask.

The old man struggled up on his elbows, only to be urged back down by Henri. "The bride, the little Anne?"

"She is here with you," Julie said. "She is fine, as we all are." Then after a moment, "And your grandsons too."

"Charles?" he asked, his eyes on her face.

"And Armand," she said firmly.

His eyes narrowed in that skull of a face. "Armand?" he asked. "How is that?"

"With Margot," Julie told him quietly. "He is very pleased with his grandpère who promised that his papa would come and the promise was fulfilled." Her eyes dared his reply.

The old claws picked at the coverlet so that his eyes did not have to meet those level golden ones. His voice, so strong with curiosity the moment before, assumed the whine of an invalid. "I am an old man and weak beyond my years, I needed an heir."

"So does Antoine," she reminded him.

"But these lands," the old man said, his voice suddenly vibrant again and his eyes bright with cunning. "Come, dear daughter Juliette. You are the daughter of a businessman. You seem to have a sound head yourself for a female, in spite of some weakness for adventuring. Let me have the account books brought to you. Henri, find a map of the estates! Let me show you what will be yours and Antoine's and later be there for the boy Armand."

Julie laughed merrily. "You are behaving like a silly old man, which you are not." she said tenderly. "I shall forgive you that silliness because of the illness you have been through. We are not to be bought or sold for lands or account books." She glanced at Henri, who was glowering fiercely at her from his corner. "And quit scowling at me, Henri. It will take more than you to keep me from scolding this father-in-law of mine. And now that I think of it, do go and fetch the others. They deserve to know with what great strength and power he has come back to join us."

Henri's anguished glance at the old man was met by a shrug.

"Do as she bids, Henri," the old man chuckled. "They cut petticoats from a different fabric on the other side of that sea."

"Seriously, do you feel well enough to let them see you for a moment?" she asked more gently.

"I am a man who has come through a long dark tunnel to see a sudden possible light," he said softly, watching her reaction with a crafty expression. "God has delivered me."

"God and Henri," she corrected him matter-of-factly.

He started at her words and darted his eyes about nervously. "Who knows of that?" he asked.

"Antoine and I, Charles and Anne," she said quietly. "And of course Margot guessed at once."

"I would not have had the guts for it," the old man admitted. "But the love of that father for his son was the great force." Then he sighed. "You were a long time coming to me, daughter. Can you bear the touch of an old man's hand on that radiant flesh of yours?"

"Only in love," she told him and took the dry claw of a hand between both her own.

The old man shook his head as Antoine entered the room. "You have won again, Tony," he ceded. "But you are blood of my blood no matter how long you protest it. I have been bewitched by this wife of yours. What is there in those colonies that this great Dame France cannot give you? The title is yours, Tony, and the lands and the honors. The whole of it, for you and then Armand."

Armand, twisting free of Margot's grasp, shot to his father's side with a great scowl. "Don't listen to him, Papa, don't even listen to him. I want to go home."

"Listen here, you young scoundrel," his grandfather began, rising on his pillow.

Julie laughed merrily. "Why do you want to have this savage son of ours when you have a perfectly decent heir of your own?" she asked softly. "He will even take a wife who will adorn the title of Countess of Rivière."

The old man stared at her dumbfounded before turning his gaze toward young Charles, who stood, as always, with Anne close to his side. He stared at them a moment, puzzled. Then he chuckled. "By God," he said laughing. "Old Bérénice gabbled on about the two of you...said that two such hot-blooded children should not be let to walk out together. She said it from the first, before the wedding even. Is it that way with you two?"

Charles flushed a deep crimson as he nodded. "I am in love with her, Grandpère," he said quietly. "She has consented to be my wife when her period of mourning is past."

The old man's eyes narrowed. "In France?" he asked.

"In France," Charles replied.

"And what will your hot-headed father say to this?" the old man asked.

"Uncle Tony tells me that my father's years among the Natchez turned him to gentleness and a quiet wisdom," Charles said. "But even if they had not, by the time we are able to marry I shall be my own man, sir."

"And you, madame?" he turned to Anne.

When she nodded at him with a slow shy smile, he raised his shoulders with delight. "A quiet woman," he sighed. "God's greatest gift to cottage or castle."

"But only if that is what a man wishes," Antoine corrected him with his arm across Julie's shoulder.

"Well . . ." The old man looked around the room with such delight that he was forced to produce something caustic. "Is there more news that you need to tell me? Just while you are doing all this behind my back?"

"Only that we have waited a confirmation of your recovery to return to our home," Antoine said quietly.

"But why so hasty?" the old man whined. "Stay a bit and—"

"We have to go home right now," Armand broke in, his bright face close to the old man's. "I miss my dogs, you see, and the white cat who has kittens all the time in the stable. And anyway I get to be cabin boy on my own papa's ship on the way."

The old man's eyes lingered hungrily on the boy's face.

"Are you sure you would not like to stay in France with Henri and your pony and Margot?"

"Oh, Margot is going with us," the boy explained. "Papa has promised me. But I have to go home. France is not home."

When the old man grew gray with fatigue, Julie finally got him to agree to their leaving him to rest. As they passed his doorsill Antoine caught Julie by the arm and hustled her along the corridor toward the room they shared. With the door bolted behind them he seized her with joyful passion.

"My God, Julie, we did it. We did it, and I thought we would never be alone together again."

"I was afraid," she confessed, "afraid that you might wish the property and all that for Armand."

"To hell with it," Antoine laughed. "And to show you how much I think of all that stuff, I want to change our name to a good solid colonial name. How does 'Rivers' sound to you?"

She couldn't stop the giggle even as the look of offense darkened his face. "Come on, Antoine," she laughed. "Be realistic. With that wild hair of his that boy will be called 'Red' no matter what. How does 'Red Rivers' really sound to you?"

He laughed with her, then paused. "Very New World, my sweet. It sounds very New World to me. And that's what we have, by God, a very new world of our own. And would you tell me why in hell you have all those clothes on when I am burning with need for you?"

"Because it is eleven o'clock in the morning," she explained, loosening her blouse as she spoke.

The rattling at the door was accompanied by Armand's commanding voice. "Maman, Papa," he shouted. "The sun is shining. Come and play!"

"Later," his father called out. "Go find Charles or Margot. We will be along later."

"Promise," the boy insisted.

"We promise," Antoine replied.

Julie was waiting for him, sitting upright in the bed with nothing but her hair loose on her shoulders. "The sun is shining," she whispered to him. "Come and play."

He stilled her laughter with his own lips. Enclosing his lean body with her arms, she felt a new serenity flow in the passionate rhythm of their lovemaking.

"*Ma générale*," he whispered teasingly against her flesh.

As many times as they had joined their bodies in love, as many times as her flesh had thrilled to his touch, she was always to remember that hour as something apart. The anguish of their early lovemaking was gone. There was nothing frantic or desperate in their search for each other. The wildness had sifted from Antoine in his new role as father and husband. And she herself? Antoine had tamed her as she had watched the Cherokee tame their wild ponies, by giving her enough head that she not feel prisoned in the wide pastures of their marriage. She lay at peace beneath his body, devoid of need, devoid of restlessness.

"You aren't laughing like you usually do," he pointed out.

"There are joys even beyond laughter," she whispered, her fingers tangled in his hair. "Past laughter, past delight...past belief."

The pressure of his arms about her told her that he understood.